CW01467920

The Raven and the Wolf

Mark of the Hunter Trilogy - Book Three

Morgan Gauthier

Midnight Tide Publishing

The Raven and the Wolf (2023)

Map by Gonzalo A. Mendiverry (IG: @gonzalom.art)

Cover by Klára Dostrašilová (IG: @artzzofkae)

Edited by Ada Charlesworth

Dust Jacket and Naked Cover Formatting by Xyvah Okoye

www.midnighttidepublishing.com

Library of Congress Control Number:

ISBN (paperback) 978-1-958673-28-7

ISBN (ebook)

To my Mom, who said she was "distraught" reading this last book.
And to my Dad, who said I should be a writer and not an actress.
I couldn't have had two more supportive and loving parents than you.
I love you both.

Adalore
N
NE
E
SE
S
W
W
NW
Taybourne Mountains
Northwind
Caelestus
Petram
Elisor
Black Forest
Oakenshire
Borg
Tree House Forest
Gomorrah
Bone Mountains
Sarurai
Forbidden Forest
The Hollow
Fennor
Valley Pass
The Sisters
Hidden Tavern
Port Daelon
Dead Man's Lands
Traders Bay
Enchanted Swamp
Jannat Sin
Caverns of the Undead
Isles of Myr
Pulau
Numbio

artzzofkae

Kae
artzzofkae

Kae
artzzofkae

CHARACTERS

Northwind (North)

Niabi, Queen, Mistress of Shadows
Salome, Exiled Princess, The Hunter
Crispin, Exiled Prince
Gershom, Niabi's Second in Command
Pash, Commander of Shadows, Gershom's son
Ophir, Gershom's Brother, Pash's Uncle
Rollo, Niabi's Son, Prince (Deceased)

Borg (West)

Zophar, Crispin and Salome's Guardian
Benaiah, King of Borg
Ivar, Captain of the Drakaar
Ragnar, Prince of Borg
Lahki, Princess of Borg

Elisor (Andrago)

Tala, Niabi's Most Trusted Advisor, Oldest Friend
Leoti, Tala's Daughter, Niabi's Daughter-in-Law
Dichali, Niabi's First Husband (Deceased)
Chua, Dichali's friend

Gomorrah

Matildys, Queen
Cyler, King (Deceased)
Thanos, Prince, Ranalda's Twin
Ranalda, Princess, Thanos' Twin
Thrak, Cannibal Soldiers

Sakurai (East)

Jinn, Prince and Heir to the Jade Throne
Kai, Ryoko Naga and Prince Jinn's Protection
Kenji, King of Sakurai and Jinn's father

Caelestis (Immortals)

Ethereals:

Harbona, Seer
Lavena, High Counselor
The Eldaar, King and Queen of the Immortals, Harbona's parents
Keeva, Lavena's Daughter (Demi)
Bellators:
Kayven, Leader of Immortal Warriors
Abba, Leader of Immortal Warriors

Numbio (South)
Osiris, King
Heru, Prince
Rayma, Royal Healer
Inaros, Rayma's brother
Memucan, King's Advisor (Deceased)
Amunet, High Priestess

Isles of Myr
Nym, Queen, Grandmother of Niabi, Salome, and Crispin (Deceased)
Zara, Princess and Heir to Bronze Throne
Bilhah, Niabi, Crispin, and Salome's mother, (Deceased)
Damaris, Princess and Oracle of Myr
Mika, Princess and Red Maiden (Deceased)
Marina, Princess (Deceased)
Utara, Mika's Daughter
Seraphina, Qata Vishna, Rosalina's Twin
Rosalina, Qata Vishna, Seraphina's Twin

Pulau (Misfit Island)
Uri, The Pirate King
Nezreen, Shadow Wielder
Palma, Diviner (Deceased)

The Sisters (Blind Order)
Neempo, Sovereign (Deceased)
Penn, Master of Keepers
Balor, Master of Witnesses

Crew Members of the *Shadow of Death*

Haldane, The Captain
Rahab, The Stabby One
Corwin, The Quiet One
Phex, The Explosives One
Ondrej, The Giant One
Rafi, The Pint-Sized One
Leeondris, The Missing One

Members of the Order (Rebel Force)
Oden, Leader, formally known as Lord Maon
Nubis, Stormcrag
Ziggy, Call Girl from Borg
Makeda, Manages *The Whispering Fox* Tavern

Stormcrags (Mountain Men Tribe)
Cato, Scout
Torrin, Leader
Oifa, Torrin's Right Hand

Krazaks (Mountain Men Tribe)
Gerd, King of the City of Bones (Deceased)
Rune, Militia Leader
Hanzo, Rune's Right Hand, Archer
Orn, Giant Warrior (Deceased)

Other Characters
Adonijah, "The Wanderer"
Odelia, Enchantress of the Swamp
Vilora, The Old Witch of Endor
Diron, Captain of *The Golden Rose*
Anaktu, The Last Nephilim, Niabi's Iron Guard

Prologue

Niabi – 12 Years Ago

As the sun peeked over the horizon after a night of bloodshed, it became evident, the White City of Northwind belonged to another. The stench of blood and burnt rubble was entombed in the city by the looming smoky haze. The Northerners who survived the attack were guarded by the invading soldiers to ensure their submission. Inside the White Keep, the castle attendants were ordered to scrub the blood and ash from the white stone walls and dispose of the dead bodies strewn throughout the halls.

Still in his throne room, Issachar sat with the remains of his loved ones until their bodies were removed. The captured king stared at the pools of blood on the floor and cried until he did not have a tear left to shed. Surrounded by enemy soldiers, he awaited his fate.

The grand wooden doors flew open and she entered. Dressed head to toe in black armor, she slowly walked towards her defeated foe. Protecting her left arm was an intricate metal sheath that perfectly wrapped around her arm and spanned from her shoulder to her fingertips. Underneath her hood, her long raven black hair rested against the back of her neck and the black war paint smeared across her olive face only accentuated her piercing green eyes. Tall and fit, she glided towards her prey with undeniable excitement. The people of the Ten Kingdoms of Adalore knew her as the Green-Eyed-Raven, but Issachar only knew her as Niabi.

With Gershom, Tala, and her nine-foot-tall Nephilim behind her, she marched up to Issachar and stopped a few feet in front of him.

"Hello, Father."

Her icy greeting seemed to rattle him. "After all this time?"

"I told you I would come for you."

His swollen bloodshot eyes met hers. "Why?"

"You know your sins," she snarled, "and now you will pay for them."

"You have murdered my people and ravaged our homeland for power?" Issachar spat at her feet. "The White City burns because of you!"

"The city burns because of you!" She corrected him as she gazed out the floor to ceiling windows. She breathed in the smell of the burning city, but satisfaction eluded her. "Their blood has been spilled for those you stole from me."

"I don't even remember their names." Her father's words stung.

Enraged, she lunged toward him on bended knee and grabbed him by his throat. "You know their names," she gritted her teeth as he gasped for air. "You know their faces. You know I loved them."

"Why did you not let them kill me with the others?" Issachar hissed, eyeing the men that stood silently behind her, with blood still smeared on their hands.

"You are *mine* to kill." Her blood thirsty gaze remained locked on her conquered foe.

"And when I am gone, Gershom will take my throne leaving you with what?"

Niabi laughed, releasing her choke hold. "Surely you do not believe the mastermind who brought your city to its knees was Gershom? It was me. It has always been me." The warrior queen flashed a triumphant smile. "And when my time is up, my son will rule the White City, forever eradicating your name from existence."

"You would have that half-blood sit on the throne of our ancestors?"

"Have you so quickly forgotten that all of your children were half-bloods?" She tilted her head. "Or is it because my son comes from a people you deem lesser than yourself?"

"History will remember what happened here today." Issachar held his head high, indignant to the very end.

"I swear not even the Almighty One himself will be able to find your remains once I have finished with you." She slowly rose from her crouched position and looked down on his tear-stained face. Her twin daggers dropped from her sleeves into her hands, and she clenched them tightly in her palms.

Issachar stared into her ruthless eyes, "You are not as strong as you think you are, Niabi."

"It does not take strength to kill a man," she retorted.

"May the Almighty One have mercy on your soul." Issachar closed his eyes.

With a determined swiftness, Niabi sliced through his throat, nearly decapitating the once King of the North. "Mercy is for the weak."

Chapter One

Harbona

Harbona had barely slept in days. Looking into Salome's future did not bring him any comfort. Death's presence was strong. He felt her reaching out to him and he heard her cries for help, but when he responded, she did not answer. The one time he spotted her in a vision, she was covered in blood and soot. He wasn't sure if the blood belonged to her or someone else.

Every version of her future varied slightly but ultimately ended the same way. Death was near and she wouldn't be denied this time.

Harbona clung to the hope that there was one way he could save her, but it would take a miracle and he was running out of time.

Pacing Lavena's dining room like a crazed animal, he mumbled and replayed the visions in his mind until he became nauseous. The only reason he had joined Lavena, Kayven, and Abba for breakfast was because Odelia, the Enchantress, dragged him like a defiant child out of his room. He did not notice when she finished her meal and left but the silence of his fellow Immortals in the room did not ease his stomach.

"You are sure about what you saw?" Lavena's voice shattered the silence and Harbona stopped to stare at her. She was sitting at the head of the glass table with the sun's rays beaming through the window behind her making her look more like a goddess than a mere Ethereal.

He nodded solemnly, rubbing the heel of his palms against his bloodshot eyes. "It is the only way to save her."

Her voice did not waver when she said, "Then she is lost."

Harbona refused to let that be the end of it. "If we do not act quickly, Salome will be executed, but not before she is tortured by the Thrak. I cannot and will not let her suffer this fate. Not if I can help it."

"You said you were not here for aid," Lavena nonchalantly raised her cup to her lips, discussing Salome's life as if it were the equivalent to choosing whether or not to add sugar to her tea.

"It was not my intent, but things have changed."

Kayven leaned forward, his elbows resting on the table. Even seated he looked like a battle-ready warrior. "What do you need us to do?"

Before Harbona could say a word, Lavena narrowed her eyes at the Bellator seated to her left. "Until the Eldaar has sanctioned our involvement, you will do nothing."

"It is not just her life at stake, Lavena," Harbona stroked a hand through his disheveled hair.

"You can make me the villain, but unless you want Kayven and Abba to share in your banishment, you will need the Eldaar's blessing."

"Then I shall meet with them."

The room suddenly stilled. The brothers stared at each other across the table before looking at Lavena, who was hastily consuming her meal.

"What is it?" Harbona's gaze shifted from Lavena to the Bellators. "What are you not telling me?"

"The Eldaar do not hold audiences anymore," Kayven began but Lavena hissed his name to silence him.

"Since when?" Harbona took the seat next to Kayven and shoved the plate of food away from him.

"For the last several months" Kayven continued, "they have only granted Keeva an audience."

"Before you ask," Lavena's voice was cold and venomous, "I will not involve my daughter in this matter, Harbona."

"Lavena, please -"

She vehemently shook her head, "My answer is no."

"It is the only way to save Salome," the Seer pleaded. He would do anything to protect the Hunter, to protect Lykos' sister.

"So, your plan is to ask the Eldaar, the parents who banished you, their only son and heir, to send Bellators to fight in a mortal war?" Lavena slapped her linen napkin on her half-eaten plate. "It would be a miracle if they even permit you entry into the Holies."

"Salome is your sister by marriage."

Her nostrils flared."That may be the case, but I will not risk my daughter's future to save her. I am sorry." Harbona noticed a flicker of sorrow behind her cold, grey eyes.

"Then I will meet with my parents with or without their permission," Harbona declared, reclining in his chair.

"They might have you executed," Abba said softly, aimlessly pushing his fruit around his plate with a fork. "Are you willing to risk your life to save this mortal?"

"I would rather die trying to save my friend than live another thousand years with my cowardice." Harbona pushed back from the table and glanced at Lavena, Kayven, and Abba. "I am not asking any of you to come with me."

Kayven and Abba stood. They always had Harbona's back in every situation and this issue was no different.

"You are fools to think you will be allowed before the thrones of the Eldaar." Lavena rubbed her temples in small circles. "They will not see you and if they do, you will not walk out alive," she whispered, worry lacing her words.

"Then it should please you to know that I have already arranged an audience with the Eldaar on your behalf, Harbona." Keeva's young voice sliced through the tension in the room as she walked in.

Lavena rose from her seat, planting her palms on the tabletop. "What is the meaning of this, Keeva?"

Keeva reached in front of Abba and snatched a pear from the spread on the table and took a bite. "The Eldaar have agreed to meet with Harbona as long as I accompany him."

"I cannot allow it," Lavena's voice cracked and Harbona saw the terror in her eyes.

Keeva made her way to her mother and stood before her. "I know you fear for me and my future, Mother, but if I can use my gift to save my aunt from a fate worse than death, how can I not?"

Lavena cupped her daughter's face in her thin fingers. "They will ask too much of you," she whispered as a tear slid down her pale cheek.

"I know," the demi wiped her mother's tear away. "I am willing to pay the price."

Harbona took a step toward the girl. "What are you talking about?"

Keeva looked over at him. "Your father is fading. The Eldaar intend to journey to the After but without an heir..."

Understanding flooded him and it made his heart ache. His eyes shot up to meet Lavena's watery gaze and it served as confirmation. "They want you to take their place. To take... my place."

Keeva nodded. "If that is what they require of me to save my aunt, then that is what I am willing to do."

Harbona knew the high price Keeva had agreed to, but he wasn't sure he could consent to it. To be an Eldaar meant attaching your soul to your partner and ruling the Immortals as one being. Any sense of freedom, autonomy, or choice would be gone, and Keeva would never be able to leave Caelestis. She would endure in the Holies for thousands of years until she bore a son or daughter to take her place when she grew weary of existing and her mate agreed to journey to the After, where they neither lived nor died.

When he was a youngling, Harbona had no interest in ruling, nor any interest in becoming the Eldaar. His banishment was a gift. He now understood why Lavena was unwilling to let her daughter spend time with the Eldaar, why she kept her close, and why she trained the demi never to make deals with the rulers of Caelsetis. They wanted an heir, and who better than the only other Seer in the known world? Harbona had been stripped of power, titles, and responsibilities, but now they would fall on the shoulders of a twelve-year-old girl. Her life would be over before it had a chance to begin.

Keeva grabbed his hand, interrupting his thoughts. She smiled up at him. It was Lykos' smile, and it brought peace and warmth to his soul.

"You need not worry for me, Harbona," she whispered. "It is time to go."

While Harbona and Keeva waited outside the throne room doors, he couldn't help but admire the demi. Even though she was only twelve years old, she was wise for her age. Lykos would be so proud of her, and the seer knew his friend would have doted on her endlessly.

Keeva slowly glanced up at him and smiled. "What troubles you, Harbona?"

"Are you sure about this?" he asked, guilt twisting in his stomach knowing the magnitude of her sacrifice. "I can go in alone."

Keeva gently shook her head and grabbed his hand. "I know what I am doing. Trust me."

"Why are you doing this? Why are you so willing to give up your freedom to save someone you do not even know?"

She crinkled her nose, looking confused. "Why must I know her to want to save her?"

The sides of Harbona's eyes crinkled as he smiled. "You remind me so much of your father."

"Did you know him well?"

"Oh yes," Harbona clasped his hands behind his back. "I was there the day he was born, and I knew him up until the day he..."

"Died."

He nodded sadly, "Yes."

She shifted her weight and asked, "Was he really as wonderful as my mother says he was?"

"I have walked this world for nearly three thousand years." He met her gaze and smiled. "And your father was one of the greatest men I have ever known. It was an honor to call him my friend."

The doors opened before she had a chance to respond. Walking into the throne room with Keeva by his side was humbling. Because of this twelve-year old girl and her selflessness, he was granted an audience with his own parents. He never felt so small and insignificant.

The golden throne room of the Holies had not changed. It was exactly how it was a thousand years ago when he stood before the Eldaar for his sentencing. The floors, the walls, the ceiling, the chandeliers: everything was gold. And the Eldaar, the rulers of the Immortals, sat in their twin golden thrones basking in their glorious glow.

His father, Oleon, didn't appear older. His platinum blonde hair, pointy ears, and clean-shaven face were in pristine condition, but his cold, grey eyes weren't as piercing as they used to be. Keeva was right. He was fading. It wasn't surprising that after ruling for five thousand years, he was now ready to journey to the After.

His gaze fell upon his mother, Soline, who was radiant as ever. Her golden crown fashioned to look like the sun's rays sat upon her long platinum hair, and her golden silks splashed around her thin frame like waves against the shore. Her pointy ears were adorned with the finest glistening jewels, and her straight nose, thin lips, and sharp chin were perfectly sculpted. But when he looked into her calculating grey eyes, he remembered the last time he stood before them, she had been the one to brand him with the banishment mark.

Instinctively, he brushed his fingertips over his right eye where the banishment mark was and felt the Eldaar's judgmental glare.

Regretting his unintentional move, he sheepishly turned to Keeva for direction. Her long dark brown hair, rounded ears and warm smile reminded him of Lykos and it calmed his nerves. She took the lead and stepped toward the dais, tugging Harbona forward and together they bowed at the waist. They only rose up when the Eldaar, in unison, said, "Rise."

Though a thousand years had passed, Harbona had not forgotten royal etiquette. He knew he could only speak when called upon, so the four of them stood in utter silence until it was nearly unbearable.

"So, you have returned," his father's deep, melodic voice echoed.

Harbona had to remind himself to stand tall, and not shrink before them. The Seer bobbed his head, meeting his father's intense glare. "I have returned."

"Keeva requested this audience," Soline began, her fingers gripping the golden armrests of her throne, "but let it be known that we are not pleased to see you. You sullied these halls and the legacy of our family one thousand years ago and seeing what you have become is pathetic."

The words stung, but Harbona kept a straight face. To react would be mortal and he could not afford to appear weak before his parents.

"It is noted." He nodded his head which seemed to satisfy his mother.

"Why are you here?" Oleon drummed his fingers on his thigh, looking disinterested.

"I had a vision that a dear friend of mine is in need of help," Harbona took a steadying breath. "I have come to ask for your aid."

The Eldaar did not react. They merely stared at their son; that was answer enough. But he couldn't accept anything less than their cooperation.

"I would ask you to send a company of Bellators to the Mainland to save the Hunter from death."

"You want us to send our Bellators to save this mortal?" Oleon scoffed; disgust written all over his pale face. "You are more of an embarrassment than I thought possible. Have you not learned your lesson from a thousand years ago?"

"Those mortals you snub your nose at have more character, courage, and integrity than you can fathom."

Soline held up her slender hand to silence him. "You have no right to come before us as a banished heir and disgraced Ethereal to ask anything of us. You are fortunate to have Keeva for an ally, for she is your only one."

"What must I do -"

"Nothing," she interrupted him. "There is nothing you can do to convince us to help you or those mortals."

"But she will be tortured," Harbona's voice cracked, anger bubbling in his gut. "She will die."

"Such is the way of mortals." Soline laid her hands on her lap. Her movements were graceful, but her eyes were vicious.

All hope he had of convincing them to help was quickly fading. He had nothing to offer them, nothing to barter or trade. In their eyes, he was no longer their son. He was no longer important and had no sway in these halls.

"Then I implore you to make a deal with me," Keeva finally spoke; all eyes fixed on her.

"Keeva?" Oleon tilted his head in confusion. "What are you saying?"

Keeva took a step forward, still paying proper respect and reverence to the rulers. "Send the Bellators to aid Harbona and the mortals in their war and I will be your heir."

The Eldaar both sat straighter in their thrones; a feat Harbona didn't think was even possible. He exchanged a glance with Keeva before she continued.

"There is one more stipulation I require before I agree to be your successor."

Soline scoffed. "You dare request more of us in addition to sending our warriors to fight in a mortal war?"

"If you want me to agree to be your successor, to rule for thousands of years and give up my freedom so you may go to the After, then yes, I require more." Keeva held her ground, tilting her head higher. "With all due respect, Eldaar, I am your only hope of leaving this world for the next."

The Eldaar squinted. Everyone in that throne room knew Keeva was now firmly in charge. With a prince for a father and an ambassador for a mother, Keeva was destined for politics. Harbona had no idea how influential and knowledgeable this twelve-year old was. Every great leader knows to successfully negotiate, you need to possess something the other person desperately wants or needs. Keeva held the fate of the Eldaar in her tiny hands. And they all knew it.

Olean motioned for her to continue. "Speak, Keeva. What is it you desire?"

"I would like to spend the next six years traveling the mortal world. I desire to see my father's homeland before I am forced to remain in Caelestis. On my eighteenth birthday, I will wed a suitable partner and take my vows as the Eldaar."

"You want us to wait another six years to journey to the After?" Oleon asked in disbelief.

"You have ruled for five thousand years," Keeva shrugged one shoulder, "I do not believe six more will make a difference."

Harbona couldn't deny he was impressed with the demi, and became misty-eyed thinking of how proud Lykos would be if he could see her now. She might look like an Ethereal, but her heart was mortal.

The Eldaar exchanged a meaningful glance, as if they were reading each other's mind, before bowing their heads. “We agree to your terms, Keeva.”

“Alert Kayven and Abba to ready the Bellators.” Soline glared at Harbona. “May our paths never cross again. You are dismissed.”

With one final bow, Harbona and Keeva walked out of the Holies. He had entered his ancestral home and walked out alive. He was one step closer to freeing Salome, but instead of feeling triumphant, his heart felt heavier. He knew his parents would never forgive him and he accepted that, but he couldn't stop thinking how Lykos would be heartbroken by the price his daughter paid. He would forever be indebted to Keeva.

Chapter Two

Salome

Salome wasn't sure how long she'd been sitting in the dark and damp cell, but she knew the back wounds she ended up with to save Kai were being treated by the Gomorrian healers and were beginning to mend. By all accounts, she should have died from her injuries, but Death wasn't ready to claim her. Had she not been in the dungeons beneath the Black Tower, she wouldn't have believed she was a prisoner at all. She was given two meals a day and was visited often by the royal healers.

What worried her the most was she hadn't seen Zophar since her capture in the Bone Mountains. She'd been unconscious most of the journey to Gomorrah, partly due to her injuries and partly due to being drugged. The Thrak didn't want her to become a problem on the way, injured or not, so they pulled the arrows from her back, slathered on a salve to ward off infection, and stitched her up. That was the extent of their mercy.

When her thoughts weren't consumed by the impending torture she was sure to endure at the hands of the vicious Gormorrian queen, she thought of Jinn. The fear; the sorrow; the love, she saw in his face and the last words she communicated to him through their bond.

"I should have accepted your proposal when I had the chance."

She wasn't sure why she said it, but at that moment, she meant it. She hurt him by choosing Adonijah over him, rejecting him when he confessed in the City of Bones that he was in love with her.

Her stomach churned at the thought of Adonijah and his betrayal, his lies, and his true identity as Gershom's son. She gave him her heart and her trust, and he'd broken both. She still loved him, but if she were to make it out of Gomorrah alive and encountered him, she wasn't sure how she would react to him.

Tears burned her eyes, so she rubbed the heels of her palms against them. How had she screwed this up so badly? She wasn't one to act impulsively or venture out without being properly armed, but hearing Kai's report about Adonijah felt like a knife to her heart. She had a hard time breathing and being inside the mountain made her feel claustrophobic. Without giving herself a moment to think, she sprinted out of the city and into the forest to find a sense of normalcy. She needed the fresh air, the trees, the sounds of the birds chirping, the crunch of the sticks and mulch under her feet. That was her way of coping with what she had no control over.

But she had been rash, and her actions put her in a life-threatening position.

She tried several times to use her magic to reach out to Jinn and Harbona to ask for help, but neither responded. Whenever she visualized extending the bridge to them, there was no one on the other side. Perhaps, being so far below the city was affecting her in more ways than one.

In a last-ditch effort, she reached out to her mother, but she too was absent, and the only thing Salome could think about was the warning her mother gave her during her time in the Isles of Myr.

"When the time comes and you find yourself standing on your own, you will have a choice to make. Rise from the ashes or crumble into dust."

"Will I be alone for the rest of my life?"

Bilhah smiled, cupping her face, "No, Sweetness, you will not spend the rest of your days alone. But the choices you make during your loneliest moments will determine who you will find on the other side."

Salome was alone. Alone in a cell. Alone to face an enemy she'd never met but had hunted her for weeks. Alone with her fate. Alone with her thoughts. *Alone*. Her worst fear was now her reality.

But she had a choice to make: rise or crumble.

Footsteps behind the wooden cell door interrupted her thoughts. Like she did every time someone came to see her, she stood with her back to the wall. If someone made an attempt on her life, she wouldn't go down without a fight, weapons or not.

Keys jiggled and jangled until the door flew open and instead of the healers or a servant with her meal, she saw two Thrak. The one with iron shackles in his grasp spat on the blood-stained, stone floor.

"The queen wants to see you," said the other Thrak and motioned her forward.

She wanted to deny them, wanted to tell them to go to hell, wanted to demand the queen drag her ass to the dungeons to talk to her, but she wasn't going to press her luck. Stepping forward, she eyed the manacles.

"Are those necessary?" she asked, trying to mask her trepidation. "I have no weapons. You can't believe I am a threat to your queen."

The first Thrak shoved the irons forward with a disgruntled huff. "Queen's orders."

Everything in her screamed not to allow this. She could fight her way out. Disarm them and slit their throats before they knew what was happeneing, but her mind flashed to Zophar. She had no idea if he was dead, alive, or worse, and she couldn't risk harm coming to him if she lashed out.

Reluctantly, she held her wrists out and the Thrak slapped the manacles on. They were heavier than she imagined, and she let her arms fall in front of her dirty, ripped up trousers.

The Thrak that bound her slipped an enormous hand around her bicep to escort her, but she pulled away from his grasp.

"I do believe these," she lifted the irons up for him to see, "are enough to keep me compliant. I can walk without assistance."

The Thrak eyed one another, looking confused and irritated but with a grunt from one and an eye roll from the other, they motioned her to walk forward.

Salome must have been deeper in the dungeons than she originally thought because the trek up the chilly, weaving incline had the back of her thighs screaming in pain. She hadn't been active during her recovery but how could she have gotten so out of shape that she struggled to march up to the main level of the Black Tower?

Once they made it to the Black Tower foyer, she got a glimpse of how the Gomorrian royals lived and it didn't surprise her. Everything was black: black marble floors, black walls, black chandeliers, and small windows to keep it dim. Whoever designed the castle was inspired by death. Salome found it hard to breathe in the stuffy palace, but she swallowed her panic and focused on taking in the details of her surroundings.

The main entrance was closed off by two iron doors with guards stationed outside. At the foot of the black, spiral staircase, stood two, stoic Thrak. They ignored her as she followed her escort up to the third floor where more Thrak patrolled the circular level. Along the far side of the wall were two massive doors guarded by a couple of Thrak, who were waiting for her.

The doors opened and she scanned the throne room. On the dais sat four thrones, two of which were occupied by females with blonde hair. Behind them was a balcony that spanned the width of the room, making it the brightest room in the Black Tower. Mother and daughter, Salome assumed. They shared the same features and were very pale. The only exception was the woman wearing the black crown with spikes had calculating, blue eyes.

Out of the corner of her eye, she saw something shift. It was Zophar, on his knees bearing the same manacles she had. Other than needing a bath, he looked unharmed and she breathed a sigh of relief and thanked the Almighty. He looked her way and offered a feeble smile, before she gave the queen her full attention.

Matildys stared hungrily at Salome which made her skin crawl, but she refused to show her fear. Salome lifted her head and stood tall remembering she was a queen in her own right as she locked eyes with the queen.

After a moment of sizing up one another, Matildys spoke. "So," her eyes ran up and down Salome. "You are the one causing me all this trouble. I imagined you would look more regal."

"And I imagined you'd be more grotesque as the product of incest."

The Thrak who had escorted Salome smacked her for the disrespect, drawing blood, but Matildys shrieked at him to back off. Salome licked the blood from her bottom lip and refocused on the queen. Though her eyes were misty from the slap, she had nothing but rage in her gaze.

Matildys smirked and seemed almost pleased. "You've got spirit. That'll make quite the show when you are executed tomorrow." The queen leaned forward in her throne, her long, black fingernails scratching the onyx armrest. "I look forward to the Thrak breaking you in every sense of the word," she said in a low, predatorial voice.

Salome didn't bat an eye, though her heart pounded in her chest. It all made perfect sense now, why she had not endured torture, why she'd been treated by the healers, and why they fed her twice a day. Matildys wanted her to be in tip top shape when she unleashed her beasts to tear her apart piece by piece for the Gomorrians' pleasure. She shivered at the thought that had she not been injured in the skirmish outside of the City of Bones, she might have already been mutilated for sport.

She needed to show this barbarian queen she was not afraid of her. She would not shrink back no matter how desperately she wanted to beg for mercy because she knew she would receive none.

"Did you receive my gift?" Salome asked knowing it would get under the queen's skin.

Matildys' smirk faded and the girl sitting beside her squirmed in confusion.

"Ah," Salome purred, "I see your daughter has no idea what I'm talking about."

"That's enough," Matildys hissed.

"Did I strike a nerve?"

The queen straightened in her throne, hands gripping the armrests so tightly the whites of her knuckles showed. "You will hold your tongue."

"What gift?" the princess whispered to her mother.

Salome smiled wickedly at the young girl who believed her mother to be all-powerful, a queen to be feared and revered. A faith, she would take great pleasure in shattering.

"Fifteen Thrak were sent to capture me in the Isles of Myr. I sent their heads back to your mother in a sack." Salome smirked at Matildys, feeling stronger with each eye-opening revelation. "They failed *her* mission, and we all know what the penalty for failure is in Gomorrah."

Fury flared in Matildys' eyes but was gone in an instant. "Tell me where the City of Bones is, and I might order the Thrak to go easy on you tomorrow."

A lie if Salome ever heard one. She knewthere was a great possibility the queen would ask her about the Krazak's secret city, but if she was going to die, she wasn't going to give Matildys the satisfaction of knowing she broke her. Salome pursed her lips and shrugged, "Never heard of it."

"We all know the Krazaks came to your aid in the Bone Mountains when the Thrak attacked and captured you. So tell me. Where is Fennor? Where are the Mountain Men?"

Salome lifted her shackled hands to scratch her chin, feigning confusion. "Doesn't ring a bell. Sorry."

"You refuse to tell me," Matildys hollered, "even when I hold your life in my hands?"

"I would rather die."

Matildys rose from her throne and grinned. "You would rather die?"

"It seems that is to be my fate." Salome watched the queen slither down the five steps from her dais to the black marbled floor. By the time she noticed the glint of a small blade clutched in the queen's hand, it was too late. "No!"

Matildys veered away from Salome and lunged at Zophar, plunging her dagger in the Westerner's gut.

Salome knocked down the Thrak standing next to her as she fought to get to her guardian, but the second Thrak yanked her by her hair, keeping her from Zophar. She stared at him with panic-stricken eyes.

"Zophar," she whispered his name as an apology. She'd forgotten he was in the room during her exchange with the queen.

Matildys grabbed Salome's chin forcing her to look at her, instead of Zophar. A triumphant smile spread across her face. "Put them in the same cell. Tonight, you will watch him bleed to death and tomorrow, I will watch you beg for death as I ensure your suffering lasts for an entire week."

"I swear to the Almighty, I swear to Death herself, if it is the last thing I do, I will kill you!" Salome hissed, not backing down from the queen's threats.

Matildys kissed Salome's cheek and whispered in her ear. "Maybe in the next life."

Chapter Three

Crispin

Captain Ivar, the captain of the *Drakkar*, was personally assigned by the King of Borg to chaperone Crispin and the company of pirates until further notice and he seemed to take his assignment seriously. He made sure every suite the pirates had been offered in Halfrond Keep was guarded by some of the best soldiers in the king's army, and to ensure their obedience, Ivar took it upon himself to stay inside the shared lounge. Crispin figured the captain was either there for information, or he was extremely worried about the pirates doing something stupid on his watch, so he stayed close. But after weeks of waiting for the king to grant them an audience, they were all becoming restless, although they were grateful they weren't sitting in the dungeons.

Most of the crew refused to be in the same room with the Westerner and kept to themselves, but Crispin, Rahab, Ziggy, and Nubis didn't seem to mind the captain's constant presence.

When Crispin thought about it, he could honestly say he'd grown fond of the grumpy seafarer. Ivar was orderly, inquisitive, and from what Crispin could tell, he was quite intelligent coupled with a dry sense of humor. If Ivar and the pirates weren't on opposite sides of the feud between kingdoms, the prince was positive the captain of the *Drakkar* and the captain of the *Shadow of Death* could be great friends.

Ivar let out a groan as he reclined in the same leather chair he sat in every day, with a small plate filled with dried meats and cheese. He glanced over at Ziggy who was sipping a cup of hot tea. As she softly blew the billowing steam, she noticed him staring at her.

Crispin watched as she shifted uncomfortably and observed how tense Nubis was next to her on the couch.

"How long have you two been together?" Ivar asked, lifting a piece of jerky to his mouth, hiding a devilish smirk.

Ziggy and Nubis exchanged a quick glance and Crispin noticed her blush.

"We have been friends for a couple of years," Ziggy answered, running her fingers across her throat where blotch was blossoming.

Ivar quirked his eyebrows, "I see. Just friends then."

"Friends," Nubis repeated the word, but it sounded bitter coming from his lips.

"So, how did a Borgian befriend a Stormcrag and find themselves aboard a pirate ship with the lost prince of Northwind?" Ivar seemed almost giddy with his line of questioning. Although Crispin wanted to come to their rescue, he, too, was curious to hear their answers.

Ziggy cleared her throat before setting her teacup down on the small table in front of her. "My parents were killed when pirates invaded our seaside village." Rahab shifted in her seat, keeping her eyes glued to the wooden floor as Ziggy continued. "Those of us who survived were taken and sold at different ports. I was sold to a ship builder in Northwind until my master offered me up as payment when he lost in cards. The man who won me, freed me."

Ivar and Crispin exchanged a glance. Crispin didn't know slavery was staining his kingdom and by the irritation flaring in the captain's gaze, Crispin knew it had been going on longer than he realized.

"Is *he* the man that freed you?" Ivar looked at Nubis, but Ziggy shook her head.

"No, a man named Oden freed me." Ziggy rolled her shoulders back to sit up straighter. "He is now my employer."

Ivar was quiet for a moment before turning his attention to the Stormcrag. "And you? Do you have a similar story?"

"Oden found me when I was in need. He saved my life." Nubis kept his answers short and vague seemingly on purpose, and Ivar accepted it.

"This Oden," Ivar scratched the two-day old stubble along his jawline, "what business is he in?"

"He owns a tavern in the Night District." Nubis stated in a matter-of-fact tone, suspicion brewing in his eyes.

"The Whispering Fox?" Ivar tilted his head with a gleam in his eyes.

Ziggy and Nubis paled. There weren't many people who knew about Oden since he kept himself hidden and had Makada manage the tavern.

"How do you know about The Whispering Fox?" Nubis demanded to know, a frightening edge in his voice.

Ivar shrugged his shoulders, not bothered by the Stormcrag's tone. "It is my job to know things."

"What kind of things?" Rahab asked, scowling at the captain as she brought her knees to her chest and wrapped herself in a blanket.

Crispin envied that blanket. He wished he were the one wrapping his arms around her. Since they had arrived in Borg, they'd had no time alone, and it was bothering him more than waiting for an inconsiderate king to grant him a meeting. He wanted to toss Rahab over his shoulders, carry her to his room a few doors down the hall, and cradle her in his arms until they fell asleep. He missed her head resting on his chest, the smell of the salty sea in her hair, and her roaming hands. He craved her kiss and missed catching her with a smile on her face, knowing he was the one who put it there.

"Lots of things," Ivar replied, cutting into the prince's daydream. "I am the Captain of the Drakkar. I am the king's eyes at sea. If there is something or someone to know about, I will make it my business to know it."

The room fell silent.

Ziggy mustered the courage to finish her tea which was growing cold.

Rahab tugged her blanket tighter over her shoulders.

And Nubis glared at Ivar across the room, though the Westerner paid him no mind.

When Crispin could no longer tolerate the silence, he shifted in his seat like a petulant child and huffed to draw the captain's attention.

"We've been here for weeks now," the prince griped. "How long do we have to wait until His Majesty grants us an audience?"

Ivar's nostrils flared, but as quick as the irritation flashed, it was gone. He leaned forward and smacked Crispin's boots off the coffee table. "When His Majesty decides he's ready to speak to the likes of you."

"You seem to forget," Crispin placed his hands on the back of his head and reclined in his seat, "that you're mistreating a prince."

"You may be a prince by birth, but a prince of nothing is what you are now. You should consider yourself lucky the king granted you and your *companions*," he said it with an air of disgust, "suites in the Halfrond Keep and did not toss you lot in the dungeons where, quite frankly, you belong."

"And here I was thinking after weeks of playing our nursemaid, you were growing fond of us." Crispin smirked. "Why did they assign you to watch us anyway? Aren't you too important to be with the likes of us?"

Ivar kicked one leg over the other. "Perhaps the king believed me to be the only one capable of keeping you devils in line."

"Or," the prince lifted his index finger, "he hates you and put you on our detail as punishment."

Ivar scoffed when the others snickered. "For a prince, you lack decorum."

Crispin shrugged a shoulder before sinking further into the plush chair. "Exile will do that to a person."

The room fell silent once again.

In the stillness of the room, Crispin sensed Rahab eyeing him, so he looked her way. He could tell she missed him just as much as he missed her. He winked at her and though she tried to hide her grin underneath her blanket, the sides of her eyes crinkled showing him exactly how she felt. One way or another, he would make sure they were alone, and soon.

"Where have you been all this time?" Ivar broke the silence with an oddly personal question and seemed genuinely interested in the answer.

"Not far from here actually." Crispin cracked his neck. "It was a small village called the Tree House Forest."

Ivar paled. "It would seem that village no longer exists."

"It's gone?"

"From the reports we received, Shadows slaughtered the villagers and burned most of the village to ash." Ivar cleared his throat. "Of course, we can't prove it was the Northerners, but it fits their methods, and there were reports they were riding through our lands looking for someone."

Crispin knew exactly who the Shadows were looking for but didn't offer the information to the Westerner. The thought of the village where he'd grown up, spent twelve years of his life, and the people he knew, being destroyed and erased as if they didn't matter, churned his stomach. He never wanted to establish roots there but knowing the tree house he'd call home was gone, pierced his heart.

"Before we could track the Shadows or find out who they were searching for, the raids stopped." Ivar rolled his shoulders back, his military mask back in place. "I guess they found who they were looking."

"I'm sorry to hear the village is gone," Crispin cleared his throat when his voice cracked. "There were good people there."

Ivar nodded, but before he or anyone else could say anything, there was a knock. The captain hopped up and opened the door to find a soldier offering an envelope. He grabbed it, shut the door, and retreated to his chair to read the missive.

Crispin watched the captain's eyes glance over the letter's contents before Ivar read aloud, "His Majesty, King Benaiah of Borg, grants Prince Crispin of Northwind an audience upon receiving this message."

Crispin slowly stood up and cracked his back. It was about time he was granted permission to meet with Benaiah. Perhaps, he could come to a fast resolution with the king so he and his companions could be released by nightfall.

"I suppose we should let Captain Haldane and Master Penn know," Crispin made his way toward the door when Ivar's voice stopped him.

"The king granted *you* permission, no one else." Ivar made his way toward the prince and met his irritated gaze. "I will escort you." He turned back to face the others. "As always, your rooms will be guarded, so please, don't do anything stupid while I'm gone."

Rahab hissed something under her breath that neither Crispin nor Ivar caught.

"What was that, pirate?" Ivar snorted, puffing his chest like a ruffled peacock. "Care to say it a second time?"

Rahab flashed a menacing smile toward the Westerner. "Give the king my regards." Her sing-song voice didn't fool anyone, and Crispin couldn't help but chuckle when Ivar's shoulders tensed.

Ivar refrained from engaging with Rahab further and motioned for Crispin to follow him to the throne room.

The only time Crispin had been able to see the city of Borg was when they first arrived. The lodge style homes and buildings were similar in style and were intricately carved with unique details etched into the wood. The craftmanship reminded Crispin of the toy houses Zophar used to whittle for him when he was a boy. The arched doorways and sloped roofs added to the ancient feel of the city and although, some of the buildings were newly constructed, they looked as if they had been there for a thousand years.

The citizens: men, women, and children alike with their red hair, fair skin, freckles, and blue eyes reminded him of the villagers in the Tree House Forest. But unlike the villagers who were thin and more open to outsiders, the Borgians were built with broad shoulders and prickly dispositions. Their plaited braids, and leather and chain mail garments also differentiated them from the villagers.

Halfrond Keep was impressive and could be seen from the harbor. Pine trees strewn throughout the kingdom made it feel as if he had stepped back into the forest where he'd grown up. Although considered a captive and criminal, Crispin oddly felt at peace in Borg.

Everyone stepped aside when he and his pirate companions were escorted to the Halfrond Keep as guests of the king instead of being thrown into the dungeons as the criminals the Westerners believed them to be. And they weren't wrong.

Crispin wasn't a pirate, but he had blood on his hands. There were times he would close his eyes and flashes of him driving the knife across Memucan's neck disturbed him. He'd killed an unarmed man and although his reasons for doing so were considered righteous and deemed necessary, he was still fighting a twinge of guilt that stung his heart.

When they entered the keep, Crispin was awestruck, because the inside was just as majestic as the outside. Wood beams, high ceilings, iron chandeliers lit with hundreds of candles and beautifully woven tapestries were everywhere, but the animal heads mounted on the wood and stone walls attested to the ruthlessness and hardened ways of the Westerners. He wished Zophar were there to experience the capital city with him, but he'd be thrilled to share his adventures with the old man once they were reunited.

Crispin received his own private quarters while the rest of the crew were ordered to share the remainder of the rooms in the wing available to them. From the outside, the enormous wooden structure didn't look like it had hundreds of rooms inside, but Crispin was pleasantly surprised of the luxury the Borgian royals were accustomed to.

Now marching down the wood paneled halls, walls decorated with artwork depicting the king's accomplishments and bear skin rugs strewn throughout, Crispin wondered what type of man Benaiah was going to be. He'd heard stories of the king from the villagers who ventured into the city to sell some goods or bring back supplies for the harsh winter season, but their reports were never glowing.

Ivar stopped before a large set of doors with two warriors stationed on either side. If Crispin was reading the captain right, he would say Ivar was nervous, but he didn't understand why that could be. As if he could hear Crispin's thoughts, Ivar glanced at him.

"Mind what you say," Ivar whispered so softly Crispin almost didn't hear him. "You are in dangerous territory."

With a nod to the guards, the doors opened slowly. Crispin couldn't even imagine how heavy the doors were. The soldiers pushed with all their might and their muscles bulged with the effort. Crispin waited for Ivar to make the first move before entering the den-like throne room.

At the far end of the room, directly in front of them, sat Benaiah. His once red hair and beard now faded, his blue eyes not kind nor cruel, and his broad shoulders that filled his wooden throne carved into the likeness of a hissing dragon were relaxed. His enormous hands rested on the claw armrests and his feet were firmly planted on the slate floor. Crispin didn't notice a crown on the king's head until they were within twenty feet of the dais. He then saw the simple gold band around the king's head, the only adornment to declare his title. Benaiah's presence alone exuded his power and Crispin forced himself to stand tall, to show he wasn't intimidated by the man who had ruled the Borgians for forty years.

When they were a few feet from the throne, Ivar bowed at the waist and Crispin followed suit. He could at least pay proper respect to the man who held his fate in his hands.

The king ran thick fingers over his braided beard. "So," his voice was coarse, as if he'd been screaming all night long, but there was an undeniable power behind it, "you are Issachar's only surviving son?"

"Yes, Your Majesty. I am Crispin of Northwind."

"Your father prided himself on one thing, and that was the number of sons his wife bore him," Benaiah flashed a crooked smile. "A shame his first born was a disappointment to him."

Somehow, Crispin was offended by the remark about Niabi, and he didn't know why. Perhaps, it was the insult to his blood, but Crispin kept his princely mask in place and smiled. "It seems you and my father knew one another well."

"I'd say. Your father bet his firstborn would be a boy and I bet it would be a girl. He lost a lot of money." The king laughed and the other members of the court in the room laughed with him. Benaiah raised a hand silencing the courtiers. "Now, Prince Crispin, what is this business about you being captured aboard the *Shadow of Death*? Were you kidnapped?"

"No, the crew of the *Shadow of Death* provided me safe passage out of Pulau." Crispin looked at Ivar standing stoically next to him, his hands firmly planted behind his back. "Captain Ivar brought us here because Master Penn of The Sisters and I requested an audience with you."

Benaiah snapped his stubby fingers and a hunched servant scurried toward the throne with a silver tray. The servant took a sip of the wine and once the king was satisfied the drink was not poisoned, he grabbed the goblet and shooed the man away. "Well, as you know, the Pulauans are our enemy. They pillage our outlying villages and have killed more of our people than I care to think about." Benaiah took a long sip, making Crispin wait until he was finished. A classic power move. The king wiped his mouth with his forearm and flashed a toothy grin at Crispin. "I am prepared to make a deal, Prince Crispin."

"You have my attention." Crispin noticed Ivar seemed to tense, as if he was holding his breath.

Benaiah leaned forward. "I assume you have become quite fond of the crew of ruffians you have been traveling with, is that so?"

Crispin wasn't sure if he should truthfully answer that question. Ivar's warning before entering the throne room rang in his head: *Mind what you say. You are in dangerous territory.* He didn't want the knowledge of how he felt about the crew to be used against him. But if he said they meant nothing to him, he was afraid of what Benaiah might do without them as his bargaining chip.

He noticed the king's eyebrow arch and answered, "I hold them in high regard."

Benaiah chewed on that bit of information before continuing. "Normally, we hang pirates on sight, but your *friends* have been given special treatment and housed as guests of the crown because of *you*." The king tugged on his beard. "I can pardon them for their crimes if they swear fealty to me and join the armada under Ivar's watchful command."

Crispin could see Rahab and Haldane slitting their own throats before bending a knee to the Westerner. But the king didn't need to know that. "I can't make that decision for them, Your Majesty. I am not their leader."

"No, but the alternative is finding themselves dangling from the end of a noose." The king's smile sent chills up Crispin's spine. Benaiah most likely knew the pirates would never agree to his terms. The pirates would die, and Benaiah would be seen as benevolent.

Crispin cringed at the thought of Rahab, Haldane, Phex, Corwin, Ondrej, Rafi and the other deckhands hanging lifelessly from the gallows for thousands to gawk and spit upon.

"What is it you want from me?" Crispin decided to play the political game, so he could get out of Borg alive and ensure the safety of his friends. "Surely, you wouldn't pardon pirates, your sworn enemies, and offer them a life amongst your people, if you didn't gain something from it."

Benaiah let out a booming laugh that filled the throne room. "You are definitely Issachar's son. He had a nose like a bloodhound when it came to political dealings." The king seemed proud of that fact, but it made Crispin nauseous. "Word has reached me that you intend to wage a war against Niabi and reclaim your father's throne."

"You've heard correctly."

"I cannot engage in a war with Niabi." The Westerner shook his head sadly, though Crispin could tell it was all an act. "I have too much at risk to anger her, and to be honest, I have no quarrel with her. Your father was a bastard." His words stung. "He was responsible for my son, Antilles', death and I was not sad to hear of his passing."

"That is quite the accusation to put at my dead father's feet." Crispin's nostrils flared.

"There is evidence of his crimes." Benaiah seemed just as angry, but waved a hand in the air. "But no need to worry. Your sister has seen to it that those responsible for assassinating my son, her betrothed, met their deaths gruesomely."

"So, you are asking me not to engage in a war with Niabi? Is that it? To protect your alliance."

"On the contrary, my boy," the king's smile was unsettling. "Wage a war. Kill your sister. It does not matter to me if she survives. She is not my blood nor is she my daughter-in-law."

"But you said -"

Benaiah stood up and made his way toward Crispin. He was much taller and his shoulders boarder than he first appeared, making Crispin feel small.

"*I* will not wage a war against her," the king stopped a foot in front of Crispin and whispered, "but I will not prevent you from starting one. If you lose," he shrugged, "I lose nothing. But if you should win, there is one thing I would ask of you to ensure your friends are granted clemency."

Crispin felt uneasy but asked anyway, "And what is it you want from me?"

"Should you win and become King of the North, I want you to marry my only daughter, Princess Lahki."

Crispin and Ivar both seemed to suck in a breath at the same time. "What?"

"Your father and I made an agreement decades ago that Niabi would wed my second-born son, Antilles. But the idea of my son becoming king didn't sit well with him and he had my son eliminated and married your sister off to the King of Elisor. I have no more sons to marry off. Antilles is dead. Ehrik, my heir, is married, and Ragnar, my spare, is betrothed. But Lahki is available and will make a fine queen."

Crispin's head was spinning. Marry the princess of Borg? His father would have arranged something similar if he were still alive, but Crispin's heart was already set on another. But if it was the only way to ensure his friends survived in enemy territory, he might have to consider it.

"Well?" Benaiah's husky voice sliced through his tormented thoughts. "Do we have an agreement?"

"Might I have some time to consider your offer, Your Majesty? I don't want to rush an important decision." Crispin needed to buy himself some time. He needed to think of how he could get out of this situation unscathed.

The king tried to mask his displeasure but failed. "Take one day. We will reconvene tomorrow, and I expect to be toasting to our newfound alliance."

Chapter Four

Niabi

Being pregnant didn't deter Niabi from having Tala and a small host of guards accompany her to Elisor on the sixteenth anniversary of Dichali's death. Her deceased husband's grave was nestled between a meadow of wildflowers and the Ameyalli River. She had never missed paying her respects and this year would be no different, except for the fact, that next to Dichali's marker was a freshly covered gravesite where their son's belongings had been buried.

She cleaned their markers, making sure their names wouldn't fade, and laid fresh flowers at the base. Sitting cross-legged on the grass, she sat in silence as the early morning breeze wisped strands of hair around her face.

In Elisor, she didn't don her royal finery. She wore no crown, no jewels, no expensive dresses. Here she was truly herself. Hair down, make-up free, wearing a traditional Andrago maiden dress, she felt at peace sitting with her departed husband and son. For a moment, she felt whole, until she opened her eyes and saw their tombstones instead of their beautiful faces.

Dichali was unlike any other man she'd ever met. And even though she found love with another man and was carrying his baby, her heart would always belong to the Andrago king.

"Do you remember the day we met?" she whispered, grazing the tips of her fingers across her husband's marker with a small smile. "I wanted so badly to hate you, but I belonged to you the moment you kissed my hand."

She closed her eyes once more, knowing Tala was keeping watch over her. She listened to the rushing water of the Ameyalli River, the chirps of the songbirds welcoming the morning light, and the bleating of a nearby flock of sheep. All the sounds Dichali loved.

Niabi's mind drifted back to the first time they laid eyes on one another.

Her father, Issachar, was seated on his throne, stroking a finger through his salt and pepper beard, as she approached the dais. To Issachar's right was her younger brother, Lykos, with the newly appointed Master of War, Zophar, beside him. Lord Maon, her father's Second in Command, sat on Issachar's left and next to him was the Immortal Seer, Harbona. The small council, made up entirely of men, summoned her, the rightful heir to the White Throne, as if she were a commoner.

She stood before the council, dressed in black mourning clothes. Her betrothed, Antilles, the Prince of Borg, and his company had been slaughtered in the Black Forest during a hunt. Her father wasn't surprised by the attack, nor did he seem bothered his alliance with the Westerners was now in jeopardy. Her marriage to the prince was the only thing keeping peace between the two mighty kingdoms. She figured her father had summoned her to inform her she was to wed another Westerner.

King Benaiah of Borg, wouldn't allow her to marry Ehrik, his heir, because he was promised to another. And Ragnar, his third born son was only six years old. Though she was against an arranged marriage, when she finally met Antilles, they immediately bonded. She was happy for the first time since her forced return to Northwind from the Isles of Myr. Antilles understood her and accepted her as she was. Her father despised the fact that she learned to wield a weapon in her mother's homeland, but Antilles celebrated it. In Borg, women were not only encouraged to learn the way of the sword but expected to. When Niabi and Antilles weren't attending royal events, they'd steal precious moments in the early morning or late night to spar with one another and share their desires and goals.

Zophar had been Antilles' protector and had seen to it that neither of them were discovered when they were alone. It would have been considered improper, but neither of them cared if they were caught. They were in love and couldn't wait to spend their lives together.

Now Zophar sat next to her brother, Lykos. The King of Borg had blamed him for failing to protect his son. His face was brutally scarred and even the beard he was regrowing didn't hide the smile scars. She could see the pain in his eyes. He, too, mourned for Antilles, but he didn't don black clothes because her father ordered everyone to shed their mourning clothes before the traditional grieving period was supposed to end.

Issachar tilted his head to the side. His judgmental gaze roved up and down her appearance. "Mourning clothes?"

"I mourn my betrothed," she said.

"Antilles is dead," Issachar spat viciously. "Nothing will change that. But today is a joyous occasion for I have found you a husband." His smile was unsettling and normally meant trouble for her.

Niabi quickly glanced at Lykos and saw the fury in his brown eyes. She turned to face their father and straightened to her full height. "Antilles' body has not yet grown cold, and you disrespect his memory by promising me to another?"

"How dare you use that tone with me?" Issachar narrowed his eyes and hissed, "You ungrateful, bitter witch!"

"Your Majesty -"

The king lifted a hand to silence Harbona's protest. "You should be thanking me on bended knees for finding you another suitor. Most men wouldn't touch a bride with a deceased betrothed. It's bad luck."

She crinkled her nose but kept her voice steady. "I will not grovel, nor will I thank you for forcing your will upon me. I grieve -"

"A boy who died," he interjected.

"The man I loved. But you wouldn't know anything about love. You are cruel and wicked and selfish."

"Enough, you vile creature!" He slammed his fists on the armrests of his throne and shot down the stairs of the dais.

"Father!" Lykos jumped up to stop him but wasn't fast enough.

Issachar raised a hand to strike her, but she unsheathed the knives hidden in her sleeves and held one to her father's throat and one against his groin. Everyone in the room froze in place. If she wanted to, she could have slit his throat before any one of them so much as blinked, but she held her weapons at bay.

"You will not touch me," Niabi growled, maintaining eye contact with her red-faced father.

"I will have you whipped until there's nothing left of your back but bone," the king hissed.

"If it is your intent to disfigure my future wife, King Issachar, then our agreement will be null and void."

The deep voice sliced through the room, startling everyone. Three Andrago marched into the throne room and Issachar's nostrils flared in irritation at the interruption.

The leader of the trio walked directly to Niabi and stood by her side. "The future queen of the Andrago will not suffer such torture to satisfy your wounded ego."

Issachar reluctantly stepped away from Niabi which surprised her. When she pulled her weapons on her father, she didn't expect to walk out of the throne room alive. She glanced up at the newcomer and found he was already eyeing her. He didn't look angry, he looked amused.

"King Dichali," Issachar cleared his throat. "You arrived sooner than expected." He shot a vicious glance at Niabi. "Put your knives away, girl, and show your betrothed the respect you fail to give your king."

So, this was the King of Elisor. The Leader of the Andrago. The Lord of Horses. She didn't lower or sheathe her weapons but gave him a look over to assess if he was more of a threat to her than her father.

Her lack of obedience infuriated Issachar. "You wicked girl," he seethed. "I ordered you to lower your weapons and show King Dichali respect."

"Why would I show him any more respect than I show you?" Niabi's gaze sliced from her father to the Andrago. "His people are responsible for Antilles' assassination. Do you hate me so much that you would hand me over to his murderer?"

Dichali's face softened. "Despite the malicious rumors circulating that we were responsible for Prince Antilles' death, I can assure you, we are not to blame."

"How dare you speak his name," she wheezed. "I would rather die than marry you, you devil."

"That can be arranged," Issachar fumed, reaching for her, but Dichali raised a hand to block him.

"May I speak with the princess alone?"

Issachar's eyes widened and his cheeks reddened but after a second's hesitation, he reluctantly agreed. The king motioned for everyone to leave the room.

One of the Andrago standing behind Dichali stepped forward. "You sure you want to be alone with her?" He whispered, but not low enough for Niabi to miss it. She still held her knives and he was wise to question leaving his king alone with her.

Dichali nodded with a smile, his gaze fixed on Niabi. "I'll be fine, Tala. Take Chua and wait outside."

Tala shot her a look that screamed, *touch him and you die,* and she bobbed her head in understanding. He turned on his heel and she watched the two Andrago warriors leave the room. Once they were alone, Dichali circled her. He was sizing her up, so she took a moment to do the same.

The King of Elisor was certainly handsome. His bronze skin and black hair that rested just below his shoulders were Andrago staples. His brown eyes were oddly comforting. He was clean shaven, and his thick, black eyebrows bounced playfully when he stopped in front of her.

They didn't say a word, soaking one another in, maintaining unwavering eye contact that was so intimate it nearly stole her breath. But despite what he said, she was unwilling to believe his people weren't somehow involved in the attack that killed Antilles. The Andrago were known to be fierce and would attack trespassers but slinking into the Black Forest and killing her betrothed was too much for her to forgive or forget.

As if he could read her mind, he said, "I did not order the attack on your departed."

"Andrago weapons were found at the..." she held back the tears and swallowed the knot in her throat. "If you didn't order it, then you are woefully incapable of keeping your people in check."

Dichali smiled, unbothered by her insults. "I see why your father was threatening you when I first walked in. You are fire itself."

"I am more than threatening." She stood her ground, even when he took a small step closer to her, clasping his arms behind his back. "I am a weapon, and he knows it. That is why he fears me."

"Should *I* fear you?" He smirked and she noticed the small, intricate braids plaited against his head.

She fiddled with her daggers and flashed a contemptuous smile. "You would be wise to fear me."

Dichali ate the distance that remained between them. He towered over her and looked down at her. She tilted her face upwards to make eye contact with him and made note that his shoulders were broader than she first thought, and he had dimples that softened the hardness of his masculine jawline.

"I believe we share something in common, Princess."

"Which is?"

His perfect smile sent a shiver down her spine. Being this close to him, she could smell the tobacco and pine clinging to his clothes. It was frustratingly intoxicating.

"We both hate your father," he whispered in glee.

She hadn't expected that response. "Then why ally yourself with him? Why take me for your bride?"

"Because he stole your birthright as his firstborn," he didn't hesitate in answering. "You are destined to rule, not to be in a man's shadow. I want to restore your crown, even if it isn't the one of your ancestors."

"Why?"

He shrugged a shoulder and grinned. "I can't think of a better way to piss him off."

Niabi took a step back and made sure he saw her sheathe her knives up her sleeves. She quirked an eyebrow and crossed her arms across her chest. "What do you gain from marrying me? What do you want from me?"

Dichali walked toward one of the floor-to-ceiling windows that overlooked the White City. "The Andrago have been at war with the North for generations. I do not wish for that cycle of bloodshed to continue. I want my people to live in peace."

"I will never love you."

He turned to look at her, unfazed by her statement. "Maybe you will never love me, but I am being truthful in my desire for peace. I need a woman who is bold and commands attention. I want a queen who will fight for both of our peoples. A wife who will ensure peace. All I ask from you, is your loyalty and your partnership."

"And if I should say no?"

"Then you will never see me again. Unlike your father, I will not silence you or force your hand. In Elisor, women and men are equals. Your choice matters. Your voice matters. Your desires matter. I will not force you to be mine, Your Highness, but I would be honored if you chose a life by my side."

She walked toward him and stood on her tiptoes to whisper in his ear, "How do you know I won't slit your throat the second I have the chance?"

Niabi knew he was smiling without looking at him. "Because you are a warrior and a true warrior is honorable. You won't harm me, just as I won't harm you." She pulled back to meet his gaze and saw a sincerity in his eyes that pierced her heart. "If you want to remain in your father's castle and live under his cruel and crushing will, then I will respect your decision. But, if you want to claim a position of power, ensuring everything he stole from you is restored, then be my queen."

There was something about the king she couldn't figure out. He was charming, but his hellacious reputation that she had heard so much about, now seemed exaggerated. He was speaking from his heart to hers and he was right. If she stayed, her father would crush her in every way.

She met the king's tender gaze. "Children."

He tilted his head to the side. "What about them?"

She jutted her chin, trying to appear taller. "Do you require them?"

"I desire them," he stroked a hand through his dark locks, "but I would not force you to bear them."

"And if I should bear you a daughter?" She held her breath.

Dichali rested a hand over his heart, as if he were swearing an oath. "I will love, protect, teach, and prepare her to rule when I am gone." He lifted his hand and when she flinched his eyes filled with rage and sorrow. Tenderly and slowly, he thumbed loose strands of hair from her face and tucked them behind her ear. "Not all men are like your father, Princess. There are some of us who have compassionate hearts and see the value of a woman. You needn't fear me."

After a moment to think, she said, "I will marry you on one condition."

"Name your terms."

"I want my own horse."

Dichali laughed and it was a deep, melodious sound that set her heart ablaze. "What an odd request from a princess with a stable full of them."

She stared at the white marble floor. "I was never allowed to ride one. I want to learn on my own horse."

The king shook his head, still chuckling. "No." She shot him a look, but he continued before she could lash out. "You want to ensure you have freedom to flee, should you decide to leave me."

Dichali was more intuitive than she gave him credit. A mistake she wouldn't make again. "Is that a bad thing?" she popped a hip to the side and smirked.

"It's a smart thing." He crossed his arms over his chest and even with his breastplate on, she could tell he was muscular. "If there's one thing the Andrago can teach you, it's how to ride." He looked deep into her eyes, clearly seeking the truth behind them. She didn't back down and maintained eye contact until he was satisfied. "I think I have the perfect horse for you, my lady."

Niabi extended her hand. "Are we agreed then, Your Majesty?"

Amused, he took her slender hand in his calloused one and nodded. "As long as you call me Dichali."

Her heart swelled at the contact. "Are we agreed, Dichali?"

He smiled. "We are agreed, Niabi."

"Niabi?" Tala's voice tore her from her memories.

She opened her eyes and tears streamed down her face. He extended his hand to help her up.

"Are you ready to go home?"

She knew he meant Northwind, but Elisor was her true home. And she missed it terribly.

What if she took Pash up on his offer and just left Northwind? Abandoning her kingdom, her crown, her throne. She never truly cared for them. It was always about revenge. Her power wasn't tied to a throne. She was power. Perhaps, she could give it all up. Run and never look back. Start over.

But seeing her father's smug face mocking her reminded her exactly why she would never run away. Why she would never give up what she took with blood and tears. If she retreated, left everything behind for a life of anonymity, she would be proving her father right. She wasn't capable of being queen. And she would be damned if she allowed him to rejoice in the afterlife.

"Niabi?" Tala's eyes were filled with worry, so she flashed a small smile to ease his nerves.

Reluctantly, she accepted his help and stood up. She kissed Dichali's and Rollo's tombstones, whispered her goodbyes and reminded them how much she loved and missed them.

"I am ready." It was time she dealt with Gershom's treason once and for all.

Chapter Five

Adonijah

After nearly two weeks of being detained in Pash's military camp, surrounded by Shadows like the countless ones he'd slaughtered over the years, Adonijah was growing antsy. He tried thinking of a way to get word to Salome that he was alright, that he was thinking of her, and trying to figure out a way to return to her, but his brother's good graces only stretched so far.

Pash had ensured he wasn't chained or mistreated, but Adonijah saw how the soldiers looked at him. Their hunger to see him hanged was evident. Every time he stepped outside of his brother's tent to smoke, stretch his legs, or get some fresh air, they watched him with hate in their eyes.

His brother was busy most days strategizing and readying his men to launch an attack on Gomorrah. And good riddance to the Gomorrians and the horrific Thrak. Adonijah wouldn't mourn any that died during battle. But observing Prince Thanos skulking about the campgrounds didn't instill confidence the Gomorrians would be any better under his crushing thumb.

Since the night he'd been captured, he hadn't seen the Nameless Rider and Pash reminded him periodically not to get himself into trouble while being his guest. Guest. Prisoner. It all meant the same thing. He wasn't free to leave. He wasn't free to participate in meetings. He wasn't free to wander much farther than a few tents down from his brother's shelter. Pash insisted it was for his safety, but he and his brother both knew Adonijah was instructed to stay in the tent for the safety of Pash's soldiers. Adonijah was lethal. And if he really wanted to, he could try to slip out of the camp, slaughtering a few Shadows on his way out. But he wasn't going to be reckless. That would jeopardize his brother's life and he didn't want to repay his kindness with betrayal. That wasn't his way of doing things.

The only highlight of his long and boring days was at night when he and Pash would stay up late talking. Getting to know his brother again after so many years apart felt fulfilling. He'd been alone so long he almost forgot what it was like to have family. Of course, there was Salome, but that was different. His brother was the only blood relative he had left – other than their father – but Adonijah refused to include him in the family tree.

Leoti, the Andrago maiden, would stop by their tent nightly to eat dinner with them. He thought at first, she and Pash were having an affair, but his brother was far too honorable for that, especially knowing how loyal he was to Niabi. As wretched as Adonijah believed her to be, Pash would light up every time her name was mentioned, and he knew his brother was hopelessly in love with her.

The Andrago maiden was intriguing. She was soft-spoken but bold at the same time. She held her ground when arguing with Pash and didn't bat an eye when challenged. There was a refreshing quality about her that Adonijah couldn't quite put his finger on. There was no denying she was beautiful. Her long black hair was always in an intricate braid and her round eyes and full lips were enticing. But it was her bluntness and calm demeanor that nearly hypnotized him every time she spoke. Whenever she walked into the tent, he felt a wave of peace wash over him and for a second, he would forget all his worries.

That night sitting at the circular dinner table in Pash's tent, despite Leoti's presence, Adonijah didn't feel relaxed and wasn't at peace. He had been stunned into silence and stared at Pash across the table.

"Are you certain?"

Pash took another bite of his venison, the blood sauce dripping back down onto the plate. He nodded. "Our spies are well informed, Adonijah. The Thrak were seen carrying a woman that matches Salome's description along with a middle-aged Westerner. From what we know, they are being held in the dungeons beneath the Black Tower. The square is being prepped for a significant event."

"You mean, they are planning to torture her." Adonijah couldn't eat another bite and pushed his nearly full plate away from him.

"That is what we suspect." Pash glanced at Leoti who sat upright in her chair and hadn't said a word since she entered the tent, nearly thirty minutes ago.

"You have to rescue her." Adonijah leaned forward, tears welling up in his eyes at the thought of Salome being brutalized by the Thrak, while the Gomorrians cheered at her screams.

Pash rested his hands on the table and the look plastered on his face was one Adonijah knew well. It was sympathetic and apologetic, and it enraged him.

"You will sit by and do nothing to save her?" Adonijah fumed. "Does your queen not have a bounty on her head? Surely, she would want you to bring her back to Northwind before letting the Gomorrians have their way with her."

"My orders are to attack the city and claim it for Thanos." Pash wiped his mouth with a linen napkin. "If we can get there in time to extract Salome, we will, but that is not our objective."

"Then let me go," Adonijah pleaded. "Let me go, I can save her."

Pash slowly shook his head. "I'm sorry, Adonijah, but I can't let you do that. If you're captured, it could jeopardize our assault."

"How?" He leapt to his feet, his chair falling to the ground behind him. "You think if they capture me, I'll tell them about you and your army?"

"It's nothing personal," Pash remained calm, straightening in his seat. "We march at dawn. If the Thrak are aware of our plans, I could lose hundreds of men and I am not willing to risk their lives to save one or two people."

"She is not just some random prisoner -"

Pash stood up silencing his brother. "You will stay here. Do not give me a reason to lock you in the pit."

Adonijah flinched. His brother had never sounded so militaristic with him before.

"Please," Pash's voice softened. "I am already sticking my neck out for you by keeping you here, alive, and treated as my guest. If you were any other trespasser, I would have hung you by now." He rounded the table to stand in front of Adonijah and rested a hand on his shoulder. "I swear, I will do what I can to save her when we launch our assault. But I cannot do my job and worry about whether or not you listened to my orders."

"If it were Niabi who had been captured and I asked you to stay put, would you be able to?" He asked, rage coursing through his entire body.

A flash of fear flickered in Pash's eyes, but as quickly as it appeared, it disappeared. "I would want to do everything I could to rescue her."

"Yet, you still expect me to stay behind and do what exactly?" Adonijah shrugged his brother's hand off his shoulder. "If something happens to her -"

"I am asking you to trust me." Pash grabbed the belt that held his weapons and strapped it on. "I have rounds. When I get back, we can talk more." He made his way to the flap entrance and stopped. Looking over his shoulder he said, "My hands are tied, Adonijah. I'm sorry."

Pash left and Adonijah started pacing the room, kicking tables, chairs, and other random objects out of his way. He prowled to the decanter of wine and poured himself a hefty serving. He swallowed the contents in one big gulp and turned back around toward the table where the remainder of his dinner sat. It was then he noticed Leoti sitting quietly at the table, and it startled him. He had forgotten she was in the room. He felt foolish. She'd watched him throw an adult version of a two-year-old tantrum.

"Pash is right," she finally broke the silence, her round, brown eyes fastened on him. "If you get involved, it will give Ophir ammunition to use against not only you, but Pash as well. He might be Pash's uncle, but he's only loyal to himself."

"What is that supposed to mean?" Adonijah picked his chair up and sat back down, kicking his feet up on the table.

"It means, Ophir was passed over as the Commander of Shadows years ago and he hasn't forgiven Pash or Niabi for the insult." Leoti spoke softly, as if she was concerned someone would overhear. "If you interfere with Pash's operation, it will make him look inept and that is the kiss of death for any leader. He stuck his neck out for you when you were captured. Give him a chance to help Salome while fulfilling his duty."

"I'm sure he'll do his best to save her," Adonijah said sarcastically, rolling his eyes.

Leoti smacked his boots off the table and stood in righteous fury. "Your brother and I might not see eye to eye, but no one can accuse him of being dishonorable. If he said he will do his best to save her, you better damn well believe he will fight to his dying breath to get her out of there. Not just for your benefit, but because he cannot fathom an innocent person suffering at the hands of the Thrak." She spat on the ground. "The Thrak are an abomination. A stain on humanity. No one, enemy of the queen or not, should suffer such a fate."

Adonijah was stunned into silence for a second time that evening. This petite woman had humbled him, putting him firmly into his place. He stood up and looked down on her. He was a full head taller than her and to her credit, she didn't shrink back from his encroaching figure.

"I'm sorry," he said, which seemed to surprise her. "You're right."

Leoti flicked her braid behind her with a huff. "Of course I am, and don't you forget it." After a brief moment of maintaining eye contact with him, she took a step back and headed for the tent's entrance. "I know you probably won't, but try to get some sleep, Adonijah."

Once she left and he was truly alone, he sank into one of the leather chairs, pulled out his pipe, and lit it. He exhaled a puff of smoke up to the ceiling folds and groaned. Had he not left Salome, maybe this wouldn't have happened. How had she been captured by the Thrak, anyway?

Pash had never failed to keep his word before, and he had no reason to believe his brother would fail him this time. All he could do now was pray that Pash wasn't too late to save her.

Chapter Six

Salome

Salome and Zophar were dragged back to the dungeons beneath the Black Tower and thrown into Zophar's cell. The Thraks' rough treatment would be evident in the morning. Salome was positive her arms, legs, and torso would be covered in bruises. She could already feel her bottom lip swelling from the smack she received in the throne room. But none of her injuries mattered. She was running on pure adrenaline and the pain did not register. Zophar's groan forced her to lift herself up from the damp prison floor to help him.

"Zophar?" She knelt in front of him and ripped the bottom half of her shirt to press against his wound. "Zophar, I am so sorry. This is all my fault."

He coughed. "No, it isn't. You did what I would have done."

"But you're hurt."

"I've been stabbed worse than this," he flashed a half-smile. He lifted his hand to touch her jaw where a bruise was forming. "Your face."

"I've been struck harder by children," she snorted, drawing a laugh from him.

"You always did have a mouth on you."

Salome pressed the torn piece of cloth against the wound again, making him wince. She looked around the cell to see if there was a way to escape. "I'm sure the guards will come back soon."

Zophar's eyes were filled with pain, but he cleared his throat and said, "You should lie to them about where the City of Bones is to buy yourself some time."

"You know they will never let me walk out of here alive."

"You need to try. When they come back, tell them you want to make a deal."

Salome shook her head. "They will kill you or worse if they find out I've lied."

"I am prepared to die."

"I am not prepared to let you," her voice cracked.

"Salome, please."

"We are both leaving alive, or we are dying together. I will not leave you."

"Our people need you. You cannot die here."

"I will not lose another family member." She pressed his hand to the wound while she took a turn around the cell. "I will not add another band to my arm."

"You need to think of everyone else before me," he said in an oddly calm voice, which rattled her.

"You know me well enough to know I won't." She found a broken piece of rock that fell off the wall, lying on the damp floor. Picking it up, she turned it over in her palm and noticed there was a sharp edge to it. If she needed to, she could use it in lieu of a dagger. Not the cleanest of kills, but it would do the job in her hands. She plopped back down on the floor next to Zophar, resting her head on his shoulder. "How did you get those scars on your face?"

Zophar looked at her, but she didn't meet his gaze. "Why ask me that now?"

"I was always too afraid to ask before."

"The possibility of death brings boldness." He propped himself up as much as possible without groaning. "I was a captain in King Benaiah's army. I swore to protect his son, Antilles, who was betrothed to your sister, Niabi. When it came time for them to meet, they fell hard for one another and were inseparable. We spent a few months in Northwind and once we were ready to return to Borg, we went on a hunting excursion on the way back to the Western Lands. We normally would have travelled by ship, but the pirates of Pulau were aware of the prince's visit. If captured, they could get quite the ransom for him. What we didn't anticipate was being ambushed by the Andrago. Only one of our members managed to make it back to Northwind for aid."

"What happened?"

Salome wasn't sure he would finish the story but then he cleared his throat and continued. "By the time your brother, Lykos, arrived with reinforcements it was too late. My leg was severely broken, and I was unable to get Antilles to a healer. He died in my arms. Your brother helped me bring the fallen bodies to Borg. The king was angry, distraught over losing his son, and sentenced me to be executed."

"But it wasn't your fault."

"The king didn't see it that way. Thankfully, your brother intervened. He broke me out of my cell that same night and took me back to Northwind."

"But the scars?" She looked at his smile scars barely noticeable underneath his bushy beard. Now she wondered if he'd purposely grown it to hide them.

"My punishment before my execution. One to remind me I had failed my king. The second because I had disgraced our people."

"You've never gone back to Borg?"

"If I go back, my life will be forfeited." Zophar reached for her hand and squeezed it. "The Northerners accepted me. Lykos was a better friend than I could have asked for, and I owed him my life. But perhaps, my time has now come."

"Death would have come for us by now, if that were the case."

"She will not be long, I imagine."

Salome stood up and paced. She couldn't sit still anymore. "We need to get out of this cell." She wasn't going to give up that easily. He needed to get to a healer, and she would burn the city to the ground, if that's what it took to save him.

"There is no way out of here, Salome. Gomorrian prison cells are inescapable."

"Then we fight our way out." She whipped around to face him, determination and worry in her face. "We don't end like this. This is not how we die."

Zophar's blue eyes filled with tears. "Your father would be proud of the woman you've become," he whispered.

She knelt in front of him. "Are you proud of me?"

He looked as if the question confused him. "Of course I am."

"Then that is all that truly matters to me." Before he could protest, she continued, "You saved us from our enemies. You raised us, protected us, trained us, and loved us as if we were your own. You have been more of a father to me than Issachar. And if I'm being honest, from what I now know about him, the Almighty blessed me with you."

"Salome, I have been honored to be your guardian," his voice cracked, "but I could never replace your father. Blood is blood."

"Give me your hand." She grasped his outstretched palm and took the sharp rock she'd found earlier and sliced the tip of his finger, then sliced her own. She placed their fingers together letting their blood mix. "Now there is no doubt. We share the same blood. From this day forward, you are my father, and I am your daughter."

"Salome-"

"Say it," she interrupted him.

Zophar's bottom lip quivered, but the burly Westerner's voice boomed with confidence. "From this day forward, I am your father, and you are my daughter. Blood is blood."

She leaned forward and kissed his chilled forehead. "I promise you," she whispered, "you will not die here."

Chapter Seven

Crispin

Crispin and Ivar didn't utter a sound as they trekked through the halls. The captain seemed on edge and even though Crispin was dying to ask why, he kept his mouth shut and his thoughts to himself. There was no way he wanted to agree to an arranged marriage, but he wasn't sure what other options he had to ensure the pirates' safety. To ensure Rahab's safety.

Ivar delivered him to his quarters where two guards were stationed outside, reminding him that even though he was free to roam the designated rooms he and the pirates had been assigned, he was still a prisoner in a foreign kingdom. Still at the mercy of a king who seemed to have held a grudge against his father for two decades.

Once the door to his lavish room closed and he was finally alone, he sat on the edge of his fur-lined bed and hung his head. He rubbed the heels of his palms against his eyes as he listened to the crackling fire in the stone hearth, irritation and exhaustion plaguing him. To agree to the king's demands would go against everything his heart wanted. What would Salome do if she were in this position? He grumbled to himself knowing his sister would do anything in her power to secure an alliance.

But there was something gnawing at him. He didn't trust Benaiah. The king had a sinister look in his eyes. He couldn't have survived as sole ruler for forty years without learning a few wicked and deceitful tricks. What was he missing?

Marry Lahki and he would be free, the pirates would be granted clemency, and no one would be executed. Simple. His ancestors had made alliances forged in marriage countless times. It was politics. But he wasn't sure if the nausea he was battling was because he would be agreeing to marry a woman he'd never met, or he would have to give up the woman he wanted, or if deep in his soul he felt the king wouldn't hold up his end of the bargain.

Crispin flopped down on the soft mattress and laid his forearm over his eyes to block out the bright light pouring in the tall, narrow window.

He could ensure Rahab's safety, the entire crew's safety, if he agreed to Benaiah's terms. It was the most logical choice, but he couldn't convince himself to agree. He would rather plot, destroy, and fight his way out of Borg, if it meant he could be with Rahab. What had that pirate done to him? Had he never met her, he wouldn't have hesitated to marry a princess. If he were still marching through the halls of Northwind, his father surely would have arranged a match similar to this, one that would benefit the North. It was what was expected of him, and in another life, he would have agreed without a second thought. But things were different. He was different.

Consumed wholly by his thoughts, he didn't hear his door creak open, nor did he hear the footsteps approaching him until it was too late. His eyes shot open, and he swung his arm to protect himself but found Rahab standing at the edge of his bed, arms folded over her chest.

"Did I startle you, Your Majesty?" Her left eyebrow arched in teasing, but her smirk vanished when she looked into his eyes. "What is it?"

Crispin sat up and shook his head. "Nothing. I'm just tired is all."

Rahab popped her hip to the side and shot him an angry glare. "You're a terrible liar, Crispin. If you are to be king, you will have to work on that."

"Why would I need to be proficient at lying to be a good king?" He scoffed. "I thought honesty was what made a leader worth following."

Rahab ate the distance between them, her knees bumping his legs planted on the wooden floor. "Honesty is admirable, but it could cost you your life if you aren't careful."

Crispin didn't want to burden her with what he and the king had discussed because he already knew what she would say. She would insist he marry Lahki, reminding him of her lot in life. He refused to let her push him away or make the decision for him. But if their relationship had a chance of working, he knew he'd need to include her in important matters, especially if she would one day be his wife, his queen.

He raked a hand through his hair before snatching her wrists and pulling her on top of him. Once she was straddling him, he wrapped his arms around her hips and stared into her suspicious hazel eyes.

"I spoke with the king."

"And?" she prodded when he didn't offer more information.

"And..." Crispin sighed and decided to tell her the truth. "He made me an offer that would ensure the crew's safety."

"We would be free to go?" Rahab sat wide-eyed before her skepticism kicked back in. "What exactly are you expected to do?"

He bit his bottom lip before breaking eye contact with her. "I must agree to marry his daughter and make her my queen." He felt Rahab's body tense up and he wished he hadn't told her. He forced himself to meet her gaze and was surprised to see the hardened pirate he'd first met in Pulau was staring back at him. She didn't look surprised, she didn't look heartbroken or even angry, and it frightened him.

They stared at one another in silence until Crispin couldn't take it any longer. "Say something, Rahab."

Rahab slid off his lap and stood before him. "What would you have me say? I will not weep when we both knew this was inevitable. You are the future king of the north. I'm a pirate. We had some fun and now it's time for you to marry a princess like we both knew you would."

"Rahab -" He reached for her but she side stepped his advances.

"On behalf of the crew of the *Shadow of Death*, we appreciate you securing our release." She bowed her head slightly, as if dismissing herself from his presence. "I will let the captain know."

She turned on her heel, cold and mechanical, and marched toward the door. Before she was able to touch the doorknob, Crispin was on his feet and upon her. He grabbed her arm and whipped her around to face him. She two-hand shoved him away, but he refused to let that be how things ended between them. She reached for the door again, but he slipped between her and the exit, blocking her path.

"Get out of my way, princeling."

"Rahab, would you stop being stubborn and listen to me for once in your damn life!?"

"What else could you have said?" Rahab's eyes were fiery, and he could feel the pain radiating from her like a cornered and wounded animal. "We both knew this would happen. Why prolong the inevitable?"

"Because I didn't agree to it!" Crispin slammed his fist against the door behind him. "I couldn't agree to it."

"Well, that was stupid." She huffed, backing toward his footboard. He pushed up from the door and stalked toward her.

"You are without a doubt, the most frustrating woman I have ever met. You drive me crazy and half the time we're together, I would like nothing more than to toss you overboard." Crispin closed the gap between them and cupped her face in his hands. "But you are also the one woman I cannot stop thinking about. The only woman I want and need."

"Crispin," she whispered, but he pressed on.

"I am deeply, madly, irrevocably, and helplessly in love with you. I want you. I need you. And I will have you as mine, everyone else be damned."

"Your honesty is going to get us all killed once the king finds out." Rahab rested her hands on his chest.

He bent down so his lips brushed against her ear. "Tell me you do not love me, that you do not want me, that you do not desire me as I desire you, and I will accept the king's offer." He heard her breath hitch and he silently prayed she wouldn't say any of those words. He'd taken a gamble and he needed her to abandon her stubbornness and forget her pride and admit the truth. "Say it," Crispin pressed when she remained silent, "and we will end things between us now."

"I can't say it," Rahab finally whispered, dragging her lips across his stubbled cheek as her hands travelled from his chest up his neck and through his tresses. "Because it is not true."

"Then swear you will be mine," Crispin's lips hovered above hers. "Promise me, when this war is over, you will be my wife, that you will be my queen."

Her eyes widened, as if she was sobering up from a drunken stupor. His heart skipped, thinking she would push him away, or slap him, or flat out reject him. But she planted her hands on his bed, lifted her body over the footboard, and laid back on her elbows. Crispin crawled over her and ran his fingers through her hair.

She gently dragged her thumb over his bottom lip. When he released a shuddering breath, she gripped his chin between her fingers and forced him to look at her. "When this war is over, I will be your wife, your queen, and anything else you require of me. You have ruined me in every possible way, and I intend to live and die by your side, my king."

Crispin claimed her mouth and pressed his chest against hers. They would find another way out of Borg, but he wouldn't sacrifice his love for her to play the political games of kings. He wouldn't be like his father or his ancestors marrying for selfish gain. He would marry the pirate who loved him before he had a throne. He would give his people a queen who would not only fight for them, but alongside them. She was worth the price he would pay for angering the West.

Chapter Eight

Niabi

Niabi's craving for blood fueled her to drag her aching body out of her soft bed to march to her throne room. She had arrived from Elisor the day before, and although Tala told her the meeting could wait one more day, so she could rest, she adamantly refused. She was looking forward to the meeting and wouldn't miss it for the world.

When she sent written word to Gershom to join her in the White Throne Room, she sealed it with a grin. Tala had asked why she was smiling and all she said was, "One down, two to go."

Her enemies would remember her name. They would regret coming for her crown, her throne, her loved ones. They would beg for mercy but as always, none would be given.

Gershom's treason was now confirmed. His ties to Lord Memucan of the Numbio would be the final nail in his coffin and Niabi couldn't contain the excitement humming through her body as she slipped into her throne and waited for her prey to fall into her trap. Because once he stepped foot into the room, he would be dragged out in chains.

With Tala and Anaktu on either side of her, Gershom entered the throne room with his head held high, but Niabi saw the fear in his shifting eyes as the doors closed behind him. She smiled when she recalled the moment she sliced off his ear months earlier.

Gershom didn't bow before her, most likely because he knew what was about to happen and she relished in the moment she'd dreamt of for years. "You sent for me?"

Niabi ignored his blatant disrespect when he didn't address her by her title. Licking her lips, she flashed her teeth. "We found Lord Memucan's body in the Night District. His neck was slit from ear to ear. Any thoughts on why the Southerner was in Northwind?"

Defeat. She could swim in the despair flooding his muddy brown eyes.

"It seems to me," his voice came out as a raspy hiss, "you already have the answer to your question, Niabi."

"Was it worth it?" she cocked her head to the side, a menacing smile stretched across her face. "Was your failed attempt to usurp my throne worth the years you will spend rotting away in my dungeons? So close to the throne you crave and will never have?"

"When I escape your dungeon, because I *will* escape, I will make sure you suffer greatly, until you beg for a death that will never come."

Nabi stood up from her throne, her hand cradling her swollen belly, and slithered down the steps of her dais to tower over Gershom, who had been forced to his knees by her soldiers. "*If* you escape," she growled. "No one will miss you. No one will mourn you. And soon, no one will remember you. You are a worm and for the rest of your miserable days, you will taste of your failure."

Gershom attempted to fight off the soldiers clamping manacles on his wrists and ankles. "I swear on the Almighty -"

"Oh please," Niabi cut him off and laughed, "your words bear me no threat. You are a broken man with broken dreams." She dragged her fingers over the hole where his ear once was, and said, "To think you had everything and threw it away for nothing."

"Was I supposed to be grateful for your scraps?" he snarled.

She patted his head. "What else would you feed a dog?" She quirked an eyebrow before whistling a laugh. "I would say, until we meet again, but we both know this is the last time we will see one another." Niabi waved her hand and her guards dragged Gershom toward the doors.

"You will pay for this!" Gershom screeched, resisting them. "This isn't the end! This is just the beginning!"

She let out a long sigh. "To think I once thought you mighty."

"Go to hell!"

"You first."

The doors slammed shut once Gershom was dragged out, but she could still hear his screams and curses echoing down the halls. Tala walked to her side and glanced from the doors to her.

"Now what?" he asked.

She met his awaiting gaze. "Prepare for war. My siblings won't be long now I imagine."

CHAPTER NINE

SALOME

Salome sleepily opened her bloodshot eyes and lifted her head off Zophar's shoulder when she heard keys clatter outside their cell door. Determined to get Zophar out of Gomorrah one way or another, she laid face down on the floor, geared to ambush their enemy. Her heart was pounding, her hand tightly holding the sharp rock she found in the cell. She wouldn't let Zophar die in a dungeon. She wouldn't let this be their end.

The door squeaked open, footsteps rushed toward her, a hand touched her, and she whipped around forcefully swinging her weapon, but the blow was blocked.

"Jinn?" Salome whispered, tears filling her eyes. "You're here." She touched his face to make sure he was real and not a figment of her imagination. He'd come to rescue her.

"I'm here." The prince thumbed her lip where a fresh bruise sat, as if he could wipe it away.

"I never thought I'd see you again." Salome wrapped her arms around Jinn's neck, feeling his heartbeat against her chest but quickly pulled away. "Zophar is hurt. We need to get him to a healer, and I don' think he can walk on his own. And before you argue with me, old man...." She turned to smile at Zophar and noticed he was slumped over. To anyone walking by, it would look as if he were sleeping, but she knew something was wrong.

"Zophar?" She crawled to him as her heart thrashed in her chest. She could feel it pounding in her ears as she cupped his face. Everything around her slowed, as if frozen in time. "Zophar?" she whispered with tears streaming down her dirt-stained cheeks. When he didn't respond, she rested her forehead against his cold one. Her tears dripped onto his cheeks making it appear as if he was also weeping. "Please, don't leave me. I just got you back."

Hanzo and Oifa entered the cell, cradling a bundle of weapons. She spied her three daggers, including her wolf knife, and the handle of Zophar's battle axe. The Stormcrag and Krazak were silent as they took in the sight of Salome holding her departed. Hanzo dragged his middle finger from his forehead to his chest, paying the Westerner respect.

Jinn knelt next to Salome; eyes filled with sorrow. He hesitantly reached for her hand. "We need to get you out of here."

"I promised him he wouldn't die here," she choked. "I promised to get him out. I failed him."

"This is not your fault." Jinn swiped the tears from her cheeks. "We don't have much time. We need to leave before it's too late."

"I won't leave him here!" She felt the panic rising. "I can't leave him!"

Jinn held her gaze, his golden-brown eyes filling her with warmth amid feeling numb. "We will bring him with us." He motioned for Hanzo to step forward to carry him. "But we need to move quickly before our army launches an assault."

Salome didn't hear a word the prince said. All she saw was Matildys' dagger plunging into Zophar's body. She heard his groans, saw the pain in his eyes, and felt the fear in his shaky hands. Suddenly, her grief turned into a full-blown rage. She felt the fury spark in her toes and spread through her body like a poison. She leapt up, snatched her wolf dagger and Zophar's axe from Oifa's arms, and sprinted out of the cell.

"Salome! Salome, wait!" Jinn called, but she didn't hear him. She was on a mission to cut the queen's black heart out of her chest. Not even the Almighty could stop her now.

She sensed Death's presence. She had come for Zophar, gathering the souls of those Salome loved most, biding her time until she claimed hers.

"Not today." Salome let Death know she would have to keep waiting. She would bring Gomorrah to its knees if it was the last thing she did.

Jinn, Hanzo, and Oifa had killed the Thrak guards in the dungeons on their way to find her, so it made her ascent into the Black Tower easy. As soon as she stepped onto the black marble floor, her eyes zeroed in on the two Thrak stationed at the foot of the stairs which led to the royal sector.

One of the Thrak gurgled a warning, then drew his sword. She couldn't decipher what he'd said, nor did she care. They were between her and revenge, and they wouldn't be able to stop her. She held her weapons tightly and walked with determined steps toward the guards.

The one with his sword drawn ran toward her, ready to strike her down. He swung his blade at her and if it had struck true, she would have lost her head. She ducked, tumbled, and twisted her body like the Qata Vishna had taught her, before she lodged Zophar's axe into his thigh, bringing him to his knees. With cat-like swiftness, she slid behind him, pulled his head back to look into her eyes and slid her dagger across his neck, watching his fear and hatred fade as his life ended.

The second Thrak whipped his mace around, but Salome used the dead Thrak's body as a shield to get closer to her attacker. Bloodied, bludgeoned, and broken, her human shield allowed her to get within striking distance. She threw her wolf dagger at him, but he stepped out of the way to avoid the brunt of the blow. He wasn't fast enough to avoid the blade slicing his arm before it clanged to the floor. He quickly examined his wound and turned to face her with a smirk, but his smile disappeared when Salome, battle axe in hand, leapt at him and two-hand slammed the axe into his head, the crunch of his skull echoing through the rotunda.

She stood over the bodies, blood splattered all over her face, hands, and clothes. She was the monster parents warned their children about, but she relished the power rushing within her.

"Salome?"

She slowly turned around when she heard Jinn's voice behind her. He stared at her in what she hoped was wonder and not terror. The prince tentatively made his way to her but before he reached her, a boom in the distance rattled the tower.

"What was that?" she asked as dust shook free from the chandelier swinging above them, sprinkling down on them like snow.

"I told you the army was launching an attack on the city," Jinn explained, drawing her attention. "We will have to fight our way out now."

Salome caught sight of Hanzo and Oifa appear in the doorway. Hanzo had Zophar draped over his shoulders like a stag on its way to be skinned. Sorrow and anger once again surged through her. She'd rather die facing the queen than flee the city.

"You go," Salome commanded. "I'll meet you as soon as I can."

"Where are you going?" Jinn grabbed her.

"I have unfinished business."

Jinn turned to Oifa and Hanzo, "Wait here. We'll be back."

"You don't need to come -"

"I came to bring you home," Jinn interrupted her. "I won't leave your side until I do."

Not interested in arguing with the prince any further, she tucked Zophar's axe into her belt loop before sprinting up the stairs, taking them two at a time. The double doors leading to the throne room were within sight and she knew Jinn had cloaked them when the guards didn't notice them. Marching up to the guards, unaware of the danger lurking, and with swift precision, she stabbed them in their chests, and watched them drop to the floor.

She turned to face Jinn, his tachi blades drawn, ready to fight by her side, ready to face any demon hell sent to keep her safe. "When I walk through these doors, don't try to stop me from doing what I must."

Jinn nodded his head in acknowledgement. "I'm with you."

"Uncloak me." Jinn obeyed.

She stepped over the guards, pushed the doors open, and locked eyes with Matildys sitting on her onyx throne with a smugness Salome was itching to wipe off her pale face. If the queen was surprised or fearful to see the blood-stained Salome, she didn't show it.

"Did he die?" Matildys purred. "Did you suffer as greatly as I hoped you would by watching him take his last breath?"

Salome held her wolf dagger in her left hand and Zophar's axe in her right, making sure the queen made note of them as she approached the dais. "I have come to make good on my promise."

Matildys sipped from her goblet of wine, not a care in the world, and waved Salome off. "It seems your *friends* have come for you. Why don't you run off and join them before you die here?"

"You stole from me," Salome kept her approach steady. "You will pay dearly for it."

Matildys glanced around the empty room. All the Thrak were either patrolling outside of the throne room, dead, or at the wall to battle the army Jinn had brought. Apart from Salome and Matildys, Jinn and Ranalda were the only ones in the room.

Ranalda sat at the edge of her throne and when Salome was in reach, she launched herself down the dais and fell to her knees, crying. "Please," she begged, "I did nothing to harm you or your friend. Spare me. Please."

Salome stared at the Gomorrian girl and felt nothing. No compassion, no sympathy, no mercy.

"You are a disgrace, Ranalda!" Matildys hissed.

Salome yanked Ranalda up to her feet, spun her to face her mother, and put a knife against the girl's neck. The princess whimpered, but Salome did not yield. "You killed a good man."

"And I'd gladly do it again," the queen stood up, nostrils flared. "What are you planning to do, *Princess*? Are you going to slit my daughter's throat in my own throne room? Are you going to stoop to my level? Are you -"

Salome ran the blade across Ranalda's throat and let the girl drop to the floor. She reached for her mother for help, but both women knew there was nothing that could be done to save her. Matildys showed a hint of grief and helplessness but quickly returned to her heartless self. When Ranalda's gurgling stopped, Matildys latched her wicked, cruel, hate-filled eyes on Salome.

Salome motioned to the princess sprawled on the floor in a pool of her own blood. "I came here with the intent to gut you, but perhaps I should let you live knowing you will have to bury and grieve your dead for the rest of your miserable days. My army will wipe your filthy city from existence so you can no longer call yourself a queen over anyone but the ashes of the fallen. You stole from me. I am glad to have returned the favor, Matildys."

Matildys stood in utter silence; a silence that would have made Salome's skin crawl, had she not already felt dead on the inside. Salome realized what the queen was about to do before it happened, and then it all happened in slow motion.

The Gomorrian finished her glass of wine and shattered it against the floor. She glided to the balcony, turned to face Salome one last time, anguish and rage brewing in her eyes, and let herself fall backwards to the ground below.

Salome made her way to the banister and glanced over the edge to see a mangled Matildys lying dead in the infamous Square, where thousands of Mountain Men had been tortured and mutilated for generations. The same square where she was to be tortured at dawn the next day. Dogs so skinny their rib cages protruded, found their way to the queen's body and began to lap up her blood. She turned her focus from the dead queen to the fires raging at the city gates. Smoke billowed, people screamed, metal clashed against metal as the battle raged. They'd come for her. Her friends, her allies. They had waged a war to save her.

Remembering she wasn't alone in the throne room, she turned around to see Jinn staring at her. She was suddenly afraid of what he might be thinking of her and what she had done. But the prince extended his hand with compassion in his eyes.

"Are you ready to go home?"

A simple question, but she didn't have a home. She hadn't had one in a very long time and the man who had loved her as his own daughter, who had sacrificed everything to give her a bit of normalcy growing up, was gone. The gravity of Zophar's death finally gripped her heart and twisted it until it was nothing more than a broken, mangled mess.

She stared at the body on the floor. Ranalda wasn't much younger than her, but there she was, eyes wide open, neck split, dead.

Salome recoiled at the sight of what she had done. The way she let her grief and her anger manifest into a murderous rage. She was the Hunter. She was meant to avenge the blood of the innocent. What if Ranalda wasn't cruel like her mother? Did she take the life of an innocent girl, just to hurt her enemy?

And then it hit her. She'd said it before when talking to her grandmother, Nym, in the Isles of Myr.

"If you were Niabi, what would you have done?" Her grandmother had asked.

"I am *Niabi. We share the same story."*

She judged her sister for seeking revenge for those she'd lost, for all she had suffered. She hated Niabi for what she'd done, and Salome had now done the exact same thing. She and Niabi weren't different at all. They were two sides of the same coin. Perhaps, it was in their nature to be bloodthirsty and in the end, they would share the same fate.

"Salome?" Jinn's honey-smooth voice brought her back to the sight of the body on the floor and she shuddered. Her stomach twisted in knots to the point of needing to wretch. She was grateful she hadn't eaten all day.

She stared at blood-stained hands and broken fingernails, then lifted her gaze to meet Jinn's. "What have I done?" she whispered so softly she didn't think the prince heard her.

But he did, and reached her in three long strides. He wrapped her in his warm embrace; one hand on her back, the other cradling her head.

"I...I killed her. I killed that girl to hurt her mother." Salome sobbed into Jinn's leathers, tucking her forehead into the crook of his neck. "What have I done, Jinn? I'm turning into Niabi."

"Don't say that. You're nothing like her." He rested his chin on top of her head and tightened his grip around her.

She wished that were true, but despite Jinn's words, she knew the truth and had just proven it.

I am Niabi.

Chapter Ten

Pash

The guilt Pash felt for forcing Adonijah to stay at the camp instead of joining the fight, was eating him alive. He knew his brother, no matter which side of the war he was on, would never betray him or do anything to harm him, but as the commander of Niabi's forces, he needed to think about his men first. If Adonijah had to choose between rescuing Salome or following his orders, Pash knew what his brother's choice would be. He couldn't fault him. If their roles were reversed, he would have burned the enemy campsite to the ground to find Niabi.

One thing was certain, Pash would keep his word to do everything in his power to save the lost princess from the monstrous clutches of the Thrak. No one, not even his worst enemy, should endure such an end.

After hours of riding, Gomorrah was within reach. Once Pash led his army over the tree-lined ridge, the city would be in sight and the battle would begin. The greatest advantage Gomorrah had was its location. The city sat in the middle of flatlands which enabled them to see invaders up to a mile away. Though they may see them approaching, Pash had full confidence in the ability of his soldiers to outmaneuver and outsmart the Thrak. When it came down to it, the Thrak were barbarians with weapons, but Pash and his men were bred for war.

A noise to his right caused Pash to look over at Leoti, who rode by his side in silence. He'd spent enough time with the Andrago to know she was deep in thought, but before he could ask her if she was nervous about the upcoming battle or if something else was bothering her, Thanos' grating laugh pierced his ears.

"By this time tomorrow," the prince flashed a triumphant smile to no one in particular, "I will be King of Gomorrah."

Leoti's reaction didn't go unnoticed. Pash knew they were thinking the same thing. Gomorrah was a stain in Adalore and the Thrak were an abomination. It still didn't sit well that they were there to put this spoiled boy on the throne, but he was a soldier and would serve his mistress well.

"And once I am king," Thanos continued,"I will resume the search for those murderous mountain men and their cave city."

"Murderous are they?" Leoti chimed in with a disdainful chuckle. "Last I checked, the Krazaks and Stormcrags didn't hunt down, imprison, and mutilate *your* people for pleasure."

If looks could kill, Thanos would have killed Leoti eight different ways in the span of two seconds. Pash could have kissed Leoti on the forehead like a proud father would for her retort.

The Gomorrian prince narrowed his blue eyes and licked his dry lips. "Perhaps, I will enlist your services to complete my mission, *warg*. I think you would be a most useful companion in more ways than one."

Pash wanted to wipe the lustful grin off the boy's face. The need to protect Leoti thundered in his chest, but he didn't get a chance to put the would-be king in his place because Leoti straightened in her saddle, doing her best to appear taller than the Gomorrian, and said, "I'd rather bathe in pig slop than be associated with an impudent product of incest."

"Why you little bit-"

"Stay your tongue or lose it," Pash growled, causing the prince to shrink back.

"You will pay for this disrespect, Commander." Thanos promised under his breath. " I will delight in seeing to your punishment personally."

"I am your only hope to claim your throne," Pash met Thanos' cruel gaze, unfazed by the temper brewing within the teenager. "I suggest you mind your manners."

Suddenly a blare rang out, then another, drawing a curse from Pash. There was no way the Gormorrians had already spotted them. His scouts would have decimated any Gomorrian lookout. Pash kicked the sides of his horse to reach the top of the hill to assess the situation. To his amazement, the alarms weren't signaling his army's arrival, but that of another army laying siege to the soot-stained kingdom.

Leoti was by his side a moment later, her mouth agape. "Who is that?"

Pash shook his head in bewilderment. If he hadn't been there to see it with his own eyes, he might not have believed it. "If my eyes aren't deceiving me, that would be the Krazaks and Stormcrags fighting alongside one another. Perhaps, they've finally united to battle the Gomorrians."

Leoti pointed to a small group running alongside the Mountain Men. "Are those warriors from Numbio?"

That didn't make sense. Sure, the Krazaks and Stormcrags had a long-standing feud with the Gomorrians but the southerners had no... Realization hit Pash like a wave crashing against the shore. "They're here for the princess." Relief and satisfaction flooded him. Maybe Salome would be rescued after all, and his brother would be put at ease.

Thanos' horse pulled up and the prince screamed, "What are you waiting for? Attack!"

None of the soldiers moved, waiting for Pash's orders. His mind was racing as to what the best course of action would be. To interfere would put his men at a higher risk. They had come to fight the Gomorrians, but if they attacked, the Mountain Men would believe they were being ambushed and would turn on him and his men. The only ones who would profit from his interference would be the very people he came to destroy.

Pash lifted his hand in the air, silently commanding his troops to stay put. "We wait here."

"What?" Thanos yelled. "You are supposed to-"

"Do not tell me how to command my men," Pash interrupted. "You look stupid." Before the prince could respond, the commander glanced at Leoti. "I need eyes."

The Andrago maiden nodded and dismounted her horse. She took Tiki out from his crate and untied the blindfold. Stroking the bird's feathers, she whispered something to him, and the bird shot into the air. Leoti sat on the ground cross-legged, leaning her back against a tree, and the moment she blinked, her brown eyes were washed over with solid white ones.

Pash's attention bounced from Leoti up to the falcon. All he had to do now was wait.

An unease slithered through Pash as he turned toward Thanos, but the prince's gaze wasn't on him, but fixed on Leoti. Pash knew he'd have to keep an extra eye on the Andrago. If Thanos had his way, he'd kidnap and enslave her to do his bidding and that wasn't going to happen. Not on his watch.

Pash hopped off his horse, spurring his men to do the same and keep themselves hidden behind the tree line. He walked toward Leoti and stood between her and Thanos, blocking his view and garnering a wicked glare. Crossing his arms over his chest, Pash silently willed the boy prince to stand down and to his surprise, Thanos steered his horse in the opposite direction.

The Gomorrian might not see a crown upon his head if he kept ogling Leoti in that manner.

Fixing his gaze on the city before them, Pash hoped and prayed he wouldn't have to deliver heartbreaking news to his brother.

Chapter Eleven

Salome

Salome and Jinn found Hanzo and Oifa exactly where they'd left them in the dark foyer. There were a few more dead Thrak bodies scattered across the room but neither the Stormcrag nor the Krazak looked fazed. Hanzo had placed Zophar's body on the floor, crossing the man's arms over his broad chest; a small gesture of respect, but one that punched Salome in the gut.

Oifa was picking at her fingernails with a dagger, leaning against the wall, as if the battle raging around the city didn't affect her in the least. She glanced up as the duo descended the staircase and straightened to her full height. Though she was slightly shorter than Salome, she was more muscular and broader in the shoulders. A true warrior's frame.

"Ready?" Oifa asked, her pointed gaze roaming over the blood coating Salome's hands and clothes. She didn't make any remark about her appearance and Salome whispered a prayer of thanks for that.

Salome nodded in response to her question and the group readied for their escape. They would more than likely run into more Thrak on their way out of the city, so Jinn would cloak them, but if someone bumped into them, they would be released from his magic. They had to stay together and stay close.

Salome whimpered as Hanzo picked Zophar up and threw him over his shoulders, but she didn't say anything when her eyes collieded with the Krazak's.

"Follow me." Jinn's voice pulled her back and she obediently trailed after him as he led them toward the exit of the Black Tower. Before opening the doors, he turned around to look at Salome. "No matter what you see outside, stay close to me."

"What do you expect us to see?" she asked.

"Death."

His response felt like a bucket of cold water had been dumped over her head. Of course there would be death. She'd never been involved in a true battle before and this would be her first taste in the horrors of war. Jinn's golden-brown eyes were kind, but once she nodded, a hardness washed over his face. She could tell he was prepping himself mentally, emotionally, and physically for what was on the other side of those doors and what was on the other side of the walls surrounding Gomorrah. No one would openly admit it, but those lost lives, their blood, was on her hands.

It was the smell that immediately assaulted her when the doors flew open. Burning wood, sulfur, smoke, blood, and the scent of decomposing flesh filled her nostrils and stung her eyes. Sound followed swiftly. It was incredibly loud and so chaotic in the city streets that it made it difficult to focus. Screams of the citizens, metal clashing against metal, collapsing buildings, Thrak roaring. It was overstimulating. As shocking and nauseating as the smell and sound of battle was, the sights were unmatched. Dirty children hiding behind their mothers' skirts, covering their ears, tears streaking down their ashen faces. Thrak stomping through the city, pushing anyone who got in their way to the ground. Fire raging at the city walls as smoke billowed toward the darkening skies. Hungry dogs feasting on freshly fallen Gomorrians.

It was chaos.

But even with all the dead strewn throughout the streets, she didn't see any of their allies. They were still at the city gates, surrounding the walls to ensure no one escaped but them. So, who was killing the citizens?

And if she hadn't seen it with her own eyes, she wouldn't have believed it. Thrak were killing men, women, and children in their own kingdom. Had they lost their minds? Were they following Matildys' orders? What did they gain in slaughtering their own people?

Jinn was right. War was ugly. But she never imagined the true horror until that moment. The Gomorrians were not just ruthless with their enemies, but with their fellow countrymen as well.

She slapped a hand against Jinn's back and closed her eyes. This was too much for her to take in all at once. She felt trapped, claustrophobic, and was terrified she was going to stop dead in her tracks and panic, giving one of the Thrak the perfect opportunity to stab her through the heart. And they would be right in doing so, because she had blood on her hands as well.

Jinn took her hand in his and squeezed it without looking back at her. A silent comfort. He must have felt her heart thundering in her chest and the anxiety washing over her entire body, but he never once looked back. He kept pulling her forward and she knew the others were right on her heels. Oifa had kicked her calves a couple of times to remain as close as she could to the magical prince.

They weaved up and down the streets for what seemed like an eternity. The Black Tower was in the center of the city, so to get to the wall was quite the hike. She knew Hanzo was getting tired of carrying Zophar's body, she could hear him breathing hard and his footsteps became heavier and slower. Oifa made sure he didn't fall behind and if he needed a break, she'd let Jinn know.

For two people who supposedly hated one another, Salome observed they made quite a good team.

After the fourth or fifth five-minute break, Jinn knelt in front of the others and whispered, "We are almost to the wall. There's a small grate to let sewage out. We'll have to slip out through there."

Salome was already covered in blood, dirt, and sweat. What was a little sewage? She bobbed her head in agreement.

Hanzo picked Zophar back up and his legs wobbled. Jinn volunteered to take over, but as he did the last few times the prince offered, the Krazak archer refused.

Jinn made sure everyone was huddled together before turning the corner, but as soon as he did, he slammed into a bloodied, broad-chested Thrak. The cloaking magic was broken, and a horde of enemy warriors quickly surrounded the group.

With weapons pointed at them, the Thrak leader stepped forward. He had a grotesque scar down the middle of his face and half of his nose was missing. Salome wanted to look away but couldn't. Fear was beginning to take over. Her hands shook as she searched and found her wolf dagger and unsheathed Zophar's battle axe. They would have to fight their way out or die, and she wasn't interested in the latter option.

"Well, well, well," the Thrak leader said in a gravelly voice. "What do we have here?"

Jinn was already armed with his tachi blades and put himself between the Thrak commander and Salome. He tilted his head to the side, looking almost amused by the disfigured soldier. "What happened to your nose?"

The question surprised not only the Thrak soldier but Salome as well. What was Jinn doing?

As the Thrak opened his mouth to speak, Jinn kicked up dust from the street, blinding the Thrak. Taking advantage of the brief moment of confusion, the prince sliced the soldier's head off and watched as it bounced against the street.

As intimidating as the move was, the other Thrak were unmoved, and charged as a unit.

Salome gripped her weapons, but as two Thrak approached her, she froze. Every bit of her training seemed to vanish from her mind and her fear overtook her. She felt like she was wading through quicksand and was sinking. Looking around, Oifa and Hanzo had already accumulated a pile of bodies.

Salome was an expert marksman, but Hanzo was quick with his bow, faster than anyone she'd ever seen. And Oifa was ferocious, using her axe to strike any Thrak within arm's-length. Blood was splattered across her face, and she didn't seem bothered. She looked as if she relished the feeling of slaughtering her enemies.

Jinn was holding his own, whipping his blades around effortlessly, almost like an ancient dance. His gaze met hers and she saw her fear reflected in his eyes. "Salome!" he shouted as the two Thrak neared her, swinging their weapons.

Something in her snapped and she ducked, dodged, and eluded their attack. Her muscles ached with the effort. Her back was still healing, and she almost didn't get back up on her feet. Adrenaline was the only reason she jumped up to fight off her attackers. No one was going to be able to help her. They were being overrun with the company of Thrak. She batted her attackers' weapons away, clearly on the defensive.

Salome risked a glance at Oifa when she heard the Stormcrag yelp, and saw she had a slice across her thigh. Hanzo stepped in front of her and whipped out a blade from his belt and shielded her from attack. Oifa bit her bottom lip and forced herself to her feet, putting her back against Hanzo's and defending him from Thrak on the other side.

Jinn was dripping in sweat, his hair falling from its place and sticking to his forehead.

They weren't going to make it. She knew it. All of them knew it.

Salome managed to kill four Thrak, but she was quickly tiring. She'd not had anything to eat in almost two days and her injuries were still not completely healed, and according to the Gomorrian healers, wouldn't fully heal for months.

She heard Jinn hiss and turned around to see blood trickling down his arm. Instead of landing a fatal blow, the Thrak attacking Jinn backed off. The new Thrak leader had thrown his hand up in the air and halted the assault. The four of them were surrounded by the enemy, but it looked as if the Thrak were no longer interested in killing them. Capturing them and torturing them to a slow and painful death was more their speed and Salome was terrified that was in their future.

"I'm sorry," she sent through their bond. It was the first time she'd been able to access her magic since the Gomorrians had imprisoned her. *"This is all my fault."*

Jinn shook his head, pressing his forehead against hers while holding his injured arm. *"In life and death, we go together."*

"Bind them!" the Thrak leader bellowed.

A few Gomorrians stepped forward with manacles but before they were able to slap them on, something large thudded to the ground, shaking the foundation, and knocking everyone off their feet. Several more equally destructive quakes vibrated the ground, toppling buildings, and rattling bodies.

When the dust settled, Salome didn't see angry Gomorrians or bloodthirsty Thrak surrounding them. She found herself in a small crater and saw Zophar's body lying a few feet from her. With a groan, she crawled to his body, tears streaming down her cheeks, dirt itching her eyes. She had just managed to clutch his pale, limp hand in hers when she caught sight of a winged warrior approaching through the smoke. His bronze skin, dark hair, and golden eyes were hypnotizing. His white feathered wings and gold armor shimmered in the streaks of setting sun, signaling he wasn't mortal, but she wasn't sure what or who he was fighting for.

"Who are you?" she asked the warrior now hovering over her.

"I am Kayven, Commander of the Bellators." He extended his hand to her. "It is time to go, my lady."

Salome glanced over at Jinn, Oifa, and Hanzo, all of them injured and trying to find their bearings from the sudden blast. "My friends..."

"Will be coming with us." Kayven smiled and nine Bellators stepped into view, all muscular and battle ready.

"Please," Salome was feeling lightheaded, her hand still in Zophar's lifeless one. "Please don't leave him."

The Bellator Commander motioned one of his winged warriors to collect Zophar's body. Only then did she release him from her white-knuckled grip.

Salome thought she heard Odelia's voice. Glancing around, she squinted at a faint figure in the distance, and saw the Enchantress thrusting her hands into the dirt. She was making the streets and the ground beneath them move. Had Salome hit her head so hard that she was imaging it all? A loud rumble sounded, and screams echoed in a chorus as buildings collapsed and dust rose around them like a sandstorm.

"Princess?" Kayven drew her attention. He was crouched before her, unfazed by the chaos. "Are you ready?"

Salome sucked in a breath and nodded. "I'm ready." She grabbed Kayven's enormous, outstretched hand and once she was cradled in his muscular arms, he said, "Hold on tight," before rocketing into the sky.

She clutched Kayven's neck so tightly she was afraid she'd strangle him. If she was hurting him, he didn't show it. Her stomach churned with each second they climbed higher into the sky. She wasn't sure if she was afraid of the sudden ascent or invigorated by it. Burying her face in the crook of his neck, she took a deep breath of the eucalyptus and leather coating his skin. It was intoxicating enough to ease her upset stomach and calm her frayed nerves.

Mustering the courage to pull her face from his neck, she looked down. A part of her screamed, to be put back down on solid ground, but the other part craved to go higher into the sky to dance in the clouds. From their height, she could see sections of Gomorrah still under siege and sections collapsing into the earth. Odelia was using her magical powers to tear down buildings and she beckoned the earth to do her bidding by swallowing up the unholy city. She was destroying Gomorrah single-handedly. Salome saw a trail of rubble where soot covered buildings use to stand. A ghost of what was. A ghost that would haunt her for the rest of her days.

"You left her!" Salome panicked seeing the other Bellators flying behind them. "You left Odelia, you have to go back for her."

"She is in good hands, my lady." Kayven's voice was soothing, and it instantly calmed her, as if he had cast a spell over her, and she was forced to obey.

When she looked back down, there was a Bellator with shaggy hair standing beside her.

"My brother, Abba, will make sure she escapes unscathed."

Salome nodded, exhaustion beginning to claim her.

What was left of the sadistic Thrak continued to fight the Krazaks, Stormcrags, and Numbio, at what remained of the black stone wall. They had come for her – waged war, shook the very foundation of the entire kingdom, to save her.

Behind her, the Bellators carried her friends and she remembered where she'd heard the term Bellator before. They were in one of the history books her brother, Lykos, used to read to her. They were Immortal warriors. And if they were Immortals, that would mean they knew Harbona.

"Is Harbona...?" She wanted to finish the question with "alive" but wasn't sure she was ready to hear what the Bellator Commander would say.

Kayven met her nervous gaze and grinned. “Who do you think sent us?”

Her bottom lip quivered as tears slipped down her cheeks – a dam broken. He’d survived the Eldaar and answered her plea for help. He was alive. He'd come for her.

“Where are you taking me?” She asked when Kayven and a few of the Bellators headed away from the Bone Mountains.

“Oakenshire.” Kayven's grip on her tightened, securing her to his chest for the long journey. "Rest, my lady. You're in safe hands."

Chapter Twelve

Adonijah

Adonijah had been driving himself mad with worry since the moment he found out Salome had been taken captive by the Thrak. He should have been there to protect her. He never should have left her side and now, he was a prisoner in his brother's camp, forced to stay put and let other people handle it. He was cursing himself and his reckless decisions for the thousandth time when he heard the pounding hooves of the Northmen returning from Gomorrah. They hadn't been gone long enough to lay siege to the city and he was terrified of getting an update from Pash.

He was pacing back and forth in Pash's tent when his brother entered and beelined for the wine decanter, pouring himself a healthy serving. Before his brother could take a sip of his drink, and before Adonijah could ask him what happened, Prince Thanos stormed in, nostrils flaring like a pissed off bull.

"You failed your mission, *Commander*!" He yelled at Pash with an air of superiority that rubbed Adonijah the wrong way. "You were supposed to conquer my city. Instead, you watched it fall to ruin! You worthless piece of sh -"

Pash drew his sword from the sheathe attached to his hip and pointed the tip against Thanos' chest. He eyed him silently, finally taking a sip of his drink. Once he swallowed, Pash said, "I would choose your next words carefully, *boy*."

Thanos' face reddened. "You dare threaten the Prince of Gomorrah?" he seethed.

"As of a few hours ago," Pash brushed past the whiny prince and slumped into one of the leather chairs, "the Kingdom of Gomorrah no longer exists, thanks to the Immortals."

"The Immortals?" Adonijah's eyes widened and Pash glanced over at him, looking surprised by his brother's reaction.

"Bellators leveled the city to rescue your princess. It would seem she has powerful and timely allies we did not realize she had."

"Your queen will hear of your failure." Thanos hovered above Pash who rolled his eyes.

"Scream of it from the tallest mountain, Thanos, no one will weep for you. No one will mourn the filth that was your kingdom. We should thank the Bellators for ridding Adalore of your cruel and wicked people."

Thanos was going to say something, but Pash waved him off with an irritated huff.

"Now, get out, before my patience and good graces run out." Pash stared at the pouting prince. "You live now because I allow it. You are a prince of nothing. Do not forget it."

Opening his mouth again, but thinking better of it, Thanos marched out of the tent just as furious as when he entered.

Adonijah snickered as he joined his brother for a drink. "I think you made him piss himself."

Pash smirked, "He might lose the appendage required to piss if he speaks to Niabi in that manner."

A silence settled between them as Adonijah downed the contents of his glass in one gulp. "Salome is alive?"

Pash nodded and rubbed his fingers around his temples. "From what we could see, she was in the midst of being rescued, when she was surrounded by the Thrak. The Bellators arrived in time to get them out of the city before it was leveled. All that remains of that unholy and cursed kingdom is the black soot that stained its people and walls."

Adonijah breathed a sigh of relief knowing she had escaped captivity. Her allies had leveled a kingdom to get her back. He wouldn't mourn Gomorrah. In fact, no one would. But he still felt sick to his stomach with the news of how she was rescued. "I should have been there."

"Even if I allowed you to ride with us, you couldn't have done anything to help her." Pash finished his drink and set his glass on the table between them.

"Who rescued her?" Adonijah asked.

Pash's exhausted gaze shot toward his brother. "Were you not listening, brother? The Bellators -"

"No, before," Adonijah cut him off. "You said she was in the midst of escaping when they were surrounded. Who was rescuing her?"

Pash's eyebrow arched as he reclined in his seat. "Is there a name you are hoping or dreading to hear?"

"Indulge me."

"I wish I could, little brother," Pash shook his head. "I don't know names, but I can give you descriptions. There was one male Krazak, one female Stormcrag, and a male dressed in black that Leoti said looked to be from the Eastern Lands."

Adonijah knew based on description alone, Jinn had been the one to rescue Salome and it made his heart ache. It should have been him rescuing her. Not the prince. "How did Leoti know all of that?"

"She's a warg; she's my eyes." Pash closed his eyes and threw a cold rag over his face. Adonijah hadn't seen him soak the towel, but he wasn't paying much attention to anything but the thought of Jinn and Salome together.

Adonijah nodded, having already forgotten the Andrago maiden's affinity. A useful one in battle to be sure.

Pash reached over and smacked Adonijah's chest. "You should be rejoicing that your princess is safe from the Thrak. Yet, here you are looking just as sullen, if not more so. What troubles you?"

Adonijah had a lot troubling him. Salome being captured by the Thrak and him not being the one to rescue her, was eating away at his soul. Jinn vying for her heart and being the one to set her free from captivity, left a bitter taste in his mouth, but he wasn't going to admit any of this to his brother.

"Adonijah?" Pash's voice ripped him from his jealous thoughts. "Is everything alright?"

"Aye." He nodded and pulled his pipe from his jacket pocket. "I need some fresh air. I think I'll take a walk around the camp."

"She's alive. You needn't worry about her safety in your absence."

It wasn't her safety he was concerned with.

Adonijah ducked out of the tent and lit his pipe. He strolled through the camp observing the differences between the Northern army and the Shadows. They kept to their separate groups; to Adonijah's left were the army soldiers and to his right were the Shadows. Both troops were in black armor, but the mercenaries were far more menacing, even while seated, eating and drinking. There was one Shadow he couldn't seem to find in his scanning. He knew he shouldn't be looking for the Nameless Rider because if he found himself alone with the monster, he wouldn't heed Pash's instructions or warnings. He would slit the beast's throat, avenging his mother, and accept whatever punishment his brother dished out.

He walked deeper into the camp, weaving through the different pathways, passing tent after tent, until he saw a large shadowy figure in the corner of his eye. He turned towards it and saw the back of the Nameless Rider. He wasn't alone. Adonijah's curiosity drove him closer. He could hear a muffled groan and high-pitched whimper, but the rider's bulky body was blocking his view. He stopped dead in his tracks when he realized it was a woman.

He hadn't seen many women in their camp. In fact, the only one he could recall was Leoti. He tip-toed closer and heard the Shadow hiss, "You will not deny me, witch."

"You forget who you speak to. I am the queen's daughter-in-law -"

"Your husband is dead. You are cursed. And I don't mind." The Nameless Rider yanked her by her braided hair and tilted her head up. "If you cooperate, you might enjoy yourself."

Leoti spit in his face and the beast smacked her across the jaw, sending her tumbling to the ground.

"I guess we'll be doing this the hard way." He smiled and tugged at his trousers when Adonijah interrupted.

"Lay another finger on her and I will cut your favored appendage off and feed it to the crows."

The monster whipped around, fury and intrigue flashing in his one blue eye. "Ah, the sell-sword. Come to play?"

Adonijah took another step, tossing his dagger haphazardly hand to hand. "Do you remember a woman named Satara?"

If the Shadow was caught off guard by the name or question, he didn't show it.

"Let me refresh your memory, monster. She lived on a farm north of Gomorrah, not far from here, actually. She had blonde hair, freckles, and brown eyes. Gershom ordered you to fetch her son, but instead you murdered her and burned down her cabin."

The beast flashed a sinister grin. "I remember her well. Sometimes, I even dream of her with her hands on my -"

Adonijah threw his dagger, and it pierced the Shadow's groin forcing him to his knees. He squatted in front of the screaming one-eyed man and whispered, "I have been looking for you for quite some time. And even though I shouldn't, I'm going to flay you here in your own camp, consequences be damned. My mother will finally have peace, and you will never terrorize another being again."

The Nameless Rider reached for his sword, blood pooling around his knees, but Adonijah whipped his second dagger out and thrust the blade into the giant's neck. He watched in satisfaction as the monster gurgled, drew his last breath, and keeled over onto the blood-soaked ground.

Adonijah retracted his daggers from the dead man's throat and privates, knowing he'd need to move the body before anyone came looking for the Shadow. But that could wait until he made sure Leoti was alright. She hadn't moved from her position on the ground and held her knees to her chest, eyes wide, and breathing steady. He hesitated before gently resting his hand on her arm. She didn't flinch, but her eyes shot to where his fingers were, then dragged up to meet his gaze.

"Are you alright?"

Leoti nodded, exhaling a breath as if she'd been holding it. "I'm alright."

He maintained eye contact with her as he explained what they needed to do next. "You need to get to your tent. If you aren't comfortable being alone, go to Pash's tent. He'll keep you safe until I come back."

"Where are you going?" A flash of concern lit her brown eyes.

"I need to get rid of the body before someone finds it." Adonijah glanced back at the dead Shadow. "Pash is going to kill me when he finds out."

"He won't find out from me." Leoti promised, releasing her knees from her white-knuckled grip. Whatever fear that had marred her features before was gone and in its place was fury. "Where will we hide his body?"

Adonijah was slightly taken aback but shook his head. "*We* won't be hiding his body. *I* will be hiding it-"

"You can stop with the theatrics. I am more than capable of helping you bury a body."

He furrowed his brow but realized she was going to be stubborn about this and he didn't have the time to waste arguing with her. "Fine. But if Pash finds us, I won't be able to protect you from whatever punishment he inflicts."

"Afraid of your older brother?" she teased.

He narrowed his eyes and huffed, "Hardly. But I am still technically behind enemy lines, so I won't be taking my chances in angering him."

"Enough talk." Leoti stood up and looked down at him. "What's the plan?"

Adonijah lifted from his crouched position, eyes fixed on hers, until he was towering over her. "I was planning to cut him up and scatter his body parts around the outskirts of the camp, but if you're too squeamish at the sight of blood- "

"Please," she puffed, quickly redoing her braid. "I learned as a youngling to hunt, skin, and dismember animals. He will be no different."

Adonijah didn't know whether to be impressed or bothered by her spunk. She was bold, he'd give her that.

"Alright, my lady," he motioned a hand toward the body, "after you."

She brushed past him but before she could get close to the dead man, they heard voices nearing.

"Damn." Adonijah grabbed her forearm and pulled her behind him. He went to unsheathe his daggers, but she tugged him to face her, and shook her head.

"What exactly is the plan here?" Her whisper held a bite to it. "You can't fight every soldier in a military camp. We need to get out of here. Come on." She pulled him to weave behind a row of tents.

She was right and for some reason that irked him. He reluctantly followed her, but before he was behind the tents and out of sight, two Shadows turned the corner, caught sight of their dead comrade and Adonijah creeping in the distance.

"You!" One of them cried, and they both drew their weapons.

Adonijah ducked behind the canvas and sprinted after Leoti. Thunderous footsteps boomed behind them and shouts alerting the other soldiers of what happened echoed through the camp. There was no way to escape unscathed.

Leoti sharply turned to the left and grabbed Adonijah by his shirt and pulled him into a dark corner where the tents met the rocky bottom of the mountain. There wasn't much space between them. Their chests rose and fell against each other and as fast as his heart was beating, so was hers.

Adonijah glanced down at her, his chin skimmed her forehead. Even in the dark, he could feel her gaze piercing him. He leaned forward until his mouth was touching her ear and the stillness of her body sent a shock of electricity through him. He wasn't sure he understood what it meant, but he pushed it to the back of his mind.

"I need you to find Pash and tell him what happened. Don't leave his side."

Leoti tilted her face to look at him. Her breathing was shallow. "What are you doing? You aren't seriously considering giving yourself up to them? They'll demand you be executed."

"Is that concern I hear in your voice, my lady?"

"Someone needs to be concerned about you. Clearly you don't care about saving your own skin."

"Just get to Pash. He'll know what to do."

"We can get out of here." Leoti seemed panicked and he wasn't sure why. "You killed a Shadow. They won't care why. Pash won't have a choice but to give you over to them."

"I guess I'll have to trust you to make sure that doesn't happen." Adonijah glanced over his shoulder to the narrow opening leading to the pathway where footsteps were nearing. "They didn't see you. They only saw me. I promise, I've been in worse situations. Now go. Find my brother."

Leoti clutched his shirt as he tried to leave, and he stared at her. "I didn't thank you for what you did."

"You don't need to." He placed his hand atop hers until she released him and for some reason he couldn't explain, he didn't want to leave her side. His eyes dragged down from her eyes to her full lips. "Find Pash." And then he stepped into the pathway, hands held above his head, a smirk across his face. "Looking for me?"

Shadows and soldiers alike surrounded him. Ophir, the bald Shadow and the man he learned was his uncle, marched toward him, fists clenched.

"You look angry, Uncle. What could possibly be troubling you this fine evening?" He lowered his arms and pulled his pipe out of his pocket. "Smoke?"

"You murdered one of the Shadows. One of our brothers." Ophir stared hostilely at him as he lit his pipe and pressed it between his lips.

"How good of a brother was he though?" Adonijah exhaled. "Were you two close? Should I offer my condolences?"

"You won't be laughing when we riddle your body with arrows."

"You have such a way with words, Uncle."

"Stop calling me that."

"Touchy, touchy." Adonijah tsked. "Pash said you had a temper, but he failed to mention that when you get angry your bald head turns red."

"You're lucky you're Pash's brother. Otherwise, you would have been slaughtered on sight. Chain him. Throw him in the pit." Ophir motioned for two soldiers to slap manacles on his wrists.

Adonijah extinguished his pipe and tucked it in his jacket before offering his wrists. "You really should be careful being out in the sun too long, Uncle. It might scorch your head and you'll look permanently flustered."

Clearly having had enough of Adonijah's taunting, Ophir took the hilt of his sword and struck him on the back of the head, knocking him out cold.

Chapter Thirteen

Salome

It was dark by the time Salome and Kayven hovered above the ancient castle of Oakenshire. In some sections of the walls, there were gaping holes, and what was once a bustling city, the center of the old world, was nothing more than dilapidated houses and deserted businesses. But even in its raw form, Salome could see the potential for it to be an ideal base of operations. The treeline of the Black Forest skirted in the distance around the outer wall of the once capitol kingdom and gave the watchtower a clear view of any approaching parties. On the opposite side of the keep, the Ignacia Sea stretched as far as the eye could see. When their allies arrived, by land or sea, there would be a place for them to stay.

Kayven tightened his grip around her back and underneath her knees, drawing her attention.

"Tired?" she asked, fearing he'd exhausted himself carrying her the distance from what used to be Gomorrah to what remained of Oakenshire.

"No, my lady," he smiled. "Harbona would never forgive me if I dropped you as we descended."

The mention of Harbona's name warmed her. She scanned the bailey for the Immortal's face until she found him standing on the moss-covered steps that led inside the keep.

Kayven landed gently and whispered in her ear, "Are you able to stand, Princess?"

After being off her feet for hours, she hoped she wouldn't fall flat on her face the second her feet hit the stone pavers, but she nodded and the Bellator gently set her down.

When she turned her attention to the steps where she'd seen Harbona, she saw he was already running toward her, brewing a fresh batch of tears to stream down her face. As quickly as she could, she hobbled to meet her friend.

The Immortal Seer crashed into her, wrapping his arms around her, refusing to release her. "Thank the Almighty you're alright," he murmured against her face.

"You're alive." She sobbed into his pristine robes, pulling herself away to get a good look at him. He looked young, not a wrinkle in sight, and the Immortal glow was back, though his banishment mark was still around his right eye.

Harbona nodded, relief washing over him. "Alive and in my true form."

Tentatively, she reached her hand toward his face and trailed a finger down his jaw. "You heard my cry for help."

"I'm just thankful we were able to get to you in time." Harbona said with a sadness that reminded her that not everyone made it.

Her lip quivered. "It's my fault, Harbona. Zophar's dead and it's all my fault." Harbona tried to comfort her, but she shook her head, grief once again ripping her heart in two. "I promised he wouldn't die in that cell. I failed him. I failed to save him. I failed to keep my word."

Harbona wiped the tears from her cheeks as the Bellator carrying Zophar's body arrived. When the warrior's feet thudded to the ground, the pavers beneath her shook. It wasn't a bad dream. Zophar was truly gone, and it was all her fault.

"No," she rasped, crumbling to the ground.

The Seer knelt before her, tilting her chin up to meet his gaze. "We must send him to the ancestors."

Salome's eyes snapped from her friend to the Bellator carrying Zophar's body. The bronze warrior marched to a small boat by the shoreline. It was decked out in furs, weapons, and flowers; then it hit her. It was already made up for a traditional Western burial.

"When did you know he was going to die?" she asked, her gaze fixed on the boat.

"I have many visions, Salome," he replied. "I only knew for sure he was gone, once he passed."

She sucked in a breath, biting her bottom lip to keep from sobbing. "Did you see this when you first came to us?"

"I saw Zophar's death the moment I met him."

That statement caught Salome's attention and she turned to Harbona. "You could have warned him."

"Death is not definite. I have seen Zophar die at least a dozen different ways." He slid bits of his platinum hair out of his face. "There was no way for me to be certain and if I warned him of all the ways he could have met his end, he would have been too afraid to live."

Salome couldn't argue with that logic, although she wished there had been something she could have done to save her guardian. Something she wished Harbona could have done to prevent his death. But it was all wishful thinking and far too late to do Zophar any good. He was gone and she would blame herself for the rest of her days.

Watching the Bellator carefully lay Zophar in the rowboat and slowly push it off into the sea tore at her heart and for a split second, she couldn't bear the thought of never seeing the Westerner again. She pushed Harbona away from her, sprinting toward the sea.

"No!" she cried. "Come back, Zophar! Come back! You can't leave me! I need you!" She waded into the sea, clawing at the water, desperate to get to the boat before he was swept away forever. "You can't leave me!"

The icy water was up to her neck by the time she made it to the boat, gripping the edge to steady herself. She ran her wet hand across Zophar's chest and shoved him, as if he was just in a deep slumber and needed to be woken up.

"Zophar?" Her bottom lip quivered as she rested her head against his chest. There was no heartbeat; she knew she wouldn't hear one, but she couldn't bring herself to let him go. "I'm so sorry, Zophar. It should have been me. It should have been me."

A strong hand clamped down on her shoulder. "Princess?" Kavyen asked softly, spurring her to wiggle out of his grasp.

"Leave me alone!"

"You need to let him go." Kayven didn't attempt to touch her again, but his golden eyes stared so deep into her soul, it almost hurt. "He has returned to the ancestors."

"It's not fair," she whimpered. "I just got him back."

He extended his hand, "We need to get you out of the water. It is far too cold - you will get sick."

"I'm not letting him go!" she howled like a wounded animal, baring her teeth at the warrior.

"Then I am sorry for what is about to happen, my lady."

Before she had a moment to react, the Bellator grabbed ahold of her and dragged her back to shore. All the while, she kicked, screamed, cursed, and clawed at him like a rabid beast.

"Let me go! Let me go!" She watched as Zophar's boat slipped further and further into the distance. "Please," she pleaded, tears flowing like a broken dam. "Please, let me go to him. It's all my fault. It's all my fault."

Once they returned to shore, a small crowd, including a distraught Harbona, had gathered to watch. Kayven held Salome firmly in his arms, not allowing her an opportunity to escape. She fought against him, but he held her close against his body in what could only be described as a hug.

Kayven tilted her chin up to look at him. "Rest, my lady." The Bellator thumbed a golden powder underneath her nose, and everything faded to black.

Chapter Fourteen

Crispin

The next morning, Captain Ivar escorted Crispin back to the throne room where not only King Benaiah awaited his answer, but the royal family and court did, too. The king was seated in his throne, a mighty figure that exuded power. To his left sat his latest wife who looked to be only a few years older than Crispin.

To the king's right was Prince Ehrik, the firstborn and heir to the throne. Ivar's description of the prince was spot on, even down to the scraggly red beard and cunning blue eyes that narrowed as he approached the dais. He was Benaiah's spitting image and Crispin imagined they were similar in personality as well.

There were two more thrones on either side of the lower level of the dais. Next to Ehrik was Prince Ragnar, the spare. His eyes were blue, but weren't like Benaiah's eyes, they were like the sea, calm and wild all at the same time. His red hair was pulled back in a half knot and he rubbed a ringed index finger across his stubbled face.

Next to the queen lounged a hauntingly beautiful woman with long, wavy red locks that hung loosely right above her hips. Intricately plaited braids weaved along the sides of her head signifying though she was royalty, she too, knew how to wield a weapon. If Crispin were a gambling man, he'd bet she was Princess Lahki.

Crispin and Ivar bowed at the waist when they reached the dais and waited for the king to receive them. Those gathered fell to a hush, all eager to know the prince's answer.

"Prince Crispin," Benaiah motioned for them to stand. Though he smiled, Crispin could sense the venom behind the king's polite words. "Have you considered my generous offer? Agree to marry my daughter," he sliced an enormous hand through the air, pointing at the woman next to the queen, "and your friends will be pardoned of their crimes."

Crispin glanced over at Lahki, who didn't return his gaze. Her brown eyes were looking at Ivar who was standing next to him. Daring a look at Ivar, he found the captain stoically staring forward, his shoulders tense and lips tightly sealed. It appeared as if the captain was holding himself back or stilling his tongue.

"I have considered your offer, Your Majesty." Crispin forced himself to stop reading into Ivar and Lahki's behavior and answer the impatient king. "And I am afraid, I must decline." By the gasps and whispers of the courtiers, Crispin braced himself to incur the king's fury. Even Lahki and Ivar jerked in surprise, or relief, Crispin couldn't tell which.

"You decline my generous and merciful offer?" Benaiah's nostrils flared and his knuckles whitened as he gripped his armrests.

"I am sorry, but I cannot marry your daughter." Crispin turned his full attention to Lahki who met his gaze for the first time, and he realized she was relieved. "I assure you, this has nothing to do with you, Princess, but my own heart. I beg your forgiveness, if I have offended you."

Lahki's lips parted to respond but before she could utter a word, the king jumped from his throne and pointed an accusatory finger at the prince.

"You have not only offended me and my daughter, but you have proven yourself to be no ally of the West. You are like your father in every way, and you shall pay greatly for this dishonor."

Benaiah waved his hand, and the guards surrounded him, pushing Ivar away from the prince. Crispin whipped his head toward Ivar who looked completely caught off guard. The prince protested as soldiers slapped iron shackles on his wrists and bound his hands behind his back, but his cries fell on deaf ears. He was dragged from the throne room and taken to a cell in the dungeons beneath the castle. Once he was thrown into the barred prison, and his eyes adjusted to the dim lighting, he realized the crew of the *Shadow of Death* were already sitting in matching cells around him.

"Crispin?" Rahab's voice sounded to his right. He saw her sitting in a cell next to Ziggy. He was the only one in a holding cell by himself. Haldane, Phex, Corwin, Ondrej, Rafi, Nubis, even Master Penn and her Keepers were stuffed into cages.

Crispin slammed his hands against the bars rattling them. "That bastard!"

Rahab stuck her arms through the bars and Crispin embraced her from his side. He kissed her forehead and whispered, "I'm sorry."

"The king wasn't going to let any of us walk out of here alive." Rahab tilted his chin up to meet her gaze. "We were targets before we even met. If anything, you spared us from being executed on the spot."

"We've been in worse scrapes before," Haldane chimed in from the cell across the hall. "We'll find a way out of here, too." He winked and grinned, but Crispin sensed his panic.

He'd failed them and underestimated Benaiah. Had he agreed to marry Lahki, he'd only be signing his life away to serve the Westerners. He never would have been free to rule the North, not with Benaiah playing puppet master.

A couple of hours later, footsteps dusted the stone steps leading into the dungeons. Crispin hopped up and made his way to the cell door to see who was coming. His heart was lodged in his throat imagining Benaiah sending soldiers to haul the pirates away and having them hanged in the town square. But when Ivar rounded the corner with a torch in hand, he breathed a little easier.

"Ivar?" Crispin waved at him, and the captain walked toward him. "What are you doing here?"

"His Majesty doesn't know I'm here," Ivar whispered and looked over his shoulder at the stairs. "I don't have much time. The king..." the captain rubbed his forehead and grimaced. "I didn't know what he had planned until it was too late. I assure you I wouldn't have let this happen to you or your friends."

Rahab scoffed from her cell, her back flush against the cold stone wall, legs stretched out across the damp floor. "Oh, I'm sure you're real torn up about it."

Ivar narrowed his eyes at her, but instead of a snide remark the Westerner replied, "I'm sorry. This wasn't supposed to happen. This is not honorable."

"What does the king intend to do now?" Crispin asked, nausea and guilt bubbling in his gut.

Ivar met his gaze and he looked positively exhausted. "It would seem the king has sent word to your sister in Northwind that he has you as his prisoner. He intends to hand you over to her once the ship arrives."

Crispin wasn't surprised by that, but it wasn't his main concern. "And the crew? What of Master Penn and her Keepers?"

"Master Penn and her Keepers will be released in a couple of days and escorted back to The Sisters." Ivar paused and Crispin's heart sank. "He has ordered the crew of the *Shadow of Death* to be executed by the end of the week."

"Why wait?" Rahab growled. "Why not execute the lot of us now?"

"It seems our king -"

"*Your* king." The pirates said in unison which brought a smile to Crispin's face.

Even Ivar couldn't hide a smirk at the blatant defiance. "The king has declared your execution a day of rest for the citizens of Borg. There will be a festival and all Borgians will be in attendance to watch you die."

Crispin rested his forehead against the iron bars. "Why are you telling us this?"

"I found this before the king's soldiers could go through your belongings." Ivar dug through his breast pocket and fished out a rolled-up parchment. Crispin recognized it and it appeared Rahab did too when she leapt up from her lounged position.

She rushed across her cell and hissed,"That's mine!"

Ivar took a step away from the adjoining cell, just out of her reach. He kept an eye on her when he unraveled it and asked, "What do you know of Leeondris?"

"What do *you* know of Leeondris?" She shot back.

"Look," he lowered his voice and once again looked over his shoulder toward the stairs. "I want to help you, but if you don't tell me how you know Leeondris, I won't be able to do anything."

Rahab and Crispin exchanged a glance and the prince nodded for her to tell him. Reluctantly, Rahab explained how the pirates knew Leeondris. How he'd saved her life and after years of being a member of their crew, he just disappeared. When they received word that he was in trouble, they set out to The Sisters to get information from the Witnesses. Rahab hadn't had the heart to open the parchment, fearing he was dead.

"So, you never opened this?" Ivar asked, clearly skeptical.

"Like I told you," Rahab rested her elbows against the bars, "I was afraid it would say he was dead. I wasn't ready to know the truth."

Ivar handed her the note and she nervously read it before gasping. "He's alive?"

"And in Borg." Ivar snatched the piece of paper back, rolled it up, and stuffed it in his pocket. Scuffling at the top of the staircase alerted Ivar to the shift change. "My time is up. I have to go." He turned his focus to Crispin and extended his hand through the bars. "You may be in enemy territory, Prince Crispin, but you have friends."

Crispin clasped Ivar's hand and shook it before the captain pulled away, grabbed the torch, and retreated up the steps.

Chapter Fifteen

Adonijah

Cold water splashed Adonijah's face, waking him up in an instant. He had no idea how long he'd been unconscious and made a mental note to pay his dear uncle back tenfold for the welt on the back of his head.

"Wake up." A familiar voice barked with a swift kick to his boot.

Adonijah opened his eyes as he wiped the water from his face. His gaze rested on Pash and Ophir's frowns, prompting him to grin. "What a delight to wake up to your smiling faces."

Ophir took a step forward but stopped when Pash held out his arm.

"It appears you're still cross with me, Uncle."

"Shut up, Adonijah." Pash hissed. "Do you know what kind of trouble you're in?"

"Enlighten me, brother."

"The Shadows are demanding your execution." Pash admitted with sadness in his eyes.

"And?" Adonijah motioned for him to continue.

"Show some respect, bastard." Ophir spat at Adonijah's boots.

Adonijah shook his head. "Truly, Uncle, you need to reign in that temper of yours. It'll stop your heart one day."

Ophir muttered a string of curses before Pash ordered him to leave. Reluctantly, the old man left the brothers in silence.

"Someone really should talk to him about his health. He looks unwell," Adonijah smirked.

Pash sat on the ground in front of him and released the tension he'd been holding in his shoulders.

"When am I to be executed?" Adonijah asked.

Pash peered at his brother, raking a hand through his hair. "Why'd you do it? We had a plan."

"Did Leoti talk to you?"

Pash nodded. "She told me."

"Then you know why I did it."

"You didn't have to kill him."

"Was I supposed to ask the monster nicely to leave the lady alone?"

"Damn it, Adonijah, you're not taking this seriously." Pash rubbed a hand down his face. "My hands are tied. You murdered a Shadow, one of the brothers. You are to be executed at dawn."

Adonijah nodded his head. "When you see our father again, tell him, I send my regards."

"That's all you have to say?" Pash scoffed, fury raging in his eyes.

"If you're looking for an apology, I haven't one to offer. If you're looking for an explanation, you've received one." Adonijah leaned forward. "What else would you like me to say?"

Pash stood up and brushed the dirt off his pants. "I can't save you," he said softly, averting his gaze.

"I know." Adonijah bobbed his head in understanding. "Make sure Leoti isn't there to watch."

Pash looked like he wanted to say something else but decided against it. He walked through the flaps, leaving Adonijah chained to a pole in a tent he could only assume was a makeshift prison. He knew when he first left the City of Bones to kill the Nameless Rider that there was a chance he might not make it back to Salome, but with his execution looming, he wished he could hold her one more time to tell her that he was sorry for leaving. Maybe he could make it up to her in the next life.

Knowing there were only a few hours left before dawn and his inevitable execution, caused sleep to elude him. He was honest when he told Pash he wasn't issuing any apologies, but that didn't mean he was going to accept his fate easily. He'd break free or die trying when the Shadows collected him for punishment.

As his mind plotted any feasible escape, he heard two thuds outside the flaps of his tent. Two figures dressed in black and armed with longswords entered, dragging the two soldiers posted to guard his prison inside.

Adonijah sat straighter. “It’s a little early to fetch me, isn't it? Even I can see the sun has yet to make an appearance.”

“Are you always this annoying?”

“Pash?” Adonijah tried to get a look at the man beneath the hood.

Pash flipped his cloak back. “We don’t have much time.”

“You’re rescuing me?” Adonijah didn’t see that coming.

“You really thought I wouldn’t?” Pash almost looked offended.

“We don’t have time for this,” Leoti hissed. She unlocked Adonijah's manacles with the keys she yanked off one of the unconscious soldiers. The second he was free he twisted his fingers around the raw area of his wrists. “Well, come on. We haven’t got all night.”

Adonijah hopped up and grabbed her arm, turning her around to face him. “Thank you.”

“A life for a life.” She bowed her head slightly and Adonijah couldn't take his eyes off of her.

“Oh, it’s fine. I’m just the one who hatched the entire plan in the first place. No need to thank *me*.” Pash poked his head out of the tent to take a quick look before they darted for the outskirts of the camp.

“I’ll thank you once we get out of your camp intact.”

Pash grinned, “Oh, we’ll get out alright. It’s keeping ahead of the Shadows once we escape that’ll take some skill.”

“We’ll manage.” Leoti stepped forward to join Pash at the entrance. “With my warging affinity, your Shadow training, and Adonijah’s tracking, we’ll remain hidden.”

“I appreciate your enthusiasm,” Pash rolled his eyes, “but don’t underestimate Her Majesty’s Shadows. They’re an elite killing force for a good reason.” He handed Adonijah a leather case that held his daggers and tossed him his longsword. “I trust you will only use that if you have to.”

Adonijah placed the daggers in their holsters and sheathed his blade. “I will do my best to refrain from slaughtering everyone in sight.”

"Ass." Pash shook his head before taking one last look outside and nodded. “Let’s go.”

Swiftly, but quietly, the trio weaved through the camp. Pash knew exactly where the guards were posted and managed to avoid them. After a few minutes, the outskirts of the camp were within sight. But Pash stopped suddenly, halting the other two.

“What’s wrong?” Leoti whispered.

A soldier had crawled out of his tent to relieve himself in the direct path they were headed. Their exit was blocked. They could either wait until the soldier finished and went back to bed, they could eliminate him, or they could try to flee a different way. Adonijah knew what he would do, but followed his brother's lead. Pash had them hide behind tents and wait for the soldier to finish. But instead of going back to his tent, the soldier decided a midnight stroll was what he needed instead.

Pash grumbled something Adonijah couldn't quite make out. The brothers made eye contact and Pash mouthed, "Knock him out."

"Slit his throat?" Adonijah cupped a hand to his ear and feigned confusion.

Pash narrowed his eyes and shook his head. "Knock. Him. Out."

Adonijah smirked and nodded that he understood. As the soldier neared their hiding spot, Adonijah waited for him to pass, then locked his arms around the unsuspecting man's neck from behind. He held him there until he passed out and they deposited him back inside his tent. With nothing blocking their gateway to freedom, the trio slipped out of the Northern camp and headed north until the darkness swallowed them.

Chapter Sixteen

Salome

Salome woke up with a splitting headache. Lifting a palm to her forehead, she could feel the throbbing beneath her fingers. She squinted as she looked around the room, realizing she wasn't in the Gomorrian dungeon. Then she remembered she had been brought to Oakenshire, and the uninhabited castle of King Greygor was now their new base of operations. But that wasn't the only thought that flooded her mind. Everything slammed into her like a crashing wave beating against the rocky cliffs. Zophar was dead. She failed to save him. She thought of her arrival, seeing Harbona again, after weeks apart, only to crumble into a shadow of her former self.

She flashed back to Zophar's funeral and how she lost herself in grief. She swam out to the boat that carried him to the next life but was held back. She fought the Bellator who grabbed ahold of her, wishing she could follow her guardian. The Bellator that saved her apologetically wiped a powdered substance under her nose and that was the last thing she could remember.

Now, she was in a large bed that was nowhere near as comfortable as the one she had in the Isles of Myr, but it beat the damp dungeon floor beneath the Black Tower. She pushed herself up slowly, her head still throbbing. The curtains in her room were closed, shrouding her bedroom in darkness. It reminded her too much of her prison cell. Struggling to get on her feet, she shuffled to the window, gripped the heavy velvet drapes, and ripped them open. She coughed as dust rained down on her but once she was able to see clearly, she stared out her window at the most breathtaking view: The Ignacia Sea. It was so close, she wanted to jump out of her window and feel the cool water swash against her skin.

Her attention turned toward the castle walls. Even though part of the grey-stone wall was crumbling, she saw men and women from different kingdoms in Adalore working together to refortify the former capitol city.

She withdrew her gaze from the people in the bailey back to her room and was pleasantly surprised that after hundreds of years of neglect, it wasn't in complete shambles. There was dust and cobwebs in the corners of the ceiling and the mirror attached to the ornate vanity was so dirty she couldn't make out her own warped reflection. She ran her fingers across the floral wallpaper, a dirty film stained her fingers and she wiped her hand clean against her pants.

It was then she noticed someone had changed her out of the blood-stained, tattered clothing she had worn in Gomorrah, before her escape. She now had a clean pair of brown trousers, a loose white shirt, and sitting neatly at the foot of her bed was a new pair of leather boots. She sat on the edge of her mattress, hearing the creak of her weight sinking, and strapped her boots on.

Curious, she walked over to the mirror and used one of the towels that had been left on the vanity next to the wash basin to wipe the glass clean. It took some effort, but once she saw herself clearly, she started to examine her injuries. Her lip was still swollen and bruised from the Thrak backhanding her in Matildys' throne room. She slipped off her shirt and saw bruises along her ribcage. Slowly, she turned to get her first glimpse of the scars the arrows she'd taken to the back left behind. Two ugly, fresh scars marred her back. She exhaled a deep breath. She really should have died from the injuries.

Death does not want me yet, she thought. That was the only logical explanation. The Gomorrians had put a lot of effort into healing her, making sure she not only survived, but that she was in the best condition possible for her public torture and execution. She shuddered at the thought. Had Jinn not arrived when he did...

Where was Jinn? How long had she been asleep?

She shook her head, rattling the questions free for now and returned to examining her body. Thankfully, apart from the bruises, some cuts on her arms, a busted lip, scars on her back, and exhaustion, she was physically alright. But mentally, the nightmares and flashbacks would take months, if not years, to recover from.

Tears ran down her face when Zophar's face flashed in her head. Her heart ached and she retched, but there was nothing in her stomach to throw up. Overwhelmed with grief and anger, she snatched a candlestick off the vanity and threw it against the wall. The thud echoed in the room and Salome heard feet shuffling toward her wooden door. The doorknob jiggled and she instinctively lunged for her dagger sitting on her nightstand. Whenever she heard footsteps approach her cell in Gomorrah, she wasn't sure if it would be the healers, a servant with her meal, or the Thrak finally coming to harm her.

The door swung open, and her hand shook as she clutched her wolf dagger tightly. But there were no Thrak coming for her. She'd been rescued. The people who entered were ones she recognized, ones she loved. Kai and the Qata Vishna twins, Rosalina and Seraphina, stopped when they took in her appearance.

"Are you alright?" Kai grabbed Salome's shirt from the vanity and slowly approached, offering it to the princess.

Salome opened her mouth to speak but no words came out, only a whimpering cry, and the tears weren't far behind.

"Bring a healer," Kai whispered to Rosalina who immediately turned on her heel to obey.

Salome didn't want Rosalina to fetch anyone looking the way she did, but the twin was gone before she could object.

Seraphina made her way to Salome and helped her sit on the edge of the bed then knelt before the princess. "You are safe, my lady. You can rest."

"Zophar's really gone." Salome's voice was raspy from disuse and a fresh batch of tears dripped down her jawline. "I didn't save him. It should have been me."

Seraphina grabbed Salome's hands and said in a gentle tone that was unlike her, "Do not blame yourself for surviving. I know for a fact your guardian would say the same thing."

"If I hadn't been careless and left the City of Bones without protection, Zophar would still be alive." Salome buried her face in her hands. "This is all my fault."

Kai stepped forward, "You can't do that. You can't blame yourself for his death. Death called -"

"No matter what you say," Salome interrupted the Easterner, "I will always blame myself."

The room fell silent. Kai and Seraphina busied themselves with cleaning and organizing her room until Salome was ready to speak.

"How long have I been asleep?"

"About a week," Kai answered.

"A week?" Salome's eyes widened.

"Harbona believed it necessary for you to rest," Seraphina chimed in with her no-nonsense tone. "You wouldn't have followed the Healer's orders otherwise."

Seraphina was right, but a week? That was far longer than she had originally estimated. She thought she'd been sleeping for a day or two. But an entire week?

"I want to speak with Harbona." By her tone, Seraphina realized Salome meant she wanted to see the Immortal immediately, so she bowed her head and left the room to find him.

Kai was leaning against the wall next to Salome's vanity, arms crossed over her chest.

"Has anyone heard from Adonijah?" Salome bowed her head and stared at the splintered floor.

Kai shook her head. "No."

Her bottom lip quivered, "I'll never understand why he did this to me. Why he left, why he lied."

"I wish I could give you an explanation," Kai said softly, pushing up from the wall, "but I don't know why he left or why he hid his identity from you. Maybe, if your paths cross again, you can get the answers you seek."

"If I ever see Adonijah again, I'll kill him."

Kai reached to touch Salome's shoulder but stopped. "You're angry, you're hurting, and you're grieving, but don't allow that to corrupt the goodness in you." The Easterner shifted her weight from one foot to the other, clearly uncomfortable. "Maybe there is someone who can give you answers."

After the healer examined Salome and gave her a cup of herbal tea to help ease her pain and speed up her recovery, she left the princess so she could speak with her awaiting visitor and promised to check on her again that evening.

Salome sat in the receiving area attached to her bedroom and silently stared at a fidgeting Jacobi. He looked healthier, obviously eating well now that he was out from under the Shadows' thumb. His right knee bounced, and his eyes looked everywhere but at her.

Kai stood in the corner, watching quietly like a predatorial cat and for a second Salome wondered why she was guarding her and not Jinn. She'd meant to reach out to Jinn through their bond but wasn't sure what she'd say to him. 'Thank you' seemed inadequate for what he did to rescue her, and she preferred to tell him in person.

Jacobi coughed and Salome's gaze darted across the coffee table to look at him.

"Kai told me you showed Adonijah the way to the Northern Military encampment." Salome watched him with a calculating stare.

That wasn't the only thing Kai had told her about Jacobi. He'd joined their ranks and, in an attempt to redeem himself for his cowardice in the Tree House Forest, he'd become the head baker in Oakenshire. He took his duties seriously and made sure everyone on castle grounds was well fed. Salome was oddly proud of the redhead, but this wasn't a friendly catch-up session. This meeting was strictly to find out what he knew about the night Adonijah left.

Jacobi nodded his head. "Yes, I showed him how to get there. He told me the Shadow who gave the order to slaughter the people in our village was the same Shadow who killed his mother." The baker swallowed hard before continuing. "He said he could kill him, if I took him."

Salome was oblivious to Adonijah's past and didn't know his mother had been murdered by Shadows. She motioned for the baker to continue. "And once you got him there...?"

"He told me to stay hidden and if he didn't come back, that I should return to the City of Bones and deliver a message to you."

"What was the message?" Her breathing quickened but she steadied herself. What were his last words to her?

"He told me to tell you he was sorry."

Somehow, even with an answer to one of her questions, she didn't feel any better. She almost felt worse. He left knowing there was a possibility he wouldn't return. He left knowing he'd be sorry when she learned the truth. He left knowing he'd lied to her about his past, his true identity, and that he'd leave her shattered in his absence.

He left.

She had to continue to remind herself that Adonijah was Gershom's son, and although that part of his past was hard to swallow, she never would have held it against him. The fact that he hid it from her when he demanded transparency and trust from her made her want to vomit. He didn't trust her. That's what it boiled down to. And where there was no trust, there was no love.

Salome realized Jacobi was watching her in silence and she collected herself, forcing the neutral mask back on her face.

"Thank you, Jacobi." She stood up, signifying their conversation was over and he jumped to his feet, making sure to grab his chef's hat from his lap. "And thank you for joining our company. Kai has raved about your pastries."

Kai stood stoically in the corner, but Jacobi beamed over his shoulder at the Easterner. "She is welcome to have as many as she likes."

The warrior flashed a half-smile which might as well have been her doing a full-blown cartwheel. Jacobi bowed to Salome before Kai opened the door for him to leave.

Salome slumped back into her chair and Kai made her way forward. There was a slight limp in her gait where she'd taken an arrow during the skirmish outside of the City of Bones, but otherwise, you'd never know she'd been wounded. "Should I send for the healer?"

The princess waved the idea off and motioned for the Easterner to sit. Once Kai obliged, taking the spot Jacobi vacated, Salome asked, "Why are you guarding me?"

"What?"

"You're Jinn's protection, his Ryoko Naga." Salome cocked her head to the side, eyes fixed on every slight move or twitch Kai made. "Why aren't you with him?"

"The prince instructed me to guard you while he is away."

Salome's heart sank. She'd hoped to see him, even if she didn't know what exactly to say. "Where is he?"

"Not all of the Bellators flew straight to Oakenshire. Prince Jinn, Oifa, and Hanzo all stayed behind for their minor injuries to be tended to and they were to make the trip with the remainder of the army."

"When will they arrive?" she asked.

Kai shrugged one shoulder. "From our reports, they should be here any day."

"So," Salome's eyes bounced from Kai's face to the leg that had been struck by an arrow. "Are you guarding me because of what happened when the Thrak captured me?"

Kai's body tensed. "I have been meaning to thank you for what you did, Princess -"

"You would have done the same for me."

Kai nodded solemnly. "And that is why I will watch over you, until I am no longer needed."

Chapter Seventeen

Crispin

Days passed, and they hadn't seen or heard from Ivar. They were given some water and a poor excuse for a meal once a day, but no one seemed to be interested in eating. Any day now, all the pirates would be executed and there wasn't anything Crispin could do about it. He tried asking the soldiers who brought their meals to take him to the king, but they acted like they didn't hear him, as if he were invisible. It was then it hit Crispin, that once again, his title meant nothing. He had no riches, power, throne, crown, or army to back him up. He was just as ordinary as the next person and had little sway in enemy territory.

Even though the pirates tried to keep their spirits up, sharing stories of their adventures, telling crass jokes, or hurling friendly insults at one another, Crispin could tell they were all worried, frightened even.

Crispin had not rested well in days, but when sleep finally summoned him, he laid on the cold, stone floor and shut his eyes. He wasn't sure how long he'd dozed off for, but when Rahab reached through the bars and tapped his foot, he sat up instantly and stared at two cloaked figures standing at the entrance to his cell. He couldn't see their faces, and they didn't immediately identify themselves.

"Who are you?" Crispin tried to mask the fear lacing his voice. "What do you want?"

The two figures exchanged a quick glance before pulling their hoods off their heads. Crispin stood up and rubbed the heels of his palms against his eyes. Surely, he must be imagining them, but then he heard them speak and it confirmed he was wide awake, and they weren't figments of his imagination.

"Prince Crispin." Lahki gripped the bars of his cell. "I apologize on behalf of our father. He does not speak for all Borgians."

"Princess Lahki," Crispin bowed his head in a show of respect and Rahab folded her arms over her chest. His gaze bounced from Lahki to her brother, Prince Ragnar, leaning against the bars lazily. "Prince Ragnar, this is a surprise."

Ragnar brushed a thumb over his jawline before standing up straight. At full height, the prince towered over Crispin's six-foot frame by a few inches. It had been quite a long time since Crispin felt small.

"Captain Ivar told us that we have a friend in common." Ragnar's voice was smooth as honey despite his rugged appearance. Crispin noticed the black tattoos on the prince's wrist and wondered if they extended up his arm.

"It would appear we do," Crispin nodded.

"Then I would like to make a deal with you."

"Forgive me, but I don't know if I believe you will uphold your end of the bargain."

Ragnar's smile crinkled the corners of his eyes. "I am not my father, Prince Crispin."

Crispin was inclined to believe him, his eyes spoke truth, but he was still wary. "What is it you want?"

"We can get you and your friends out of here," Ragnar leaned forward and lowered his voice, "but you will owe me a favor in the future."

"What kind of favor?" Crispin's eyebrow arched.

"I will send word when the time comes." Ragnar reached into his cloak and pulled out a ring of keys, making sure Crispin could see them. "Do we have a deal?"

Crispin wasn't sure he should agree, but what other choice did he have? If the prince had learned of the pirates' relationship with Leeondris from Ivar, clearly, they were friends or at least on the same side. He glanced over at Rahab, then scanned the faces of the weary pirates and relented.

"You get us out of Borg, and I will owe you a favor."

Ragnar flashed a wicked smile and unlocked Crispin's cell door. "Nice doing business with you, *vargr*."

Crispin eyed him suspiciously. "What does that mean? Vargr?"

Ragnar chuckled and offered Lahki the keys to unlock the other cells. "It means 'wolf' in Borgian."

Before Crispin could respond, Lahki had opened all the cells and given the pirates their confiscated weapons before Ragnar led them deeper into the dungeons.

"Stay close," Ragnar ordered as he marched before them, guiding the group with a flaming torch.

"And keep quiet." Lahki added as she walked next to her older brother.

The deeper they traveled through the sloped dungeon halls, the spookier it became. The smell of decay mixed with the humidity made it difficult to breathe. But they continued to follow Ragnar and Lahki, hoping it would lead to their freedom and not an ambush.

After hours of silently trekking forward, Crispin could hear the chirping of birds and could see light. When they reached the end of the tunnel, the prince realized they had been led out of Borg completely underground and were now at the edge of the forest that he had grown up in. Dawn was upon them; they'd walked through the night and were free. Or at least, Crispin hoped they were free.

Ragnar paused at the mouth of the tunnel before motioning the group forward. When they were all standing in the light, hooded figures stepped out from the tree line. A tall man with broad shoulders marched toward them. Every pirate reached for their weapons but Ragnar, held out his arms to embrace the vigilante.

The Western prince turned toward the group, patted the newcomer's chest, and smiled. "I believe, you know one another."

The man removed his hood to reveal himself. The crew of the *Shadow of Death* stood speechless, as if they were seeing a ghost. Rahab slowly approached the red bearded man. She reached a hand out and touched his freckled face.

"Leeondris?" she whispered reverently.

Crispin had always wondered what the mysterious Leeondris looked like and was surprised to find a man not much older than himself. It looked like Leeondris and Ragnar were around the same age, mid-twenties, and his long, red hair and grey-blue eyes identified him as a true Westerner.

"You're a pretty sight for sore eyes, Ray," Leeondris' deep voice boomed, and a set of perfect white teeth flashed. He leaned in to embrace the pirate, but Rahab seemed to snap out of her stupor and punched the Westerner square in the chest. Hooded rebels lurched into attack positions, but Leeondris held a fist up and the vigilantes relaxed. "It would seem you haven't changed a bit." Leeondris smiled.

"That's for leaving," she snorted, popping a hip to the side.

"And what do I get now that you've found me?" His eyes danced as he wiggled his eyebrows.

Rahab nearly tackled the rebel to the ground in a bear hug. "Stars above and seas below. I thought you were dead."

Leeondris smiled against her temple, stroking a large hand through her icy blue locks. "I'm not so easy to kill."

Crispin felt a pang of jealousy pool in his chest at how close – how familiar – they were. He was tempted to clear his throat to remind Rahab he still existed, but she beat him to the punch when she ripped herself from Leeondris' grasp and met his gaze.

"Leeondris, this is Crispin. Prince of Northwind."

"So, you're the man who insulted not only the king, but our princess as well?" Leeondris eyed him with an air of suspicion. "Why did you turn down the chance to marry our princess? Did she not suit your Northern desires?"

Crispin's eyes darted to Rahab before returning to the burly Westerner. He was ready to puff out his chest and put the rebel in his place, when he noticed Ragnar smirking beside Leeondris, his eyes dancing in mischief.

Leeondris bellowed a laugh when Lahki swatted his arm. "You brute. You shouldn't give the prince a hard time."

"Oh, come on, Lahki," Leeondris wiped a tear from his eye, a wide grin plastered on his face. "Did you see the look on the princeling's face?"

"That *princeling* now owes us a favor for helping him and his friends escape." Ragnar's voice hummed in delight, drawing all eyes.

"And when will you be calling in that favor?" Crispin asked, wishing he wasn't in the prince's debt.

“At the proper time.” Ragnar’s smile reminded Crispin of a fox and it made him nervous. He turned to Leeondris. “I trust you can ensure safe passage for the prince and his company out of our lands?”

Leeondris bobbed his head, a seriousness washed over his features. "Consider it done."

"Good," Ragnar seemed pleased. "This is where my sister and I leave you. We must return to the city before anyone notices our absence."

Crispin extended a hand to the prince who looked at it quizzically. "Thank you."

Ragnar hesitated a moment before snatching Crispin's hand in his. His palm was littered with callouses and proved him to be just as much a warrior as he was a politician. "It was a pleasure doing business with the future King of the North. Our paths will cross again, Crispin." And with that, the prince turned and marched toward a carriage awaiting to take him back to Borg.

Lahki paused in front of Crispin and gave him a peck on the cheek. "Thank you, Prince Crispin. Have a safe journey." Not waiting for him to respond, she turned and quickly followed her brother to the royal carriage and hopped inside. The driver whipped the horses, and they raced back to Borg.

Crispin couldn't shake the feeling that Ragnar would pop up at the most inconvenient moment and he'd have no choice but to honor the Western prince's request.

Leeondris turned to face the group of pirates and lifted his arms out to his sides and said, "Come! We'll get you back to our camp and prepare you for your journey."

Chapter Eighteen

Adonijah

The trio couldn't stop to rest, if they were going to keep out of the Shadows' reach, but when they became too tired and hungry to continue, they set up camp and sat around the campfire to keep warm from the forest chill. They only had one small tent and the brothers wholeheartedly agreed, Leoti should be the one to have it. She disagreed, but when the distant roll of thunder echoed through the woods, she changed her mind.

Adonijah easily caught three rabbits and Pash had already stoked a roaring fire to roast their dinner. Leoti showed no signs of squeamishness when she took the animals from Adonijah and skinned them, prepping them for their humble feast.

Though they spent the wee hours of the night speaking of their adventures, upbringings, and travels, Adonijah found himself tuning out of the conversation every so often with one person on his mind. He had to keep reminding himself that Salome had escaped. She'd been rescued, despite the fact, he wasn't the one there for her, as he once swore, he would be. His failure, his broken promise to protect her, was slowly eating away at him. But thinking of Jinn being the one to risk everything to get her out of Gomorrah – thinking of the prince with his arms around the woman he loved, and being countless miles away from her, was a new form of pain and torture.

Would she wait for him? Would she even want him anymore? Would he ever see her again?

Though deep in thought, he couldn't shake the feeling he was being watched, so he glanced up and across the campfire, he caught Leoti staring at him.

"You must see something you like, if you're gawking that hard," Adonijah rolled his shoulders back with a devilish smirk.

Leoti didn't look away. "Rollo used to stare off into the distance when he was deep in thought, too."

He shifted uncomfortably. "He's the queen's son?"

"He was."

Adonijah suddenly remembered hearing the prince died unexpectedly and felt like a cad for remarking about him so flippantly. "I'm sorry for your loss."

Something in Leoti's eyes made him feel like she saw Gershom when she looked at him and he hated it. He hated feeling the need to apologize on behalf of his father's transgressions.

As if she could read his mind, she shook her head. "I do not blame you for your father's sins."

"If only everyone saw it that way," he sighed and focused on his rabbit.

"This princess of yours..."

"What of her?" His eyes narrowed, expecting her to attack or slander Salome.

"You said she doesn't know who you really are." Leoti picked up a piece of roasted meat and chewed it. "If you care for her as you claim, why lie to her?"

"I didn't lie to her," he huffed.

"Omitting the truth is still lying." She set her plate on the ground by her feet and leaned forward. "Why did you not tell her?"

He hesitated. "You don't blame me for Gershom's sins, but she might think differently."

"Maybe it isn't her opinion you're frightened of. Maybe it's your own."

He looked up at her. "What do you mean?"

"Has she given you any reason to suspect she would hold an innocent person responsible for someone else's wrong doings? Do you truly believe she would blame you for assassinating her mother and brothers? Has she ever blamed anyone for their deaths, other than Gershom?"

Adonijah smirked, baring his teeth in a predatorial way. "Just your queen."

"Which is understandable," Leoti didn't miss a beat. "If I were in her position, I would blame Niabi, too."

Pash made his way back to the campfire after relieving himself in the woods and plopped down on a stump. "Tread carefully, Leoti. Your words sound treasonous."

"Funny," she scoffed. "My words seem like the last thing we should be worried about, seeing as we are on the run from Her Majesty's Shadows."

Pash shrugged a shoulder. "A misunderstanding."

"Your brother gutted a Shadow," Leoti snapped. "You think our queen will forgive a *misunderstanding*? On top of it, we are helping him evade capture, making us traitors- "

"For the greater good," he interrupted with a bite in his tone. "Once we kill Gershom all will be forgiven."

"So you say."

Pash motioned his hand toward the blackened forest. "You can leave at any time, if this is too much for you to handle."

Leoti looked at Adonijah. "What do you say?"

Adonijah swallowed his food, confusion written all over his face. "What?"

"Do you think I should leave?" Leoti asked.

Adonijah seesawed from the Andrago to his brother. Both were irritated, but he wasn't sure what to say to ease the tension. She was right. She and Pash were now fugitives alongside him. They had committed treason to rescue him and whether the queen loved Pash or not, with her reputation, they might not be forgiven.

"If you want me to leave," Leoti's voice sliced through his thoughts and he met her fiery gaze, "then I will leave."

"Why do you care what I think?" he asked.

There was a mischievous twinkle in her eyes when she said, "I trust you to be honest."

Adonijah knew what she was doing. What she was implying. He hadn't been forthcoming with Salome, hadn't been completely honest. He hadn't lied, but he hadn't been truthful. She was giving him a chance to grow, to redeem himself in a way. Even though Pash would be irritated, they had a better chance of completing their mission if they banded together, instead of pushing her away. And whether he wanted to admit it or not, he hoped she wouldn't disappear in the middle of the night.

"Stay." Adonijah cleared his throat and tried again. "I want you to stay."

Pash rolled his eyes and refocused on his dinner.

With a satisfied grin, Leoti stood up and made her way to her make-shift tent. "Goodnight."

As soon as Leoti disappeared into her sleeping area, Pash flashed a disapproving look at Adonijah. "What is going on?"

"We need her – "

"We don't," Pash interrupted, "but that's not what I'm talking about."

"Then what are you talking about?" Adonijah lit his pipe, bored with his brother's question.

"You have feelings for her."

Not a question. An accusation. A statement.

Adonijah stretched his legs in front of him and scoffed. "Because I told her to stay, I must have romantic feelings or ulterior motives?"

"You can deny it all you like, but I have eyes, and I am very good at reading people," Pash maintained his intense glare. "In fact, I've made a career of it.

"Then I suggest you request a healer examine your eyes, because you are clearly reading into this."

"Am I? I haven't seen Leoti smile in months." Pash sipped water from his sheepskin and wiped the excess from his lips with his sleeve. "And don't think I haven't caught you eyeing her when you think no one is watching."

Adonijah's face flushed, and he attempted to hide it by scratching at his beard. "My heart belongs to another."

Pash tossed the rabbit bones into the fire and set his plate on the ground before standing. "Your heart may belong to Salome, but your attention is fixed on Leoti."

"You're wrong." Adonijah hated that he sounded like a child in his denial.

Pash planted his foot on the stump he'd used for a seat and rested an elbow on his knee. "Let me ask you this. Where do you see yourself in the future? You've killed your mother's murderer and we are on our way to kill our father. Forgetting about this inevitable war between Niabi and Salome; what do you want, should you survive?"

Before answering, Adonijah took a minute to think. Pash was right. His mother's murderer was dead. He and Pash were on their way to kill their father. After that, he had no other passions or goals. His entire life had been so centered on revenge that he never thought about what else he wanted in life.

"I..." Words failed him.

Pash reached forward, clamping a hand on his brother's shoulder. "I'll tell you what I want, should I live through this war. Family. I want Niabi and I to escape the madness of Northwind, to live a life where no one knows us, to live in peace, and to raise our child without fear of someone harming him or her." Adonijah's eyes flashed at the mention of a child and Pash nodded with a smile. "She told me before I left the city. So, what is it you want?"

Adonijah shrugged. "I wish I knew."

"Do you believe Salome would choose a life roaming Adalore with you?"

He knew she wouldn't, and the thought pained him more than he cared to admit.

"She would choose her people before you, then?" Pash asked and it was like a punch to Adonijah's gut.

"How do you do it? Living in your queen's shadow and being second to her crown?"

Pash sank to the ground and sat next to his brother. "You come to realize the woman who bears the crown is different than the woman without it. If you desire a life free from the responsibilities of titles, thrones, crowns, and rulers, then let Salome go. There is no happiness for you there."

"You say that because you do not wish for me to be higher ranking than you, when she wins this war." Adonijah smirked but realized if Salome did win the war, that would mean Niabi would most likely be dead and Pash's dream would be unattainable. That thought didn't sit well with him.

Pash bumped his elbow into his brother's arm playfully. "I say it, because should you choose someone who shares the same goals and desires, you might find yourself content. The Andrago way of life isn't for everyone." He glanced at Leoti's tent. "But it might be perfect for someone like you."

"Were you not just lecturing me about having feelings for Leoti?"

"Not lecturing. Just pointing out my observations."

"Why don't you like her?" Adonijah exhaled a puff of smoke.

"It has nothing to do with her." Pash looked up at the twinkling stars before continuing. "Her father, Tala, and I do not see eye-to-eye. He is Niabi's oldest friend, and he is very protective of her. I don't blame him. Truthfully, I'm grateful he watches over her when I'm not there."

"Are you sure there's nothing more between them?"

Pash shook his head. "She was married to his childhood best friend. They both lost their spouses and rocked the very foundation of Adalore to right Dichali's death. Their bond will always be a strong one, but her heart belongs to me. Of that I have no doubt."

Adonijah shifted his weight. "I wish I had your confidence."

The Shadow patted Adonijah's back as he stood. "Love can be a blessing and a curse." The brothers stared at Leoti's tent again when they heard movement, but she didn't emerge. "A decision like this doesn't need to be made tonight. Get some rest, brother. Tomorrow will be a long day and I have a feeling, Niabi's Shadows aren't too far behind." Pash retreated to his sleeping bag on the other side of the campfire and settled down for the evening.

Once his brother was fast asleep, Adonijah's thoughts flooded him. He thought about Salome and their future together, Pash's goals and desires, Leoti and the Andrago way of life, and the heartache that one, or both of them would suffer, if they didn't get what they wanted. There was a great possibility that one, or neither of them, would make it out of the war alive, and he wasn't sure which one he'd rather it be.

Chapter Nineteen

Salome

Once the healer cleared Salome to start physical activity again, she jumped at the chance to work out the kinks in her still recovering body. Kai, Rosalina, and Seraphina helped her get ready and escorted her to the section in the bailey that had been set up as a training arena. Numbio, Stormcrags, Krazaks, Easterners, Qata Vishna – they were all exercising and sparring together, learning new tricks and techniques.

"You made it!" Cato's cheerful face instantly brightened Salome's mood and she embraced her Stormcrag friend.

"It's good to see you, Cato."

"I've been wanting to check on you but someone," he rolled his eyes at Seraphina, "forbade me from doing so. Something about you needing rest."

"Well, you can visit me whenever you want now." Salome smiled. "I've been cleared for activity."

"Well, then," Cato scratched his short white hair and took a step back, motioning toward the sparring grounds, "after you, my lady."

"Don't be a fool," Seraphina hissed. "She isn't sparring with you."

"Oh no?" He grinned at the Myridian and playfully bounced his eyebrows. "Does that mean *you* want a piece of me?"

Seraphina whipped out the blades strapped in her back holsters. "I'd prefer *all* of you."

"Gross," Rosalina crinkled her nose and waved them away. "Go on, love birds. Get out of here."

Salome turned to Kai and Rosalina once Seraphina and Cato walked off together, to spar or kiss, she wasn't so sure of anymore. "What was that about?"

"You missed a lot while you were gone," Kai muttered.

"It's almost obscene," Rosalina rolled her eyes. "Seraphina is... *happy*."

"You say that like it's a bad thing," Salome laughed and the Qata Vishna stared at her and shrugged.

"It's weird. I've never seen Seraphina happy." Rosalina scratched her chin. "It's almost unsettling."

"And you don't have your eyes on someone?" Kai's question sounded more like an accusation.

Rosalina blushed and instinctively her eyes drifted to a handsome Numbio warrior across the bailey. "Damn you, Kai, and your Ryoko Naga observations."

Kai shrugged. "I see things."

"And by the looks of it," Salome elbowed Rosalina's arm, "he might think the same about you."

The three of them glanced over at the Numbio Rosalina identified as Obi. With his smooth, dark skin, brown eyes, and muscular body, it wasn't difficult to see why Rosalina found him irresistible.

"You should go talk to him," Salome insisted.

"She won't," Kai snorted. "She will keep watching him from afar wishing he'd make the first move."

Whether Kai was goading the Qata Vishna or just picking on her, Salome didn't know, but either way, it spurred the Myridian to march her way toward Obi. His smile was bright, and though Salome was ecstatic for her friend, it felt like a kick to her gut. She had two men smile at her that way and now, neither one was with her.

"Come on, Kai," Salome nudged the Ryoko Naga to the sparring grounds, refusing to feel sorry for herself any longer. "I guess that leaves you and me."

If Kai was reluctant to spar with her, she didn't show it as they quickly took their stances. The Easterner pulled a couple daggers from her belt and Salome mirrored her by pulling her Qata Vishna blades from her back.

Though her body was sore and seemed rusty from weeks of disuse, muscle memory kicked in and propelled her in the match-up. She suspected Kai was pulling her punches and purposely left herself open to an attack to test her theory. When Kai didn't take the opening, Salome growled in frustration.

"Why are you holding back?"

Kai didn't deny it, nor was she surprised when she was called out. "This is your first session back. I didn't want to hurt you."

"Don't do that," Salome hissed, eyeing her friend. "Don't treat me like I'm fragile. Fight me like you would fight any of them," she motioned around the bailey.

"Princess -"

"Fight me!" Salome wiped sweat from her brow. "Fight me or find me someone who will."

A moment passed and Salome wasn't sure if her friend would do as she asked, until Kai took her fighting stance again. Salome readied herself and when the Easterner flew at her, she braced for impact. As Kai's leg swept through the air, aimed at Salome, something in her slowed. Instead of eluding the blow or blocking the attack, Salome froze. Moments flashed in her mind in the blink of an eye:

Hugging Crispin before they parted ways.

Zophar being stabbed.

Blood gushing from Ranalda's slit throat.

Kissing Adonijah in the City of Bones.

Touching Jinn's face in the dungeons of Gomorrah just to make sure he was real.

Watching Zophar's cold, lifeless body float away.

The stench and chaos of battle raging around her.

Death's presence thick in the air, not quite ready to claim her.

Her hand shaking every time she clutched her weapons, her fighter instinct quiet.

The Easterner's foot slammed into Salome's chest knocking her off her feet. Everyone in the bailey stopped their individual exercises and sparring sessions to gawk at Salome lying on her back, muttering a string of curses under her breath. The princess lifted herself up on her elbows as Kai approached. The Ryoko Naga's normally neutral face was filled with worry which angered Salome.

Kai offered Salome a hand, apologetic for harming her, but Salome waved Kai's hand away and quickly told everyone to get back to their sparring. Before anyone could stop her, she stormed off, embarrassment and rage stewing in her belly. She stared at her hands and noticed them trembling. Balling her hands into fists, she held them tightly at her sides and marched back to the castle, hoping no one noticed.

The moment she crossed the threshold into the castle and turned down the long hallway, a winged warrior stepped out of a dark corridor in front of her, blocking her path. She stopped and stared at Kayven, the Bellator who had rescued her and flown her to Oakenshire. She then noticed no one was around and she wasn't naïve enough to believe it was a coincidence.

"What do you think you are doing, Princess?" Kayven folded his arms over his enormous chest and quirked a dark eyebrow.

"I could ask you the same question, Bellator. Now move." She was not in the mood for lectures or games.

"Move me."

"What?" she growled.

"If you want to get by," Kayven said a bit louder, "make me move."

"I don't have time for these mind games, Bellator." She attempted to side-step the Immortal, but he stepped with her, remaining a huge obstacle in her path.

"I said, make me move."

She looked up at him, tears welling in her eyes from immeasurable anger. "Why are you doing this? Let me pass."

He towered over her and glanced down at her weary face. "Running will not make you stronger."

"Sometimes it's best to retreat before it's too late."

The sternness in Kayven's face softened. "Look, Princess, I know what it feels like to lose a loved one. I know how it feels to see your friends fall in battle. I have lived long enough to taste the bitterness of being the one to survive and wonder why Death called them and not me. I see all the same signs in you, and I beg you not to run."

Salome quickly surveyed the corridor making sure they were still alone. She met his golden gaze and whispered, "I don't think I can do this. I've done terrible things. "

"What are you running from?" he asked.

"I was born with two different color eyes; everyone thought I was cursed," she spoke so softly she was afraid he wouldn't hear her, but she pressed on before she could change her mind. "I didn't want to believe them, but I am starting to. Everyone I love, anyone who gets close to me, ends up dying and I'm left to pick up the shattered pieces of my heart, wondering who might be next. Praying that it's me so everyone else may be spared."

"Death -"

"Comes for us all," she interrupted and rolled her eyes in irritation. "I know that already."

"If you run now, you will not stop." Kayven stepped closer, towering over her. "You are not weak for being afraid," he whispered.

Her bottom lip quivered, and she cleared her throat to keep from weeping. "I'm so tired."

Kayven's feathered wings flared. He wrapped her in his wings giving her privacy in case someone came inside. He gently tilted her chin up to look at him. "That is why you have us. Your friends, your allies. We are here to lift you up when you feel you do not have the strength to go one step farther. Together, we will win. But we need our leader to keep pushing with us." His eyes were burning bright and were filled with hope. "I can help you get through battle fright, but you have to want my help."

"Battle fright?" she asked.

"You have been through things most mortals will never experience. Trauma haunts us all in different ways. I can see it in your eyes. You are having flashbacks even with a weapon in your hand." Kayven lowered his voice, as if he were telling her a secret. "You have stared Death in the face and said, *'not today'*. You survived for a reason. It is time you remember why."

Salome knew the Bellator was right, but she wasn't ready for anyone else to know. "They will all lose faith in me, if they see I can't wield my weapons," she shifted her feet.

"Then we shall practice in secret." Kayven said, matter of fact. "Meet me and Abba at midnight on the practice grounds." He retracted his wings, arms clasped behind his back, the vision of a true soldier.

"Why are you doing this?" She had to know.

Kayven hesitated, and for a moment she was afraid he wouldn't answer, but then he said, "Harbona spoke highly of you mortals. Said he would willingly die by your side than live another thousand years without you. He gave up his birthright, his title, and his home, to walk amongst you. I did not understand why he valued you mortals more than his own people, but seeing you fight, seeing you overcome your deepest fears and fiercest enemies, made me respect you. And if Harbona would willingly lay down his life to save you, then I can make damn sure you are equipped to win your battles."

"And if I can't overcome this? This battle fright?"

Kayven smiled, "I swear on the Eldaar, you will wield your weapons again, my lady." He bowed and turned to leave, but she grabbed his forearm.

"Kayven." He glanced back at her. "Call me Salome."

He bobbed his head. "Until tonight, Salome."

Salome spent the rest of the afternoon in her chambers resting. When darkness fell, she went about her normal bedtime routine, but instead of slipping into her warm, inviting bed, she donned her sparring clothes and crept down to the training grounds. More than once she thought she should just ignore the

Bellator and figure out this battle fright on her own, but if Zophar were present, he'd fuss at her for being far too stubborn for her own good. She swallowed the tears that itched to be released and before she could talk herself out of the midnight training, she strutted into the bailey.

Kayven and Abba were already there waiting. How long had they been there? She was five minutes early and they were lounging, as if they had been there for hours.

"Ahh!" Kayven hopped up from the ground and dusted off his pants. "You are finally here."

"What are you puffing on about?" she rolled her eyes. "I'm early."

"Well," the Bellator pulled his shoulder-length hair out of his face, looping a hair-tie around half of his locks. "Show me what I am working with."

She glanced over Kayven's shoulder at Abba, who was leaning against the stone wall, one foot pressed against the castle, arms crossed. She was curious about how he got the scar that ran down the side of his face but kept her questions to herself. She didn't like when people asked her about her two-colored eyes, so she refused to put Abba in that uncomfortable position. "And what is he supposed to be doing? Lurking in the shadows?"

Kayven barked a laugh and turned to look at his brother. "It is better that you spar with me. Abba is too advanced for mortals."

"So, what I'm hearing is he's the better brother," Salome teased, and it was Abba's turn to chuckle.

"Now, I will have none of that," Kayven snorted. "If you are to learn to defeat battle fright, you will have to pay attention."

Salome was trying to make light of the situation but her attempt at humor seemed to offend the Immortal which was not her intent. "I'm sorry," she extended an olive branch. "I didn't mean to upset you."

"Upset me?" Kayven cocked his head to the side, looking more amused than anything. "You will have to do a hell of a lot more than tell a bad joke to hurt me, Princess."

"I can't do this anymore!" She flung her hand in the air to stop Kayven's attack. A solid hour had passed, and she was no better than before. Her hands were still shaking, and the flashbacks still haunted her.

"Stand up, Princess." The Bellator motioned for her to rise from her crouched position.

"I'm tired." She shook her head, sweat dripping down her forehead. "It's not working. I'm not getting any better."

"Did you really think you would be back to normal after an hour of training?"

"I at least thought my hands would stop shaking," she snorted. "Or the flashbacks would..." She bit her bottom lip to keep it from quivering and slowly stood up, a foot shorter than the muscular Immortal. His bronze skin glistened in the moonlight, a light film of sweat coated his arms, but he didn't look remotely tired.

"Where are you going?" Kayven asked as she dragged her sore legs toward the castle entrance.

"I'm going to bed." As she brushed past him, she caught Abba's golden eyes. He didn't look disappointed or surprised – he almost looked as if he'd expected her to give up and she wasn't sure why it bothered her so much.

"We are not finished," Kayven barked. "I told you I would help you overcome your battle fright. It will take some time, but I believe you can do it."

She waved him off, not looking back as she shuffled away. "I'm done."

"What would Zophar say if he saw you like this?" Kayven challenged. "What would he think of you quitting?"

She spun around, fury raging in her eyes. "Don't speak of Zophar!"

"What would he think," the Bellator commander pressed, "of the girl he raised to be a warrior running away from her fear instead of facing it?"

She clenched her fists, her nails digging into her palms. "I said, don't talk about him!"

"You are angry."

"Yes, I'm angry!"

"Good." Kayven smiled and removed his shirt, exposing his bronze, muscular torso. He motioned for Salome to punch him. "Take your best shot. Let go of your anger."

"I'm not going to hit you."

"Your anger will consume you, if you harbor it."

Salome shook her head. "My anger is what fuels me."

"Anger will not win you battles." Kayven took a heavy step toward her and to her credit, she didn't shrink from the Bellator's encroaching figure. "Anger will cost you your life when the dust settles. Anger is an emotion. Emotions are fickle and change from day to night. But your training, your discipline, and your level-headedness is your constant. It is your beacon of light in the darkness. It is your salvation. Training will not fail you at the end of the day. Your emotions will. Now, hit me. Let go of your anger, Salome. Let go of your hatred. Neither will serve you well."

Tears streamed down her cheeks as fire raged in her eyes. Kayven motioned her toward him again with a comforting smile. "Hit me, Salome. I promise, I will not break."

Faces flooded her mind. Zophar. Nym. Mika. Korah. Lykos. Her mother. Her brothers. Ranalda. When Crispin popped into her head, the possibility that he was also gone, caused her to fly into a rampage. She clenched her fists and screamed. She could have sworn the very foundation of the castle trembled beneath her feet. Salome launched herself across the practice grounds, landing blow after blow against Kayven's rock-hard chest. She punched him repeatedly, screaming, crying, wailing, until she was too exhausted to hit him anymore. She threw her head back and yelled again, releasing her fear, her anger, her grief. Her knees gave out and she started to crumble to the ground but Kayven's strong arms caught her and held her against his chest. The Bellator didn't say a word as she released her sorrow and battled her demons. When she opened her eyes, she saw he not only kept her firmly in his embrace, but had shielded her with his wings. She heard his heart beating and the rhythm brought her peace. She pushed away and gazed into his eyes.

"How do you feel?" he asked, retracting his wings.

"Free," she replied. "I feel free."

Kayven smiled. "Choose your weapon."

Abba stepped forward, "Perhaps the mortal needs to rest, Kayven."

The Bellator nodded. "I forget you mortals do not have the same stamina -"

"I choose blades." Salome interrupted him and swiped the Qata Vishna knives from the holsters on her back. She risked a quick glance at Abba who seemed satisfied by her response. As the quiet Bellator leaned against the stone wall, retaking his familiar stance, she turned her focus back to Kayven. "If you are too tired, we can call it a night. I know you're pretty old."

Kayven smirked, cracking his neck. "Some would say, I am in my prime."

"How old are you?" she asked, curiosity getting the better of her.

"I am three thousand years old." He answered without missing a beat and unsheathed a pair of knives.

Salome's mouth dropped open, but she quickly closed it before he could make a snide remark. She flipped her knives around her hands and flashed Kayven a playful grin. "I'll go easy on you this time, old man."

He took his stance and snorted, "Do your worst, mortal."

Chapter Twenty

Crispin

The rebel camp was filled with tents and everything they had was meant to be easily packed, in case the group needed to move at a moment's notice. From what Leeondris shared with them that night around the crackling fire, the King of Borg had lost the favor of the people and change was in the air. Leeondris had received word from Ragnar that he needed his help, if he was going to overthrow his tyrant father and provide a better life for his people. But more importantly, Benaiah was planning to launch a thousand ships to destroy the Pulauans once and for all, and Ragnar couldn't – wouldn't – let that happen. So, Leeondris dropped everything and left the pirate life and his Pulauan family behind, to aid and serve his childhood best friend. As Ragnar and Lahki worked in the inner circle of the royal court, Leeondris rallied the people to their side and their cause, and Ivar kept his eyes on the seas. They were a formidable team and serving their people was the highest honor. When the time was right, Ragnar and those loyal to Borg would make the move to overthrow Benaiah and keep Ehrik from taking the throne and following in their father's footsteps. It was a dangerous game they were playing, but one Leeondris said he would give his life for.

With that information planted in his brain, Crispin could only imagine what the rebel prince would ask him to do when he called in his favor. Hopefully it wouldn't cost Crispin something he valued.

Even though Crispin spent most of his life in the Treehouse Forest in the Western Lands, he never kept up with the politics of the capitol. He couldn't blame Ragnar for the coup, and if what Leeondris said about Benaiah was true, he had a gut-wrenching thought that Rahab would band with the members of the crew that planned to join in on the fight to protect their home against the

Borgian King. The thought of her not continuing the journey to Oakenshire, pained him.

Ziggy readily agreed to stay with the rebels when Leeondris asked her to help, since she was back in her homeland. And wherever Ziggy went, Nubis was sure to follow. Crispin happily gave them his blessing to fight with the Borgian rebels. He had grown quite fond of the lively redhead and the broody Stormcrag but he wasn't going to drag them to Oakshire to fight for him.

Once everyone had eaten and ushered to their tents for the night, Leeondris bade them goodnight and informed them they would be fully prepared for their journey in the morning. Crispin was relieved when Haldane, Phex, Corwin, Ondrej and Rafi assured him they would be continuing with him until he was seated on the White Throne of Northwind.

"We've come this far," Haldane said, clasping his hand on Crispin's shoulder, "and I believe I've got some unfinished business to settle with a bastard king and conniving witch."

Crispin still bore the weight of Palma's torture and death and he swore he would do everything in his power to help Haldane and his crew get their revenge.

Once he was escorted to his tent, Crispin slipped inside, kicked off his boots, stripped off his shirt, and groaned from exhaustion, before he stretched out on the small cot. He knew they would have to pass through what was left of the Tree House Forest on their way to Oakenshire, and he was terrified of what he was going to find. Or not find.

Korah, his young friend who had been killed by the Shadows months earlier, popped into his head. He remembered the boy's laugh and how excited he was when he agreed to teach him how to use a bow. He missed the freckle-face redhead tremendously and it broke Crispin's heart that the boy was nothing more than a memory.

He ran a hand down his face, swiping a lone tear from his eye and rested his palm on his chest. He'd be a liar, if he said, he wasn't thrilled to be back in the Western Forests, after what seemed like a lifetime of traveling to exotic places. While lying in his tent, he came to realize he was tired and wanted to go home. He wanted to sleep in his own bed, eat Zophar's venison stew and be surrounded by the people who loved him. But that life was gone and the home he took for granted, even cursed on some occasions, no longer existed. How spoiled and selfish he had been months ago when he wished for a life outside of the small village. Now, he would give up just about anything to go back to the comfort of his old life.

His thoughts drifted to Salome. He hadn't seen or heard from her in months. He prayed she was alright and safely waiting for him in Oakenshire. The stories he would swap with her and Zophar put a smile on his face. He couldn't wait to see them. To hug them and maybe feel at home, again. It would only be a few more days before they are reunited, and he couldn't wait.

Exhaustion was setting in and his heavy eyelids closed. He was drifting to sleep when suddenly, lips were pressing against his. Startled, he opened his eyes and there was Rahab, now putting her weight on top of him. Crispin grabbed her hair and gently pulled her back to look at her. She groaned in frustration, and he chuckled.

"I didn't realize we were assigned roommates." He stroked his fingers up and down her tattooed arm.

Rahab flashed him a smile that made his heart flutter. "Thank your lucky stars I'm your bunkmate and not Phex or Rafi."

"I don't know," he shrugged, wrapping his arms around her. "I think it would be fun to cuddle with Rafi. How does he get his mustache to end with such sharp points?"

She giggled and kissed his chin. "Rafi sleeps with his eyes open."

"And how do you know that?"

"Because he tends to sleepwalk, too. It's horrifying."

Crispin barked out a laugh and twisted to his side, pulling Rahab onto the cot beside him. "Well then, I guess I'm lucky the First Mate is sharing my bed."

He couldn't help but think this might be the last time they would cuddle up together. Back in the city, she had promised to be his queen, but after hearing Leeondris' report, he knew there was a good chance she might want to stay and help. Although scared to hear the answer, he had to ask anyway.

"Do you want to stay here?" he whispered.

Rahab tilted her head back and stared into his eyes. "Stay? Why are you asking me that?"

He shrugged, "Because of what Leeondris told us about Benaiah's plans to attack Pulau."

"Do you..." she cleared her throat, "do you want me to stay?"

"No," he shook his head, "but I also don't want to ask you to fight in my war, when your people need you."

"What makes this your war, princeling?" She pushed herself up onto an elbow and glared down at him.

He mirrored her posture and leveled the playing field. "It's about my kingdom-"

"You cannot claim a war, Crispin. This isn't just about you anymore." Rahab's brow furrowed. "Uri and Nezreen are involved now, and they were our enemies long before they were yours. When all is said and done, you will end up on the White Throne, but it's not just about seeing you crowned king. It's about avenging our dead and taking back our freedom." She wiped hair off his face and leaned closer. "Where you go, I go. That's that."

"I can't argue with that."

"Then kiss me already."

Crispin laughed, "Greedy."

"I'm a pirate," she whispered, inching closer to his lips. "I take what I want."

"And what do you want, Rahab?"

"You."

"You have me."

Rahab leaned across his chest and blew out the candle on the small, wooden end table. "I intend to."

Bidding farewell to Leeondris, Ziggy, Nubis, and other crew members of the *Shadow of Death*, wasn't easy. Crispin was off to Oakenshire, with Penn and her Keepers and a handful of heavily armed pirates – thanks to their rebel friends. He knew they would have to cut through the Tree House Forest and as they drew closer, his stomach soured. At the rate they were walking, they would be forced to set up camp in the small village and he wasn't looking forward to it.

It was dusk when they finally reached the Tree House Forest and seeing what had become of his childhood home was worse than he imagined. Disaster. That was the best and only word he could use to describe what little remained of the burnt village. The once bustling community was wiped out, and the very spirit and soul of the town had vanished.

Memories of his childhood flashed before his eyes: their first night in their new home; Zophar reading to him and his sister nightly by the fireplace; sparring with Salome as children and seeing their skills improve throughout their teenage years.

He turned and looked from the main square where Korah had been killed and spotted his treehouse. Little remained, but the front steps and first floor were surprisingly intact. His breathing slowed; and for a moment, he felt like he was drowning.

"You hard of hearing, lad?" Haldane slammed his hand down on Crispin's shoulder, freeing him from his thoughts. "Are we to camp here for the night?"

Crispin scanned what remained of his once home and nodded, holding back tears and taking deep breaths. "We'll rest here tonight."

The captain bobbed his head in agreement and began ordering his men to set up camp for the night. Phex volunteered to start the fire, but the pirates unanimously agreed the explosives expert shouldn't be within ten feet of the fire lest they all blow up by mistake. Ondrej and Rafi gathered firewood from some of the dilapidated houses and were in charge of lighting the bonfire. Phex and Corwin set up the sleeping bags that Leeondris had sent with them, and Haldane worked on cooking the food they had in their packs.

Penn and her Keepers pulled their weight during the trek; the fact they were blind didn't hinder nor slow them down and Crispin enjoyed speaking with the Master of Keepers during their walk through the Western Forests. She lived an interesting life and whenever they took short breaks, he insisted she show him some of her fighting moves. She used the vibrations in the ground and her heightened senses, to fight her opponents. Every time they faced off, he got his ass handed to him and loved every second of it. Remarkably, he began to improve and started to hold his own against her.

She must have sensed him watching her because she stopped what she was doing to face him. Her smirk crinkled the black wrap around her eyes. "Another lesson tonight, Prince Crispin?"

"If it's all the same to you, Master Penn, I think I'll let you take a stab at the pirates tonight."

Phex, Corwin, Ondrej, and Rafi all stopped what they were doing and scowled. Penn flashed a wicked smile in their direction and nodded. "Yes, perhaps I will take a stab at the pirates."

"Meaning?" Rafi crossed his arms over his chest.

"Meaning," Penn clasped her hands behind her back and stepped toward the crew, "we will be facing the enemy head on in battle. There will be no ships to keep you at a safe distance and you will need to learn better hand-to-hand combat if you wish to live."

Corwin threw a dagger directly at Penn, but as the knife approached, she kicked up her spear and used it as a shield and blocked the weapon. The dumbstruck pirates stared at Corwin.

"I guess it wouldn't hurt to pick up a few tips." Corwin shrugged and bobbed his head, as if he hadn't tried to kill the Master of Keepers.

"Let's begin then," Penn smiled, stabbing her spear into the ground.

Crispin smiled; grateful the pirates and Keepers were with him on this journey. But while they laughed, poked fun at one another, and bickered like a true family, Crispin used the distraction to slip away and visit the treehouse where he'd grown up. Despite a few missing boards, Crispin easily made his way across the swinging bridge. The sight from a distance was depressing but stepping onto the front porch where he and Salome used to sit and talk for hours while Zophar puffed on his favorite pipe, pierced his heart.

The prince ran his fingers over the charred wood beams where the front door once stood. Stepping across the threshold, he stood in the main room of their cozy lodging. All of Zophar's books were gone and the chipped plates and mugs Salome used to obsessively clean, were shattered into hundreds of little pieces on the floor. He crouched down, scooped up a kettle Zophar used to make tea, and admired it fondly.

He grumbled to Zophar about how much he hated it – how he wished for an adventure that would whisk him away, so he'd never have to return. But now standing in the rumble and remembering how Zophar hid them in the treehouse after losing everything the night Niabi attacked, and how it quickly became their safe haven, filled him with regret. He fought the tears, but he couldn't hold them back, they streamed down his cheeks and he quickly wiped them away with the back of his sleeve.

It was a small mercy that Zophar hadn't been traveling with him – the state of their house, of the village, would have crushed him.

"So," Rahab's whisper startled him, "this is where you grew up."

Crispin thumbed away what evidence remained that he'd been crying and slowly stood up, facing her as she waited in the doorway. "I was six when Zophar brought us here."

"That's a long time to live in the same place," she said.

"All those years, I hated living here. I woke up every morning for twelve years saying one day I'd return to Northwind, to my true home." Crispin dusted the debris from Zophar's favorite armchair and sat in what little remained. "It wasn't until I left that I realized how much of a comfort this treehouse was – how much love filled these creaky walls."

"You can have that feeling again," Rahab assured him and carefully stepped toward him. "Maybe not here, but when you reclaim your kingdom."

He raked his fingers through his hair with a heavy sigh. "I just wish I had appreciated this place more, appreciated everything Zophar did for us. He took two wanted children and raised us as his own. He sacrificed so much for me and my sister. I just... I can't wait to thank him properly when I see him again."

Rahab leaned against part of a wall where the fireplace used to be, twisting a lock of her hair. "What's she like?"

"Who?"

"Your sister."

"Salome?"

She nodded, meeting his gaze. "Is she just as insufferable as you?" she smirked.

Crispin let loose a laugh and it felt good to release the tension in his chest and shoulders. "Oh, even more so, I imagine." He grinned and she offered him a small smile in return. He motioned for her to sit with him and she obliged. She slipped into his lap, and he wrapped his arms around her waist, tugging her close. "Salome is an excellent hunter. She's bold, cunning, and doesn't have a problem speaking her mind. She is also one of the kindest people I know and she's my best friend. If all fails, I know she will be by my side fighting as the world burns around us."

"You miss her."

"More than I thought I would," he caressed her arm and smiled. "We've always had each other. We were born less than a year apart and have wreaked havoc together since we could crawl."

"Do you think she'll like me?" she whispered. It was odd hearing any sort of vulnerability coming from the pirate's mouth.

Gently, he squeezed her hand. "Oh, my sweet pirate queen... no."

"What?"

Crispin chuckled, tightening his hold on her when she tried to wiggle free. "She'll love you."

Rahab punched his chest, nostrils flared. "That's not funny, princeling."

“You know what else she’ll love? He honed in on the dagger with the ruby hilt dangling on her hip. “She’ll love the hardware. She always carries three knives wherever she goes.”

"Sounds like my type of woman," she bounced her eyebrows playfully.

"Should I be worried you'll like my sister more than me?" he teased.

"Oh, absolutely." She smiled and dragged her fingers down the curve of his jaw. Something flashed in her eyes, and he wished he could read her mind.

"Why are you looking at me like that?"

"To think I almost let Kubantu have you."

"You cruel, wicked woman," he shook his head. It seemed like a lifetime ago they'd fought the sea beast in the Obsidian Sea, where he pushed her out of harm's way, sparing her a watery death. She rescued him in return, even though she claimed she felt nothing but hatred for him.

Her laugh filled the empty space and sparked a bit of comfort and joy in him. "Oh, princeling, I don't know what I'd possibly do without you now."

"I told you I'd grow on you."

She ran her thumb over his lips and whispered, "That you did."

Glancing across the bridge, Crispin noticed the pirates had managed to start a fire, but Phex had gotten too close to it, and was told to get away.

"It's cold out here," Phex hissed, slapping his hands on his hips. "You can't expect me to -"

"Empty your pockets!" Rafi shouted, blocking Phex's path.

"I'm not emptying my pockets," the explosives expert grouched. "Captain, tell him I can sit by the fire like everyone else."

"Aye, you got a right to keep warm, same as the rest of us," Haldane bobbed his head as he stirred the stew over the flames.

"See!" Phex whipped his hands around to emphasize the point.

"But," Haldane held the ladle out, blocking Phex from getting too close, "for the safety of the crew, empty your pockets, lad."

"Captain!"

"It's not that we don't trust you, Phex," the captain held firm, "but I'd like to be able to sleep well tonight without worrying one of those inventions of yours will roll into the flames and blow us all to hell."

Phex glanced from the captain to the quiet Corwin sharpening his knives to the giant Ondrej already sprawled out in his designated sleeping area, looking for them to come to his aid. He even dared a glance at Penn and her Keepers, but they sat stoically around the fire, scooping spoons full of stew into their mouths. When no one defended him, he reluctantly, muttering every curse word he knew, emptied his pockets of all its trinkets, and stomped toward a log in front of the fire and plopped down with a huff.

"Happy?" Phex flashed a menacing look Rafi's way and the halfling pirate glared right back.

"And in one piece," Rafi snorted.

"How long do you think it'll take before Phex blows something up just to scare the piss out of Rafi?" Crispin chuckled.

"Phex always gets his revenge when you least expect it," Rahab winked before she slid off of his lap and motioned for him to follow her back to camp. "Best eat and get some sleep, princeling. We've got a long way to walk tomorrow."

Chapter Twenty-One

Salome

When Salome was informed Jinn had finally arrived early that morning, she abandoned her breakfast, forgot about the aches and pains of training the night before with Kayven and Abba, and walked as fast as she could toward the room Kai told her he'd been assigned. But when she finally stood outside his door, she felt nervous. What would she say to him? What could you say to someone who'd risked everything to save you from certain death? Someone who'd brought an entire army to rescue you and who slaughtered every Thrak who stood in his way. *Thank you* seemed terribly insufficient.

Before she lost her nerve, she took a deep breath, and pushed the door open to see a shirtless Prince Jinn. The left half of his back was covered in tattoos, as was his entire left arm. When he turned around to see who had burst into his chambers, she saw the tattoos continued to the front left side of his chest and stomach as well. Ancient Eastern runes, dragons, and the history of his ancestors were etched in permanent black ink on his skin. She stopped in the threshold; her heart beating rapidly as their eyes silently roved over one another. His signature black pants hung low on his hips exposing his chiseled abs. She knew he was muscular, but she didn't expect his body to be riddled with scars. Just as her body told a story of brutality and survival, so did his.

Jinn looked as if he wanted to say something, but words failed him. He looked at her as if he'd seen a ghost and she forced herself to speak to slice through the tension.

"I – I'm sorry. I should've knocked." She couldn't hide her blush and forcefully averted her gaze from his half-naked body.

Jinn stared at her as he reached for his shirt. He slipped his arms through the sleeves, but didn't fasten it, leaving the center of his chest exposed.

Salome met his gaze and inhaled deeply to keep from crying at the sight of him. "You came for me."

"I'll always come for you."

She wasn't sure what to do with her shaky hands, so she stuffed them in her pockets. "You've saved my life three times now. I owe you -"

"You don't owe me anything," he whispered, cutting her off.

Once again, silence settled between them. She slowly closed the door behind her, maintaining eye contact with the prince who hadn't moved a muscle.

"Kai told me you tried to see me this morning," she said, "but the twins wouldn't let you wake me."

"Those three don't seem to care I outrank them and insisted I get some rest before seeing you."

His small smile eased her nerves. "You think you would have learned not to question them by now," she teased.

He took a step toward her, hands buried in his black pants pockets. "If I were a smart man, I would have learned by now, but I've been told more than once, that I'm a bit hardheaded." Jinn stopped a few feet from her, soaking her in. He studied her quietly, his eyes scanning her like he wanted to scoop her in his arms but refrained. "I was afraid you were..."

"Dead?" she filled in the blank.

"I tried reaching out to you. I know that's not how our bond works but..." he stared at the floor between them.

"I thought about you," she admitted, earning his gaze. "I was so far beneath the Black Tower; I couldn't seem to access my power."

"Did they hurt you?" he whispered.

"Not as much as we hurt them."

But they had hurt her. They had taken Zophar and in turn, they had taken a piece of her good nature when she slit Ranalda's throat. The nightmares were constant and unrelenting. She blinked and saw Zophar with a knife plunged into his abdomen. She blinked again and saw Ranalda lying in a pool of blood with a gash across her neck. When she blinked a third time, Jinn was watching her with a deep sadness in his golden eyes.

"I'm sorry I didn't protect you that day in the mountains."

She lurched. "Jinn-"

"That moment plays over and over in my head." He raked a hand through his dark locks. "The look in your eyes, as if you knew I wouldn't reach you in time. I see it when I close my eyes. It haunts me when I try to sleep. I don't think I'll ever forget how I felt at that moment. Powerless and afraid. I not only failed to protect you but watched as my entire world crumbled around me."

Salome cupped his face, his smooth skin cool against her warm hands and pressed her forehead against his. Her touch silenced him; his hands rested on her waist, as they drank one another in, falling into a rhythmic breathing.

"I'm sorry I didn't protect you," he whispered again.

"It's not your fault. It's mine." She let him pull her closer until their bodies were flush. "You saved me when I lost hope. Had I not left the City of Bones, Zophar would still be..."

Jinn kissed her forehead and wrapped his arms around her. She rested her head against his chest and listened to his heartbeat, inhaling his scent, and when she realized her cheek was against his bare chest, her face flushed, and her heart skipped a beat.

She pulled away and whispered, "Can I show you where I go when I need peace?"

Jinn nodded as she slipped her hands down his neck and rested them on his exposed chest. His breathing was shallow and his eyes expectant.

She wasn't sure this would work, but she closed her eyes and pictured herself standing in the gardens of the White Keep, extending the memory to Jinn. She and her brother would run around, ducking and dodging all the palace workers, and avoiding their nursemaids. The memory filled her with warmth, peace, and comfort.

"Where are we?" Jinn asked, standing beside her in the frostbitten garden.

Salome gently tapped the frost covered purple crocus and looked over her shoulder at Jinn and smiled. "This was once my home."

"We're in Northwind?" Jinn noticed the white stone walls of the White Keep.

"One of my memories." Salome glided through the crisp snow, pushing it with her foot. "When I was a little girl, there was a late snowfall during spring. It froze the gardens, the flowers, the trees. I remember waking up and seeing the snow on the rooftops in the city and sprinting to this very garden. It was the most magical sight. It felt like I had stepped into a fairytale."

Jinn walked next to her as they toured the snow-covered garden.

"I've always liked the cold. It's one of the things I miss most about Northwind. It's why I named my horse Snow. It's this memory that brings me a sense of peace and wonder. Whenever I feel overwhelmed, whenever I feel lost, I come here." She stopped to breathe in the coolness of the rare, spring snowfall and noticed Jinn smiling at her.

"What?" she asked.

"This is amazing. How is this even possible for me to see?"

"Back in the Isles of Myr, I touched Harbona's hand and was able to see his memories flash before my eyes." She lifted a shoulder. "I thought it might be possible to share a memory of my own with someone I share a bond with." She motioned around the garden. "It reminds me that even in hardship, a flower can flourish. I've lost so many people." She choked up when Zophar came to mind. She reached for a red rose that had icicles nestled between the satiny folds. "This place may not bring you the same peace it brings me, but maybe it will bring you the slightest comfort, and that will be enough for me."

He cupped her face in his hands, forcing her to meet his gaze. "Thank you."

Tears welled up in her eyes and the vision of the frozen garden was lost. When she blinked, they were back in Jinn's quarters.

"What's wrong?" he asked.

She pulled away from him, wrapping her arms around herself. She already felt the heaviness of his absence, missed his hands against her face. "I ..." She couldn't seem to get the words out.

"What is it?" he asked again.

"In Gomorrah, in the throne room..." *When I slit Ranalda's throat and watched her die,* is how she wanted to finish that statement but couldn't.

Jinn straightened. By his stance, it was evident he knew what she was referring to, but waited for her to continue.

"If you see me differently because of my sins, I understand, but please know that I regret my actions."

"You don't need to explain yourself to me, Salome."

"But I do."

"Why?" He tilted his head to the side and strands of black hair fell over his forehead.

Because she was afraid he would judge her and distance himself.

"Salome?"

"Forget I said anything." She swatted her hand in the air and headed toward the door.

"Where are you going?"

She grabbed the doorknob and he pressed his palm on top of her hand, preventing her from leaving. She could feel his breath on the back of her neck, his chest rapidly rising and falling behind her. She wanted to lean into him, surrender herself to his embrace, tell him she made a mistake by not choosing him and feel his soft lips against hers, but instead, she turned to face him with her back pinned against the door and said, "I need to meet with Hanzo and Oifa. They're expecting me -"

He planted his hands flat against the door on either side of her. His gaze was unrelenting, searching her eyes for the truth she refused to share. She felt a bead of sweat drip down the center of her back. She didn't know if she was more nervous about him finding whatever he was looking for or the electricity she felt in his presence. She closed her eyes and inhaled his familiar and comforting scent of cedar and springtime. It took every fiber of her being not to jump into his arms and kiss every inch of his body.

"I should probably go," her voice cracked, and Jinn leaned forward so his lips hovered above her ear.

"I'll be here whenever you're done with your meeting." He said *meeting* as if he didn't believe her.

She tried not to shiver at his proximity but failed. "What makes you think I'm interested in your whereabouts?" she fired back.

Jinn pulled back far enough to meet her gaze, if she leaned forward just an inch, they'd be kissing. "Have you already forgotten I can see how you look at me?" He smiled. "I'm inclined not to let you out of my sight, for your own protection, of course."

"Of course." She hid her smile, but her treacherous heart pounded far too quickly for her to appear calm and collected. She cleared her throat. "If you plan to escort me around the castle, I suggest you button your shirt before you catch a chill."

The prince's low chuckle warmed her belly. He pushed up from the door and started buttoning his shirt slowly, eyes still glued on her. She knew he could tell exactly what she was thinking. If she didn't get out of his room and put a few feet of distance between them, she wasn't sure she could keep her hands off of him. Knowing exactly what he looked like without his shirt, his sculpted torso, muscular back and his half-body tattoos would definitely cause her to dream about him later. When he finished looping the last button, he flashed a longing smile at her. She blinked away the hunger in her eyes, but he had already noticed.

"Consider me your bodyguard until further notice." He motioned toward the door behind her.

"You mean my watchdog?" she teased as she twisted the knob, but then Adonijah's face flashed in her mind. Her stomach instantly soured.

What was she doing? She chose Adonijah. But he left her. He'd lied to her. She didn't think she could ever trust him again. But she knew she hurt Jinn when she rejected him. Although she was grateful she and the prince were picking up where they left off in their banter and friendship, she didn't know if his proposal was still on the table or if he had moved on. And she wasn't about to ask, afraid of what he might say.

Chapter Twenty-Two

Adonijah

The charred remains of where the cabin used to be, was the ghost that haunted his dreams nightly. This place was what spurred him to dedicate his life to finding his father and those who were complicit in murdering his mother and robbing him of what remained of his childhood. This place marked the beginning and end of everything that molded Adonijah into the man he had become.

"What is this place?" Leoti stopped beside him, eyeing the rubble.

"This used to be my home," Adonijah whispered.

Pash stood silently where the entrance once was with his arms crossed over his chest. He'd been forced to visit the farmhouse a handful of times before the soldiers came and burned it to the ground, forcing Adonijah to flee when the Nameless Rider killed his mother and grandfather.

Leoti dragged her middle finger down the center of her forehead until she reached her chest. "You lost someone?"

His mother's face flashed before his eyes, and he shook the image of her freckled face free. "My mother died protecting me from the Nameless Rider, the Shadow our father sent to find me." Pash seemed to tense at the mention of Gershom. "I've walked Adalore for years alone and never once came back here."

"What happened?"

"Gershom wanted to take me to Northwind, separating me from my mother. She wouldn't let him, so the Nameless Rider broke her neck and set the house on fire. I was able to get away but..."

"Satara was a good woman." Pash sat next to him and patted his back. "She can now rest knowing you avenged her, brother."

Adonijah nodded his head, but he wished he could have done more to save her all those years ago.

"Can I ask why your father never married your mother?"

Pash met Leoti's inquisitive gaze. "Satara was betrothed to our Uncle Ophir before Issachar imprisoned our father in Northwind. When our uncle freed him, he brought him here for his wounds to be treated."

Adonijah cleared his throat and picked up where Pash left off, knowing the next part of the story was gruesome. "Gershom forced himself upon my mother when no one was around. When she told my grandfather what happened, he blamed her. He said she'd defiled herself and the union he arranged for her. I never knew it was Ophir who was betrothed to her, but once she became pregnant with me, Gershom insisted Ophir refuse to marry her because she now belonged to him."

"Your father is a monster." Leoti had tears in her eyes and wiped them away with her thumb.

"One that will be dealt with soon enough," Adonijah bobbed his head. "I would start a fire, but we are out in the open and I don't want to attract any unwanted attention." He glanced at Pash and Leoti. "We'll need to sleep close to keep warm."

Pash and Leoti looked uncomfortable, but eventually nodded in agreement. The cold months were upon them. To survive the trek north, they'd have to do whatever was necessary.

They laid their sleeping bags in a row inside the only tent they had and even though it was cramped, they were out of the blistering cold. Leoti was in the center since she was the smallest and needed the most warmth. But in the middle of the night, she wiggled free from the brothers and before she was able to slip outside, Adonijah grabbed her arm.

"Where are you going?" he whispered.

"I'll be right back."

"Leoti, where are you going?" He glared at her with a seriousness that caused her to narrow her eyes.

"If you must know," she hissed. "I need to relieve myself, if it's alright with you. Or would you like to come watch?"

Releasing her arm, he felt foolish thinking she was going to disappear in the middle of the night. He mumbled an apology as she left and he laid back down. But he couldn't fall back to sleep until she returned. He wanted to make sure she was safe. When a few minutes had ticked by and she hadn't returned, he grabbed the knife underneath his head and made his way to the flap of the ten.

It was then he heard a high-pitched scream spurring him and Pash to fly out of the tent. They caught sight of Leoti a few paces away, with Thanos behind her, poking a knife to her throat. As the brothers glanced around, they noticed Thanos' soldiers had surrounded them, and knew they were at the mercy of the deranged boy who wanted to be king.

"Let her go, Thanos." Adonijah sheathed his dagger and raised his hands to show he was unarmed. "She doesn't need to be harmed."

"*You*," the prince seethed, jutting his chin at Pash. "You cost me my kingdom."

"There was nothing to be done to-"

"Shut up!" Thanos interrupted Pash. "You thought you could escape me so easily?"

"Thanos," Adonijah pleaded again, his eyes fixed on the knife at Leoti's neck. "Let Leoti go, she had nothing to do with you losing your crown."

"No, I suppose she didn't." He yanked her head back by her braid, causing her to wince. "But she will help me restore it, once she uses her warging abilities to show me where the City of Bones is. I will take their throne for myself and do what my ancestors couldn't. Destroy the Mountain Men."

"Take me instead," Pash took a step forward.

"Pash," Adonijah growled in warning.

"If you are going to have any chance at restoring your crown, you will need money to fund an army," Pash continued, ignoring his brother. "Take me as your hostage and Niabi will give you what you want. Let Leoti go."

"You raise an excellent point, Commander," Thanos flashed a sinister grin. "But who said I was here to make any deals?"

"Than-"

"We're taking all of you and will use you as I see fit." Thanos tucked his nose against the crook of Leoti's neck and sniffed. He ran his tongue from Leoti's neck up the side of her face, eyeing Adonijah and Pash with a glint of wickedness. "She will be more exciting in my tent, I'm sure."

Adonijah lunged forward, "Why you little-!"

"Ah, ah, ah!" Thanos tsked and his soldiers advanced, weapons drawn. "Not another step, rebel. Any trouble you cause will be taken out on your lover here and believe me, I am not-"

One of Thanos' soldiers screamed before he was launched across the field. Adonijah whipped around and saw a large black bear stampeding the guards, clawing and ripping their limbs from their bodies. He scooped his sword from the tent to attack the beast, but Pash grabbed his arm and held him back.

"Adonijah, don't!" Pash ordered. "It's Leoti! It's Leoti!"

"What?" Adonijah had been so concerned about Pash giving himself up to Thanos that he hadn't realized that his brother was giving Leoti the distraction she needed to warg into the bear who was within distance of her magic. He glanced at her face and noticed her eyes were white. Even in Thanos' grasp, she was destroying his soldiers, bit by bit.

The Gomorrian prince released Leoti from his grasp, unaware she was the one controlling the bear, and attempted to flee the campsite. But the bear didn't give up on the chase and knocked Thanos to the ground, hovering above him, flashing its blood-stained teeth.

"Please," Thanos cried, "spare me."

Leoti cocked her head to the side and the bear mimicked her gesture. Her grin sent a shiver through Adonijah, but before he or Pash could protest, the bear attacked the Gomorrian and mauled him to death.

Once the prince stopped twitching, Adonijah reached for Leoti, but Pash once again prevented him from touching her. "Not while she's in her warg state," Pash shook his head.

His first instinct was to shove his brother away to check on Leoti, but once he took a deep breath, he decided to heed his brother's warning. He nodded his head and Pash released his grip on his forearm.

Once the bear took off and disappeared into the woods, Leoti blinked and her eyes turned brown again. The Andrago slumped to her knees spurring Adonijah to kneel before her. He lifted her chin and the look in her eyes pierced his heart.

"Are you hurt?" he whispered, maintaining eye contact with her.

"No," she shook her head.

"Are you frightened?"

"No." Her voice was raspy. "I've never killed anyone before."

Adonijah gently swiped loose strands of dark hair from her face. "Killing a man is never easy. You did what needed to be done-"

"I enjoyed it," she interrupted him, her eyes hardening, "and I would do it again, if I had to."

Adonijah sat back on his heels. He didn't expect her to say that, and honestly, he had no idea how to respond. When he looked at Leoti he saw a woman full of heartache, a woman who had someone she loved stolen from her, and a woman who wanted revenge. Her peace had been ripped from her and he understood better than most how she felt. When he lost his mother, he set out on a journey to avenge her death, to kill those who had taken her from him. He had killed more men than he cared to admit in his quest, and at this point, he was numb to death. But watching how this woman let her shattered heart and unquenchable rage finally consume her and boil over into using her magic to wipe out nearly a dozen men, was oddly relatable. He wished he could reach out and hold her, to take her heartache and bear that burden himself, but he couldn't. All he could do was help her weather the storm and help her find peace again.

He reached his hand out to her, "Let's get you cleaned up."

Leoti stared at him a moment longer, looking unsure, but when he held steady, she slipped her petite hand into his calloused one and let him hoist her up from the ground. He looked down at her and offered a small smile, hoping she recognized he wasn't judging her, but that he understood.

Adonijah dragged his thumb across her neck where Thanos' blade had been. Her breath quickened and his eyes skipped up to her lips and then her eyes. The need to protect her was strong, but she had not only protected herself, she saved him and Pash as well. The urge to kiss her was consuming his thoughts and without realizing it, he lowered his face as she lifted her head, but the moment was interrupted by Pash clearing his throat.

He glanced at Pash who had his arms crossed over his chest. Adonijah wondered what was going on in his brother's head. Was he trying to keep him from kissing Leoti? Was he being smug about being right that he did have feelings for the Andrago?

As if Pash knew he was silently flipping through questions, he said, "Just wanted to remind you I'm still here."

Adonijah understood what Pash was actually trying to say. He had been so adamant about being in love with Salome and here he was about to kiss another woman. He took a step away from Leoti, rubbing the back of his neck.

"I'm glad you're alright." Adonijah cleared his throat and snatched a piece of cloth from his pocket and handed it to her. "You have some dirt on your face."

"Thank you." Looking as if she too had sobered from what had almost happened between them, she took the cloth, walked toward the sleeping bags, and sat down to wipe herself clean.

The brothers exchanged a quick look. Pash opened his mouth to say something, but Adonijah held up his hand "I already know what you're about to say and it's unnecessary. I know where my heart lies."

Pash slanted his head to the side and smirked. "I was going to say, I owe you an apology. I was opposed to Leoti joining us, but your insistence she stay with us was the right decision." He took a step closer to Adonijah and lowered his voice, "But I'm glad you're following your heart, brother." By his tone, Adonijah knew his brother didn't believe him.

"We'll have to burn the bodies." Adonijah walked toward Thanos' nearly unrecognizable body and dragged it toward the others. "Then we'll have to move before your Shadows find us."

The Almighty One willing they'd be long gone before those masked riders picked up their trail.

Chapter Twenty-Three

Pash

It took about an hour to gather the bodies, or what was left of them, and toss them into the fire pit. The smell of burning flesh was overwhelming and Pash knew if they didn't get a move on, they were sure to attract the Shadows who were probably not too far behind Thanos' group. Packing up the camp site, they walked northward. Pash was hopeful they would reach the Black Forest before anyone else picked up on their trail.

He glanced behind to ensure his brother and Leoti were still following, because they were undeniably distracted by one another. Even the members of the blind order of The Sisters would be able to see they had feelings for one another. Though Pash should be sickened by the clearly in denial love-struck duo, he found himself secretly rooting for them. Maybe once they killed their father, Adonijah would choose to live in Northwind and abandon fighting in the war. Despite being separated for years, he knew his brother well enough to know he would never turn his back on those he had sworn an oath to.

A soft whistle captured his attention, and he stopped dead in his tracks, glancing around the densely populated forest.

"What is it?" Adonijah was by his side, looking around.

"Did you hear the whistle?" Pash asked.

"Is it a signal?"

Before Pash could answer in the affirmative, several thuds sounded around them as Shadows dropped in from the trees, surrounding them. One of the mercenaries grabbed Leoti but as she fought back, the Shadow hit her on the back of the head, knocking her out. Adonijah growled as he looked at Leoti's limp body dangling in the Shadow's arms, but Pash wrapped his hand around his brother's bicep, keeping him rooted.

"Lower your weapons." Ophir stepped forward, looking angry and disappointed. "Don't make this any more difficult than it has to be, Pash."

Pash shook his head, refusing to obey. "Afraid I can't do that, Uncle."

"I, more than anyone else, understand what it's like to be loyal to your brother," Ophir appealed to him. "That's why I'll give you one more chance to redeem yourself, Pash." He stepped closer. "Lay down your weapons, join us, and all will be forgiven."

"You want me to give up my brother to save myself." Pash shook his head. "My answer is no."

"Think of Niabi, my boy," Ophir played on his emotions. "Think of your unborn child. She need never know of your betrayal."

"Your words sound sweet, Uncle," Pash's eyes watered, "but they're poison. We both know you'll never let me walk free and I won't have my brother's blood on my hands."

The care and sincerity in Ophir's face vanished and his face reddened. "Then you will die together." With a flick of Ophir's wrist, the band of Shadows launched their assault.

Adonijah and Pash unsheathed their weapons and fought their attackers with the same brutality they were shown.

Pash knew if they didn't fend off the men he'd spent most of his life training with, they'd execute him, no questions asked. The men he had led into battle, had fought beside and bled for, were now his enemies and a piece of his heart broke with the understanding that he was going to be the one to steal their last breath. A part of him wanted to lower his sword and let them chain him, if it meant sparing them, but with his back bumping against Adonijah's back, he knew whose life he valued more. So, he swung his sword ferociously against his friends and comrades, striking them down one by one, knowing their faces would haunt him until the end of his days.

Despite their best effort, Pash and Adonijah were simply outnumbered, and it was only a matter of time before they tired and fell to the Northmen.

Pash risked a glance at his uncle and all the warmth had drained from his face. Is that what their enemies saw when they faced Ophir? His muscles were aching; sweat beaded and dripped from his forehead. He didn't have much fight left in him. He was going to fail Adonijah.

Pash watched his brother fend off two Shadows and wished he could have spent more time with him. The truth was: they weren't going to win this battle. He hoped no matter what Ophir told Niabi, she'd remember how deeply he loved her.

One of the Shadows lunged at Pash, and he braced himself for an impact that never came. Two arrows zipped past his shoulder and pierced his attacker square in the chest, downing him. Arrows from different directions flew toward the Shadows, picking them off.

Knowing they were now the hunted, the remaining Shadows, including Ophir, scattered into the woods, escaping the hidden assailants.

Pash turned to face Adonijah, but he wasn't behind him. He was on his knees, cradling Leoti in his arms. Slowly, her eyes fluttered open, but the commander was more concerned with who had saved them, than hovering over his brother and the Andrago.

His question was answered immediately when a group of ruffians stepped into view. They didn't have any armor or banners hailing their kingdom, but from their appearance, they looked to be Puluan. But what were pirates doing this far inland? The man who Pash assumed was their leader pulled his hood back, revealing his face. Pash couldn't believe his eyes. For months, he'd stared at his wanted poster and now, in the middle of nowhere, Pash was standing before him.

"Are any of you hurt?" the man's voice sliced through Pash's thoughts.

Adonijah found his way back to his brother's side, ushering a dazed Leoti with him, and when Pash saw the astonishment on his brother's face, his suspicion was confirmed.

"You're Salome's brother?" Adonijah's question took the ruffian leader by surprise.

"Most people just call me Crispin," he smirked, cocking his head to the side. "You know my sister?"

Pash and his brother exchanged a look.

"Aye," Adonijah finally spoke, drawing a skeptical look from the prince. "I know her."

"Then it seems we have a lot to talk about." Crispin eyed them both suspiciously. "Especially the part about a Shadow fighting off his own men."

The lost prince was no fool and was very observant. Pash bobbed his head, knowing the journey to kill Gershom was now on hold. He was going to be detained as a prisoner in the prince's company, there was no getting around it. And though he desperately wanted to spill the entire story about how they planned to assassinate Gershom, that they were on the same side, he knew at the end of the day, they would never be allies. So, he kept his mouth shut and met Crispin's gaze.

"To free my brother, I turned my back on my men."

Crispin stared at them, giving nothing away in his facial expressions. "A Shadow with a conscience. I never thought I'd see the day."

"So," Pash swallowed his retort. "Are we your prisoners?"

"I prefer the term *unexpected guests.*" The prince smiled and it was oddly comforting even though Pash knew they were talking about the same thing. "What are your names?"

"I am Adonijah."

"I am Leoti."

Crispin fixed his eyes on Pash, and the commander reluctantly said, "My name is Pash."

"By the pin on your chest," he pointed to the raven pin Niabi had awarded him upon his promotion to commander, "it would appear you're a high-ranking Shadow."

The prince really did know too much for his own good. But there was no use in lying, it wouldn't be long before someone recognized him and exposed his true identity.

"I am the Commander of the Shadows."

Crispin grinned and Pash wished he could wipe the smugness off his face.

A woman with blue hair rounded the prince and said in a low voice, "We need to move before they return." Crispin nodded in agreement before glancing at the Andrago.

"Are you able to walk?"

"Yes," Leoti nodded her head.

"Good." The prince pointed in the direction they were headed. "Then we should get moving."

"You aren't going to bind our hands?" Pash quirked an eyebrow.

"With their aim," Crispin cast a thumb at the motley crew behind him and smirked, "you wouldn't get far, if you tried to escape."

And by the hardened looks on the pirates' faces, Pash knew they wouldn't hesitate to shoot him in the back, if he attempted to flee. He was now Crispin's prisoner, and he was well aware wherever he was headed to next was going to put him behind in his quest to assassinate his father and return to his queen. But he was alive, and that was all he could hope for in a situation like this. He was determined not to give his captors any trouble, to earn their trust, and when the moment to escape presented itself, he would jump on it. He would return to Niabi, if it was the last thing he did.

A strange look in Crispin's eyes caused Pash to become paranoid. Had the prince managed to read his thoughts? Had the prince figured out what was running through his head? If he knew, he didn't speak on it. He motioned for the trio to walk with them. East. They were headed east which wouldn't lead them to Northwind, but to the abandoned city of Oakenshire.

"Where are you taking us?" Pash boldly asked his captors.

"I'm sure a man of your military prowess already knows the answer to that question." Crispin slipped his hood back over his head, masking his face in shadows, but Pash saw the prince flash a sinister grin.

"Tell me," the prince's attention honed in on Adonijah, "how does the brother of the Commander of Shadows know my sister?"

Adonijah stiffened but kept a steady hand on Leoti's arm as he helped her trek through the darkening forest. "We met months ago when Harbona found me in the swamplands."

"Are you the Wanderer?" Crispin asked, a twinkle in his eye.

"I was, but that title doesn't seem to suit me anymore."

"Are you no longer wandering then?"

"I suppose you could say that."

Crispin held his arm out, blocking Adonijah's path. "Who are you to my sister and why are you not with her now?"

The need to defend his brother engulfed Pash and he took a step toward the prince, nostrils flared. "He doesn't need to answer your questions."

As if his tone alone triggered the pirates, they all pointed weapons in his direction, reminding him that he was no longer giving orders, he was taking them. Pash took a small step back, raising his hands to show he meant the prince no physical harm.

"When it comes to my sister," Crispin hissed, "any question I ask will be answered." He turned once more to Adonijah and asked, "Why are you not with my sister?"

The brothers exchanged a quick look before Adonijah said, "I left her in the City of Bones to find the man who killed my mother. He was in my brother's camp at the foot of the Bone Mountains."

"And why were you and your Shadows this far south?" Crispin's eyes darted to Pash and Adonijah nodded for him to tell the truth.

"The queen ordered us to aid Prince Thanos in retaking Gomorrah from his mother."

"And did you?"

Pash swallowed hard and shifted from one leg to the other. "My army made it to the outskirts of Gomorrah, but we didn't get the chance to engage the Thrak in battle, because another army had beaten us there."

Crispin's eyes narrowed. It was evident the prince knew he was omitting something in his tale.

Rubbing the back of his neck and again exchanging a look with his brother, Pash continued. "The Stormcrags, Krazaks, a small force from Numbio, and a host of Bellators destroyed the city of Gomorrah, because they were trying to rescue someone."

"Rescue who?"

"Your sister," Adonijah chimed in with a raspy whisper. "After I left, somehow the Thrak captured her and -"

In a flash, Crispin pinned Adonijah against a tree and had a dagger against his throat. Arrows and spears pointed at Pash and Leoti from every angle, keeping them rooted in place.

"Please," Leoti's voice trembled, "don't hurt him."

The prince either didn't hear Leoti's pleas or it fell on deaf ears, because Crispin pressed his forearm in Adonijah's chest, drawing a grunt from him. "You abandoned my sister and let her be taken by the Thrak?"

"She's alive!" Pash shouted, hoping to diffuse the situation. "The Bellators rescued her before they leveled the city. Your sister is safe!"

Crispin cocked his head toward Pash, not releasing his hold on Adonijah. "She might be alive, but can you guarantee she is in one piece?"

The woman with blue hair approached the seething prince and slipped her hand on his forearm, squeezing until he met her gaze. "The sooner we get to Oakenshire, the sooner we can see your sister."

The prince's body relaxed and slowly, he lowered his weapon from Adonijah's neck, releasing him.

"I'm sorry," Adonijah raked a hand through his hair. "Had I not left, maybe I could have protected her."

"You speak of her like you have feelings for her," Crispin's voice had a bite to it.

Pash noticed Leoti's shoulders tense up.

Adonijah bobbed his head. "Aye, she means a lot to me."

"Not enough." Crispin sheathed his knife and motioned the group to lower their weapons. "Move out."

As he traipsed down the path, Pash thanked the Almighty that the prince didn't slit his brother's throat in anger, but he knew there was a good chance once they set foot in Oakenshire, they would never leave.

Chapter Twenty-Four

Salome

Salome sat in her makeshift throne with Jinn standing on her right. The prince had kept his word by escorting her everywhere. Clearly, he wasn't going to jeopardize her safety again. And if she were honest with herself, she fully enjoyed having him nearby. She caught herself staring at him, but before she could look away, he noticed her longing gaze. He smiled and winked as the doors to the neglected throne room opened and Oifa and Hanzo entered, a few feet apart but in stride. Once they reached Salome, they bowed.

"I wanted to thank you both for joining Prince Jinn in rescuing me. I am forever in your debt."

Hanzo shook his head, hands clasped behind his back. "You owe us nothing. We volunteered, knowing the risks. I am just sorry we didn't make it to you sooner."

Salome repressed the tears begging to be released. Had they arrived earlier, maybe Zophar would have survived the Gomorrians. She rattled the thought free, dwelling on the what ifs wouldn't bring her guardian back.

"I appreciate you both," Salome forced a smile. "There is another reason I asked you to meet with me."

"And what reason would that be?" Oifa narrowed her eyes, suspicious to her very core. She swatted rebellious strands of her lavender hair from her face.

Salome took a deep breath. She wasn't sure how either one of them would digest what she was about to suggest, but it was the only solution she could think of to unite the two clans. "Are either of you married or betrothed?"

Oifa and Hanzo exchanged an equally hateful and confused glance. Both shook their heads. "No."

"If there is one thing I've learned about politics and the ways of kings and queens," Salome continued before she lost her nerve, "alliances are forged in blood or marriage. I propose you marry to unite your tribes. Rule as king and queen, as equals."

Oifa scoffed, crossing her arms over her chest. "Have you gone completely mad?"

"Show her some respect," Hanzo jumped to Salome's defense, eyes raging. He clearly took her being the new leader of the Krazaks seriously. "She is trying to help our people."

"By suggesting *we* get married?" Oifa shook her head, practically foaming at the mouth. "That will put you in an early grave."

Hanzo looked up at Salome with pleading eyes. "Is there another way for the Krazaks and Stormcrags to have peace?"

"There are a couple ways to conquer a throne. Through war and bloodshed or through marriage and unity. I believe unless you consider marriage, you will continue to have bloodshed between your two mighty clans. You might not like one another, but you make a formidable team. I saw how you worked together in rescuing me. How you protected one another and fought valiantly side by side. If you join forces, you can change everything for your people."

They all stewed in silence. Oifa tapped her foot against the cracked stone tiles, fire raging in her eyes. "You truly expect me to marry *him*?

"Because you're such a prize?" Hanzo spat back, earning a hiss from the Stormcrag.

Salome stood up and walked toward them, shaking her head. "I don't expect anything from either of you. But I will not rule a people I have no business overseeing. The Stormcrags and Krazaks have lived for one thousand years as enemies. You have an opportunity to heal your city. All I ask is that you consider peace and break the cycle of war."

Oifa scoffed, drawing everyone's attention. "You're asking us to agree to an arranged marriage for the sake of peace while we prepare to shed the blood of your sister and your people."

She heard Jinn take a step forward, whether he was offended by Oifa's tone or felt she was a threat to Salome, she didn't know, but she extended her arm to stop him.

Salome locked eyes with Oifa. "You're right. It's hypocritical of me to ask you to choose peace while we prepare for war. Would it mean anything if I told you I never wanted to be involved in this war? That I never wanted the burdens, responsibilities, or scars that titles and power have thrusted upon me? If there was another way to reclaim my home, do you not think I would take it to avoid bloodshed?" Oifa glanced down at the floor. "Like I said before, there are two ways to conquer a throne. Bloodshed or unity. In my future, there is blood. Your future doesn't have to end like mine."

The room stilled and no one said a word. Salome knew she was asking a lot of them, but if she could fulfill her destiny without another person dying, she would jump at the chance. She'd do anything in her power to avoid this inevitable war.

She extended the bridge to Jinn, feeling the anxiety creeping in. *"They're more liable to skin me than agree to this."*

"Don't let them see you sweat. Peace won't come easily. All you can do is steer them in the right direction. That's what a queen does." Jinn's voice calmed her nerves, and she stood a little bit taller.

"I'll do it," Hanzo said, breaking the tension in the crumbling throne room.

"What did you say?" Oifa's eyes were wide, confused.

"She's right." Hanzo turned to the Stormcrag, rolling his shoulders back to make himself appear taller. "Oifa, I think you're crass and rude and lack basic manners -"

She planted her hands firmly on her hips and scowled at him. "Oh, is that all?"

"Even though I may not care for you romantically -"

"Or at all."

Hanzo continued, unfazed by her attitude, "My people mean everything to me. I have lived with Death my entire life. I may not know what peace looks or feels like, but I'd like to try to give it to those who come after me." He met Salome's stunned gaze, "I choose peace. If this woman will agree to the marriage, so will I."

Salome, Hanzo, and Jinn stared at Oifa with expectation. "What say you, Oifa?" the princess asked, hoping her plan would work.

Oifa took a minute to think. Scratching her chin with her long nails until she looked up from her feet. "We would rule as equals." A statement, not a question.

Hanzo nodded. "As equals."

"The Stormcrags will dwell in the City of Bones, if they should so choose." Oifa squared her shoulders to his, looking every bit of a warrior queen even without a crown.

He mirrored her body language, focusing on her as if no one else was in the room. "And the Krazaks will dwell in the Tears of the Gods should they so choose."

Oifa took a step toward her enemy. "I promise not to slit your throat while you sleep."

Hanzo ate the remaining distance between them. "I promise not to raise an unkind hand to you or treat you lesser than myself."

"And do you expect me to warm your bed at night?" She asked with a softness Salome didn't realize the Stormcrag possessed.

"If you should so choose." Hanzo smirked at her; his eyes hazy.

Salome cleared her throat to remind Hanzo and Oifa they weren't alone, drawing scowls from them. Maybe they weren't as opposed to the idea as she originally thought.

"There are two people we need to include in this decision for this to work," Salome said, and by the looks on Oifa and Hanzo's faces, they knew who she was referring to.

After explaining what they had discussed and agreed upon, Rune and Torrin were oddly and uncharacteristically quiet.

Salome shifted in her throne, poised like a queen, but anxious the two leaders would demand she be flogged for even suggesting the marriage. "What say you, my lords?"

Jinn, Heru, and Harbona were witnesses to the potential peace treaty and held their collective breath.

"Should you both provide your blessing," Salome continued when their silence extended a bit too long for comfort, "your tribes will be united. You will have peace and your children will have a future without bloodshed."

Rune glanced at Hanzo, ignoring everyone else. "Is this what you want?"

Without hesitation, the archer nodded, "To bring our people peace, yes."

Torrin rubbed his bald head before taking a step toward Salome. "Forgive me, my lady, but what will become of our positions amongst our peoples? I have led the Stormcrags for decades."

Salome let loose a breath she'd been holding in for far too long. At least they were talking. "I've thought of that. Though Hanzo and Oifa will rule over a united Mountain Men tribe, the Stormcrags and Krazaks will need spokesmen, ambassadors if you will, during the transition." She maintained eye contact with the Stormcrag, "Torrin, you will remain in the Tears of the Gods and Rune," she met the Krazak's gaze, "will be in the City of Bones. You will maintain the peace and secure the new reign. Together, the four of you can build what your ancestors couldn't."

Rune slammed his hand on Hanzo's shoulder. "I have spent most of my life serving King Gerd. I trust you and Oifa will not follow in his wicked footsteps." Hanzo placed his hand on top of Rune's and nodded. A silent promise.

Torrin turned to Oifa, stroking his long, scraggly beard. After a moment of hesitation, he met Oifa's gaze. "You have served me with a ferocious loyalty since you could walk. May Death take me, if I do not serve you in the same manner."

Salome's heart skipped a beat. Had they all really agreed to unite their clans? "Then we are agreed?"

The four of them nodded their heads in agreement. They had chosen peace.

Salome stood up, clapped her hands together, and smiled, "I think we have a wedding to plan."

Chapter Twenty-Five

Crispin

Crispin wanted to throttle Adonijah the night before when he heard that his sister was captured by the Thrak. He heard the pirates' stories about the Gomorrians and the thought of his sister in their cruel hands was more than he could bear. Had Rahab not soothed him, he would have killed the trio for no other reason than they were clearly enemies and deserved to be executed before they could betray him.

Safe.

Salome was safe according to his unexpected guests and he held on to the hope that she was not only in Oakenshire, but had escaped any brutality and torture in Gomorrah. Would he even recognize her when he saw her again? Was it possible she succumbed to her injuries, and he would never get the chance to say goodbye?

He casted out those tormenting thoughts as he sat by the crackling fire the pirates built at their new campsite. Haldane brewed a warm, rum-spiked drink that Crispin welcomed, hoping to drown his anxiety.

Adonijah approached him slowly from across the bonfire and motioned to the area next to the prince. "Mind if I sit?"

Crispin wanted to tell him to piss off, but with eyes on him from around the camp, the prince chose to be diplomatic and patted the ground next to him.

Once the sell-sword made himself comfortable, taking a sip of Haldane's concoction, he cleared his throat and said, "Not a moment goes by that I don't blame myself for failing to protect your sister when she needed me the most."

"I don't want to talk about her."

"Your sister is the bravest woman I know," Adonijah persisted, which irked Crispin. "I've seen her face assassins and bring them to their knees. I've seen her risk her life to free men and women being led to their executions. I've seen her face monsters, both human and creature alike, and come out bloodied, but victorious. I've never met a woman like her -"

"I know how incredible my sister is," Crispin cut him off. "I do not need you to tell me what I already know."

"I failed to protect Salome in her hour of need," Adonijah whispered as he stared at his tin mug, "but I swear, that is not a mistake I will make again. I will live, fight, and die by her side."

Crispin heard the conviction, the sorrow, the truth in the sell-sword's voice and although he desperately wanted to blame him for what happened to his sister, he could hear Salome's voice in his head urging him to give Adonijah a chance. That he wasn't truly at fault for her capture. Adonijah looked broken and then it hit him.

"You're in love with her, aren't you?" Crispin asked. Adonijah stared at him, and by the look on his face, Crispin knew the man was conflicted. "You speak as if you are in love with my sister, but the way you look at your Andrago companion tells me differently." Crispin smiled, but there was nothing kind in the prince's eyes.

Adonijah raked a hand through his dark hair. "I love your sister."

"But?"

Adonijah's eyes fell upon Leoti, who was on the other side of the camp showing the pirates her falcon, Tiki. "Our paths crossed for a reason, but I do not know if your sister and I are headed in the same direction."

"Meaning, she's a princess and you're a sell sword?" Crispin tore a piece of the rabbit from the skewer and chewed it. "If there's one thing my sister isn't, it's a snob. Your title and rank wouldn't make a difference to her."

"I meant no offense to you or your sister," Adonijah corrected himself. "What I meant to say is she has responsibilities I will never truly understand or willingly volunteer to help her with. I am not suited for city living. Not suited for confinement."

"And the Andrago way of life would neither confine you nor thrust you into a life of civil service." Crispin bobbed his head as he glanced across the camp at Leoti, neither angry nor offended.

"That makes me sound selfish."

"Is it selfish to know what would make you happy and to pursue it?" Crispin locked eyes with him, a seriousness in his tone that hadn't been there before. "You would be doing yourself and my sister a disservice by pretending. I don't know you, but I know for a fact my sister deserves better than that."

Adonijah took a bite of his food and chewed silently until Leoti's laugh drew his attention. Crispin watched with great interest as Adonijah's face lit up as he watched the Andrago.

"Does she know how you feel?" Crispin asked, forcing Adonijah to meet his gaze.

"No, and I am not sure what I feel exactly." He rubbed the back of his neck as he stretched his legs out in front of him. "I care deeply for Salome," his eyes found Leoti once more, "but I feel drawn to Leoti and I don't understand why."

Crispin leaned forward and whispered, "I'd make your intentions known, if I were you. And soon."

Adonijah frowned. "Why?"

Crispin jutted his chin toward the group of pirates surrounding Leoti and smirked. "Because if you don't, I guarantee one of those scallywags will."

"Does this mean you won't slit my throat in my sleep?" Adonijah asked as Crispin rose from his seat, cracking his back.

The prince stared at him, his eyes revealing none of his thoughts, but after a moment's hesitation, Crispin pat Adonijah on the shoulder. "Not tonight."

"There's something else you should know." Adonijah tapped the side of his mug rhythmically. "Something I wish I had told Salome but didn't have the courage to."

"And what's that?"

"Pash and I are half-brothers," Adonijah said after taking a deep breath. "We share the same father."

"I already know you are brothers. I learned of it the night we met."

"Our father is Lord Gershom." The confession stole Crispin's breath, and he stepped back. "We were on our way to Northwind to assassinate him when you found us."

Part of Crispin's brain urged him to stab Adonijah through the chest and be done with it, but the other part of him demanded he spare the man. He had willingly confessed who he was – who his father was – and even though Gershom had slaughtered his mother and brothers, Adonijah wasn't responsible for their murders. He even said they were on their way to kill their father – which could be a lie, but when he looked into Adonijah's eyes, he just knew he was telling the truth. He had borne his soul and his true identity to him, and if Zophar were with him, he would insist Crispin give him a chance to prove himself a worthy ally.

The prince once again patted him on the shoulder and mumbled, "We are not our fathers."

He refused to wait for a response. He turned on his heel and walked toward Rahab who was sharpening her knives by her sleeping bag. He knew if anyone would be able to cheer him up, it was her. He felt safe in her embrace, felt seen in her presence, and felt peace when she spoke to him. She was his saving grace, and he needed her now more than ever. The image of what Salome might have endured at the hands of the Thrak was consuming his thoughts, but now Adonijah's confession took up residence in his head.

"Let's hope one of those knives doesn't have my name on it," Crispin smirked as he hovered above the pirate.

She caught his gaze and winked. "Time will tell, princeling."

He laid flat on his back, placing his head on her lap. "I like when you say sweet things to me."

Rahab rolled her eyes but didn't attempt to hide her smile.

"There's that smile I love." Crispin grinned and she swatted at him with a huff.

"You'll have me looking soft to the crew and I can't have that." She shook her head as she ran her fingers through his curls.

"And if they saw me kissing their First Mate?" His eyes danced with mischief and desire.

She pointed one of her freshly sharpened daggers at him and quirked an eyebrow. "Keep your sappy expressions of love to yourself, Your Mightiness."

"Last I checked," Crispin sat up and leaned close to her, even though the tip of her knife poked him in the chest, "we're on the Mainland now."

"Your point?"

"When we're on the seas, I do what you say. When we're on dry land, you do what I say."

Rahab chuckled darkly, "Is that how we're playing this game, Crispin?"

Hearing his name come from her lips excited him and seemed to wash all of his troubled thoughts away. He tilted his head and slowly moved closer. "What say you, Queen of the Seas?" he whispered against her lips.

"I say," she said in a low, raspy voice, "you're in for a heap of trouble once we get back on a ship."

Crispin smiled, "I think I'll take my chances." He pressed his lips against hers and his heart leapt when she kissed him back, running the tips of her fingers along his beard.

Rahab pulled away sooner than he wanted her to, but she gripped his chin between her fingers and said, "I look forward to ordering you around the moment your boots land on the deck of my ship."

"Whatever my queen commands."

She tipped his chin up, forcing him to look into her hazel eyes. "I know you're worried about your sister, but the important thing is she's alive."

A tear slipped down his cheek. "What if she's not the same..."

"Whether she was harmed or not, she will never be the same as she was before." When his bottom lip quivered, she brushed her fingers through his hair and whispered, "Strength will find her. I speak from experience, princeling. When I was left for dead in Uri's dungeons, I knew I would never be the same, if I made it out alive. It's been years, and I'm still not over what happened to me," she cupped his face and leaned her forehead against his. "I survived and she will too."

All Crispin could do was hope and pray she was right.

Chapter Twenty-Six

Niabi

When the army Niabi dispatched to claim Gomorrah for Prince Thanos returned, she demanded for Pash to be brought to her private quarters immediately, to give his report. So, when Ophir, Gershom's brother, entered her office, she was not only confused but irritated. She didn't bother hiding her disregard for the oldest member of the Shadows. She had only permitted him to join the order she founded as a show of goodwill when she first allied herself with Gershom. Now, over two decades later, she still hadn't warmed up to him.

Tala motioned the Shadow inside and he marched up to the queen's desk and bowed.

"I sent for Commander Pash," Niabi eyed the bald man up and down. "Yet, you stand before me. Why?"

Ophir didn't bat an eye at her tone as he straightened to his full height. "I bring sorrowful news, Your Highness." He glanced around the study before suggesting, "Perhaps, my brother should be in attendance for my report?"

"Bold of you to suggest who should be privy to your report, Ophir." Niabi glared at him, fighting the urge to throw him in a cell next to the disgraced second in command just for good measure.

"I meant no offense," Ophir stammered. "I just thought -"

"Lord Gershom has been arrested for treason." Niabi cut him off and motioned for Tala to shut the door as Anaktu took his place standing to her right-hand side.

"Treason?" the Shadow's eyes widened. "Is my brother...?"

"Dead?" She shook her head and straightened in her chair. "Not yet."

"Your Highness, might I ask -"

"You may not." She narrowed her eyes, her patience had run thin, and she wanted to know why Pash hadn't come to give his report. "What is this sorrowful news you bring me instead of your commander?"

"It is about my nephew."

Niabi's heart jolted but she kept her expression unreadable. She perfected her nonchalant glare over the years, and she was grateful it was finally paying off. "What about the commander?"

"While we camped, awaiting to launch our assault on Gomorrah, a sell-sword found his way to our site. It turned out the trespasser was Pash's half-brother, Adonijah."

"Half-brother?" Niabi didn't know about Pash having any siblings.

"Yes, my queen." Ophir nodded. "Bastard born, but a son of my brother, nonetheless. I wanted to have him executed for trespassing, but Pash wouldn't allow it, wouldn't listen to reason. He had Adonijah confined to our camp while we left for Gomorrah, but when we arrived, we found another army had laid siege to the city. Krazaks, Stormcrags, Numbio, even Bellators fought to rescue your sister from the Thrak."

"The Thrak had Salome?" She hadn't expected her sister to be a part of Ophir's tale, but then her thoughts drifted to why Matlidys would capture Salome and not try to cash in on the reward money Niabi had offered.

"From what Leoti could see, your sister was rescued, and the city was destroyed. Pash ordered us to return to camp which angered the young Prince Thanos."

Niabi couldn't help but chuckle at the thought of the prince throwing a tantrum over the turn of events. But when Ophir stopped recounting his tale, she rolled her eyes and motioned for him to continue.

"What is this sorrowful news you continue to tip-toe around?" Niabi didn't truly care about Gomorrah's fate. She didn't even care that her sister's army had destroyed the wretched place. But what she did care about was Pash. "Where is the commander?"

"When we returned to our camp, his half-brother killed one of the Shadows and Pash and Leoti helped him escape before his execution," Ophir met her gaze. "We tracked them down. I even asked Pash to rejoin us, that you would be forgiving of his temporary lapse in judgment, but he chose his brother over the crown. We ended up drawing swords against him, but my group was ambushed by vigilantes, and they took Pash with them."

Niabi cocked her head to the side. "Are you trying to tell me that Pash deserted his post?"

"I am trying to tell you, Pash is a traitor. His half-brother serves your sister and if Pash chose to stay with his rebel brother, if Pash chose to desert his command and aid an enemy of the crown, then he has committed treason."

Niabi forced herself to meet Tala's worried gaze. "And Leoti?" she asked. "Did Pash force her to accompany him against her will?"

Ophir shifted side-to-side, most likely feeling the weight of Tala's gaze boring into the back of his skull. "The warg joined the brothers of her own free will."

"Is there anything else you have to report, Ophir?" Niabi could sense Tala's growing anger and didn't want him to say anything about Pash or Leoti in front of Ophir. He was not to be trusted. If anyone would try to usurp Pash's position out of spite, it would be his uncle.

He shook his head. "No, Your Highness."

Niabi waved him away and Tala opened the door to let the Shadow out. "That will be all."

Though he looked like he wanted to say something else, he'd been dismissed, and like a good soldier, Ophir bowed and left. Once the door was closed and he was well out of earshot, Tala took a step toward Niabi.

"Do you believe him?"

Niabi poured herself a glass of water and offered Tala one which he declined. "Ophir is many things, but I do not believe him to be the teller of tall tales."

"So, you believe Pash deserted his command to join up with the rebels? You believe my daughter would abandon us?"

Tala's voice was on the verge of rage and brokenness which spurred the heavily pregnant queen to stand up and approach him. She grabbed his hands in hers and forced him to meet her gaze. "Tala, listen to me. There is more to this story than what Ophir is telling us. I do not believe for a moment that Pash and Leoti are traitors."

"Then what do you intend to do?" he asked, taking a deep breath.

"There is nothing I can do." She reached behind her and grabbed her glass from her desk and took a sip. "All we can do is wait for them to return."

"And what if these ruffians, who supposedly captured them, are torturing them? Or what if they've already killed them?" Tala was unhinged and all Niabi could do was speak softly and hope she soothed his frayed nerves.

"Tala, we will see them again. Pash is the Commander of Shadows and Leoti is a powerful warg. If anyone could escape their captors and make their way back home, it would be them." She squeezed his hand. "And if Pash did desert his post to save his brother, then he must have had a good reason."

Tala stared into her eyes, searching for something. "You trust him that much?"

"He has never given me a reason not to trust him." She cupped his face in her hands and offered a small smile. "We will see them again. I promise."

"You would have me do nothing then?"

It pained her to say it, but she nodded. "Your place is here, with me. If I lose you, I will be vulnerable, and I already have too many enemies to fend off."

She slipped her arms around his neck and hugged him tight. "We will see them again."

She said it again more for her benefit than Tala's. On the outside, she appeared calm, but inside, her heart was breaking. Pash had chosen to save his brother when they were on opposite sides of the upcoming war. He had deserted his command, left his men in the hands of his scheming uncle, and for what? He'd never mentioned this brother to her before, how close could they actually be?

Drawing back from Tala, she cradled her swollen belly and for the first time was nervous that she might raise this child without the man she loved. It felt too much like how she raised Rollo without Dichali. She'd guarded her heart and had always kept Pash at arms-length so she wouldn't get hurt again, but now that she'd let him in, now that they were expecting a child together, she couldn't help but feel like she was drowning, and there was no one there to rescue her.

Chapter Twenty-Seven

Salome

When word was sent to Salome that three war ships from the Eastern Lands had arrived, she quickly made her way to what used to be the throne room, now overrun by greenery and roots protruding through the slate floors and took her place upon her wooden throne.

Jinn took his place at her right-hand side, straightened his clothes, and slicked his hair out of his face. He seemed relieved that his father had sent aid and that they had arrived rapidly, but the second the Eastern delegation entered the room, the prince paled. The elderly man leading the small group shared similar features with Jinn, but while the prince was clean shaven and had dark features, the man using an intricately carved wooden cane to steady himself, had long white hair and a matching mustache.

"Is that...?" Salome started.

"My father," Jinn nodded. "I didn't expect him to come with the reinforcements," he whispered.

"Why do you think he came?" she glanced up at him.

Jinn met her curious gaze but whatever he was thinking, he kept to himself.

"Jinn?" she sent down their bond. *"What is it?"*

She felt a sudden shiver crawl up her spine as Jinn's attention shifted from her to the old man hobbling toward them. The King of Sakurai reached the dais and smiled. He acknowledged his son then fixated on Salome. The way he held her gaze was odd, like he had a deep, dark secret, and she wished she could get him to stop staring at her so unabashedly.

Jinn's shoulders tensed, as if he too was put off by how his father was looking at her. Clearing his throat, the prince drew the king's attention. "Father, I didn't expect you to make the journey from the Jade Palace."

Kenji took a step forward, stretching his hand out for Jinn to grasp. "It's been far too long since I left our shores." The king's gaze once again found its way to Salome. "And I wanted to meet the lost princess for myself."

Salome stood from her throne and made her way toward Jinn's father. Offering a slight bow of her head in respect, Salome said, "It is an honor to welcome you to Oakenshire, Your Highness. Thank you for sending aid."

"Of course," he smiled brightly, crinkling the corners of his eyes.

"You've had a long journey," Salome motioned toward the double doors the king and his entourage had come through. "Perhaps you would like to see your rooms and have refreshments -"

"If it would be alright," the king politely interrupted, causing Jinn to stand straighter. "I had hoped to have a private audience with you, Princess." Kenji's eyes darted to his son but before Jinn could get a word in, he said, "One leader to another."

Salome bobbed her head, even though her heart was thrashing in her chest. Forcing a smile, she motioned them toward the secluded terrace outside of the throne room. "Of course, Your Grace."

Sparring one last glance Jinn's way, Salome led the Easterner outside where a cool breeze was blowing. Once seated at the table, drinks and plates filled with dried meats and fruit were served. Taking a long sip of her wine, Salome waited for Kenji to initiate their meeting. She remembered enough of her lessons on proper etiquette in dealing with other royals to know since the King of Sakurai asked for an audience, it was up to him to bring up the topic at hand. It seemed like a small eternity before he finally set down his glass and spoke.

“Thank you for agreeing to meet with me, Princess.” Kenji sat in the seat opposite her overlooking the Eastern ships docked in the harbor.

“It's the least I can do to thank you for bringing aid in our time of need.” Salome poured a second glass of wine, offering it to the king who gratefully accepted. After taking another gulp, she placed her glass down on the table, the clink drawing the king's eyes. “What is it you want from me, Your Majesty?

His eyes were filled with confusion. He tilted his head, his white hair falling across his forehead in the same manner Jinn's did. “Want from you?”

She squirmed in her seat, shifting her gaze from his face to the sea. Jinn was the spitting image of his father and in the sunlight, his eyes were the same warm golden-brown. She cleared her throat, lifting the glass to her lips again. “It seems everyone wants something from me these days.”

He bobbed his head in understanding. “A crown is a heavy burden to bear.”

She shot the king an intrigued look. "Are you saying you aren't here to ask me for something? Money? Promises? An alliance written in blood?"

The king shifted his weight before meeting her gaze, as if what he was about to say was hard for him to bring up. "I want to talk to you about my son."

Her heart raced. "So, you want a formal alliance, then."

He chuckled. "You misunderstand. I don't expect you to marry Jinn, but there is something you should know about him. Something he would never tell you himself."

She was both eager and afraid for the king to continue. She'd already gone through the heartache of Adonijah keeping secrets from her and it cost her dearly. If Jinn had also been lying to her, she didn't know if she would be strong enough to lose him too. "You have my attention."

Kenji leaned closer, as if he was going to share a secret with her. "When Jinn was a little boy, no more than six or seven, he told us he'd been having strange dreams. Dreams of fire, of ash, of blood. Dreams that scared him, but dreams that he said felt real."

Salome cocked her head to the side. "Are you telling me Jinn used to have nightmares? No disrespect, but it's not uncommon."

"That's what my wife and I thought as well," he held up an index finger to stress his point. "Just nightmares. But he'd have these dreams almost nightly, so we had our Healers examine him. They said nothing was wrong with him. So, we had the oracle speak with him. The only thing Jinn would constantly talk about was a girl. He saw her in a burning city. He saw her in a forest training with different weapons. He saw her riding a horse, watched as she stalked through the woods hunting, watched as she got tattooed."

Salome froze in her seat, her eyes glued to the king.

"As he grew older, so did she. The oracle said he was dreaming of his future love – the woman who would bring peace to his heart. Once he reached the age of marriage, he rejected every suitor to his mother's dismay. He kept saying one day, he'd find her. I am ashamed to say, I never believed he would."

Salome gulped. Even though there was a cool breeze wafting around them, she felt like her skin was on fire. "What changed your mind?" she whispered so softly she was afraid he hadn't heard her.

Kenji reached into his robe and pulled out a folded parchment. A letter by the shape of it. "May I?" Salome nodded and motioned for him to read it aloud. "This is the letter Jinn sent me asking for me to send troops to aid you in reclaiming your ancestral throne." He unfolded it and handed it to her. She warily grabbed ahold of it and let her eyes scan over the neat penmanship.

Kenji pointed to the bottom where Jinn signed the letter. "At the end, he said, '*Father, I found her.*' You see, that girl he described had wild curls and two different color eyes."

Kenji pulled out two more sheets of paper from his pocket and flattened them on the table, smoothing them out with care. When Salome glanced at the drawings, it took her breath away. One was of her when she was no more than seven or eight years old, and the other was a recent sketch of her.

"My son never thought he had any talent, but I think he captured your beauty perfectly."

"Jinn drew these?" She didn't dare touch them, fearing she'd smudge the charcoal. She let her hand hover above them an inch or two. Her mouth was suddenly bone dry, so she picked up her wine glass to coat her throat.

The king pointed at the recent rendering with a smile. "He drew this one a year ago. They are yours, if you want them."

"Why are you telling me this?" Her voice came out raspier than she expected.

"For as long as I can remember, he's been searching for you and here you are." Kenji reached for her hand and patted it gently. "Jinn always believed he had a greater destiny than to be King of Sakurai."

"What could be greater than being king?"

The king smiled and it reminded her of Jinn. "Being of service. I have known for years that Jinn was not interested in being my successor. To be fair, he was never meant to be. Jinn is my last son, but he wasn't my only son. I've lost two sons and a daughter. Nobu, my first born, drowned when he was eight. Itsuki was ill, had a cough for months that wouldn't go away and finally succumbed in his teenage years."

Salome fought the urge to get up and hug the man. "I'm sorry. I know about loss."

"It is a heavier burden than a crown, I dare say."

"And Anka?" Jinn mentioned his sister was betrothed to her eldest brother, Lykos, and had died a few years ago. "What happened to her?"

Tears welled in Kenji's eyes. "My sweet daughter was betrothed to your oldest brother, Lykos. When he died, she was devastated. Some of our older citizens believed she was cursed, and no man wanted her, fearing Death followed her. After years of being rejected by suitors, ostracized by our people, losing her two brothers, and her beauty fading, she couldn't defeat the darkness that clouded her mind and poisoned her heart. She..." The king wiped his eyes and cleared his throat before continuing. "She was found days later, washed up on the shore."

"I'm so sorry, I didn't know."

"Jinn is my last born. He was never meant to sit on the Jade Throne."

Salome placed her hand on top of his. "He loves his people, and he knows his duty to them." She meant it to be reassuring but the king shook his head and gave her a warm smile.

"For the first time in years, he is alive, and I know it's because of you." He stood and she jumped up from her seat. "I don't know what your feelings and intentions are for my son, but I thought you should know how deeply he cares for you. How deeply he's always cared for you, even before you officially met."

Salome knew she didn't owe him any explanation, but she felt she wanted to share her thoughts and feelings with him. But before she could, Cato bolted through the arched terrace doorway, breathing heavily, as if he had sprinted the entire length of the castle to bring her a message.

"Cato?" Salome turned her full attention to him. "What is it?"

"Riders approaching from the west." Cato caught his breath, hands perched on his hips.

Salome made her way to the watchtower, Cato and King Kenji in tow. Jinn and Heru were already there, watching the approaching group. They waved no flags and gave no indication of who they were or where they hailed from. She knew they weren't Shadows. The northern fighters donned their black uniforms with pride and would never stoop to pretending to be anyone else. She looked through the distant faces, trying to see if she spied anyone she knew. Instead, she saw a woman with icy blue hair, a man who looked like a giant, a halfling, and was that a pirate captain?

"Do we know who they are?" Salome asked Jinn, but he didn't respond. She glanced in his direction and saw him and his father whispering back and forth. Jinn looked rattled. She cleared her throat, drawing their attention. "Do we know who they are?" she repeated her question.

Jinn distanced himself from his father and shook his head. "No. They don't seem to be a large company, but they could be a group sent on someone's behalf to speak with you or give their lists of demands to keep from attacking us."

Salome's nostrils flared. "If they are looking for trouble, they've come to the right place." She scanned the group as they got closer, now starting to make out faces. She didn't recognize anyone, but one man's gait looked familiar. She squinted, as if that would help her identify him. She gasped, her hand covering her mouth. "It can't be."

"Salome?" Jinn reached out for her, but she turned and fled down the steps as fast as her feet could carry her. She sprinted by soldiers and castle attendants, pushing them out of her way if necessary, apologizing as she darted past. She made it to the bailey and shouted at the gatekeepers to open the gate.

"Did you say open the gate?" One of the soldiers from Numbio looked at her wide eyed.

"Open the gate!" Salome stood before the closed entrance, itching to get outside to see if it was really him.

Jinn reached her side. "Do you know them?"

She was so focused on watching the gate lift, listening to the metal gears screech, that she didn't hear Jinn's question. With the prince by her side, they made their way to the lowered drawbridge. On the other side of the bridge, the group stopped. A man stepped in front of the motley crew and pulled his hood off his head.

His teary eyes met her awaiting gaze. For a moment, no one moved or said anything. She sucked in a cool breath; her heart fluttered wildly in her chest. Almighty, was this even possible? Was he really standing a hundred feet in front of her? Was her mind playing tricks on her?

She opened her mouth, but nothing came out. The sting from keeping her emotions in check burned the back of her throat. This time, her voice came out raspy, "Crispin?"

Crispin took off toward Salome and she sprinted to meet him. Jinn motioned for the archers to stand down as Salome jumped into her brother's embrace, wrapping her arms around his neck. Tears streamed down their cheeks as they laughed and cried as if no one was watching them. She felt the tension, grief, worry, and stress leave her body the moment she reached him.

"I've missed you," Crispin whispered in her ear, running his fingers over her intricately braided hair.

"I feared you were dead." Salome pulled back, holding his face in her hands, making sure he was really standing before her. The prickle of his new facial hair tickled her fingers. "This is new," she smiled.

Crispin rolled his eyes and smirked. "Alright, let's have it. Whatever cruel thing you have to say, spit it out while I'm still in a good mood."

She tapped his face lovingly, still overwhelmed that the brother she prayed had survived the Caverns of the Undead, was standing before her. "It suits you."

He grinned, proudly rubbing his fingers across his jawline. “It’s not as long and bushy as Zophar’s, but I think the old man will still be impressed by it.” Crispin looked past Salome, scanning the people for their red bearded guardian. “Where is he? Smoking that pipe of his, I imagine.”

Salome’s bottom lip quivered, and she swiped tears from her face.

"What is it?" he asked.

“I’m sorry,” she whispered, a tremble in her soft voice.

Crispin shook his head. “No.” He took a step back. “No, he can’t be... But the Numbio...”

“Come inside. There’s a lot for us to talk about.” Salome extended her hand to him.

As the group he was travelling with made their way across the drawbridge, she caught sight of Adonijah, his hood over his head. Their eyes locked and a wave of anger, surprise, and sadness flooded her heart. She wasn’t sure if she wanted to hug him or stab him.

Adonijah stopped next to Crispin, eyes fixed on her. “Hi.”

She gritted her teeth, forcing her face to still, to hide the emotions clearly ripping her heart apart. “You’re alive.”

An awkward tension hovered over the trio until Adonijah cleared his throat and said, “We should talk.”

Salome’s nostrils flared, but before she could say anything, Crispin chimed in. “Perhaps you can find some time to speak with Adonijah later tonight? Maybe, after we eat and catch up with one another.”

Salome reluctantly agreed to meet Adonijah and once he walked away, she quickly put him out of her mind. She grabbed Crispin’s arm and led him inside Oakenshire. He was alive and well and finally back home. By the looks of the company he kept, he probably had plenty of stories to share with her and she wanted to hear every single one of them.

Chapter Twenty-Eight

Gershom

"Wait for me," Gershom called out to Issachar as they ran through the Black Forest.

They had been instructed by their fathers to stay at the hunting campgrounds, but before the sun had fully peaked over the horizon, the wild and reckless Prince Issachar had stirred Gershom from his peaceful sleep and ordered him to come along. Although they were only ten years old, Gershom already knew his place in life. It was the same as his father's. Protect and serve the crown. So, when his best friend gave him an order, he knew to obey, even if it went against his own father's wishes.

"Issachar?" Gershom cried out, hoping to catch up to his friend before one of the fabled monstrosities of the forest found him first. Or worse. His father. "Issachar -"

"Shhh!" Issachar stepped out from a bush and put his index finger to his lips. "I found something."

"We should go back before our fathers realize we've gone missing." Gershom feared disobeying Issachar since he was to be the future king one day, but his father's whippings were in the forefront of his mind. The Commander was not one for foolishness and even though it was Issachar's idea to wander off that morning, his father would state his case that Gershom should have convinced the hot-headed royal to stay put for his own safety. As if Gershom had any sway in the prince's actions. If he had the gift of persuasion, he would have been able to sweet-talk his way out of every unwarranted beating he'd incurred from his father's brutal hands.

"Issachar," Gershom pleaded once more as the prince turned his focus on something he'd spotted down the path. "I don't hear the hounds searching for

us, so there's still time for us to return to camp without anyone ever knowing we left."

"Where is your sense of adventure, Gershom?" the prince flashed a mischievous smile at his friend. "Look at what I found."

Gershom wanted to run. Run as far as he could and beg for his father's mercy, but if he left the prince alone, he'd face the king's wrath and that wasn't any better. Reluctantly, Gershom joined his companion behind the bushes and glanced in the direction Issachar pointed, where a small cabin sat nestled in the pines. The sight was odd for sure, since it was well known no one actually dwelled in the Black Forest because of all the creatures and vagabonds rumored to terrorize the woods. But right in front of him, not so much as a stone's throw away, sat a cabin with smoke wafting up the chimney.

"We should go." Gershom's mouth was dry. If someone chose to live in the Black Forest, they were not a person to be trifled with.

"Don't you want to see who lives there?" Issachar wiggled his eyebrows and Gershom quickly shook his head in protest.

"Please, Issachar." His eyes were wide, and sweat was dripping down his back. "We shouldn't be out -"

"I dare you to go inside."

"What?" Gershom stared at him in terror. "No."

Issachar narrowed his eyes, putting his princely mask in place. "I order you to go inside that cabin."

To disobey now was a guaranteed beating that would take him weeks to recover from, so he took a deep breath before slowly making his way to the clearly not abandoned cabin. Even if the house was empty at the present, the owner wasn't too far if they left something cooking in the fireplace. Once he got to the front door, Gershom risked a final pleading look where he knew Issachar was hiding, but when no order to retreat came, he raised his balled-up fist and gently knocked on the door.

Nothing. No answer.

His hand trembled as he grabbed the knob and opened the creaky wooden door. Expecting to find something similar to a torture chamber, he was pleasantly surprised and relieved to see it was just an ordinary cabin. A small cot sat to one side with a table in the center. A cauldron hung upon the open flame in the stone fireplace, but no one was inside the one room hovel. Gershom took another step inside to look around when a strong gust of wind whipped through slamming the door shut. Frightened, he turned and tried tugging the door open, but it wouldn't budge. He was stuck inside. But at least he was alone.

"You've wandered far from your camp," a woman's voice sounded, sending a bolt of fear zinging through his body.

Whipping around, he saw a beautiful woman with long black hair, green eyes, and long black fingernails stirring what he could only imagine was some unholy concoction.

"Please, don't hurt me," he cried out.

Her eyes latched onto his and she smiled. "Oh, child, I do not intend to harm you. I am here to help you."

"Help me?" He pressed his back against the door, keeping the maximum distance between them. "What do you want from me? Who are you?"

"My name is of little importance at the present," she continued stirring her stew. "What is important is that I know who you are, Gershom of Northwind. I know who you serve, and I know that if you do not heed my warning, you will not live to see your glory."

"Glory?" He took a tentative step forward. "You're a witch, aren't you?"

Her side-eyed grin reminded him of a cat that had just toyed with a mouse before swallowing it whole.

"Let me see your hand."

Gulping so loud he was positive the woman heard it, he did as she instructed, walking to her with his palm upturned. Her hands were cold and sent a shiver down his spine the second she touched him. She stroked her thumb up and down his small hand before looking into his eyes.

"You harbor a lot of anger and desire to be the one making all the decisions." Before he could deny her words, she continued. "You will betray your closest friend -"

Gershom ripped his hand away. "That's a filthy lie! I would never betray my friend."

"You will have two sons by two different women," she continued, unfazed by his protests. "Neither will love you."

"Why are you saying these things?" Gershom couldn't help the cry that escaped his lips.

"You will commit many sins, little lord. You will hurt those closest to you and will truly trust no one."

"Stop!" Gershom slammed his hands over his ears, rocking his head back and forth, hoping she would quit talking. "I'm a good boy. I know my duty. I know my place."

"You may know your place," she stood from her stool, fire blazing in her eyes, "but you are not content with it."

"I am to be the next Master of War, like my father. I am to protect the future king. I am to -"

The woman smiled, but he felt no warmth or comfort from her calculating gaze. "The penalty for your betrayal will be the Hunter's blade buried deep in your heart."

His throat tightened, but he mustered the courage to refute her false prophecy. "But there are no Hunters."

She motioned toward the door. "Your friend, the prince, is growing anxious waiting for you in the bushes up on the ridge," she said sweetly. "It is time for you to leave."

He marched to the door, but paused when his hand touched the knob. Without his prompting, it opened, but his hesitancy in leaving hadn't stemmed from wondering if the door would open.

"Ask your question." Her voice echoed behind him.

He didn't turn to look at her, but whispered, "How can I escape this fate?"

"Do not be seduced by the Mistress of Night."

"But who is -" When he looked behind him not only was the woman gone, but the entire cabin had disappeared. He stood in the middle of the Black Forest where the house should have been.

"What happened in there?" Issachar hopped up from his hiding spot and sprinted to him, looking just as confused as Gershom was that the cabin vanished.

Before Gershom could answer the prince's question, pounding hooves and howls of the royal hounds echoed around them. The king and Gershom's father, along with a host of soldiers, appeared from the trees and neither man looked amused.

Gershom hadn't thought about that day in years but sitting in a dark and foul-smelling cell in the dungeons of Northwind, he found he had nothing but time on his hands. Even though he spent most of his life obeying Issachar's commands, he still ended up being seduced by the Mistress of the Night and betraying his childhood best friend. He might be marked for the Hunter's blade, but all was not lost. Not yet. He had years to plan his revenge, to stage his coup. Sure, things looked bleak at the moment, but he had sworn years ago to make Niabi suffer, and he intended to do just that when the moment was right.

Feet scuffed against the stone pavers outside his cell door, but he didn't move from his seated position against his cell wall. If it was that slop that was deemed his dinner, he wasn't in any hurry to lap it up. But the tiny opening at the foot of the door didn't open. The slat where he could see someone's eyes staring at him slid open, and he relaxed, already knowing who the mysterious visitor was.

"What news?" he asked, voice raw from disuse.

"Everything is going according to plan, my King," the silvery voice danced in his cell, drawing a wicked smile from him.

"Excellent, Vilora." He leaned his head against the cold stone wall and glared up at the ceiling, knowing multiple stories above him, sat Niabi, unaware of his schemes. "Vengeance will be mine."

Chapter Twenty-Nine

Salome

After swapping stories of their separate adventures, and how Crispin had faced off with their fire wielding sister, they sat in a comfortable silence, drinking a glass of wine in memory of Zophar. Telling her brother about Zophar's death was the hardest thing she'd ever done. Crispin hadn't cried, he'd just listened intently to each word she spoke until he was all caught up. Months apart but they picked up right where they left off.

He cleared his throat and raised his glass. "To Zophar. The best father and friend."

"To Zophar." She clinked her glass against his and took a long sip. "I miss him."

"I wish I could have had the chance to say goodbye." Crispin swiped a lone tear from his cheek. "The last memory I have of him is in the Cavern of the Undead, when I was swept away, and he looked terrified."

She grabbed his hand and squeezed until he met her gaze. "I'm sorry I couldn't save him."

Crispin pulled her to him, her face resting against his chest. "It's not your fault."

"I wish I could have done more."

"You leveled an entire city on his behalf. I'd say you exacted your justice." Crispin kissed her forehead and held her tighter. "I'm just glad you survived. I don't know what I would have done without you."

She sat up and wiped her eyes with her palms. "Well, now that you're here, you can make all the decisions and I can go and fight a few sea monsters." Her attempt at levity was a welcome one and he laughed.

"As if you could have defeated Kubantu." He elbowed her shoulder and she swatted at him.

"Excuse me, but have you already forgotten that I fought and killed a cornigera and became the Red Maiden?" She snorted when he stuck his tongue out at her. "Maybe I should tell you again. Perhaps your ears stopped working during that part of the story."

"I do believe I missed the part about your relationship with Adonijah." He wiggled his eyebrows playfully, but she recoiled. She didn't want to think about Adonijah, let alone talk to her brother about him.

"I'm sorry," he cleared his throat. "You don't need to talk about him if you don't want to."

"How did you cross paths?"

"After escaping Borg, we ran into a horde of Shadows attacking three travelers. We decided to intervene. I have no qualms in killing Shadows. Turned out, Adonijah was with them and when we introduced ourselves, he told me he knew you." Crispin shrugged. "At first, I thought you would be happy to see him again, especially after hearing how he spoke about you."

"But?"

"I think that's a conversation for you and Adonijah to have."

"You beast." She threw a small pillow at him which he easily dodged. She twirled her curls in her fingers absentmindedly. "I loved him. He left." She shrugged, biting her bottom lip to keep from crying. "He broke my heart and lost my trust." Crispin stretched his arm across her shoulders and kissed her temple. "Did he tell you he's Gershom's son?" she asked, and he nodded.

"We are not our fathers," Crispin whispered.

Silence once again enveloped them. Salome wasn't sure what else to say. They'd both seen and experienced incredible things and suffered tragic losses. She had imagined their reunion including Zophar; the three of them laughing until their bellies hurt and smiling until their cheeks ached. But their guardian, the man who had truly been a father to them, was gone.

"I think -"

Salome didn't get to finish that thought because Crispin let loose a loud snore. He must have been exhausted to fall asleep sitting up. She slithered out from under his arm, carefully ushering his body down to a more comfortable position on the couch. Grabbing one of the blankets from his bed, she covered him, wiped hair from his face, kissed his cheek, and left him to sleep, knowing he would be perfectly safe in the castle.

Slipping out of her brother's room and walking down the hall toward her own chambers, she found she was wide awake and wanted someone to talk to; not wanting to be alone. Her thoughts drifted to Jinn. Seeing him shirtless the other day, having him so close to her, whispering in her ear and sending shivers down her spine. She wondered what it would be like to lay with him, to be wrapped in his warm and protective embrace.

She stopped when she tucked her hand in her pocket and felt the drawings King Kenji had given her. She pulled them out and looked at them, admiring the prince's exceptional talent and being in complete awe of what Jinn's secret had been. Why hadn't he told her? How was it even possible? Damaris had told her in the Isles of Myr that they must have shared a strong bond, but she thought it was because they were both magic wielders. If she had known he'd been searching for her his entire life...

Something shifted in the darkness capturing her undivided attention. Quickly, she tucked the papers back into her pocket and unsheathed her wolf dagger. Salome listened for a moment to see if whoever was lurking in the shadows would reveal themselves.

"I know you're there," she mustered as much courage as she could to sound intimidating. "Either you step into the light, or I'll gut you in the dark."

The hooded figure stepped out from behind a column and her fear vanished. "Did they hurt you?"

"Still lurking in the shadows, Adonijah?" She put her knife back in its sheath strapped to her thigh. "I suppose the darkness suits you."

"What did the Thrak do to you?" Even in the dark, she could sense the pain and grimace his face held. He was bold to ask her that question when he could have probably guessed the terror she endured.

"The question you should be asking is, what did *I* do to *them*?"

He ate the distance between them until they were standing a foot apart. She could see his face clearly once he pushed his hood back. "I cannot even begin to imagine what you must think of me but -"

She crossed her arms, "Try."

"Salome -" He reached for her, but she side stepped his advances.

"I gave you my trust," she hissed, interrupting him. "I gave you my heart. You broke both."

He raked a hand through his hair, regret in his eyes. "I know I hurt you and I'm sorry."

"I hope leaving was worth it."

"I never intended to leave you. Things got complicated." He rested one hand on his hip and the other rubbed the back of his neck. "I swore an oath to avenge my mother's death. Surely, you of all people can understand that."

"I understand loss and have come to know Death quite intimately." Seeing the sorrow in his eyes tugged at her heart and she softened her gaze and voice. Before she could think better of it, she reached out and gently grabbed his forearm. "You leaving wasn't what shattered me. It was that you lied. Lied about who you are, while insisting that I open up to you. Had you told me the truth, I wouldn't have stopped you from fulfilling your oath. I would have helped you."

"I know that now. I was a fool, but I'm back now."

She squeezed his arm. "I will always care for you, but we will never be together."

"It's because of Jinn, isn't it?" He didn't look or sound angry, but Salome still didn't appreciate him dragging the prince into their conversation.

"This has nothing to do with him."

"In my absence, I thought he would look out for you, but now I see he's poisoned you against me."

Her nostrils flared. "I think you did a good enough job of that on your own."

"So, that's it?" His voice was little more than a whisper. "You choose him?

"I choose me."

"I will fight, live, and die by your side." His eyes flicked up to meet hers and she took several steps back.

"It's dangerous to pledge oaths when one does not intend on keeping them."

"I swore to protect you and I -"

"Failed when it counted most," she spat viciously and was surprised when he recoiled, as if he'd been struck. "You failed to protect me from *you*." They stared at one another silently until she approached him, cupping his face in her hands. "I release you from your oath," she whispered as she pressed her forehead against his. "I release you from whatever responsibility you believe you owe me. I release you, Adonijah."

"I hope one day you will forgive me." He wrapped his arms around her waist and held her close.

She couldn't help the tears that flowed disobediently down her face. He pulled his forehead from hers and wiped her cheeks.

"I will always love you," Adonijah squeezed her hand.

"And I you." Her bottom lip quivered. "But we are on two different paths now. Maybe in another life, we could have been happy together."

"If you will allow it," Adonijah looked into her glassy-eyes and sighed. "I would ask for you to let me continue to fight for you. I may no longer have your heart, but you will always have my sword."

Salome kissed his cheek and nodded in agreement. Before she completely lost all composure, she backed away from him and turned toward her bedroom door. She could feel his devastation, but she pressed onward, not daring to look back.

She closed the door and slipped into her bed, but sleep eluded her. She tossed and turned for hours; her mind restless. Adonijah was fresh in her thoughts, but deep down in her heart, she knew she'd made the right decision in ending whatever was going on between them. Saying she would always love him hadn't been a lie and that's what made her heart ache. If she had stayed in the Tree House Forest, if she hadn't gone on this journey, maybe if their paths had crossed then, they would have been happy roaming Adalore together. And months ago, that's exactly what she thought she wanted.

Turning over on her side facing the window with the moonlight kissing the waves of the Ignacia Sea, Salome replayed the conversation she and Crispin had earlier that evening. He said something that she overlooked at the time, but now she was itching to know more. He faced Niabi in the White Keep and discovered their sister had fire magic. And if she had magic that meant Salome should be able to communicate with her like she could with Jinn and Damaris.

Salome sat up and leaned her back against the cushioned headboard and chewed on the tip of her finger. Crispin would probably be furious if she reached out to Niabi, but she'd be lying if she denied the strong urge to see if it would work, and what her sister would say in response.

Maybe it was all the emotions of the day running wild through her mind, or the fact she just couldn't sleep and needed to talk to someone, but she closed her eyes and reached out to a door that was shrouded in darkness. As she approached, she saw withered flowers covering the archway around the door that belonged to Niabi. This was it. She shouldn't reach out, she shouldn't expose herself or her magic to the sister who was trying to hunt her down and exterminate her, but the temptation was too great.

"Niabi?"

Chapter Thirty

Niabi

Niabi couldn't sleep. All she could think about was Pash. She didn't care about the failure in Gomorrah, but what bothered her was that he had chosen his brother – his rebel brother – over her and their unborn child. She stepped onto her balcony and rested her elbows on the stone railing. The cold, gentle breeze creating goosebumps, the sounds of rushing water, and the barely audible music rising from the Night District, brought her immeasurable peace, though her heart was aching.

She loved Pash. She trusted him. But what if he never made it home to her? What would she do without him? What would she tell their child years from now, when he or she started asking questions?

"Niabi?"

Whipping around, facing her chamber doors, she unsheathed one of her knives, ready to defend herself from the intruder that had managed to sneak up behind her, but to her surprise, and confusion, no one was there. She looked around the balcony area but again came up empty.

She sheathed her dagger and then held her belly, as she inhaled deeply to calm herself down. She could have sworn she heard someone say her name, but she had been so stressed lately she must have just imagined it. But then she heard the soft voice echo in her head again, *"Niabi?"* and she knew she wasn't imaging anything. Who could possess the ability to speak to her through her thoughts? Although she was tempted to ignore whoever was reaching out to her, she decided to soothe the itch of curiosity, and opened the door to the unknown visitor.

"You seem to have me at a disadvantage," she cooed. *"You know who I am, but who are you?"*

"It worked," the voice replied. Niabi detected excitement and hesitancy from whoever was contacting her.

"You seem surprised."

At first, Niabi didn't think the voice was going to respond, but finally, she heard her say, *"You sound so much like her."*

Niabi cocked her head in confusion. *"Like who?"*

"Our mother."

The queen gasped. *"Salome? How are you doing this?"*

"You aren't the only one that possesses magic, sister."

Niabi smirked. The only way she would know about her magic was if Crispin had been reunited with her. *"And how is our dear brother doing?"*

"Alive," Salome's voice held a bite to it. *"No thanks to you."*

"Clearly there's a reason you've gone through the trouble of reaching out to me, Salome." She admired her sister's boldness, but instead of verbally sparring with Salome, Niabi was more curious to understand why she had reached out to begin with. *"So tell me, what do you want from me?"* Her aggressive question was met with silence. After a few moments, Niabi asked again. *"What do you want, Salome?"*

"I don't know," Salome whispered. *"I needed to talk to someone."*

Niabi laughed. *"So you reached out to me? Your enemy?"*

"I saw your past." That caught Niabi off guard. *"I saw what our father did to you and I'm sorry -"*

"Sorry?" Niabi interrupted with a hiss. Her throat tightened as she fought the tears bubbling within her. *"What are you sorry for? Are you sorry the man you called father was cruel and wicked? Are you sorry for looking into my past and seeing how I became your monster? Why are you sorry?"*

"I'm sorry for what happened to you."

"No, you're not." Niabi shook her head, her left hand ignited, and it took great effort to extinguish it. *"You pity me, and there is no greater insult than that."*

"Niabi-"

"What did Damaris show you?"

"How do you know it was Damaris who showed me your past?"

"She is the Oracle of Myr. Or have you already forgotten, I too, dwelled in the Scarlet Citadel?"

"She showed me how father stole your birthright. How he forced you to leave the Isles of Myr and forced you to marry for his gain. I saw how father treated you."

"Did Damaris show you how the monster was born?" Niabi gripped the balcony banister, dragging her fingernails across to soothe her anger. *"Did she show you the night Dichali was murdered?"*

"No."

Niabi saw Dichali's face, his warm smile, the dimples he passed to Rollo. The gravity of everyone she had lost consumed her, crushing her, until she felt as if her heart would burst. Cradling her swollen belly, she straightened, determined to make her sister see the truth. Why she desired for Salome to see this moment in her grief-filled history, she didn't understand, but she was dead set on her truth being made known.

"How does your magic work?" Niabi asked.

"I can communicate mentally with magic wielders and the departed."

"Memories? If I allow you access, can you see my memories?"

"Yes."

"Then I will show you what tipped the scales, sister." Niabi made her way into her bedroom and sank into her mattress. A light breeze whirled around the room as she closed her eyes.

"Despite Issachar's intentions, I loved my husband deeply, and when our son, Rollo, was born, my desire for the White Throne vanished. I had finally found my place in the world. Ruling by Dichali's side, raising our son to be his heir, accepted by the Andrago as one of their own: I was finally free, and I was finally happy."

Niabi focused on the memory she wanted to share with her sister, mentally opening a door to her traumatic past.

"Dichali kept his promise to me the day I agreed to be his bride and gifted me a magnificent stallion named Nagrom. It was normal for me to go for nighttime rides to clear my head and enjoy the chilly breeze. But one night, when I returned from a late-night ride, I entered our tent and found three assassins making their way toward my sleeping husband and our two-year-old son.

"I unsheathed my knives and screamed for Dichali to wake up. As soon as his eyes opened, he grabbed the knife he had tucked underneath his pillow. I leapt for our son, slitting the throat of the assassin hovering over his crib. Dichali managed to kill one of his attackers, but the second was far too quick for my husband to defend himself. It was in that brief moment, that I realized, I wouldn't be able to save him.

"It all happened so fast. Dichali had taken a blade to the chest by the time the Andrago guards rushed in to arrest the last assassin.

"Tala grabbed my screaming son from his crib, as I sprinted to Dichali and held him in my arms, covered in his blood. His bronze face was draining of color and even though I beckoned for a healer to come at once, my husband reached up and turned my face to meet his gaze."

"It's alright," Dichali whispered.

"Stay with me, Dichali. Stay with me." Niabi sobbed. "I'm so sorry. Please don't leave me."

He weakly pulled her toward him, kissing her forehead. "I will see you again, my love, in the next life. Take care of our son."

"No. Dichali, please, please don't leave me."

She shook him several times when his eyes closed, but despite her screaming and crying, there was nothing she could do. He was gone. She wanted to sit there, holding his lifeless body until she woke up from the nightmare. She rocked him, pressing kisses against his forehead, softly singing Andrago lullabies in his ear.

"My queen," Tala crouched beside her, tears slipping down his cheeks. "My queen, you need to let him go."

"Where is my son?" Niabi didn't bother looking in his direction as she stroked her blood-stained fingers through Dichali's long, black hair.

"He is outside with my wife." Tala slipped his hand around her forearm, finally drawing her attention. "You must let him go, so the healers may prepare his body."

Her bottom lip quivered. "I can't."

"My queen -"

"If I let him go, then it'll be real," she bit back her sobs. "I can't, Tala. I can't let him go."

Tala squeezed her arm gently. "Niabi -"

An Andrago guard slipped into the tent and cleared his throat for permission to speak. Tala kept eye contact with Niabi as he said, "Speak."

"What would you have us do with the assassin?"

All of Niabi's grief turned molten and a fire blazed within her. "Where is he?"

"We have him subdued in the gathering tent, Your Majesty."

Niabi tore her gaze from the Andrago warrior and fixed her attention to Tala. "Take me to him."

"Niabi-"

"Now!"

Reluctantly, Tala led her to the gathering tent and upon entering, she ordered the room to be cleared. Once everyone had left, she and Tala stared upon the remaining assassin and her heart shattered. It wasn't a stranger who had killed her husband, but it was one of his best friends and most trusted soldier.

“Chua?” Niabi gasped as she glared at the familiar face tied to a post in the middle of the room. "Why?"

When Chua didn't respond, Tala growled, "Your queen asked you a question."

Chua spat on the ground before Niabi's feet. "She is *not* my queen."

Before Tala could react, Niabi unsheathed her knives and stabbed Chua in his right shoulder joint. "Why did you kill your king?" she gritted her teeth, beginning her interrogation.

The traitor screamed but refused to answer her, so she took her second dagger and pierced his other shoulder. Holding onto both hilts as his blood spilled down his arms, she said in a low, predatorial voice, "I will destroy you, piece by piece, until I am satisfied. Why did you kill your king? Why did you kill your friend?"

"We were ordered to," Chua hissed in breathless gasps.

"Ordered by who?"

Whimpering, and taking too long to answer her, she retrieved one weapon from his body and stabbed him above the knee. "Who ordered you to assassinate Dichali? Who ordered you to murder my son?" she whispered in his ear.

"Your father," he shouted. "Your father ordered their assassinations!"

Breath stolen, she quickly recovered, twisting the knife still piercing his shoulder. "Why did he order them to be killed?"

Broken, with sweat and blood dripping down his body, Chua confessed. "We were supposed to kill all three of you. Your father didn't want you or your son trying to claim your birthright. He has never forgotten how you disrespected him the day you agreed to be Dichali's wife."

"You are Andrago. Why do my father's bidding?"

"He promised I would be king, if I obeyed."

Pushing the knife above his knee deeper, relishing in his grunts and screams, she asked, "How long have you served Issachar?"

"He hired us to kill Prince Antilles," he gasped, trying to catch a breath amid the torture. "He didn't want you marrying him. He didn't want the West to support your claim to his throne."

Another betrayal. *"You* killed Antilles?"

Chua nodded, "Those were your father's orders."

Tala stood several feet from them, quiet, his eyes filled with anger and confusion. But Niabi was not done. Not even close. Chua was an extension of Issachar and she would send him a message. One the king would not soon forget.

"Is that all?" She met Chua's weary eyes.

He furiously bobbed his head. "That is everything. I swear it."

Niabi pulled the knife from his shoulder and slammed the blade above his other knee, summoning an ear-piercing scream from him.

"I told you everything!" Chua wailed. "I told you everything I know!"

"I believe you," Niabi acknowledged in a maliciously sweet voice.

Chua's bottom lip quivered, "But you stabbed me. I swore I told you everything."

Niabi leaned close to him, her hands gripping the hilts of her knives, and whispered, "You stole from me. Not once, but twice. You are a traitor, a liar, and a murderer. I promise your death will not be quick. I will bathe in your blood and let the vultures feast on whatever is left of your corpse."

Chua's gaze darted to Tala who did not move to stop their queen from furthering her merciless quest. "Please. Tala, please help me-"

"Beg all you wish," she interrupted his cries with a hateful grin. "No one can save you from me."

Endless screams echoed through the night across the Andrago kingdom. It was rumored, Chua's unearthly howls were heard for miles, as Niabi tore him limb from limb, slowly and methodically. Once the traitor was nothing more than a pile of flesh and bones, she and Tala left the tent. The sun had risen and mirrored the blood red appearance she was sporting.

"The Red Sun," Tala muttered. "The universe mourns the loss of our king."

Niabi shielded her eyes from the sun's glare. "I swear on the blood of my husband, I will destroy my father and everything he holds dear. He will not escape my wrath."

"My queen?" Tala turned to her.

"I am now the monster he always feared me to be." Niabi stared at her hands and tattered clothes covered in so much blood, she wasn't sure what the original color of her dress had been. "Take what is left of the traitor and send it to Issachar with a missive attached."

"What should the note say?" he asked.

"That I will not rest until I claim his head from his body."

Once the memory she cared to share with Salome had come to an end, she forced her sister out of her thoughts and back to the present moment.

"Niabi..." Salome started but either couldn't or wouldn't finish that statement.

"My quarrel has never been with you or our brother," Niabi cut her off. *"All I ever wanted, all I still want, is to live my life in peace. To raise the babe growing within me, away from war and the political dance of the throne."*

"You are with child?"

"I am." Niabi knew better than to reveal so much to her enemy, but despite the warnings blaring in her head, she ignored them. *"And I wish this child could have the peace I was denied. Can you not understand that?"*

"Peace?" Salome's voice was soft and shattered Niabi's heart. *"How can you possibly have peace after what you've done? After the lives you stole?"*

"Our father was cruel, wicked, and selfish," Niabi growled. *"He wouldn't have hesitated to eliminate someone whether they posed a threat or not. You remember him as your protector, your kind and doting father, but that's not who he was. Not really. Had he lived long enough to see you now, he would have sold you to whoever best suited him. Whatever would advance his power, his crown, his throne, and he wouldn't have thought twice about you, once you were gone. He never loved any of us. Had I not helped Lykos in the quiet of night to study, father would have deemed him inadequate and found some way to remove him from the line of succession.*

"Issachar hated me because of my gender. He hated me because I was smarter, faster, stronger, and bolder than Lykos. He hated me and never hid it. He never said one kind word to me. Never held me, never comforted me, never told me he cared for me. I was the stain on his legacy and a threat to his name.

"Little did our father know that he was the monster, and in his paranoia, anger, and hatred, he created something much, much worse. He molded me into the vengeful and powerful creature that I am. I will not apologize for what I did because I do not hold one inkling of regret."

"But Mother and our brothers did not deserve to be collateral damage in your hostile takeover." Niabi could hear the pain and sorrow in Salome's quiet voice and it tugged at her heart. Her motherly instinct to wrap her arms around her sister and comfort her took her by surprise.

"You of all people should understand that usurpers cannot live." Niabi reminded her of the way of rulers and leaders.

"We were children."

"Children that grew into vengeful adults." Niabi braided her hair, taking a deep breath of the cool breeze that danced around her room. *"Again, that is something you should be well aware of, Salome. I did what I needed to do to ensure my reign, to ensure my son's future reign."*

"And yet your son is dead." The words stung, but Salome was right. Rollo was dead. Niabi had failed to keep him safe.

"Because you lived, he no longer could." The words tasted bitter even as thoughts. *"Again, I ask you one last time. What do you want from me?"*

No answer came and the hollowness in her head confirmed whatever magical door her sister opened to communicate with her, had been slammed shut. Niabi felt empty, drained. She had not allowed herself to relive the day Dichali died, but after sharing it with her enemy, she knew there'd be no resting for her that night. She had more questions than answers when it came to her siblings. She might never know why Salome really reached out to her, she might never know what it was her sister wanted from her, but what she couldn't do was dwell on it. Slowly, she would begin to see Salome as her sister instead of her enemy, and it would make it that much harder to kill her when the time came.

Chapter Thirty-One

Crispin

Crispin hadn't slept so peacefully in weeks. When he woke that morning, his drool was on the red velvet couch where he and Salome had been sitting and swapping stories. He must have fallen asleep while talking to her, obviously more tired than he originally thought. Being on the run from countless enemies had finally caught up with him.

Crispin rubbed his eyes with the heels of his palms, hungrier than ever. He could smell the aroma of freshly baked bread in his room and was thrilled when he remembered what Salome told him about Jacobi the baker. He not only survived the Shadows' massacre, but he had joined their forces and now headed their kitchens. His mouth watered at the thought of sinking his teeth into freshly baked goods, instead of the jerky and dried fruits, Leeondris had sent with them. As if just thinking of food caused it to manifest before him, a knock on the door with a soldier holding a tray of food, put his growling stomach at ease.

He knew there would be countless meetings he would have to attend, and there were dozens of people he wanted to see after weeks apart, but he craved to have a moment to wander the ancient castle alone. He hadn't been by himself in a long time, and before all the chaos was unleashed, and battle plans were formulated, he was determined to have a private moment.

In the quiet of his room, his mind kept flashing back to the sight of Salome standing on the opposite side of the bridge in front of the keep. She was alive. And not only alive, but in one piece. The Thrak hadn't broken her. Before he could even think, he was sprinting to her, tears streaming down his cheeks. It was a memory he would always cherish.

Once he'd had his fill of baked goods, fruit, and meat, Crispin slipped out of his chambers and wandered the halls. Grey stone hallways, red runner carpets eaten by moths, dusty candelabras, and tattered tapestries ushered him down the corridor. On one side of the hall were windows facing the sea, on the other, doors that led to bedrooms. Weaving up and down countless halls, Crispin found himself in what was once known as the largest library in existence. Scrolls, texts, and leather-bound tomes filled with ancient tales and historical accounts of the ancestors of the old world, were stored on hundreds of shelves that spanned from the stone floors up to the dome glass ceiling. There were a few cracks in the ceiling, but nothing too grand to have caused any true damage to the treasured texts.

Memories of helping his mother in the White Keep's library and archives room put a smile on his face. What his mother would have given to stand in this dilapidated room of knowledge.

Running his pointer finger along one of the wooden shelves spurred a tornado of dust to swirl around him, drawing a sneeze from him that echoed throughout the chamber.

"Good morning, my friend." The warm, familiar voice startled Crispin. "I was hoping our paths would cross again." Heru stood with his arms clasped behind his back, a smile on his face.

Crispin grinned and bounded across the space to embrace the Prince of Numbio. "It is good to see you, Heru."

"And you." Heru patted Crispin's back. His eyes were bloodshot, and he looked as if sleep had eluded him for quite some time.

"Are you unwell?" Crispin asked, unable to hide his concern.

Heru's smile didn't stretch far. "A lot has happened since we lost you in the Caverns of the Undead."

"Tell me."

For the next hour, Heru recounted his journey. He told Crispin all about Pyke, the Queen of the Wagura, how they escaped the caverns and how Shiek Ibrahim gave them shelter. Crispin's heart ached hearing stories about Zophar and his final weeks. When Heru told him of Rayma's allegiance to Memucan, which led to the end of their relationship, Crispin could feel how hurt his friend was by the tremor in his voice. What intrigued him the most was Rayma's tale of the Grim and how he demanded she take Pyke's place.

Crispin glanced at the texts scattered on the wooden table. "So, what are you looking for?"

Heru sighed, running his hand down his full, dark beard. "A way to save her from the Grim."

"She was sent to kill you." Crispin furrowed his brow in confusion. Why would Heru even care what happened to her?

"She saved my life in the Caverns of the Undead. I owe her."

Crispin folded his arms across his chest, leaning back in his creaky chair. "You still love her."

"I will always love her," Heru admitted.

"But?"

Heru looked at the prince. "I may not trust her anymore, but she doesn't deserve to wither away for a hundred years serving the Grim. If I can find a way to save her, to outwit the Grim, I will do it."

"You're an honorable man, Heru."

"Or maybe just a very stupid one."

Crispin chuckled, drawing a smile from his friend. As Heru continued to peruse the tomes he had pulled, Crispin's mind wandered to the little black book he'd lifted from Memucan's room the night he killed him in Northwind. Inaros, Rayma's brother, was frightened by it, claiming it was evil. Crispin and Rayma had their differences, but he hoped for Heru's sake, he could find a way to spare her a life with the Wagura. Hopefully, that wicked book didn't contain the secrets his friend needed.

"Have you seen her?"

"Who?" Crispin gave him his full attention.

"Rayma."

He nodded. "I passed Rayma and Inaros as they were reunited when we arrived yesterday."

"Ah yes." Heru clicked his teeth, looking indifferent. "The brother. I'm ashamed to admit, I thought she made him up to save face when she told me of her betrayal." He glanced across the table, a thousand questions swimming in his gaze. "How did you find him?"

"In the dungeons of the White Keep. Memucan had him imprisoned for stealing his book of black magic."

Heru smirked. "It seems you have stories to share."

Crispin gladly shared his encounters with the pirates of the *Shadow of Death*, his run in with Uri and Nezreen, his failure to save Neempo the Sovereign from his sister and her witch. He also didn't hold back any details on how he killed Memucan and tossed his book into the Obsidian Sea.

Had this all happened in a matter of weeks? It seemed like a lifetime ago he was battling Kubantu and scaling one of the towers of The Sisters.

"So," Heru said the word as if he was savoring the thought. "Memucan is dead?"

Crispin bobbed his head. The Southern Lord's face flashed before his eyes as he remembered sliding his blade across the old man's throat. "Yes."

"Then Rayma is finally free of her debt."

"And she has her brother back, after all these years." Crispin playfully wiggled his eyebrows. "She has no reason to make an attempt on your life now."

Heru snickered. "Love is a funny feeling. I want to hate her..."

"But you can't." Crispin thought of Rahab. That feisty, stab-happy pirate had stolen his heart and even though some days he felt like tossing her overboard, he couldn't help but love her.

"We'll find a way to save her," Crispin found himself promising when he noticed Heru's downcast glare.

"Thank you, my friend." Heru stood up, scraping the legs of his chair against the stone floors. "I have training with my men. You are always welcome to join us."

"Perhaps tomorrow. I have some people I need to see first."

"Of course." Heru pressed his hand to his chest. "Crispin."

Once the prince left, Crispin flipped through the manuscripts spread across the table. It was a long shot to defeat or even outwit a Grim when he believed you owed him a life debt, but Crispin couldn't bear the thought of Heru watching the woman he loved suffer. So, he scanned the texts, flipping through dusty page after dusty page, hoping to find a shred of hope to give his friend. But after an hour of searching, he came up empty-handed. Maybe Inaros would know of a way, since he trained with Memucan years ago, and had been in possession of the black book of magic.

He let out a defeated sigh as he dragged his hands down his face. He was exhausted. Mentally and physically. And he was hungry. As he contemplated raiding the kitchen for more of Jacobi's freshly baked pastries, he heard footsteps approaching.

"I should have known you'd be hiding in the last place I'd look for you." Salome leaned against one of the bookcases with an impish grin.

"Ah, but you did find me, so not the best hiding place after all," he smirked.

"Speaking of hiding," she welcomed herself to the chair Heru had been using and kicked her boots onto the table. "I just met the most interesting lady pirate with blue hair."

By the look on her face, he knew she was well aware of who Rahab was to him, and instead of denying it, he readily confessed.

"You're too nosy for your own good," he rolled his eyes.

"She's pretty," Salome smiled. "I especially appreciate a woman who loves a dagger."

"I told her you'd like that ruby knife of hers."

"Does she know how to wield it?"

"Too well."

Salome laughed and he hadn't realized until that moment, just how much he'd miss the sound of his sister's voice. How comforting it was when his mind was foggy.

"Do you like her?" he asked.

Salome's stare gave nothing away. "Do *you* like her?"

He nodded, clasping his hands between his knees as he leaned forward. "Very much."

"Is she to be my future queen?"

The question threw him. By the smirk on Salome's face, he knew she was enjoying her teasing far too much.

"Salome," he warned.

She lifted her hands in surrender. "Alright, alright. I yield."

"Never thought I'd hear you say those words," he teased.

Salome's smile faded.

"What is it?"

"Rahab lit up at just the mention of your name." Salome reached for his hand and squeezed. "If you like her, I like her. I look forward to getting to know her as my future sister and my future queen."

"She cannot bear children," he whispered as Salome stood, causing her to stop in her tracks. "How can I be king and not have an heir?"

Salome was silent for a moment. "Would that hinder you from making her your wife?"

"Of course not," Crispin tried not to sound offended.

"Then why -"

"Perhaps you should claim the White Throne," he interrupted. "Produce an heir, keep the House of the White Wolf alive."

She crouched before him, forcing him to look into her eyes. "I do not want the throne. If she cannot bear an heir, then adopt a child or name a successor. You are not the first king to do so, and you won't be the last."

"Would our people accept my heir, if he is not of my blood?"

"Zophar wasn't our kin, but no one could deny that we were family." Salome once again stood, his gaze following her movements. "Your heir will continue our legacy because *you* say so, not because of what others may believe. We are wolves, Crispin, not sheep."

Crispin smiled at her and took her hand and kissed it. "You think Zophar would have approved of Rahab?"

"Absolutely," she grinned. "You need a woman who can kick your ass once in a while."

"You've always had the mouth of soldier."

Salome bowed and winked. "I never was one for the flittering life of the ladies of court, and by the looks of it, your wife-to-be has a fouler mouth than me."

Crispin barked out a laugh. Heaven help the Kingdoms of Adalore with Rahab for his queen and Salome as his right hand. None of the other kings would stand a chance against them.

Chapter Thirty-Two

Salome

Salome hadn't been able to shake Niabi's memories from her head in over a week. The horror her sister endured was unfathomable and when she slammed their connection shut, she was instantly bathed in guilt. Part of her wanted to hate Niabi, but the other half of her not only sympathized, but understood.

"You do remind me of Niabi." Her grandmother, Nym, had been right.

How could she continue the bloodshed after all the losses both sides had suffered?

Her days were filled with activities: training at night with the Bellator brothers, spending time with Crispin, getting to know the pirates her brother cared about, and preparing for Hanzo and Oifa's wedding to unite the Mountain Men, once and for all. But none of those duties weighed her down. The incredible heaviness she felt, stemmed from harboring her secret conversation with Niabi, and withholding it from Crispin. Although she knew he would angrily disapprove of her actions, something deep within her heart and soul desperately wanted to reach out to her older sister again.

Why, she wasn't quite sure. Maybe to check on her welfare after sharing her dark memory. Maybe to see if she could glean any information that would help further their war. Or maybe, she just wanted to get to know Niabi better, and that was the most frightening reason of all.

She had questions. Lots of questions. But there was no one alive that could answer them, so she reached out to the one person she knew would be honest with her about Niabi.

"Lykos?" Salome closed her eyes as she searched for her eldest brother. *"Lykos, are you there? I need to speak with you."*

The sound of the soldiers sparring in the bailey outside of her bedroom window and the cooks and attendants baking and decorating for the wedding that evening faded and was replaced with the chirping of songbirds and the gentle ripple of a stream. Her eyes flashed open and she saw Lykos standing by the largest wisteria tree she'd ever laid eyes on.

"Hello, Little Wolf," Lykos smiled and the warmth of his voice overwhelmed her.

She took a tentative step forward, closing the gap between them, and took a moment to look around paradise. Grass as far as the eye could see, a light breeze blowing the wisteria branches around them, the sunlight beaming just right casting a halo over Lykos, making him appear otherworldly.

"Where are we?" She finally managed to find her voice.

"The After."

"It's so quiet here," she met his gaze.

"That is called peace," he motioned for her to join him on a white stone bench. "Tell me, Salome, what do you need to speak to me about?"

Once she was seated next to him, she got a whiff of his familiar scent, and fought the urge to melt into his arms like she used to do as a child. Had he lived to see her grow, she was positive he would have continued their secret sparring lessons until she was better than him. He would have been a great king had he had the chance.

"Salome?" He gently squeezed her hand, ending her nostalgia. "Mortals, even a Hunter, do not have much time in the After. I suggest you tell me what you came here for."

"You always knew?"

"About you being the Hunter?" Lykos nodded. "Harbona recognized your mark and told me. He made me promise to protect you at all costs and to keep your identity a secret from father."

"Harbona never told our father?" Salome was surprised the Seer withheld that information from the king he had sworn to advise.

"There is a lot you do not understand about our father." Lykos' brown eyes held a sadness in them that made her want to bear hug him and tell him everything would be alright. "Had our father known of your mark, had he known of your potential magic, I'm not exactly sure what he would have done, but I know without a doubt, he would have used you for his own purpose."

"Niabi said the same thing."

"So, you've spoken to her?" He smiled.

"Tell me about her," Salome whispered, as if she didn't want anyone to overhear, even though they were the only two beings in the area.

"What exactly do you wish to know?"

"Was she always so... vengeful?"

Lykos shook his head. "No. She wasn't born that way. She was created." He met her eager gaze. "Niabi is many things, some of them are not good, but she has suffered much, and loved greatly. Her motivation has always been to protect her loved ones." He sighed, his fingers tugging on the purple wisteria flowers. "She should have been queen all along."

"Are you saying what she did to our family was justified?" Salome spat indignantly.

"Justified in her mind, yes, but wrong nonetheless." Lykos looked at her. "Why are wars started?"

"What?"

"What is the motive for war?" He rephrased the question, a glint in his eyes.

"Power, revenge, money, defense," she listed, and he nodded his head.

"And which of these do you believe fueled Niabi's grab for Northwind?" Lykos stood and strolled around the tree with hands clasped behind his back. "She had willingly given up her birthright to go to the Isles of Myr. She once again gave up her claim to the throne by agreeing to marry King Dichali and become his queen. She showed no signs of being the power-hungry usurper our father feared her to be, and yet, he waged a war against her. So, I ask again. What motivated Niabi?"

Power clearly wasn't the right answer, nor was money. Salome rubbed her hands against her face, "She sought to avenge those who were taken from her. She sought to defend and protect those she still had, against our father."

"You see her as the villain, but she is not so different from you or me."

"I'm not much different in my desire for revenge." Salome stood up and made her way to Lykos. "I've killed in anger because of losing someone I loved dearly. I've joined Crispin in gathering an army to march against Niabi, who lawfully is the true heir to the White Throne. Are Crispin and I..." Salome sucked in a breath, keeping tears at bay. "Are Crispin and I the villains?"

"No one is the villain in their own story, Little Wolf," Lykos cupped her face in his hands.

"I'm the Hunter," her bottom lip quivered. "I am meant to protect the lives of the innocent. I am supposed to defeat Niabi."

"Perhaps, she is not the one you were meant to defeat. Perhaps, she is the one you were meant to save."

"What?"

"Someone is calling you. Your time here is up, Little Wolf." Lykos wrapped his arms around her and squeezed so tightly she gasped for breath. "Your friends are looking for you."

"But I do not know what I am supposed to do," she pulled back from him, staring into his kind, brown eyes.

"You will, when the time is right."

He kissed her forehead and before she could protest, she was sitting on her bed in Oakenshire, as someone knocked on her bedroom door.

"Salome?"

"Yes?" She scurried to answer the door, unsure of how long the visitor had been knocking.

She opened it to Kai and the twins, Rosalina and Seraphina, who had their hands filled with items to prepare her for the wedding festivities. They didn't appear to be frustrated or worried that she'd taken too long to answer their call, so they must have just arrived.

"Is all that necessary?" Salome motioned to their soaps, perfumes, brushes, and towels.

"Did you think you could attend a wedding in your fighting leathers?" Rosalina chuckled as she pushed past Salome to begin setting up.

Seraphina smirked, "I, for one, cannot wait to see you dance."

"Dance?" Salome scoffed. "I don't dance."

"Oh, you will tonight, my lady." Seraphina teased as she helped her twin finish setting up the trinkets and tinctures. "It is expected that the host and hostess of the wedding, dance with the bride and groom."

Salome crossed her arms over her chest and laughed. "You think Oifa and Hanzo are going to dance? They don't care about tradition."

"Ah, but the rest of the kingdoms attending will, Your Highness," Rosalina turned to face Salome with a smile. "First, your bath. Then we will fix you up."

Knowing there was no resisting or fighting the Qata Vishna twins or getting past Kai leaning against the closed door, she nodded her head in agreement. If she was forced to be the center of attention at tonight's reception, she would look ravishing, if her friends had anything to say about it.

Her dress wasn't nearly as spectacular as the white silk gown she had worn to the Festival of Forbidden Fruit during her stay in the Isles of Myr, but it was beautiful, nonetheless. When she inquired why they chose the colors navy and white for her outfit, she was reminded they were her House colors. It sparkled like the night sky and even Salome had to admit she liked the feel of the off-the-shoulder, A-line gown.

The twins had pulled her wild curls back in a low bun befitting a royal hosting a wedding and did her make up subtly at her request. With her friends' approval, she made her way down to the renovated ballroom. Weeks earlier, what was overrun with vines, roots, and broken windows, was now plant free, cleaned, and decorated with hundreds of candles, wooden tables, and a designated place for people to dance.

Salome smelled the venison before she saw the magnificent spread Jacobi and his team had put together. His strength was in baking, but once tasked to prepare the feast for everyone staying at Oakenshire, the Westerner rose to the challenge and delivered a buffet kings would covet.

Over the next half hour, she greeted and chatted with guests, royal or not, and waited anxiously to see when her brother would be joining her. He had been ecstatic about attending a wedding, mostly because he loved a good party with food and ale, but he had yet to make his appearance, and it was nearing the time for the ceremony to begin.

"You look beautiful," King Kenji's voice caught her by surprise. "Oh, forgive me, Princess, I didn't mean to startle you."

She smiled at him, looking over his shoulder hoping Jinn was with him.

"My son isn't with me, I'm afraid."

For being as old as he was, Kenji didn't miss a thing. She squeezed his outstretched hand and allowed him to plant a kiss on the back of her hand.

"I'm so glad you could be here to witness the joining of the Mountain Men." She sounded so much like a politician she wanted to kick herself, but Kenji returned her smile and laughed.

"I wouldn't miss this for the world. If you could find a way to unite the tribes after a thousand years of turmoil, then I cannot wait to see what you will do next."

His kind words felt like a punch to the gut. Such a heavy burden – the expectations everyone would have of her was something she thought about often.

"I have offended you?" His eyes were filled with worry, and she shook her head.

"No, Your Highness, you did not offend me," she reassured him, patting his hand still clasping hers. "But there is something I wish to ask you."

"Ask me anything."

"You knew my father." A statement he agreed with. "How well did you know him?"

"If there is something specific about your father you wish to know," he whispered as guests wandered by, "then you may speak candidly."

If Jinn had half the discernment his father had, there would be no way she'd be able to hide anything from him. Not that she wanted to. She shook her head, freeing her thoughts of the prince and refocused on the king.

"Was my father a good man?" The question made her stomach flip. From what she'd learned of her father over the last couple of months, she already knew the answer to her question, but she had to know from a neutral third party who had personally known Issachar, if what she had learned was true. "Was he a good king?"

For the first time since meeting the Easterner, he wouldn't meet her line of sight. Everything seemed to be more interesting at the present moment than answering her question.

She was about to ask again when he finally spoke. "Your father was a strategic king and only pursued tactics that would strengthen his kingdom and further his stretch of power."

"Forgive me, Your Grace," Salome whispered, "but you did not answer my question."

Kenji sighed. "Your father was a good king. He was not a good man."

"How can someone be both?"

"Issachar was so consumed with being the mightiest king the North had ever seen that he forgot to nurture the ones who would come after him." The king led Salome to a table and sat down to relieve his aching feet. "He kept your people safe until the end."

"Do you think my sister is a monster?"

"Why do you ask me that question?" His curious gaze roved across her face.

"Above all else, I seek the truth, Your Majesty." Salome kept steady eye-contact, even though she was desperate to drop her gaze to keep him from seeing how vulnerable she felt. "Do you see Niabi as a villain?"

He took a moment to choose his words carefully, but then nodded his head. "Yes, I see her as a villain, not because of her motives, but how she handled her anger. If I were in her position, I would have sought revenge as well, but not at the price she paid."

"How else would she have defeated my father?"

"She could have rallied support from other kingdoms, staked her claim upon Northwind by the law of your ancestors, brought the King of Elisor's assassination to light -"

"With all due respect," she interrupted him. "Would you have listened to my sister, if she came before your throne accusing one king of assassinating another?"

Kenji stroked his long fingers through his white facial hair and shook his head. "I wish I could say I would have."

"But?"

"I suppose everyone can look back on their life choices and make all the right ones." The king pressed a hand to his chest, bowing his head slightly. "Forgive my judgment."

She reached over and grabbed his hand. "There is nothing to forgive. Thank you for your honesty."

"There you are!" Crispin rushed over to her, whisking curls from his face. "You need to get ahold of those Qata Vishna twins of yours, trying to, as they said, 'fix me up'. What does that even mean? Why do they have so many brushes?" As if he was just now noticing who his sister was with, he bowed slightly at the hip toward the King of Sakurai. "Your Highness, forgive my intrusion."

The old man waved him off, "It is I who have intruded on your sister long enough. Go enjoy yourselves." He smiled at Salome before she stood up and walked away with Crispin.

"What was that about?" he asked her once they distanced themselves.

She wasn't sure how to broach the topic of their sister's past with him, and minutes before Oifa and Hanzo's historic wedding wasn't the proper time, so she lied, which knotted her stomach.

"He was telling me all about Sakurai. They're a very interesting people." She looped her arms in her brother's. "Did you know Sakurai was the first kingdom Malachi the First established once he defeated Phlias?"

Crispin huffed out a laugh, "Forget I asked."

"You better be nice to me."

"Or what?" he teased.

"I'll tell Rosalina and Seraphina to rub kohl around your eyes."

"I don't know," he stopped and faced her, pointing at her eyes. "They might have used it all on you."

She swatted at his chest and laughed, but her face dropped when she looked at the dance floor and remembered what the twins had told her. "Did you know we're supposed to dance with the bride and groom after the ceremony?"

Crispin flashed her an encouraging smile and nudged her chin with his balled-up fist. "It's just swaying back and forth. Here, let me show you." He grabbed her hand and started dragging her to the dance floor, but she panicked and pushed him away.

"What are you doing?" she chastised him, trying to keep her voice low and composure collected, should anyone cast a glance their direction.

He extended his hand to her. "It's just you and me."

"You know I hate dancing."

"That's because you've never had the chance to dance with me." His cocky grin summoned a smile from her. "Dance with me."

Although she wanted to run from the room screaming, she couldn't deny her brother whatever he asked of her, so she bobbed her head and took his outstretched hand. He gently placed one hand on her waist and pulled her close.

"Must we be this close to one another?" she snarled.

"Let's hope you have better manners with Hanzo when the time comes," Crispin rolled his eyes. "Now, all we're going to do is sway back and forth."

Salome could feel the eyes of soldiers, guests, and attendants watching them as they slowly moved side to side, without music.

"Crispin, people are watching us."

"You're going to have to get used to that, *Princess*."

And he was right. They were royalty. Half of royal life was being watched by everyone around you.

"Chin up," he reminded her, and she straightened. "You're doing great."

"I feel silly."

"Why?"

"We're dancing and there's no music."

Crispin smiled, resting his chin against her forehead. He started humming a tune she hadn't heard in years. It was one their mother used to sing to them, one about a great sea monster and the men and women who united to defeat it. It had absolutely nothing to do with the wedding or dancing, but Crispin always had a lovely voice. She closed her eyes and rested her head against his chest, feeling the vibrations as he provided the music she lacked.

Dancing. They were dancing, just the two of them, before everyone in the hall, and for the first time in a long time, she didn't care what any of them were thought or said. It was as if the entire room disappeared, and she and her brother were finally at peace.

"Your Majesties."

Salome and Crispin looked up at Harbona who smiled at them. "It is time to begin."

Chapter Thirty-Three

Crispin

Crispin hadn't known the bride or groom long, but within five minutes of meeting them, two things were quite apparent. Oifa was as tenacious, as Hanzo was fearless. They would make a formidable team as King and Queen of a united Mountain Men tribe, if they didn't kill each other first.

This was also the first wedding Crispin had ever attended as an adult and it made him nervous that he was considered the host. He relied heavily on Harbona and Heru's guidance in how to behave, where to stand, how to greet people, and understand the order of festivities.

Once the hand tying ceremony was complete and vows exchanged, the music thrummed to life, signifying the start of the reception. Drinking, eating, dancing. All things Crispin whole-heartedly enjoyed.

After a couple of hours, he wasn't too proud to admit that he truly loved weddings, so much so that he tried convincing other guests not only to get married, but they should invite him to partake in the revelry.

As he looked around the grand hall filled with smiling faces, he couldn't help but wish Zophar was standing next to him, downing a pint of ale as he pointed a turkey leg at whoever he was talking to.

He spotted Salome dancing with King Kenji and beamed with pride at how happy she looked. She had grown in confidence and carried herself as true royalty. Her first dance with Hanzo after the ceremony was sweet to watch as they whispered back and forth and swayed around the dance floor. Her smile brightened the entire room.

His dance with Oifa on the other hand, was in a word: frightening. Not once did she smile. Crispin wasn't entirely sure if she knew how. Despite her answering his questions with one-word answers, he managed to survive the painful ordeal and proceeded to ask some of the older ladies who cooked, cleaned, and mended clothes for the entire camp, if they'd honor him with a dance. In fact, the prince spent most of his time on the dance floor, laughing, and for the first time in months, having a good time.

Crispin attempted to drag Rahab to the dance floor countless times over the span of the evening only to be met with a grumbled, "You're lucky I dressed for the occasion, princeling," before she continued her game of cards with the pirates.

He'd kissed the top of her head, admiring the form-fitting black dress she sported, and laughed at the thought that the foul-mouthed, cigar-smoking, gambling pirate was to be his wife and queen one day.

When he glanced around the room once more, he failed to spot his sister in the sea of jovial faces. But he did happen to notice Heru and Rayma slip out together and watched as Adonijah whispered something into Leoti's ear, before they found their way to the dance floor.

"Do you mind if I have the next dance, Prince Crispin?"

The melodic voice startled him from his shameless people-watching, and he turned to see a beautiful Immortal woman at his side. "It would be my honor, Lady...?"

She offered a tight-lipped smile as she accepted his outstretched hand and followed him to the dance floor. "My name is Lavena."

Crispin wrapped his arm around her. "I do not believe I have seen you in the halls or the bailey, my lady."

"I am an Ethereal, Prince Crispin, I am not designed for war."

"Yet here you are," he stared into her grey eyes, looking for any clue as to what she was thinking. "Who are you?"

"We met once a very long time ago." Lavena did not waver under his scrutinizing glare. "To keep my history brief, I was sent as an ambassador to Northwind, and I fell in love with your brother, Lykos. We were secretly married."

Crispin did his best to hide his surprise but failed miserably. "You and Lykos were married?"

"Before your sister attacked the White City, Lykos put me on a ship back to Caelestis. He wanted to ensure not only my safety, but the safety of our unborn daughter."

He stiffened and narrowed his eyes. "So, you're here to stake your daughter's claim to the White Throne."

Lavena shook her head, her expression giving nothing away. "You misunderstand. My daughter has no interest in claiming your ancestral throne. Her heart and duty now fully lie with the Immortals. She is planning to visit the Mainland after the war, and I wanted you to know about her, since she intends to journey to Northwind. She has so many questions about the White City and about her father, I thought maybe..."

"Maybe I could share some of my memories with her?" He picked up where she trailed off. When she nodded, he felt foolish. "Forgive me, my lady. I rushed to judgment when you reached out to me in peace. If there is ever anything I can do for you or my niece, consider it done."

"That is very generous of you, Prince Crispin."

"Crispin," he squeezed her hand. "You are my sister by marriage and shall be treated as such. You will always have a place in Northwind, should you ever desire it."

Lavena stared at him unabashedly. Whatever thoughts were running wild through her mind, she did not give away through her facial expression. "You remind me of him. There was not a person alive who did not love Lykos."

"Except Niabi," Crispin pointed out and was taken aback when she disagreed.

"No, I dare say, she loved him very much."

"She had him executed."

"If you are to be king, Crispin, there is one thing you will have to learn. It is ugly, but it is the truth." She spoke softly, but her words felt heavy on his soul. "In war there are casualties, familial and stranger alike. As a leader, you will be forced to make the difficult and often heartbreaking decision to put any who would jeopardize your reign to the sword." Lavena's grey eyes narrowed. "Lykos knew the cost of losing. Had he been able to defeat your sister, as much as he loved her, he would have had to put her down like any traitor to the crown."

"You make excuses for her treachery."

The Ethereal halted in place, keeping him rooted where he stood. "Are you not about to march an army to her gates and commit the same sins, my lord?"

"She and I are not the same," Crispin gritted his teeth. "We march to avenge my family's murders. To avenge Lykos' execution!" He angrily whispered, glancing around to see if anyone was watching their interaction. But no one noticed, far too jovial to spot a brewing storm.

"I will love your brother for the rest of my days. And I suspect, I will despise Niabi far longer than that." She slipped her cold hand against his face. "I have seen many kings come and go, Crispin. I have seen their hearts and their motives for why they war against their fellow man. Do not be so filled with pride that you justify your reason to battle your sister, and condemn her for the same."

Crispin lowered his voice, dipping his face closer to her pointy ear, "Are you asking me not to go to war?"

"The question is, are you prepared for the consequences of war?" She cocked her head to the side. "Are you prepared to see your friends fall in battle? Are you prepared to send word to the families of the fallen, that their loved ones will not be returning home? Are you prepared for your sister to claim your head should you fail to defeat her?"

The prince was short of breath and clutched at his collar, trying to loosen the top button. He had only thought of his victory over his sister – he did not once consider the consequences should he fail. It wouldn't just result in his own torment and execution, but for Salome, for Rahab, for all of their friends and allies; their lives too were at stake. Niabi would burn the known world to the ground, before she allowed any of them to escape her wrath.

He needed to find Salome. If anyone could talk him off the ledge of despair, it was her. Glancing around, he once again came up empty. He had almost forgotten he was dancing with Lavena until she spoke.

"You look ill, my lord. Do you need a glass of water?"

Crispin cleared his throat and noticed the song had ended, signifying their dance was over. He bowed. "Thank you for the dance, my lady, and for the stimulating conversation, but there are some matters I must tend to before the night is over."

Lavena barely managed to curtsy in time before Crispin beelined for the door. If he knew Salome, she'd be hiding somewhere no one would think to look. And then it hit him. He knew exactly where she'd be.

Chapter Thirty-Four

Rayma

Since arriving in Oakenshire, after the Battle of Gomorrah, Harbona set Rayma up in one of the largest rooms in the keep, where he said the apothecary had once been a thousand years ago. Whatever she needed to make her tonics, tinctures, ointments, and bandages, he provided. It was nothing like her shop back in Numbio, but after confessing to Heru about her ties to Lord Memucan and how she was supposed to assassinate him, she knew she would never be able to return to the apothecary in the southern lands. It had been the only place she'd felt safe and in control, and in the blink of an eye, it was gone.

Heru had made it clear their relationship was over and she understood why. But banishing her from her home? Where was she to go after the war was over? She survived the Caverns of the Undead, a run in with the Grim, held captive by Stormcrags, and even managed to keep her cool while healing the wounded as the soldiers battled the Thrak in Gomorrah, but she wasn't sure she would survive being labeled as a traitor and treated as an outcast. Everything she did for her people was for their betterment and even though the original goal was for her to get close to Heru, to hurt him, she secretly fell in love with him and the thought of being his wife, being his queen, brought her great joy. Together, they could continue to uphold the traditions of the Numbio, as well as protect and provide for them.

But that dream was just that. A dream.

And now all she could do was watch him from afar. How strange it was to have been so intimate with someone one minute and the next, be total strangers. She would watch him as he trained with the Numbio soldiers in the bailey. She would watch him as he interacted with the other leaders as they spoke of battle strategies. She even watched him during the wedding festivities, as he twirled with other women on the dance floor and laughed and drank with his fellow men.

Not once did he glance her way and the realization that she meant nothing to him anymore, drove her to the point of insanity. The pain of his rejection was excruciating, and she wished she could concoct a potion to ease her broken heart.

Inaros plopped down in the chair next to her and she smiled at him, thankful he interrupted her self-deprecating thoughts. When she saw him cross the bridge into Oakenshire, she thought she was seeing a ghost. The entire time she served Memucan, a part of her suspected Inaros had been executed years ago, and the old man had been using her love for her brother as leverage without any real proof he was still alive. So, to see him, scrawny, but alive, walking toward her that day, made her forget all her troubles with the Grim and Heru, and was filled with immeasurable relief.

They'd spent the last couple of weeks catching up on the years that had been stolen from them. He spent all his free time helping her in her medical ward. He willingly prepared salves and rolled bandages to prepare for the upcoming battle with the North. She was grateful Inaros was with her during the wedding, otherwise, she might have spent the entire evening alone.

He handed her a glass of wine and sipped his own, eyes fixed on her. "You are awfully quiet tonight, Rayma. What troubles you?"

She wished she could tell him everything about what happened in the Caverns of the Undead and the business concerning the Grim wanting her to replace Pyke, the Queen of the Wagura, she had killed to free her companions, but she didn't want to worry him. She'd just gotten him back and if she was on limited time, she wanted their time to be well spent and filled with happy memories.

Every spare moment she had was spent researching thousands of tomes and scrolls in the dilapidated library, searching for clues on how she could defeat or outwit the Grim, but so far, came up empty-handed. Night after night she dreamed of the Wagura and how she stabbed Pyke and how she killed Bantu, Memucan's spy, in self-defense. How she wished, she could go back to a simpler time in her life, but then she realized she never had a simple life. Maybe, simplicity wasn't meant for her.

"Rayma?"

"I'm sorry," she straightened in her chair, meeting Inaros' gaze. "I am afraid I am not very good company this evening."

"What's wrong?" his brow furrowed.

"I shouldn't be here celebrating." Her eyes latched onto Heru as he laughed at something a lady standing next to him said. She forced herself to look away to keep from tearing up. "I should be making more salves."

Inaros caught her staring at Heru. "How long have you been in love with our prince?"

She wanted to lie. She wanted to deny his keen observations but the truth was, she was tired. Tired of lying. Tired of living in the dark.

"He asked me to marry him after the war."

Inaros' eyes widened but before he could say anything, she lifted her hand to silence him.

"Memucan instructed me to get close to him. To..." she took a deep breath. This was harder to confess to him than she thought it would be. "I was to make him fall in love with me and once I had his unwavering trust, at Memucan's command, I would slip him a poisoned drink and..."

"You were going to assassinate him?" Inaros whispered, leaning closer to her.

"He promised if I did his bidding that he would release you from prison." Tears welled in her eyes, and she swiped them away before they rolled down her cheeks. "But when it came time to do the deed, I couldn't. I saved him from the Wagura -"

"The Wagura?" He gasped. "You were in the Caverns of the Undead and lived?"

"I killed their queen to save the Numbio trapped inside the caves. But the Grim came to me. He wants me to pay him back for the years and souls I stole from him. He is demanding I be their new queen for one hundred years or give up Heru for a shortened sentence." Rayma lowered her head and stared the hands she used to kill, when she took an oath to heal and save. "I confessed everything to Heru once we were out of the caverns."

"You confessed to treason, and he let you live?"

She nodded. She searched for Heru one more time, and found him dancing with the woman who had made him laugh. “He told me when this war is over, I will no longer have a home with the Numbio.”

Inaros grabbed her hand and squeezed. "You will always have a home with me, wherever that may be. You will not be alone, and we will find a way to defeat the Grim- "

"There's no way to defeat the Grim," she interrupted, letting out a whimper. "I've already tried finding a way out. There is no hope for me, brother."

"That is not necessarily true." The voice startled the siblings and when they looked up, Harbona was standing on the opposite side of their table with the beautiful woman Heru had just been dancing with. Now that she was closer, she realized she was an Immortal like the Seer, but that didn't ease her gut-wrenching jealousy.

"I don't know what you're talking about, sir," Rayma attempted to deny anything the Seer might have overheard.

"You do not need to be frightened, my dear." Harbona motioned toward the open seats, and she reluctantly waved for them to sit. "Prince Heru has already come to me and Lady Lavena with your predicament and I believe we can help you."

Rayma's narrowed eyes darted to Lavena. "And why would *you* want to help me?"

The Immortal woman tilted her head to the side, a curious but unreadable expression crossed her stoic face. "Rude or not, no one deserves to be indebted to the Grim."

Rayma should have been embarrassed that Lavena called her out for her tone, but she wasn't ashamed. She had nothing left to lose. "Perhaps your time would be better spent with the prince than helping me."

Harbona exchanged a confused look with Lavena. "Rayma, this is Lady Lavena, wife of the late Prince Lykos of Northwind and mother of the future Eldaar. Prince Heru went to her for guidance to help you outwit the Grim because she is the most knowledgeable among the Ethereals.

"I assure you," Lavena added, "there is nothing romantic transpiring between me and your prince."

Rayma felt foolish. Her cheeks burned with embarrassment, and she wished she could take back every word she spewed in jealousy. "I..." she cleared her throat. "I apologize for my tone, Lady Lavena."

"Now that you do not look as if you are going to rip my heart out," Lavena smirked with a twinkle in her grey eyes, "I believe there is the Grim to contend with."

"What can I do?" Rayma asked, hope filled her heart for the first time in ages.

"There is only one thing you can do," the Immortal woman clasped her hands together and set them on her lap. "You will have to sail to Caelestis to live out the remainder of your days."

"What?" the healer's mouth dropped.

"The Grim's reach does not stretch past mortal lands. In Caelestis, you will be able to live out your days until age claims you," Harbona explained.

"But even if I agreed to go to Caelestis, once I die, won't I have to deal with the Grim then?" Her eyes bounced between the Ethereals.

"The Grim makes deals with desperate souls to prolong their lives and once they pass, they must pay off their debt in servitude." Lavena explained. "When mortals pass, they go to the After where Death dwells."

"But the Grim demanded I make a choice. Either I serve him for one hundred years or offer Heru for twenty years as a Wagura."

Harbona leaned forward and whispered, "Have you agreed to either? Have you made an official deal with the Grim?" His eyes were frighteningly serious, and she immediately shook her head in response.

"I have made no deals," she reassured the Immortals. "He hasn't come back to me for an answer. What do I tell him when he returns?"

Lavena smiled. "I have already taken care of the Grim; he will not be visiting you before our departure to Caelestis."

"How?"

"When Prince Heru told me of your predicament, I shielded you from his sight."

"Can you just shield me from the Grim permanently?" Rayma's heart soared. "So I do not have to leave my home?"

Her questions were met with a sympathetic silence, and it extinguished her tiny spark of hope.

"I am afraid," Lavena delivered the final blow, "my abilities only work where I am. I can shield you from prying eyes, but it does not make you invisible. The Grim will not be able to find you while I am here, but once I leave for Caelestis, he will be able to track you down and he will come for you."

Rayma took a deep breath as Inaros snatched her hand in his. "Will she have to go alone?"

"Inaros," Rayma chastised, knowing what he was really asking. "You can't give up everything to follow me. I won't allow it."

"You are welcome to join us," Lavena offered, ignoring Rayma's protests.

"Then I shall go with you." Inaros said without hesitation. "Where she goes, I go."

"Inaros!" Rayma cried. "I can't let you give up your life to follow me."

"I haven't been there to protect you, Rayma," her brother met her teary gaze with one of his own. "I haven't been there during your loneliest days, but I can make up for it now. You will not be alone. Ever."

A tear slipped down her cheek as she lunged for her brother, wrapping her arms around his neck. "Thank you."

Someone behind her cleared his throat and when she turned around, she came face to face with Heru. By the sorrow in his eyes, she knew he was aware of what had to happen. Why he looked forlorn was beyond her. He'd banished her from returning to Numbio, and as reluctant as she was to leave the mainland for a land filled with angelic beings, she now had a place to call home when the war was over.

"Would it be alright, if we spoke privately?" Heru asked.

Without a second thought, she released her brother and stood up. As they walked away, the prince rested his fingers against the small of her back and led her through the crowded hall until they slipped out of the room unnoticed. She hadn't felt his touch in weeks and just the graze of his fingertips sent her soaring.

Once they entered her medical wing, surrounded by everything she had control over, she faced him as he shut the wide, wooden door. It took him a few seconds to turn around and look her in the eye, but when he did, every single wall she'd built up since their break-up, came crashing down. He was broken, and he wasn't even trying to hide it. Tears flowed down her face and there was nothing she could do to stop them. And for the first time in her life, she didn't want to compose herself. They stood in silence, staring at one another as they cried. A tightness in her chest and knot in her throat kept her from speaking and even though she wanted to rush to him and kiss his pain away, she stayed rooted to her side of the apothecary.

"Thank you," she finally managed to whisper.

"For what?"

"The Immortals told me you sought them out for aid in dealing with the Grim. It seems I will now have a place to go when the war is over."

"Rayma." He took a step forward, his voice trembled.

"It's alright." She stepped back, maintaining distance between them. "I'll be alright." But she knew that was only a half-truth. The truth was she would forever miss him.

"I will visit you in Caelestis."

"Why?"

He seemed taken aback, borderline offended by her question. "You truly need to ask?" He ate the distance between them and cupped her face in his hands. "I love you. In spite of everything that has happened, I love you, and I do not wish to see you leave for the Immortal lands."

Raking her hands up and down his muscular arms, she broke their unwavering eye contact before he could see how shattered she truly was.

"It is better this way," she said softly.

"I'll keep looking, Rayma. I swear I will find a way for you to return to Numbio to be my wife, if you will still have me -"

She put a finger to his lips, silencing him. Her lip quivered; she was about to rip his already aching heart into pieces.

"Let me go," she met his eyes and wished she hadn't.

"Rayma -"

"Heru, you must let me go," she interrupted. "One day, you will be King of Numbio. You will need to take a wife and sire children -"

"Don't," he pleaded, horror written across his features. "Please don't ask me to stop loving you."

She summoned a weak smile and stroked his tear-stained cheek with the tips of her fingers. "Our love will never die, but our paths are no longer going in the same direction."

"Don't give up on us." Heru kissed her forehead and it felt an awful like goodbye. "Give me time to save you."

"You already have."

"I'll abdicate -"

"You will do nothing of the kind." She stared into his eyes with a sternness that sobered him. "You will take your rightful place among our people, and you will do what you were born to do."

Heru reluctantly nodded and pulled her to his chest, wrapping his arms around her in a warm embrace. "Is this really how our story ends?"

"I'm afraid we were doomed from the beginning," she whispered into his chest and wished things could have been different for them.

As he pulled away, Rayma tightened her hold on him. He squeezed her in return, and she could feel her heart shatter into a million unfixable pieces. They might not have forever, but they had tonight, and she wasn't ready to let him go.

Chapter Thirty-Five

Salome

Salome's dance with Hanzo had not only been a success, but a lot of fun. She graced the dance floor a few more times with different men: King Kenji, Cato, Prince Heru, and Harbona. She even managed to convince Kayven to take a spin with her, although Abba was more than happy to stick to the wall he seemed to favor.

As she weaved around the room, greeting guests and sampling food, her eyes stopped on Adonijah, who was across the room. He smiled at her and she started to walk toward him but stopped when his attention was stolen by the Andrago maiden he had arrived with. She was gorgeous for sure, with her silky, black hair, bronze skin, and curvaceous figure, but there was something about the way he looked at the maiden that clicked in her head. For as brief as their attraction to one another had been, Adonijah never stared at her, the way he was admiring the Andrago. For a moment, her heart ached, but she quickly shooed the sting away and happiness filled its place. Though she didn't fully trust him, and they were working on rebuilding a friendship, she believed Adonijah deserved to be happy and there was no denying he'd found his happiness in Leoti.

Drawing her intrusive gaze from the budding lovers, she looked around the hall for Jinn. She'd been hoping to speak with him all evening, but hadn't seen him since the wedding ceremony. Deciding she'd had enough dancing and venison for the evening, she slipped out of the hall and wandered around the ancient keep looking for the prince.

She dared not go straight to his room to knock on his door. She might not care about what people said or thought about her dancing anymore, but she wouldn't have unsavory rumors circulating about her and the prince after a very successful evening of politics.

The kitchens were empty, save Jacobi and a few other cooks cracking jokes and enjoying some sweet treats in private. The bailey was bare, and the library showed no signs of anyone being there. It felt like she'd been wandering the castle for an hour before she thought about the roof. It was the last place she would check before giving up and turning in for the night.

As she climbed the hundreds of steps to get to the rooftop overlook, she stopped, slapping a hand to her forehead in frustration. She had magic that she could have used to ask him where he was, saving her time. *Idiot*, she thought to herself. It was too late now; she was precisely five steps away from pushing the wooden door open that led to the roof.

Muttering a string of curse words under her breath, she opened the door and was relieved to see Jinn leaning against the stone railing. The cool breeze whipped strands of his hair into his face which he swiped away. His gaze was glued to the moonlit sea and the sight of him dressed in his princely attire nearly stole her breath. Or was it the hike up the stairs?

Once she managed to catch her breath, she said, “It’s a beautiful view.”

He turned around, startled by the voice, but smiled when he saw it was her. “How did you know I would be up here?”

She returned his smile and sauntered over to join him. “I wish I could say it was easy to find you, but to my everlasting shame, it wasn't. I should have known you'd be up here though. It’s the same place I’d be, if I were trying to avoid people.” Inhaling the saltwater air and feeling the winter chill setting in, she rubbed her bare arms as she rested her elbows on the stone railing next to him.

Jinn took his cloak off and draped it over her shoulders, which she gratefully accepted and tightened around her. She loved that it smelled like him.

“I might not remember much about my childhood home, but I remember that it smelled very similar to this when the cold weather started to blow in.” She glanced out over the Ignacia Sea. She turned to look at him and saw he was already admiring her.

“It seems your idea of uniting the Stormcrags and Krazaks has been a success,” he bumped her shoulder with his, drawing a grin from her. “If the laughter and music from the wedding downstairs is an indicator, I’m sure Oifa and Hanzo will make a fine couple. I’m surprised they didn’t see the potential before.”

“They hate each other.”

“Hate is a very strong word." He arched an eyebrow.

"But an accurate one," she chuckled. "I just pray Oifa doesn't lose her temper and stab him on their wedding night." She blushed at the thought of a wedding night and cleared her throat to hide her embarrassment. "What are weddings like in Sakurai?"

The prince stiffened a bit and she wished she hadn't asked. She refused his proposal in the Isles of Myr and had turned him down when he confessed his love for her in the City of Bones. She'd chosen to be with Adonijah and knew now it was a mistake. Maybe there was still a chance Jinn would want to be with her, especially after what Kenji had told her about the prince's visions. But he was still free to decide if he wanted to give her another chance. She was just too cowardly to ask for one.

Jinn cleared his throat, "Parents make the arrangements for their children to wed." It warmed her heart that he answered, and she clung to every word that slipped from his tempting lips. "Once an agreement has been reached, the bride and groom meet. The wedding is planned for a month later. There's lots of food and lots of music, very similar to how it sounds downstairs, but I've never been a fan of weddings."

"Why not?" she asked, and his eyes met hers.

"Because I was afraid I would be forced to marry someone I didn't love, when all my life I knew there was someone out there for me, and I just needed the chance to find her."

Salome knew he meant her, and her heart skipped. Maybe there was still a chance for them to be together.

Jinn turned, squaring up with her, and offered his hand. "Dance with me?"

Had he asked hours ago, she might have said no. But with a newfound confidence in the art of dance, Salome reached for his extended hand and let him pull her close to him. His other hand landed on the small of her back and she rested her palm on his shoulder. Together, silently, they swayed with the music that drifted up from the party below. Jinn's chin touched her temple and she shivered.

"Are you cold?" he asked, concern laced his words.

"No," she shook her head, pressing herself against him.

She allowed her thoughts to wander when she closed her eyes. She pictured her future, the future she wanted. Months ago, when her journey began, it never entered her mind that she would find the person she didn't know was missing in her life. She thought it was Adonijah and maybe, in another life, she and Adonijah could have been happy, but she had grown and changed. She was ready to claim her titles, her birthright, and walk in her power. The woman she had become, belonged to Jinn, and she knew deep in her heart that she had found her equal in power and ambition.

Jinn had proposed to her in Myr, breaking a thousand-year tradition in his culture. Call it fate. Call it destiny. She and Jinn were always meant to find one another. They were always meant to be together. He rescued her from the Gomorrians. He kept every promise he made and even when she pushed him away, he never left her side. He nursed her injuries and healed her broken heart.

She tilted her head up and found him already looking down at her.

"What is it?" he asked, his voice raspy.

"Your father and I spoke of you."

His grip on her tightened and she noticed the muscles in his neck tense. Worry. His eyes were filled with it. He didn't need to ask what she was referring to because he already knew.

"Salome, I'm sorry. You were never supposed to find out that way..."

Her eyes cut down to his lips, silencing whatever excuse or apology he was about to issue. She felt his heartbeat quicken against her chest, his breathing was labored, and his eyes hungry. She slid her hand from his shoulder up his neck and cupped his cheek. Her thumb floated across his lips and his fingers pressed against her lower back gripping her dress.

"Jinn?" They stopped dancing and gazed into one another's eyes. "Am I too late?"

Jinn tilted his head, confused. "Too late for what?"

She inhaled deeply when he softly caressed her back. "When this war is over – I choose a life with you. If you will still have me."

His hand stilled, and from his expression, she thought she had made a mistake. He didn't want to be with her. She'd chosen Adonijah over him. Once the war was over, he'd find someone else, someone better.

Jinn tucked a finger beneath her chin and gently lifted her head.

"I'm sorry, I shouldn't have -"

"If I lived a hundred different lifetimes, I would choose you every time," he said softly.

A tear she had been holding back slipped down her cheek and he wiped it away.

"I have dreamed of you since we were children. I have searched for you all my life," Jinn leaned down, his lips an inch from hers. "I asked you once before and you weren't ready to give me an answer."

"Ask me again," she whispered.

"Marry me?"

"Yes." She smiled a second before his mouth crashed against hers, claiming her as his.

She was flooded with the feeling of completeness. The piece of her heart that was missing was now found. She felt a surge zing through her body, his mouth roamed from her lips down her neck and bare shoulders. She would have to thank the twins for choosing this dress for her. Her fingers plunged into his hair, tugging softly. She arched into him, accepting his loving touch, giving him her heart.

When he finally pulled back from her, he rested his forehead against hers, their breathing rapid, and their lips swollen.

"Why didn't you tell me about your dreams?" she asked, her fingers still tangled in his hair.

"I didn't know how," he answered honestly. "I didn't want you to think I was insane. I wanted to run to you the moment our eyes locked in the halls of the Scarlet Citadel. I knew, after years of hoping you existed, that I had finally found you."

"Damaris told me in Myr we had a strong bond. Now I know what she meant."

Jinn swiped curls away from her face and kissed her again. He opened his mouth to say something but didn't get the chance.

"So, this is where you two are hiding." Crispin leaned against the doorway, arms crossed over his chest, a smirk on his face.

"It's not nice to lurk, Crispin," Salome snorted, painfully aware of her disheveled appearance. Jinn took a step back, allowing her to push away from the wall her back was pinned against.

Crispin winked, "Not to worry, sister, your secret is safe with me."

"Actually," Salome took Jinn's hand and faced her brother. "There's something we want to ask you."

Crispin's eyebrow quirked. "What?"

"Jinn asked me to marry him, and I said yes." Before Crispin could respond, Salome quickly continued. "I love him, and as my brother and my future king, I ask for your permission and blessing for us to wed."

Crispin's mouth dropped. He stood up from his lazy position and took a step toward his sister. All playfulness in his gaze was gone. "You're asking for my permission to get married?"

"Yes," she nodded, "and I hope you approve."

He grabbed Salome's free hand and squeezed. "You don't need my permission to marry the man you love, Salome. I may be the future king, but I won't dare tell you what to do or who to spend your life with."

"You mean that?" Her eyes watered.

Crispin smiled, "Let's not pretend you've ever listened to me before anyways."

Salome threw her arms around her brother's neck. "Thank you!"

Crispin extended his hand to Jinn, and they shook. "She's a handful. I hope you're ready."

Salome smacked Crispin's chest and scoffed.

Jinn snaked his arm around her waist and pulled her close. "I will serve her well."

Crispin smiled at Salome, "Of that I have no doubt."

Chapter Thirty-Six

Adonijah

Even though the wedding was still raging, Adonijah slipped out to visit his brother, Pash, who had been confined to his quarters since they arrived in Oakenshire. He'd been treated kindly and hadn't been tortured or thrown into the dungeons, but he hadn't been allowed to leave his room without an escort and his weapons were confiscated. Crispin didn't want to take the chance of Pash spying on their army and resources and managing to escape to inform Niabi of their plans and whereabouts.

Adonijah felt a pang of guilt every time he thought about his brother being locked up, but he'd experienced the same treatment when Pash's men arrested him for trespassing. Pash still treated him with respect and had dinner with him nightly, so Adonijah thought it only fair to return the favor.

Once he approached the door to his brother's quarters, the two soldiers standing on either side of the frame glanced at him and nodded him through. Thankfully, even though Adonijah and Crispin didn't get along when they first met, the prince gave Adonijah free reign of the castle and even allowed him to see his brother whenever he wanted. He was surprised Crispin didn't confine Leoti alongside Pash. Maybe, the prince thought the Andrago wouldn't run away. Even if she managed to slip past the guards, Leoti wouldn't get too far on her own. She was resourceful, but she never travelled alone, so to venture through the Black Forest to get to Northwind would be a monumental task, even for a warg.

Pash on the other hand, could very well make it back to the White City on his own. He was the Commander of Shadows and had traipsed through the Black Forest more than any other man he knew. When Gershom escaped Issachar's dungeons, he and Pash set up their own camp in the middle of the cursed woods. Pash explored the area for years, and knew it like the back of his hand,

and he didn't fear the creatures that lurked there. He was born and bred for fighting and had killed many men.

At least Pash was alive. That was more than Adonijah could have hoped for when Crispin and the pirates came to their aid during their altercation with Ophir and his band of Shadows.

As soon as Adonijah walked over the threshold, the guards closed the door, locking him inside. He found Pash in the same place he always found him: the window bench. It didn't matter what time of day or night Adonijah came to visit his older brother, the commander would be staring out the window, watching the waves of the Ignacia Sea slosh around and depending on the training schedule, he'd watch the soldiers from different corners of Adalore sparring together, preparing to war with the woman he loved most.

Adonijah understood that feeling of helplessness. It was only a few weeks ago, he was doing the same thing in Pash's military camp, hoping he would see Salome again. He shook the thought of Salome wrapped in his arms free and made his way toward his brother.

Pash turned at the stomping sound of his boots and smiled. Even being locked in this room hadn't crushed his spirit.

"Sounds like a great party." Pash motioned to the plate Adonijah had in his hand. "What's that?"

"I figured I'd bring you a late-night dinner since you weren't invited to the wedding."

Pash grabbed the plate as he stood and made his way to the humble dining table fit for a party of four, and sat down, motioning for his brother to join him.

"How is Leoti faring?" Pash sank his teeth into a piece of venison.

Adonijah sat across the table from his brother and reclined, stretching his legs out in front of him. "She is doing well. Oddly enough, worried about you."

Pash smirked. "Tell the Andrago, I'll be giving her orders to disregard sooner than she thinks."

The brothers exchanged a look in silence before Pash's smile faded.

"I don't expect I'll be leaving this room for quite some time."

"I'll talk to Crispin again -"

"There's no need, brother," Pash cut him off, shaking his head. "I am fortunate to be confined to this room and not stretched out on a rack in a dark and dank dungeon being tortured for information."

"Has no one questioned you?" Adonijah asked.

"No." Pash leaned back in his seat, breaking the flaky roll apart and tossing a piece into his mouth. "I keep waiting for one of your companions to kick my door in and drag me out in chains to be executed. Waiting is its own sort of torture, I suppose."

"Salome won't let them execute you."

"I hope you're right, Adonijah." Pash chuckled, but his expression remained skeptical. "Men like me are meant to die in battle, not noosed and hanged like a common thief."

Adonijah tapped his fingers on the wooden table, drawing Pash's gaze. "You won't die here. You have a child to raise."

"I am not blind to reality," Pash whispered, tossing his half-eaten roll back on the plate. "My chances of seeing Niabi again are bleak. I may never hold my child or tell him how much I love him."

"Pash -"

"I am a prisoner of war," he interrupted, a bite in his tone. "Do not misunderstand, I am grateful that your friends have been merciful in their treatment of me, but I am still their enemy and at some point, they will understand what they must do."

"They won't execute you," Adonijah's nostrils flared. "I won't allow it."

"I know you would do your best to protect me, but the truth is, if they wish me dead, there is nothing you can do to hinder it." Pash rubbed his fingers across his growing beard. "If that time comes, I need you to promise me something."

"It's not going to happen," Adonijah stood up, scratching the floor with the legs of his chair, "so keep your request to yourself."

Pash jumped up and grabbed his brother's forearm. "If something happens to me, I need you to make sure that Niabi and my child are safe."

Adonijah slowly turned to face him. "You're asking me to commit treason," he whispered.

"I am asking you to ensure the life of my unborn child." Pash lowered his voice and Adonijah didn't miss the brokenness in his tired eyes. "Can I count on you?"

Adonijah was no fool. If something happened to his brother, he wouldn't hesitate to do whatever he had to do to protect his child. But he'd have to betray Crispin and Salome. What he needed to do was secure Pash's release, then he could fulfill his oath to protect and serve Salome and help his brother.

Pash cleared his throat, slicing through Adonijah's hesitant thoughts. He couldn't speak his agreement, but he nodded his head, and that seemed to be enough for Pash.

"I must go," Adonijah pulled his arm from his brother's grasp.

"Tell Leoti I am alright."

He nodded before rapping on the door three times and slipped through once the guards opened it. Marching down the corridors, jovial music from the wedding still wisped around the castle, but Adonijah felt a heaviness weighing on his shoulders. How could he keep both promises? Serve and protect Salome and ensure Niabi and Pash's child's safety?

He raked a hand through his hair and traipsed back to his chambers. Once inside, he ripped his cloak and tunic off and threw them on the bed before sinking into his mattress, not bothering to light any of the candles. He was comfortable in the dark and found it oddly soothing to lay in his room unable to see three feet in front of him. His other senses were heightened when his sight was hindered. He could smell the sweet pastries from the great hall below and could hear light breathing coming from the other side of his room.

Sitting up and grabbing his knife from the holster on his thigh, he growled, "If you wish to remain in one piece, I suggest you state your business."

A match flickered and a candle on his dining table was lit, revealing Leoti staring at him. Even in the dark, he felt as if she could see into his very soul and knew all his deep, dark secrets.

"Do you still intend to cut me to pieces?" she asked, a playful taunt in her voice.

He sheathed his knife and stalked toward her. As he neared, he heard her catch her breath and he realized he was only wearing his trousers and boots. Her eyes roamed the scars littering his chest. He stopped, thinking he should go back to grab his shirt, but when she slowly stood and walked towards him, he froze.

She cautiously lifted her hand and he reached for it and gently led her palm to his chest. Peering into each other's eyes, he was positive she could feel how fast his heart was beating.

"You have so many scars," she finally whispered.

"Aye." He dragged her hand lower where a stab wound he'd received a year ago was, and pressed her palm against it. "Many have tried to kill me and failed."

Leoti didn't say anything, but her gaze slowly moved up from his chest to his lips and then met his eyes.

Adonijah took a deep breath and took a step closer, so their bodies were only inches apart. His heart was racing as he lifted his hand to brush strands of hair that had fallen out of her braids away from her face. His fingers trailed down her cheek, the center of her neck, and stopped just above her breastbone. He could feel her heart pounding beneath his grazing fingertips.

"Why did you come to my room tonight, Leoti?" he whispered.

"I don't know."

He cupped her face in his calloused palms and asked again, "Why did you come to my room tonight, Leoti?"

"I feel safe with you," she confessed. "I feel alive when I'm with you, and I haven't felt this way since..."

"I know I shouldn't," he picked up where she trailed off, "but I have feelings for you."

"What kind of feelings?"

Adonijah pressed his forehead against hers and said, "I know you're still mourning Rollo, but I can't help but want you. I yearn for every bit of you that you are willing to offer. If it's just this moment, I will take it gratefully and die a happy man. But if you would have me, if you would let me, I would love you with every fiber of my heart, soul, and body. I would do everything in my power to bring you joy and to protect you. If you want me, I am yours."

Leoti was silent and he feared he had said something to offend her. She gently lifted his face and looked into his eyes.

"You are mine." Her voice was soft but confident, almost possessive. "And I am yours." Her fingers trailed down his neck and stopped above his heart. "I take all of you, just as you are. I will stand by your side as we fight, build, and grow, until Death claims me for the Great Beyond."

"Leoti." With just her name, he asked permission.

"Adonijah." With just his name, she gave it.

Slowly, he leaned down. Her eyes closed as she tipped her head up, her hands roaming his chest. He hovered over her lips; this was his last chance to turn back. But instead of letting his fear grip him, he pressed his mouth against hers and felt a shock of electricity shoot through his entire body. He'd never experienced a sensation like this when kissing a woman. He'd never had this feeling even when he kissed Salome.

Her hands went from stroking his chest to grabbing his neck and pulling him closer to her. She was intoxicating, an addiction he didn't know he had. Leoti ran her fingers through his hair, tugging to get a reaction out of him. And she got one when she bit his bottom lip, drawing a low growl from him.

He forced himself to pull back to look at her. Though her gaze was hazy, he could still see her longing for him, and his chest swelled. "You are mine," he echoed her words from moments before.

Leoti bobbed her head, "I am yours."

Licking his fingers, he extinguished the candle on the small dining table, shrouding them once again in darkness.

Chapter Thirty-Seven

Niabi

The coolness of the winter didn't deter Niabi from making her way to the royal stables where Nagrom, her black steed, was well cared for and housed. She spent as much time with him as she could and once she'd shooed the custodians out of the stable, she picked up the brush and started stroking down Nagrom's muscular body. The quiet solitude was exactly what she needed to clear her foggy mind. Nagrom nudged her with his snout, drawing a smile from her.

"You'll get your snack once I'm done brushing your coat, Nagrom," she tsked. "After twenty years, you should know the routine."

Nagrom shook his head, fluffing his mane, before refocusing on the pile of hay in front of him. She cherished his company and felt so at peace with him that she drifted back to the day Dichali gave him to her. The morning she was to depart to the Andrago lands with her newly betrothed, she found him waiting for her in the courtyard, at the bottom of the White Keep stairs, grinning.

"And what are you smiling about?" Niabi squinted, blocking the sun with her hand as she descended the stairs.

Dichali extended his hand to her once she reached the bottom, and she reluctantly accepted his chivalrous gesture, knowing her father and members of the royal court were all watching her from the top of the stairs. Just another hour and she'd be free from this city and more importantly, free from her father's crushing hand. The Andrago king kissed her hand and winked before leaning closer.

"I'm smiling," he whispered in her ear, "because I have a surprise for you, wife."

"I'm not your wife yet," she retorted, and he chuckled.

"Perhaps not," he pulled back and straightened to his full height, forcing her to look up. "But once you see what I have for you, maybe you will look at me more favorably."

Slipping his hand into hers, as if it was the most natural thing in the world, Dichali led Niabi toward his entourage of Andrago, all suited and seated on their horses for the journey. Their stares didn't go unnoticed, and she was just as wary of them as they were of her. She was the daughter of their enemy, and they were more than likely not happy their king was taking her as his bride. But if she were being honest, this arranged marriage wasn't her idea of a good time either.

Her eyes collided with the one Dichali called Tala and he stared at her unabashedly. He was bold, protective, and confident, she would give him that. He was the one to win over, if she were ever going to be trusted amongst her future husband's people – her future people. She nodded her head in a show of respect, and to her surprise, Tala's eyes softened, and he returned the gesture with a nod of his own.

The one called Chua was a slippery looking fellow. His beady eyes and serpentine smile made her skin crawl, but he was also a member of Dichali's inner circle and unfortunately, she would be seeing plenty of him. She would remain diplomatic, but if he laid one unwanted finger on her, she would claim his whole hand, consequences be damned.

Finally, Dichali stopped pulling her forward and planted his hands over her eyes. She swatted his hands away, gritting her teeth.

"I am not going to harm you, my lady," Dichali said softly, his face a mixture of sympathy and anger.

She shifted her weight foot-to-foot. She did not wish to stir her future husband's anger before they even began their journey and offending him wasn't on her list of things to do either, so she bit down hard on her bottom lip before muttering, "I did not mean to offend you, my lord."

"Offend me?" He flashed a baffled gaze her way. "What are you talking about?"

"You looked upset." Now it was her turn to be confused. "I thought -"

Dichali ate the distance between them, tucked his index finger under her chin and tilted her face upwards. "Any anger you might have seen flash across my face was not directed at you, Niabi. I hate that you flinch when I raise my hand or that your shoulders tense up when I touch you. I would ask for you to give me the names of those who harmed you, but I don't need you to, because I already know. If I could make your father suffer for his sins against you, I would. But freeing you from his prison is the best I can do."

For the first time in a long time, Niabi was truly stunned. She didn't know how to respond. Part of her wanted to agree with him, keeping her mask firmly in place, hiding any and all weaknesses he could possibly exploit, but the other part of her, the treacherous side, wanted to push up on her toes and kiss him, which was the only way she knew how to thank him. Words meant nothing to her, actions did. How could she thank him enough for all he was risking and willing to do for her. He didn't truly know her, he shouldn't even feel obligated to aid her, but here he was, standing before her ready to whisk her to a new home where she would be his queen.

"Niabi?" Dichali's thumb stroked the curvature of her jawline. "Is everything alright?"

She forced herself to nod, banning any thought of kissing him from her mind. "Where is this surprise you promised?"

His cheeks dimpled when he smiled and he motioned towards a black stallion with a saddle and no rider. "This is Nagrom."

Niabi quietly stared at the steed who seemed to almost stare back at her with a gentle strength she was unquestionably drawn to. She felt Dichali's chest settle against her back and she forced herself not to flinch at his soft caress.

"He is yours."

"A horse of my own?"

"That is what my lady requested when we first met, is it not?"

Niabi slowly turned around, missing the feel of his chest against her back. "Thank you."

The words seemed to surprise him just as much as they did to her, but he quickly recovered from his stupor and bobbed his head. "Shall I help you up?"

Niabi smiled and his eyes danced with delight. He cupped her cheek in his hand and whispered, "Do that again."

"Do what?"

"Smile," he dragged his fingers down her face. "I don't believe I've ever seen a more beautiful sight."

"Just wait until you see me riding a horse," she smirked, and he chuckled.

"Safe travels, Niabi." Issachar's menacing voice sliced through their tender moment. Together, the soon-to-be newlyweds glanced up the white stone steps to where Issachar stood with his entourage.

Lykos looked sick to his stomach, and even though she'd wished him farewell, he had spoken to her about helping her get back to the Isles of Myr to avoid their father's arranged marriage. Niabi had assured him she would be alright, that running to the Myridians would only provoke their father to act against their mother's kin, and he reluctantly conceded to her will. She hoped he would make a better king once their father passed. Maybe then she would be welcomed to the White City with open arms.

Dichali slipped his hand into Niabi's hand once more and straightened his shoulders to Issachar. "King Issachar."

"King Dichali" Issachar matched Dichali's tone before he whipped around and reentered the White Keep.

"You ready to go home?" Dichali asked her and she nodded. She was more than ready.

With his help, she mounted Nagrom and though she was frightened, she would rather die than admit her fear to Dichali, who rode by her side the whole way to Elisor. It took several days, but by the end of the trip, she felt more comfortable riding her horse. Dichali was right, the horse lords were the perfect teachers.

It didn't take long after their arrival for them to be wed. With the entire population watching them, Niabi and Dichali had their hands bound with red rope, and at sunset they invoked the traditional vows of the Andrago. The people had been so incredibly welcoming of her and rejoiced when their king not only found a bride but took a queen to rule by his side.

After a night of feasting, drinking, and dancing, Niabi was led to a spectacular tent with bright pattern rugs strewn across the floors, and pillows of all colors thrown on the white canopy bed at the back end of the room. It was well lit with candles, and she couldn't help but admire the wooden case where a host of weaponry was kept. She was more than pleased with her lodging and didn't miss her stark, cold room in the White Keep. For a brief moment, she realized she could find herself quite content amongst the Andrago, and that summoned a rare smile from her.

Someone cleared his throat behind her at the tent's entrance and when she turned around, she was pleased and surprised to see Dichali standing there. She wasn't sure how she was supposed to address him since he was now her husband.

"Am I supposed to bow to you or something?" She squared her shoulders to his. "Is there a certain title I'm supposed to use now that we're married?"

"No special titles, wife," Dichali stepped forward and shook his head. "And you do not bow to me. We are equals in all things."

A comfortable silence fell between them as they stared at each other. She was still waiting for this dream to end, half expecting she'd wake up in the White Keep, and back under her father's thumb. Dichali was nothing like what she expected him to be, but she wasn't sure how to express herself, or if she wanted to allow herself to appear vulnerable.

"I do not have to stay here tonight," Dichali's statement silenced her thoughts. "I can sleep elsewhere, until you are ready for us to..."

"Consummate our marriage." She finished for him and was oddly satisfied to see the King of the Andrago blush. "What will your people think if I ask you to leave?"

"I told you before, Niabi, women are treated as equals here. If you do not wish for me to stay, if you do not wish for me to touch you, I will abide by your wishes."

She should have told him to leave, but something deep down inside of her yearned for him to stay. The walls she'd built up around herself were there to protect her from men like her father, but Dichali made her want to tear the wall down stone by stone until there was nothing that parted them.

"Goodnight, Niabi," Dichali smiled and walked toward the tent flaps to leave.

"Wait," her voice halted him. He slowly turned to face her. "Stay," she whispered.

"What?"

"I want you to stay, Dichali," she rasped again, as if she was in desperate need of a drink of water. He didn't move a muscle. Just stared at her, as if he was the one who wasn't too keen on staying. "Please."

That word seemed to rattle him, and he met her gaze. "I could never refuse you."

As he made his way to her, she forced her feet to move and met him in the middle of their room. He stood stoically, as if he was waiting for her to dictate the pace and what would happen between them. For a second, she panicked and thought it might've been a mistake to have asked him to stay, but when she looked into his kind brown eyes, her fears vanished. Pushing up onto the tips of her toes, she slowly inched her face closer to his. His breath hitched as her lips floated beneath his. Suddenly realizing that was as far as she could go, he lowered his head and met her awaiting lips.

Fire. Ice. Shadows. Light. His kiss was everything and all consuming. Losing control of herself, she snaked her hands up either side of his face, drawing him closer. He tangled his fingers in her hair and tugged gently. Her husband. Her equal in all things.

Before she was ready for him to, he pulled his mouth from hers, but still hovered above her and stared into her eyes, appearing to be a man in search of truth.

"Ask your questions."

"Why did you ask me to stay?" Dichali asked, breathlessly.

"Why did you ask me to be your wife?" She posed a question of her own, still feeling uncomfortable with being vulnerable.

"Because you were drowning and that was the only way to save you."

"You didn't know me. You didn't owe me anything."

"No," he shook his head. "I didn't know you and you're right, I didn't owe you anything. When your father reached out to me asking me to take you as my bride to end the feud between our people, I knew he didn't mean it. I knew he was trying to use me to get rid of you. My counselors tried to dissuade me from traveling to the White City. They tried to convince me not to agree to Issachar's terms. But when I heard how your father spoke to you in the throne room and I saw how you held knives to his throat with every opportunity to kill him, and you restrained yourself - I just knew right then, I had to have you as my wife."

"I don't know how I can ever repay your kindness, Dichali," she stroked a finger through his locks, and he smiled.

"*You* are more than enough."

Their mouths collided again as they stumbled toward the bed. When the back of her legs bumped into the mattress, Dichali whispered, "Are you sure?"

"I'm sure."

Niabi was ripped from her memories when she sensed a presence flooding her head. She knew exactly who it was and although she wanted to be irritated by the sudden interruption, she found herself more curious than anything. *"I didn't think I'd ever hear from you again, sister. Pray, tell me, what is it you wish to talk about this evening?"*

Although Salome was quiet for a moment, she finally asked, *"What was our mother like?"*

The question caught Niabi off guard. She assumed Salome would want to know more about Niabi's past or their father, but to ask about Bilhah – even Niabi didn't allow herself to think about their mother often. It was too painful thinking of how their mother died protecting her brothers when Gershom came and slaughtered them all the night she took the city. She originally wanted to send her mother and siblings to the Isles of Myr, sparing them a gruesome end, but Vilora's prophecy won out in the end. There could be no survivors that would possibly attempt to usurp her reign. If she left them alive, her son would never sit on the White Throne. She supposed none of it mattered in the end since two siblings escaped, and she had to live with the burden that she was the one who signed her mother and brothers' death warrants.

"If you don't want to -"

"She was very kind and had an endless well of patience for her children," Niabi interrupted her as she continued to stroke the brush down Nagrom's back. *"She was wise, had the most beautiful voice, and was the best storyteller at bedtime. When I was sick, she would sit by my bedside, refusing the Healers' offer to care for me themselves. When a nightmare terrified me in the middle of the night, she would cuddle next to me, and when I woke the next morning, she would still be in bed with me. She was a breath of fresh air and revived me every time I felt like I was drowning. She smelled of jasmine and vanilla and when father stripped me of my birthright, she fought for me to be his heir. Ultimately, she was the one who convinced our father to send me to the Isles of Myr. She wanted me to be trained in the ways of her people and he was all too glad to get rid of me. I was so angry with her for sending me away, but it wasn't because she didn't want me to be around. It was because in her own way, that was how she could save me from him."*

"Why did you not let her go free when you attacked?" The whispered question split Niabi's heart wide open.

"I wanted to," Niabi replied with the quietness of a small child. *"But if I had let her live, let any of you live, it would have cost my son his life. All usurpers had to be dealt with, if I wanted Rollo to sit on the White Throne,"* she explained.

"I don't remember much about her," Salome's voice cracked. *"I have pieces of memories, images, flashes of happiness."*

"But?"

"As I grow older, the moments I hold dear are fading, and I'm afraid and ashamed to admit I am beginning to forget her."

"One day you shall see her again." Though the words sounded threatening, Niabi did not intend for it to come across as menacing. She was trying to comfort her heartbroken sister as best as she could, in spite of the fact she was the reason Salome would never experience more precious moments with their mother. *"Of one thing I am certain, she loved you, Salome. She loved all of us and she didn't deserve to die."*

"I suppose your hatred for our father far outweighed your love for our mother."

The words held a bite to it and rightly so. Niabi deserved that.

She shook her head, even though Salome wasn't there to see it. *"I suppose my grief for Dichali far outweighed my love for any of you. My need for revenge blinded me to all else and I will bear that burden for the rest of my days."*

"You could have let them go. Why didn't you just let us go?"

"We can talk ourselves in circles about why I did what I did, Salome," Niabi issued with a firm hand. *"But talking won't change any of it. It won't bring any of them back. It won't mend my broken heart. It won't convince you to forgive or sympathize with me. So, why bother?"*

"Because unlike you," Salome hissed, sounding more like a wounded animal than anything else, *"I wish to know the truth. I wish to know all the good, the bad, and the horrifying aspects of you, so I can convince myself that we are nothing alike. But the more I discover, the more you share, the more I realize we aren't so different after all and that scares me."*

"Scares you because you fear becoming a monster?"

"Scares me because I fear I no longer wish you dead."

Niabi was too stunned to respond. She stewed in silence for a moment and when she reached out to speak, she felt the coldness of Salome's absence. She'd severed their connection and left Niabi with more questions than ammunition. When she first realized Salome had this magic, she was hoping to garner valuable information about their whereabouts, their plans, or the number of their company, but instead, she was left with a longing to know the sister she'd never met. For the first time in years, she felt seen, felt like someone understood her, and instead of seeing her for the monster she'd allowed herself to become, she saw her for the girl she used to be, the girl she wished she could be again.

Chapter Thirty-Eight

Salome

The Bellators allowed Salome to take a few days off to help prepare and celebrate Oifa and Hanzo's nuptials, but two nights after the wedding, she heard a heavy hand knock on her bedroom door. When she opened it, Kayven stood in the hallway with a giant grin plastered across his bronze face. Abba leaned against the wall behind his brother, and she shook her head.

"We agreed to start back up tomorrow," she folded her arms over her chest in childlike protest.

"And it is a minute past midnight," Kayven motioned for her to grab her stuff. "Officially tomorrow."

Salome rolled her eyes, "Has anyone ever told you -"

"How unbelievably handsome I am?" He wiggled his eyebrows. "All the time."

Abba chuckled but offered her no help in escaping their training session. If she didn't know any better, she could have sworn Abba had grown quite fond of her over their weeks of sparring.

Knowing there was no way she was going to get out of training with the Bellators, she grabbed her weapons, and followed them to the bailey.

It felt good getting back into the routine she'd abandoned the last few days. Over the next hour she took turns sparring with both of the brothers, and even managed to swipe Kayven off his feet, but he avoided falling thanks to his impressive wingspan.

"Dare I say," Kayven smiled at her as she wiped sweat from her temples, "you might be my best student."

She made a spectacle of sweeping her hand down to the ground as she bowed. "What a tremendous compliment, Your Lordship."

"Oh, don't start calling him that," Abba huffed. "It'll go straight to his head."

"Too late," Kayven laughed.

Taking a break to drink some refreshing water, Salome eyed the hippogriffs that the Ethereals had flown to the mainland. She had been curious about the beasts since she first spotted them but didn't dare approach them since Harbona warned her that they tend to bite strangers. Kayven noticed her staring and motioned toward the stables where they were housed.

"Hippogriffs are how the Ethereals travel since they do not have wings. That one there," Kayven pointed at a magnificent looking beast, "is Harbona's hippogriff. He is one of the fastest in the herd."

"Do you have to be an Immortal to ride one?" she asked, eyes fixed on the creature.

"Are you asking to ride one?" Kayven tilted his head, a smirk appearing on his bronze face.

"Mortals aren't used to that form of travel." Abba took a step forward, uncrossing his arms, face serious. "If she should fall off -"

"One of us will catch her." Kayven's eyes danced with mischief.

Salome was excited about the chance to go on a challenging and dangerous adventure with the brothers. "Harbona won't be happy when he finds out."

"Neither will a couple of princes, I imagine." Kayven folded his muscular arms over his broad chest, standing with his feet shoulder width apart. He wiggled his eyebrows when Salome mirrored his stance and narrowed her eyes. "But what Harbona, Crispin, and Jinn do not know, will not harm them."

"You are a terrible influence." Abba shook his head, stretching his wings, as if he already knew what was coming next.

Salome bit her lower lip. She'd be lying if she said she wasn't at least curious to see what flying one of the hippogriffs would be like. If Harbona found out, she'd be on the receiving end of a severe tongue lashing. If Crispin found out, she'd have to explain why she didn't fetch him to join.

"Well?" Kayven cocked his head to the side, already leaning up against the stall where Zandaar pounded his hooves.

Salome grinned. "Let's go."

Taking off was the scariest part, but once she was soaring in the twinkling night sky, with Kayven and Abba flying at her side, she was filled with a sense of freedom, adventure, and peace. She closed her eyes as the wind whooshed around her, taking a deep breath of sea air. Crispin would be envious if he saw her flying Zandaar. He'd demand to have a turn just like a spoiled child.

"Keep your eyes open." Abba instructed. His brow was furrowed, not in anger, she realized, but in concern. He was truly worried about her falling off the flying beast. Or maybe he didn't want to face Harbona's wrath, if something happened to her.

Salome turned to the other side and watched Kayven soar through the starry night sky, looking more like an eagle than a man. She'd seen them fight in Gomorrah and knew how beautifully lethal they were in battle, but seeing them fly without bloodshed on their mind, was a memory that would forever be ingrained in her head.

"Are you alright?" Kayven must have felt her staring.

She bobbed her head and smiled, "This is amazing!"

"Zandaar does not like many mortals," Kayven glanced at the hippogriff who turned his birdlike head to look back at her. "But he seems to like you."

Salome gently stroked Zandaar's feathered head. "And I like him."

In the corner of her eye, Salome noticed a ship. It was still quite a distance from them, but she felt an uneasiness in her gut.

"Do you see that ship?" she asked the brothers.

"Ships," Abba corrected when the fleet sailed out from underneath a cloud and into the unobstructed moonlight.

"Who is it?" Salome had a lump in her throat. Even though a part of her screamed for them to turn around, she had to find out who the fleet belonged to and where they were headed. Oakenshire was as fortified as a ruined castle could be, but unless they patched holes in sections of the wall, they would be easily overrun.

"Abba and I will get a closer look." Kayven veered in front of Zandaar and held up a hand as the beast hovered. "Stay here."

"But -"

"It is for your own protection." The seriousness in Kayven's eyes made her shrink back. This was the Bellator Commander and war hero she'd heard so much about. With her, he was playful and caring. But this wasn't the time for him to make a lighthearted joke. "If something goes wrong, fly as fast as you can back to Oakenshire. Do not try to rescue us if we are captured. Do you understand?"

"I can't just leave you."

"You can and will, should they spot us." Kayven wasn't going to budge an inch on this. "Swear it, Princess."

Even though she wanted to argue with him further, maybe throw her rank in his face, she shut her mouth and nodded. She would obey. This time.

Satisfied with her response, the Bellator brothers flew toward the ships, flying high enough not to draw unnecessary attention to themselves, but low enough to spy. There was a point in which she couldn't see the Immortal warriors anymore, and she sat in complete silence as Zandaar flapped his wings to keep them steady. She listened for any sign the brothers were in trouble. Despite what Kayven made her promise, she wouldn't leave them to die, if something went wrong.

She thought they'd have more time to prepare for war. Some of their promised reinforcements hadn't arrived to Oakenshire yet. And with winter coming, she figured her sister wouldn't mobilize her troops until weather permitted.

One set of wings approaching her snapped her from her thoughts. She scanned the clouds looking for the second warrior, but still only saw one. She wasn't sure if it was Abba or Kayven, but she held her breath as the Bellator approached.

"Glad to see you did not fall to your death."

Abba. She exhaled, relieved her friend was alright, but where was Kayven?

"Where's Kayven?" she asked, terrified of the answer.

Abba grinned and pointed upward. She glanced up toward the heavens and saw a second pair of wings as Kayven lowered himself from the darkness.

"Miss me?" Kayven snickered and Salome wanted to throw something at his smug face.

"I suppose you two thought sneaking up on me would be funny?"

"Sneaking?" Kayven slapped a hand to his breastplate. "She accuses us of sneaking, brother."

"I flew directly at you." Abba crossed his arms across his chest. "How was that sneaking?"

"Valid point, Abba." Kayven purred, aware how scared Salome was and was clearly attempting to lighten the mood.

Salome scratched the side of her face, willing her heart to calm down. "Well, I'm glad neither of you got into trouble."

Kayven tilted his head to the side and grinned. "I think the mortal has grown fond of us."

"We are very likeable." Abba motioned for them to fly back toward Oakenshire.

"And handsome," Kavyen quickly added. "You cannot forget to include how handsome we are."

Salome rolled her eyes and puffed out a breath. It suddenly got chilly and she wished she'd brought a blanket or coat. "Who were they?"

Kayven and Abba exchanged a glance, but she caught the soldier flare in their eyes.

"What is it? Who are they?" Salome demanded answers.

"They fly no banners," Abba started, "but they are equipped for battle."

"The ships look Pulauan." Kayven added. "Whether your sister sent them or not, I am not sure. But they are headed for Oakenshire, of this I have no doubt."

"Are you telling me -?

"To prepare for battle?" Kayven interrupted her with a sorrowful look. "That is exactly what I am saying, Princess."

When they landed in Oakenshire, they were greeted by a group of worried and angry friends. Harbona's face was so red, Salome thought the Seer might explode. Crispin didn't appear upset, but he definitely wanted to get closer to the hippogriff once she hopped off of him. Jinn leaned against one of the stable doorways with an amused look on his face. If he was angered by her disappearance, he didn't show it.

Salome slipped down from Zandaar's back and before she had a second to breathe, Crispin and Harbona started talking at the same time.

"Do you know how risky that midnight ride of yours was?" Harbona's voice boomed. "What if you had fallen off Zandaar or worse, been seen by the enemy?"

"I can't believe you didn't come and get me!" Crispin snorted a laugh.

Jinn smirked when her eyes met his, but once he saw the tension in her face, he straightened up and made his way to her. "What's wrong?"

"We have a problem," she said.

Chapter Thirty-Nine

Crispin

Once the other leaders had been alerted to the emergency meeting and filed into the dining hall, Crispin took one last breath to steady himself before calling the meeting to order.

Salome sat to his right and squeezed his hand reassuringly under the table. He offered a nervous smile before scanning the faces staring back at him. Around the large wooden table sat Prince Jinn, King Kenji, Master Penn, Kayven, Abba, Harbona, Lavena, Oifa, Hanzo, Prince Heru, Adonijah, Captain Haldane, and Rahab on his left.

Crispin cleared his throat, "We've received a report that a fleet of ships is headed in our direction. The ships appear to be Pulauan and are equipped for war."

The leaders exchanged curious glances around the room, but no one voiced their concerns except Captain Haldane.

"Is King Uri onboard?"

Crispin peered across the table at Kayven and Abba. The former leaned forward, resting his arms on the table.

"My brother and I do not know who this Uri is you speak of, so I cannot say for certain if he is aboard. However, whoever leads the fleet has plenty of weapons and soldiers to overrun us."

Murmurs made their way around the table.

"We are fortunate to have taken the element of surprise out of the equation," Salome added, hushing them.

"They were sailing quickly," Abba revealed, rubbing his chin. "Something is giving speed to their ships."

"Is there a way to know how many soldiers they have at their disposal?" Prince Heru asked.

"We did not have a lot of time to get proper recon," Kayven tapped his fingers against the wood. "I am surprised they did not spot us on a clear night like tonight."

"So, all we know is a fleet of ships is headed our way, but we do not know exactly who we are fighting or how many men we're up against?" Oifa, the newly married queen of the united Mountain Men tribe, flashed a menacing grin as she picked her fingernails clean with a knife. "Sounds like fun."

"As my sister has already stated," Crispin steadied his voice, "we know whoever is coming was banking on ambushing us. Now that we know they're coming, we will be ready to defend ourselves."

From the silence around the room, Crispin sensed the leaders were nervous. He just wasn't sure if they were concerned about fighting an unknown foe, or if they had no faith in him.

Adonijah cleared his throat, drawing Crispin's attention. "There is a way you can get the information you seek."

Crispin quirked an eyebrow. "How?"

Leoti stood before the counsel of leaders and stared at them just as curiously and ferociously as they looked at her.

"Adonijah told us you possess certain skills that could help us," Crispin spoke softly, noticing the Andrago's eyes darted to Adonijah.

"What do you want from me?" she asked, refocusing on the prince.

"There is a fleet of ships headed our way. I need to know who is coming and how many soldiers they have."

Leoti cast a glance at Adonijah once more. He stepped up to her and whispered in her ear.

Crispin dared a quick look at Salome, but if she was bothered by her former lover moving on, she didn't show it.

"I will help you on one condition." Leoti's voice drew him back.

The Andrago was bold indeed to think she could bargain with him, but even if she refused to help, he wasn't in the business of torture, so he'd have to find another way to get the information he needed.

"What do you want?"

"Release Pash from confinement, and I will do whatever you ask."

Crispin scoffed. "He is one of Niabi's closest advisors. He's her Commander of Shadows and from what I've heard, her lover. You expect me to allow someone with his title and skillset to roam these halls free?" He shook his head, crossing his arms over his chest. "Your commander is lucky to be alive. Yet, you dare ask me to release him so he might slit my throat in the middle of the night?"

"I did not *ask* you to release him," Leoti took a step forward, her fiery eyes narrowed. "I *told* you to release him, if you want my help."

"You forget your place." Crispin cocked his head to the side. "You may be free to walk around the keep, but you are first and foremost, a prisoner of war."

Adonijah took a heavy step forward and met Crispin's ferocious gaze with one of his own. Salome stood up and joined her brother's side; a lioness protecting her future king. If Crispin wasn't careful in how he handled this situation, they might tear the alliances they'd built to shreds, and they were already stretched thin as it was.

Leoti turned and pressed a hand to Adonijah's chest, stopping his advancement, and stealing his focus. When she faced the siblings again, her eyes had softened. "We need each other," she exhaled, easing the tension in her shoulders. "Pash is a good man, and he can be an asset when it comes to strategy. At least let him prove himself worthy. Let him help you defend Oakenshire, and I, too, will do my part to help you win this battle."

"And why should I take your word that his advice will be sound?" Crispin asked, surprised he was eager to know her answer.

"Because he has people he loves, that he wants to see again. He will make sure you not only win this battle, but you annihilate your attackers."

"Even if those assailants were sent by his queen?"

Leoti and Adonijah exchanged a quick look before she nodded her head in confirmation. "He gave up his post as Commander of Shadows when he helped Adonijah escape execution. And when the Shadows caught up to us, he fought them, risking his life to defend ours. The simple truth is Pash will help you, if it means he'll be protecting those he loves."

Salome leaned into Crispin's shoulder, and he bent slightly to hear her whisper, "We have never planned for a battle of this magnitude. Perhaps, we should hear the commander out, before we dismiss him."

Crispin knew she was right, but a part of him, the prideful part, wanted to refuse and throw the bold Andrago in a room beside Pash, as a true prisoner. But he had to consider all the people in Oakenshire that were depending on him to make wise decisions. He glanced at Rahab who was still sitting in her seat. Though he expected to see her face hardened at how Leoti had spoken to him, he saw she was already waiting for him to make eye contact with her. With a slight nod, she confirmed what his sister had advised him to do.

He looked at Leoti, "If he betrays us, you will hang alongside him."

The air was sucked out of the room and Adonijah's eyes blazed behind Leoti. Before anyone could protest or interject their opinion, Leoti extended her hand to Crispin and bobbed her head.

"Agreed."

"You trust him that much?" Crispin was surprised she would trust him with her life.

"I do."

Satisfied with her fervent defense of the commander, Crispin shook her hand and ordered for Pash to be brought before the group. Once Crispin had explained what they were up against, and the penalty should he betray them or attempt to flee to Northwind, the commander agreed to aid them. When Crispin asked why he didn't hesitate to agree to his terms, Pash said, "I don't intend to die here."

The first thing they did was have Leoti warg into her falcon and fly toward the incoming fleet. Crispin had instructed her to find out how many soldiers they had, how many ships were in their fleet, what kind of weapons they were armed with, if King Uri and Nezreen the Shadow Witch were on board, and what was giving speed to their ships. Once Leoti was confident she remembered everything the prince needed answers for, she sat down and blinked her brown eyes away.

The leaders sat quietly until Leoti's eyes blinked back to normal and she met Crispin's gaze.

"What did you see?" he asked, while leaders gathered around them.

"There are seven ships," she began, but the worry in her face was unsettling. "From your descriptions, I can tell you King Uri and the Shadow Witch are onboard the largest vessel and they are heavily armed with swords, maces, spears, and bows and arrows."

"How many soldiers?" Adonijah knelt next to her, but she didn't divert her eyes from Crispin.

"They have at least twelve hundred men with them."

Crispin's heart dropped and he had to tune out the whispers amongst the leaders in the room. "How long before they arrive?"

"A couple of days," Leoti whispered. "Maybe less."

"Did you find out how they are traveling so quickly?" Salome crossed her arms across her chest. Not a stitch of worry on her face and that struck Crispin as odd. For their entire upbringing, Salome wasn't one for altercations, but here in this war room, with a fleet of ships coming to destroy them, she was the very picture of calm. Perhaps their time apart had done more than just bring her tragedy.

Leoti nodded in answer to Salome's question, horror visible in her features. "They have a man chained in one of the smaller ships. He is an air manipulator; he's the reason their fleet is so fast."

Crispin's gaze darted to Rahab. They knew of only one air manipulator and since he used his magic to save them in Northwind, he opened himself up for Nezreen's shadows to track him down.

"Oden," Rahab confirmed his suspicions.

"We have to rescue him," Crispin wouldn't budge on that.

"You know him?" Salome chimed in.

"He saved us in Northwind," the prince nodded. "I will not let him be used and tortured for that witch's pleasure."

"But we won't be able to get near him or their ships without Nezreen's shadows knowing about it," Rahab pointed out.

"There has to be a way to get around her magic." Crispin raked his hands through his hair. They had been in the war room for hours and the lack of sleep was starting to wear him down.

"I believe, I can help on that front."

Crispin turned around and saw Jinn had made his way to Salome. They were staring into each other's eyes, and it almost seemed as if they were having an entire conversation by just looking at each other.

"How can you help?" Crispin's voice tugged the lovers from their intense eye contact and the Eastern prince met his awaiting gaze.

"I'm a cloaker."

"You're a cloaker?" Crispin could hear the excitement in Rahab's tone. "How many can you shield with your magic?"

"I've been practicing," the prince scratched his chin, "and I think I can hide a small rowboat."

Crispin turned his attention to Pash. "Let's see how good of a strategist you are, Commander."

Pash bobbed his head with a flash of determination in his eyes as he hunched over the aerial map of Oakenshire and started pointing to areas around the keep. The prince hated to admit it, but Pash had a great mind for military strategy. Within a couple of hours, the leaders hashed out a plan and agreed to Pash's defense positions and ground assault tactics.

Crispin would take the pirates on a rescue mission to retrieve Oden from Nezreen and Uri's clutches. He'd saved them in Northwind, so he owed him. Jinn readily agreed to cloak the group from Nezreen's shadows as they sneaked aboard the small ship to save the rebel.

With her accuracy as an archer, Salome agreed to join the Stormcrag and Krazak archers with Hanzo on top of the wall. If a ground assault happened, Salome would take her place among the Qata Vishna in the bailey to defend the keep and the castle attendants.

Kayven and Abba were asked to have their Bellators keep the ships busy by launching their attack from the skies, to which both brothers happily agreed.

Even though Crispin was still leery of Pash fighting amongst them, he agreed Pash and Adonijah would fight alongside Prince Heru and the Numbio by the shoreline, to make sure no enemy soldiers penetrated the bailey. If any slipped through, Salome and the Qata Vishna and Master Penn and her Keepers would be ready.

Captain Haldane was more than eager for his pirates to blow up a few of Uri's ships and left the strategy meeting with a twinkle in his eye mentioning he needed to talk to Phex, his explosions expert. Rahab assured Crispin she'd keep an eye on him during the mission to ensure the captain didn't do anything stupid that would result in all of them getting killed before they could extract Oden.

Harbona, Lavena, and King Kenji would stay inside the keep to help Rayma and her team with any fallen or wounded soldiers. The thought of losing any of their bannermen weighed heavily on Crispin, but he couldn't dwell on it, otherwise he'd lose his nerve and that's what would ultimately get him killed in battle.

Crispin was well aware they were still waiting on reinforcements promised from Numbio, the Isles of Myr, and the Immortals, but there was no telling if they'd show up in time. So, they were going to deal with the numbers they had. They had less than twenty Qata Vishna, seven Keepers, a handful of pirates, twenty-five Bellators, and among the Numbio, Eastern warriors, and Krazaks and Stormcrags, they had five hundred men and women. And from the intel Leoti had provided, they were vastly outnumbered.

He rubbed a hand down his face and plopped into his chair once all the other leaders had cleared out of the room. Thinking he was finally alone with his thoughts, he took a moment to release all the tension he'd been holding in his shoulders, cradling his face in his hands. He groaned. How was he going to pull this off? The Pulauans outnumbered them nearly three-to-one, and if Nezreen saw through Jinn's cloaking magic, she'd capture him and the pirates.

Hands slipped around his neck from behind and from the salt water and tobacco scents enveloping him, he knew it was Rahab. He kissed her hand and pulled her around to sit on his lap. Straddling him, she pressed her forehead against his.

"You should get some rest, princeling."

"Even if I tried to lay down, I wouldn't be able to sleep," he shook his head. Kissing the tip of her nose, he reclined in his chair, pulling her with him. He rubbed small circles around her lower back as she stared at him. "What?"

"Tell me what's on your mind."

He sighed and said, "We are outnumbered."

"And?"

"And?" he chuckled; eyes wide. "If we're overrun, we won't make it to Northwind to face my sister."

"One battle at a time, Crispin." She raked her fingers through his curls. "First the Pulauans, then your sister."

"You're rather calm about this," his eyebrow quirked, and he stared deep into her hazel eyes, looking for a crack in her armor. "Are you telling me you're not nervous, my love?"

She grabbed the reefer tucked behind her ear, lit it, and puffed out a cloud of smoke before shaking her head. "I'm terrified."

"But you just said -"

"Come with me," she interrupted him as she hopped off his lap. "There's something I want to show you."

Crispin dragged himself out of his chair and slipped his hand in hers as she pulled him through the corridors.

"Look around and tell me what you see?" she asked, exhaling another puff of smoke away from him.

The prince watched as the other leaders ordered their soldiers to help fortify the city from attack. Castle attendants rushed around helping to prepare the keep and set up areas where Rayma could treat the wounded. Jacobi was in the kitchens getting his staff to double the workload to make sure they had plenty of food before and after the Pulauans arrived.

Rahab tugged him onward and led him out to the back patio where the Ignacia Sea raged.

"You wanted me to look at the sea?"

Rahab shook her head and used her reefer to point at the level beneath them where Salome sparred against Jinn, Kayven, and Abba. She whipped her knives and Qata Vishna blades in fury and her movements were more like a dance. He hadn't taken the time to watch her spar since he'd arrived in Oakenshire, but seeing how much her skills had improved, how much she'd grown as a warrior and a future queen, was impressive.

"You have the Hunter fighting for you, Crispin," Rahab reminded him.

"But she's still mortal," Crispin turned his eyes away from his sister to Rahab. "If she dies -"

"You think anyone will come close to harming her?" Before he had a chance to respond, she motioned toward the Bellators she was fighting off. "Most do not know, but she has been practicing with the Bellator commanders every night for weeks. The people in the keep tell stories about her – how she defeated a cornigera and bathed in its blue blood to become the Red Maiden, how she slayed the Gomorrian royals and had their city destroyed, how she united two warring tribes and fulfilled their ancient prophecy."

"What are you trying to tell me, Rahab?"

Exhaling another waft of smoke, she faced her betrothed with an oddly comforting smile. "She would follow you to the very depths of hell, if it meant putting you on the White Throne. She survived the Thrak, she survived the cornigera, she survived King Gerd in the City of Bones – she will make sure we survive this too."

"It sounds like you have more faith in her than me," Crispin teased, but a piece of him believed it and it made his stomach sink.

"A great king is only as mighty as his warriors and as wise as his counselors." She tucked her finger underneath his chin and tugged his face to look at her. "You are surrounded by the best warriors in Adalore and are armed with the most knowledgeable men and women in the ten kingdoms. We might be outnumbered, but we are united, and that is far more dangerous in battle."

Crispin focused once more on his sister fighting off three skilled warriors at the same time, and a calm washed over him. Rahab was right. He had to have faith that not only his allies would come through for him, but that his sister would fulfill her destiny as the Hunter. Their journey would not end in Oakenshire.

Chapter Forty

Salome

Two days of preparation didn't seem like enough time to prepare for an impending attack, but that's all the time they had. Salome walked around the castle grounds one more time to ensure the holes in the walls had been filled. She stopped by the blacksmiths and was pleased they'd been able to forge and sharpen all the weapons they would need for battle. Every soldier was told to eat their fill and rest that evening, because from Leoti's latest warging session, the pirates would be upon them by morning.

Rosalina had made a comment that afternoon that Salome was so calm it was unnerving, but the truth was, she was absolutely terrified. She kept thinking about how Death stalked her, waiting patiently to claim her, but first toyed with her by taking those she loved most. Salome would never admit it aloud, but she looked on her friends' smiling faces and she hoped she would see them again the following day. She made sure to check in on Seraphina, Rosalina, Cato, and Kai that day and hugged them all before they turned in for the evening.

Crispin's time had been occupied by the pirates and their bickering on how they should rescue Oden from Nezreen's clutches. She knew her brother would be protected; his blue-haired lady pirate would see to that, but the fear that he would set off in a rowboat and sail straight into Death's clutches tugged at her heart. She had to remind herself that Jinn would be sailing with him, and his magic was powerful. He'd get them aboard the ship Oden was being held captive in unseen, and he'd make sure they all returned to her.

Salome knew she should be tucked in her warm bed, resting for the day of bloodshed, but her mind was racing, and it took all of her self-control not to reach out to her sister. She still had so many questions, but she had to remind herself that though Niabi shared her blood, she was still her enemy.

Tugging her cloak tighter over her shoulders, she rested her elbows on the patio railing and watched and listened to the waves sprawl across the sandy shoreline.

"You couldn't sleep either, I take it."

Salome smirked as Crispin rested his arms next to hers on the railing. "I'm surprised you aren't visiting with a certain lady pirate on the eve before battle," she wiggled her eyebrows playfully, drawing a smile from him.

"Where exactly do you think I've been this entire time?" He bumped his shoulder into hers and she laughed, feeling a small amount of weight lift from her. "And where is your betrothed this evening?"

"Safe and snug in his bed, I imagine." Salome twisted her body, squaring her shoulders to him. "Are you alright?"

“The truth?” He gazed into her eyes, and she was struck by how sorrowful he appeared.

"Always."

"I wish I could tell you I'm not afraid," he raked a hand through his hair and sighed, "but that would be a lie."

"You aren't weak for being afraid," she squeezed his hand.

"Wise words," he gave her a tight-lipped smile.

"Don't tell Kayven that," Salome snickered. "It'll go straight to his head that you found his words wise."

"I've heard you've been secretly meeting with the Bellators at midnight to train."

"Well, I suppose it isn't much of a secret, if everyone knows about it." Salome twirled a strand of her hair in her fingers. She knew Crispin was waiting for an explanation, and as much as she wanted to keep her battle fright to herself, she couldn't deny him when he'd been vulnerable with her moments before. "After I was rescued from Gomorrah and I was cleared for physical activity, I went to the bailey to spar with Kai and couldn't do it. It was as if my arm was made of stone and my reaction time was non-existent. I kept having flashbacks of my time in Gomorrah, the people I killed, the people I lost..." she cleared her throat. "My hands trembled and I realized there was something wrong with me, but didn't know what."

"What happened?"

"I stormed into the keep like some petulant child that just got her ass whipped and Kayven stopped me in the corridor. He told me he could help me overcome my battle fright, if I let him." Salome smiled, grateful for the Bellator brothers. "Every night after everyone else went to sleep, I would go down to the bailey and spar with them. At first, I had a difficult time. I couldn't get my hands under control and the flashbacks plagued me, but Kayven and Abba didn't give up on me. And now, they're teaching me more tricks. I just wish I had wings, so I could truly be their equal in battle."

"If you had wings, I would legitimately be upset."

"Why?" she laughed.

"Can't have you looking better than me," he dodged her incoming swat and chuckled. "If you had wings that would definitely make you the better-looking sibling."

"What are you talking about?" she snorted. "I'm already better looking than you."

Crispin rubbed his fingers along his beard. When they had parted ways months ago, he looked like a kid. Now, he didn't just look like a grown man, but like a king.

"I don't know. Now that I have this beard, the ladies can't help but look at me."

Salome rolled her eyes, "Delusional to the end." She hadn't meant the words to sound so finite, especially with a looming battle ahead of them, but it put a damper on the evening, no doubt about it. "We'll be alright," she whispered.

"We'll be alright," he echoed softly.

She slipped her hand into his and squeezed, resting her head against his shoulder. "We should at least attempt to get some rest."

"We should." He nodded, but neither of them moved, as if they both just wanted to enjoy one another's uninterrupted company a little while longer.

Standing with her brother on the eve of battle, in a quiet calm, was a memory that would forever be branded in her mind. Neither alone in their fear. She prayed the Almighty would protect him, even when she couldn't. It was in that hope alone that she was able to rest her head later that evening, but a small knock on her door stirred her from her bed.

Grabbing her robe thrown over the vanity chair, she wrapped it around herself as she made her way to the door. When she opened it, she found Jinn standing on the other side, his palms braced on either side of the doorframe. His head was down, his shoulders tense, as if he was physically restraining himself from stampeding through the door.

"Jinn?" she whispered, quickly glancing up and down the corridor to ensure no one had seen the prince arrive at her bedroom that late at night. "Is everything alrig -"

In a flash, he'd slipped his hands on either side of her face and crashed his lips against hers, swallowing the rest of her question. He was relentless, a drowning man desperate for his last breath. Slowly, tentatively, he grazed his fingertips from her cheeks down her neck, down her arms, until his calloused hands rested on her hips.

Raking her fingers through his already disheveled hair, she bit his bottom lip and twisted her legs around his torso when he hoisted her up into his arms.

Salome craved him; needed him. He was the answer to every riddle, the melody to every song. The stars, the seas, the mountains, they all paled in comparison to the passion of his kiss, the lightness of his touch, the warmth of his eyes. There was no denying her love for him; he was the beginning and end of her beating heart.

Jinn pulled back, but abandoned his retreat when she wrapped her hands around his neck and tugged him closer. He was breathless, his chest rising and falling rapidly, his lips swollen, and eyes hungry. Resting his forehead against hers, he whispered, "I had to see you."

She dragged the tip of her finger along the curvature of his chiseled jaw, drawing a raspy breath from him.

"I couldn't sleep," he said as he grazed his nose along the crook of her neck, breathing her in.

"What troubles you?"

"You."

"Me?" She pulled back, slowly sliding down from his tall frame.

"You have consumed my every waking thought and now infiltrate my dreams."

She smiled but before she could respond, he glided his hand around her neck, cupping her jaw, and said in a low voice that sent a bolt of lightning soaring through her body, "A secret for a secret."

"You first." She ran her thumb across his bottom lip, relishing how he shivered from her light touch.

"I want to marry you." His smile crinkled the corners of his eyes but she rolled her eyes in response. "What?"

"That isn't much of a secret since we are betrothed, my lord."

Her use of the new pet name seemed to ignite a fire in his golden-brown eyes and the way he looked at her made her own heart leap.

Jinn leaned forward, pressing his lips against her ear. His low, sultry voice made her knees buckle. "The secret is, I want to marry you tonight."

"Wishful thinking, my lord."

"Is it?"

Salome's throat tightened. Turning her face to meet his gaze, she found no trace of humor or deception. "You're serious."

"Harbona's room is at the end of the hall," he twisted a strand of her hair between his fingers. "He could oversee an elopement."

"What about a wedding?" She knew his people were extremely faithful to keep their traditions and weddings were a huge part of that. And with them being royals, the future King and Queen of Sakurai, a wedding would be expected, if not demanded.

"After the war, we can plan a traditional wedding," Jinn tucked a strand of her hair behind her ear. "But royal weddings aren't for us, they're for our people." The prince snaked his arm around her waist and tugged her closer, pressing their bodies together. "I would marry you tonight in this rundown castle and be content knowing you're mine."

It was then Salome glanced over Jinn's shoulder and realized they hadn't closed her door when he first arrived, but his low laugh was confirmation he'd already cloaked them.

"You should save your strength for tomorrow, Jinn."

"I will worry about tomorrow when the time comes." The vibrato in his voice sent a welcome shiver down her spine. He planted an open mouth kiss against the crook of her neck. "Tonight, it's just you and me."

She smiled and tilted his chin back up to kiss his lips. "You and me," she echoed.

Chapter Forty-One

Crispin

Crispin had not gotten much sleep. Even after saying goodnight to Salome, he lay awake in his bed until he was alerted that the fleet had been spotted by the patrolling Bellators. The sun had not peaked above the horizon when the castle hummed to life. Leaders and soldiers alike dressed, prepped, and made their way to their battle positions.

Once Crispin had double checked with each leader and their group, he headed down to the beach where a rowboat filled with what remained of Captain Haldane's pirates awaited. Just to the side of the boat, Salome whispered something in Prince Jinn's ear before embracing him.

At the sound of his boots crunching the sand, Salome turned and met his gaze. The morning light haloed around her, making her appear more like the Goddess of War, than his little sister. With an arms-length of space between them, Crispin halted and offered the best smile he could muster all while battling the thought this might be the last time they ever saw one another.

"Don't," Salome shook her head, eyes tearing up. "Don't look at me like it's the last time."

"You always were too observant for your own good." Crispin kicked at some sand when he teased her. He felt like a giant hand had grabbed ahold of his heart and was crushing it. Reaching for her, he pulled her to his chest for a hug. "Fight hard," he whispered.

She squeezed his torso tight enough to bruise a rib. "I will see you soon, brother."

Reluctantly, Crispin released her and headed toward Jinn to hop into the awaiting boat.

"Take care of him." Salome's voice rang out behind him, spurring him to turn around.

"I promise to keep an eye on your betrothed," he smirked.

"I was talking to Jinn." She motioned toward the prince, eyes now fixed on the Easterner. "Protect my brother and come back to me in one piece."

Jinn bowed his head and winked. "As my lady commands."

Crispin exchanged one last look with his sister before he and Jinn pushed the rowboat away from the shoreline and into the Ignacia Sea. With a nod from Crispin, he signaled Jinn to cloak them as they made their way toward the fleet anchored in the distance.

"How do we know if your magic worked?" Captain Haldane asked Jinn, and all eyes darted to the prince.

"I can sense it," Jinn replied.

"And if it falters?" Rahab quirked an eyebrow which drew a playful grin from the Easterner.

"Then I hope you can swim back to shore, when the Pulauans sink us."

Crispin chuckled, and it seemed to relieve the tension amongst the crew of the *Shadow of Death*. He slipped his hand in Rahab's and squeezed. Her hazel eyes latched onto his and softened a bit before she transformed into the hardened pirate he first met. Mentally, she was ready, and he knew no matter what happened during the battle, he would do everything in his power to make sure she made it out alive.

The moment of truth was upon them. They were within firing range of the Pulauan warships, so if Jinn's magic hadn't worked, it would be seconds before the seafarers launched an assault to sink them. But as they continued to draw closer to the ship Leoti had described as the one Oden was being held captive in, nothing happened. No weapons were aimed at them. No soldiers aboard the ships even gave them a second glance. Their rescue mission was working.

Crispin almost breathed a sigh of relief until he saw pirates emptying from the vessels into smaller boats and rowing straight for them. There was nothing they could do but wait to see if the enemy would sail past them or attack them. They held a collective breath as the invading sailors whooshed by. At least Jinn's magic was powerful and in full effect. But as Crispin did a quick count of how many rowboats filled with enemy soldiers headed toward Oakenshire, his stomach churned. There were easily a thousand warriors making their way toward the castle. He mumbled a quick prayer of protection over his sister, before turning his focus back to the mission at hand. If anyone could lead their troops to victory, it was the Hunter.

With most of the soldiers headed toward shore, there would only be a couple hundred men left aboard the seven vessels to man them. They could easily incapacitate the sailors aboard the ship holding Oden and when they were done rescuing him, sink it. Hopefully, if Phex's trinkets worked, they could sink a couple more ships on their way back to shore. Burn the ships, then their soldiers would be stuck.

They finally made it to the first ship and one by one, slowly boarded. Jinn managed to keep them all cloaked until they were all standing on the deck. But as they were informed during the strategy meeting, the prince wouldn't be able to keep them hidden as they split up and battled the remaining pirates. Once they were ready, Jinn nodded his head, releasing them from his magic and the crew scattered around the warship, making sure to have a partner with them at all times.

Captain Haldane set off with Phex to set up explosives. If they successfully blew up this boat once they extracted Oden, Almighty willing, they'd catch the two ships on either side, burning them to a watery grave.

Ondrej the giant, and Rafi the pint-sized one, took off toward the helm to take control of the ship.

Rahab and Corwin, the quiet, knife-thrower, set off to slit the throats of the seafarers around the deck.

Leaving Crispin and Jinn to find Oden below decks.

With this vessel being the smallest in the fleet, it didn't take long for the enemy to be slaughtered. Crispin and Jinn easily found the room Oden was chained in and while Jinn stood guard outside the entrance, just in case the ship was boarded by a crew from neighboring vessels, Crispin made his way inside to free the Northerner.

"Oden?" Crispin knelt in front of the rebel and gasped when he saw the man's body.

Chained and shackled, his arms were stretched wide, and his legs were rooted to the floor, making him look like a giant X. He'd been badly beaten; his body was riddled with small cuts from his face all the way down to his bare feet. His clothing was stained with blood and had gaping holes. It was cold in the dark, windowless room and Oden's lips were turning blue. His eyes were closed, but when Crispin reached out and touched his shoulder, the man jolted awake, rattling the chains.

"It's me," Crispin held his hands up in surrender. "Oden, it's me."

Oden sighed in relief. "My Prince," his eyes darted around the room. "You shouldn't be here. It is far too dangerous."

"I've come to rescue you."

"You need to go before the witch's shadows sense your presence."

Crispin's heart ached at the fear in Oden's face. What horrors he must have endured being held captive by Nezreen and Uri. Slowly, Crispin extended his hand to the manacles around his wrists, finding the skin underneath raw and bleeding.

"We have a cloaker," the prince explained as he tugged on the chains to see how strong they were. "Once we get you out of here, we'll head back to Oakenshire."

Oden shook his head, a great sadness seeping into his bruised features. "There's no use, Prince Crispin. There is only one key that will unlock these chains -"

"Jinn," Crispin called out and the Easterner slipped inside. If Jinn was horrified by the state Oden was in, he didn't show it, his mask firmly in place. "We need to check every man on this ship for a key to unlock his chains."

Jinn and Oden exchanged a knowing look and Crispin's gaze darted between the two men.

"You know one another?" he asked.

Oden offered a weak smile and nodded. "It is good to see you again, Prince Jinn."

"I wish it were under different circumstances, Oden." Jinn's gaze roved over the chains and then met Crispin's inquisitive look. "Oden asked me to go to the Isles of Myr to see if I could find your sister. He wanted to help her before Niabi or Gershom could get to her."

That answered how the two men knew one another, but it didn't do anything to advance the rescue mission. All Crispin's questions would have to wait until later.

"We need to find the key," Crispin reiterated, but Oden shook his head.

"You don't understand, my Prince. There is only one key and that key hangs from Nezreen's neck." Oden's eyes were filled with a sorrow Crispin knew too well. "There is no saving me."

Crispin refused to accept that and started tugging the chains, hoping he might be able to rip them from the hooks tying him to the room. "I came to rescue you and that's what I intend to do."

"Crispin," Oden's calm voice made his skin prickle with goosebumps. "You need to escape, while you still can. I will buy you time."

"Don't give up," he pulled harder on the chains to no avail.

"I wish I could have been by your side when you swore your oath in Northwind," the rebel met Crispin's teary gaze. "Go. It's alright."

Crispin opened his mouth to refuse the man's plea, but when Rahab ran into the room, he redirected his attention. Apart from some sweat and a small scratch on her left cheek, she was unscathed.

"There's movement from the *Leviathan*," Rahab reported. The *Leviathan* was Uri and Nezreen's ship and was the largest and fastest in the fleet. "They know we're here. We have to go."

Crispin's face hardened as he turned back to Oden.

"You must go," Oden offered a feeble smile. "I knew I was never going to leave this ship alive."

His failure to rescue Neempo the Sovereign from his sister in Northwind weighed heavily upon him. But this. Failing Oden, the man who had saved him and Rahab when certain death was upon them; the man who had loved his mother more than himself; the man who was faithful to his king and country all his days, even as an outlaw. This failure was more than Crispin's heart could bear.

Standing to his full height, the prince rested his forehead against Oden's and whispered, "I'm sorry."

"I'm not," Oden shook his head, tears streaming down his battered face. "I get to see your mother again. Go!"

"Crispin," Rahab's voice sliced through his hesitancy, snapping him into action.

Crispin followed Jinn and Rahab to the door, but he forced himself to look back one more time. "Thank you for your unwavering devotion to my family. You will not be forgotten."

Oden bowed his head. "Long may you reign, my King."

Chapter Forty-Two

Salome

Salome watched Crispin, Jinn, and the pirates drift toward the fleet until she noticed enemy soldiers rowing their boats toward shore. They passed her brother, and she was relieved that Jinn's practice had paid off. He had successfully shielded them from the hundreds of seafarers headed her way. Footsteps crunched behind her, but she didn't take her eyes off the dozens of rowboats oaring through the sea.

"How many do you think are coming?" Adonijah asked as he stood by her.

"If I had to take a guess," she turned, "at least eight or nine hundred."

He bobbed his head in agreement.

This had been the first time the two of them had been alone, since his arrival into Oakenshire. It was then, she told him whatever was going on between them was over. She knew she'd made the right decision for herself and after seeing how he interacted with Leoti, she knew her decision was right for him, as well. But she'd be lying if she said she didn't miss their friendly banter and camaraderie.

"Are you afraid?" His voice brought her back to the present and she glanced back at the approaching force.

"Afraid for them," she smirked. "None of them are leaving this place alive."

Adonijah laughed and it filled her with an incredible sense of joy. "Smartass," he crossed his arms over his chest, shaking his head.

"You know me," she bumped her shoulder against his arm. "Thank you."

"For what?"

"Staying."

He cocked his head to the side, confusion written across his face. "Where else would I be?"

"I didn't mean to hurt you," she whispered, the light morning breeze whipping strands of her loose curls across her forehead. She'd let Rosalina braid her hair in the traditional Qata Vishna way, but her hair was stubborn and had a way of sneaking out.

Realization washed over him, and he squared his shoulders to hers. Taking her hand in his, he squeezed and asked, "Are you happy with him?"

Salome smiled. "I am."

"I'm happy too."

"So, are we friends again?" she teased, and he pulled her into his arms for a hug.

"Until Death takes me."

Taking a deep breath, she pulled away from his embrace and turned her attention to the castle they were about to defend. "I suppose it's time."

Adonijah rolled his shoulders back and cracked his neck. "I suppose it is."

Salome patted her palm against his chest. "The Almighty protect you."

He slid his hand above hers. "May Strength and her Eagle guide you."

It warmed her soul that he remembered the Virtue she had chosen as the new Red Maiden: Strength and her Eagle. She cupped his face and thumbed his jawline before turning to head up the embankment to the castle. She would take her place amongst the archers and down any pirate within distance of her shot.

Knowing Adonijah and Pash were joining Heru with the Numbio and Oifa with the united Mountain Men as the first line of defense, she swore she'd make sure they all made it through the battle. She had become deadly in hand-to-hand combat, but archery was still her first love, and she was confident in her ability. She was used to being the hunter and she would make sure all prey suffered the same fate.

Qata Vishna blades strapped to her back, three daggers in their holsters attached to her thigh, lower back, and right boot, her quiver of arrows swinging from her hip, and her bow in her hand, Salome took her place on top of the outer wall facing the Ignacia Sea.

Hanzo had the archers lined up with their bows nocked, ready to rain hell upon the intruders.

Turning to glance into the bailey behind her, the Qata Vishna and Master Penn and her Keepers were armed to the teeth and chomping at the bit, to get a piece of the action.

Although they'd done their best to patch holes and rebuild sections of battered walls, there were still gaps and weak points. That's where the troops, Heru, Oifa, Adonijah, and Pash eagerly awaited the first wave of sailors.

Salome cast her gaze toward Kayven, Abba, and their elite unit of Bellators. Their entire agenda was to destroy ships and keep Uri and Nezreen distracted from Crispin's group rescuing Oden. When the Bellator brothers saw her, she nodded, signaling it was time. They smiled, spread their wings, and rocketed into the sky. They were fast and undeniably beautiful in their lethality. She couldn't help the smirk that snaked across her face as she watched the winged warriors zig-zag through the air, cutting down pirates that attempted to fight them around the decks of the warships.

As the Bellators wreaked havoc upon the fleet itself, the enemy sailors reached the beach and began their assault.

"Archers ready!" Hanzo cried out and all the bowmen aimed their weapons at the invaders.

Salome obeyed the King of Fennor, inhaling and exhaling rhythmically to settle her nerves. They were prey – nothing more.

To her left, Kai readied her own bow, the very picture of calm. She was grateful to have the Ryoko Naga by her side.

"Loose!" Hanzo dropped his hand forward and dozens of arrows soared through the sky, downing their intended targets.

Waves of pirates fell, but many managed to slip through, stampeding toward the gaps in the outer wall and into the awaiting arms of the Numbio and Mountain Men.

"Swords!" Heru bellowed, and his men unsheathed their swords as one.

"No survivors!" Oifa pounded a fist to her chest. "No mercy!"

The Mountain Men howled in response and unleashed hell. The clashing of metal upon metal rang out and drowned all other sounds.

Death was present and she was feasting that morning. Men and women on both sides succumbed to the sword, axe, or arrow, and the grey stone pavers were coated red with blood.

Salome kept a steady pace, each of her arrows meeting its mark, offering another soul to Death. A loud grunt behind her caught her ear and when she whipped around, she saw three Pulauans swinging their cutlasses at Heru. Redirecting her attention, she grabbed three arrows and quickly fired them in rapid succession, striking all three of them dead. Heru flicked his gaze up to the wall and nodded his thanks before jumping back into the fray.

Wave after wave of pirates continued to dock and storm the castle. The marksmen downed as many as they could, but they were running low on arrows.

"I'm out," Kai shouted and motioned toward her empty quiver.

Salome, too, was out and was ready to move to the next phase of her battle assignment. Casting her bow to the side, she unsheathed her Qata Vishna blades and blew two long notes on the horn Seraphina had given her to signal the Myridians and Keepers they were needed. With Kai at her side, armed with her fan of knives, Salome made her way down the stone staircase, setting foot on a real battlefield. Adrenaline pumped through her body and she had to fight the flashbacks that kept wanting to creep into her mind. Training with Kayven and Abba gave her the strength and technique to quiet the battle fright. She couldn't succumb to her fear, not now, when she was needed most.

A small door set inside the gate leading to the bailey opened and the Qata Vishna and Keepers filed out and fell into line behind Salome and Kai.

"Qata Vishna! Keepers!" Salome called out and they stood at attention. "Slay them all."

Blades ripped from the Myridians' holsters; the united unsheathing echoed across the battlefield, alerting everyone they had arrived. As one, they sprinted toward the chaos and once they reached their allies, proceeded to flip, kick, spin, and stab their way through the enemy soldiers.

Salome swiped the legs out from under an enormous Pulauan. The ground shook when he fell. Not wasting time, she drove both her blades into his chest before ripping them back out and moving on to the next one.

"Salome!"

She recognized Adonijah's voice and whipped around. He and a handful of soldiers were surrounded by Pulauans and cut off from the rest of their allies.

"Shield!" She yelled and two Qata Vishna dropped to the ground, bracing their shields above them to propel her as soon as she jumped. Soaring through the air, she decapitated two seafarers as she landed.

Fighting their way out, Adonijah thanked her while wiping blood and dirt from his face. She wasn't sure if the blood belonged to him or not, but there wasn't time to ask as another group darted toward them. As hard as they fought, they were still outnumbered, and it was only a matter of time before they were overrun.

A sudden cold wind stirred, whipping in from the sea. Looking out toward the fleet, she saw a massive storm swirling. Crispin must have gotten to the air manipulator. He's the only one she could think of that could conjure such damaging conditions. But as she looked out and over the expanse of the beach, her heart sank. The endless wave of faces running toward them sobered her to the fact they might not win this battle. Even if Crispin was successful in his rescue mission, he and the Bellators might not make it back in time to help, or worse, they might not be able to do anything to change the outcome.

"Jinn," she couldn't help reaching out to him.

"What's wrong?" He responded immediately.

"We're being overrun. We might not make it," her voice cracked.

"Hold on, darling, we're coming."

"Jinn -"

"Don't you dare give up! Do you hear me?"

"I just wanted you to know that I love you." She slammed their connection closed, sliced a pirate's leg off at the knee, and followed it up with a blade stabbed through his neck.

A horrendous scream pierced her ears and when she turned, she caught sight of Rosalina with a knife stuck in her abdomen. Salome sprinted toward her friend, watching helplessly as Rosalina fell to her knees. The Pulauan that had stabbed her, swung his cutlass, his aim to decapitate the Qata Vishna.

"No!" Salome screamed, pushing people out of her way, but she was blocked.

Rosalina closed her eyes as the blade swung at her neck but at the last second, she ducked, ripped the knife out of her gut, and sliced the inside of both of the sailor's thighs, bringing him to his knees. Now face to face, she took his own knife, covered in her blood, and slit his throat.

Salome reached her as she keeled over, her hand pressed to her wound. Rosalina had lost a lot of blood and was frighteningly pale.

"You're alright." Salome cradled her friend. "I'm going to get you to Rayma. You're going to be alright, Ros."

"I'm sorry, my lady," a tear slid down Rosalina's cheek. "I'm afraid I will not be able to keep my oath to protect you."

Salome shushed her and attempted to lift Rosalina up, but the Qata Vishna fought off her efforts.

"Ros, I am trying to help you."

"I go to the After to join my sisters in arms." Rosalina was having difficulty breathing but met Salome's teary gaze.

"Please don't go," Salome's bottom lip quivered.

"Tell my sister, we will meet again." Rosalina pulled Salome close and kissed her forehead. "As deep as the sea," she whispered.

"Rosalina?" Salome whimpered as the battle raged around her. "Rosalina!?" She shook the Qata Vishna but there was no waking her. She was gone.

It felt like she was wading through quick-sand and she couldn't hear anything or anyone around her. She gently laid Rosalina down on the ground, covered in her friend's blood.

Feeling eyes on her, she looked up and met Seraphina's line of sight. She was frozen in place with several invaders running toward her, swords drawn. It snapped Salome out of her grief. She wouldn't lose both twins. Rushing with her blades out to defend the stricken Qata Vishna, she blocked the incoming blows and fended off the enemy sailors. Once she'd downed them, she shook Seraphina, screaming for her to fight, but her far off gaze was fixed on her dead sister. Seeing no other option, Salome slapped Seraphina, bringing her back.

"Fight, Seraphina," Salome pleaded. "I need you to fight."

The twin dragged her sight from Rosalina's lifeless body; rage replacing her pain. Together, Salome and Seraphina sliced through every pirate in their path, leaving a trail of splattered blood and splintered bones. Scanning for her friends, she was relieved to see Kai, Adonijah, Heru, Oifa, Hanzo, Cato, and Master Penn still standing. They were beaten, bloody, and exhausted, but they were alive, and that's all that mattered. The only thing they could do now was fight for their survival, and hope Crispin and the Bellators could return to aid them before it was too late.

Chapter Forty-Three

Crispin

As soon as his boots hit the deck of the warship, Crispin took in the sight of the chaos and destruction of the Battle of Oakenshire. Dead Pulauans were strewn throughout the deck. Looking up into the sky, the Bellators were zipping in and out of combat with soldiers on other vessels. But when he looked to the Mainland, where his sister was leading the battle against the invaders, his heart lodged in his throat. There wasn't an inch of that beach that wasn't occupied by an enemy soldier. He knew they were outnumbered, but seeing the invasion his sister was facing, sent him into a panic. They needed to get back to help, but what could a handful of people do? They could come up from behind to fight them, but it would still take a miracle for them to win this battle.

"Crispin!" Rahab's voice dragged him back to the present. "We have to get off this ship before it blows."

He followed her to the rope ladder to climb down to their awaiting rowboat, but as he descended, he sensed someone was watching and turned toward the Leviathan and there stood Nezreen with her shadows dancing all around her. He knew she was blind and that she couldn't actually see him, but he swore, she was staring into his very soul. A wicked grin snaked across her pale face, confirming his suspicions. She was well aware of his presence, and it was indeed time for them to escape.

Dropping to the boat, he motioned for them to leave. Pushing against the hull of the vessel that Oden would die in, he whispered, "Rest well, my friend."

Crispin picked up an oar and helped them row back to Oakenshire. He noticed Jinn stiffen, his eyes were filled with concern and his brow was knitted together.

"What is it?" Crispin asked once Jinn was set free from whatever spell he was under.

Jinn met his gaze. "It's Salome. They're being overrun."

"How do you -?"

"Her magic."

Crispin felt stupid. Of course, she could communicate with Jinn through her magic. She had told him about her power when they were reunited, but they hadn't discussed it since. And since Jinn had magic, they had a connection.

"How bad is it?" Crispin refocused and questioned the prince.

Jinn shook his head; a wave of emotions clouded his features. "It sounded like she was saying goodbye."

"Row faster!" Crispin shouted, but Haldane pressed a large hand to his shoulder.

"We're rowing as fast as we can, lad, but the tide is against us," the captain explained.

As if on cue, a gust of wind swept through, propelling them toward the Mainland.

"Oden," Crispin whispered, recognizing the magic in effect.

But the gust of wind that Oden conjured, turned into a funnel and began tearing one of the smaller ships in Uri's fleet apart. The rebel was going to fight until his last breath, once again saving Crispin from Death.

Seeing the storm brewing, Kayven warned the Bellators to avoid the twister, so Crispin took his chance to get the commander's attention by waving and shouting his name.

Kayven heard him and descended, "Prince Crispin?"

"My sister needs your help!"

Hard determination settled into the Bellator's features and the winged warrior nodded in understanding. "Bellators, to Oakenshire!"

"Take me with you!" Jinn called out before the Immortal left. Glancing at Crispin, Jinn said, "I'll make sure she's safe."

Crispin nodded in approval as Kayven extended his hand to Jinn. Once the prince was secure in Kayven's arms, the Bellator rocketed back to the castle, and it gave Crispin hope that Salome and their friends would survive.

Behind him a large explosion sounded. Crispin ducked from the debris flying overhead from the vessel Oden had been on. Phex's trinkets had worked, and the ship was nothing but a pile of floating debris. As Phex hoped, the ship next to it ignited and the flames spread quickly along the hull. The ship sank within minutes.

Crispin looked back at the *Leviathan* and Nezreen still hadn't moved from her position. Her shadows darted toward them, looking for souls to snatch, but suddenly halted and retreated. Her attention was no longer fixed on them, but on something behind her.

A giant harpoon jettisoned out of the fog and splintered the vessel adjacent to the Leviathan. Someone had come to their rescue. When Crispin saw three white ships with golden sails, he jumped to his feet to scream for joy. The Immortal reinforcements had finally arrived, and just in time. Their presence forced Uri and Nezreen to order their fleet to retreat before they lost another ship. But before they could sail away, a wall of water sped toward the vessel next to the Leviathan and crashed into it, toppling it into the sea. Whoever was with the Immortals was a powerful magic wielder, and Crispin was glad to have them on their side.

Crispin glanced around at everyone in the boat and smiled, a second wind filling his lungs. "Let's go help our friends."

Chapter Forty-Four

Salome

If she hadn't seen it with her own eyes, Salome wouldn't have believed the wall of water had destroyed one of the Pulauan warships, but that's exactly what happened. She watched as the seafarers retreated, abandoning their soldiers on the Mainland, whom they still had to defeat, but her strength – physically, mentally, emotionally – was waning. Hope stirred within her when she saw the golden sails of the Immortal ships and the hundreds of Bellators taking off from the decks and making their way to shore. Kayven, Abba, and the Bellator elite were leading the charge. Help was on the way, she just had to hold on a little bit longer.

Four Pulauan soldiers rushed and cornered her, bloody weapons drawn. She had to dig deep to muster every last ounce of fight she had left in her to survive. Ducking, dodging, and tumbling, she avoided their attacks, slicing and stabbing as she eluded them. Three fell to the ground, dead, but the fourth and largest Pulauan slapped her wrists, knocking her blades from her grip. Now disarmed, the soldier smacked her hard across the face, drawing blood. She fell to the ground and he swung his cutlass upon her, but she quickly rolled, jumped to her feet and drew her wolf dagger from her thigh, ready to poke holes in his chest. But despite his large size, he moved swiftly and landed another two blows to her face and chest, stealing her breath. He landed a large boot to her stomach and she keeled over. She tried to crawl away, but couldn't move fast enough and suffered a crushing kick to her ribcage, wrenching a scream from her.

This was it. Exhausted and in excruciating pain, she watched as he lifted his weapon over his head to deliver the final blow. "Care to beg for your life? I love when bitches beg for mercy."

Salome flashed her middle finger and spat at him in response.

Enraged, the pirate swung his cutlass at her throat, but Jinn uncloaked himself and blocked the deadly blow.

The prince whipped his tachi swords around, disorienting the Pulauan, but he quickly recovered and sparred with Jinn, landing a punch to the Easterner's chin. Jinn jumped back, eluding the swipe of the soldier's blade. Their swords clashed ferociously, but Jinn managed to get the upper hand when he elbowed the pirate in the face and quickly plunged a sword into his chest.

With a grunt, the Pulauan dropped dead, and Jinn grimaced, and fell to his knees.

"Jinn!" Salome crawled to him, horrified at all the blood seeping from his abdomen. "No, no, no, no. Jinn, please hang on." She pointed at the nearest soldier, a Stormcrag archer, and ordered him to bring a healer immediately.

"Salome," Jinn's voice was calm and washed over her like rain extinguishing a forest fire. "Look at me." He flashed her a pain-filled smile, "I'm alright."

"Alright?" her voice cracked. "There's a lot of blood, Jinn."

"I've had worse injuries." He cupped her face. "I promise, I'll be alright, darling."

"I can't lose you too," she sobbed. "We lost Rosalina today and I just can't... I can't..."

"I'm not going anywhere." Just as Rosalina had done before she died, Jinn pulled her close and planted a kiss on her dirty forehead, his blood stained her armor. Her breathing hitched and her bottom lip trembled. Noticing she was having a panic attack, Jinn tilted her chin to force her to look into his eyes. "I'm not going anywhere," he whispered in a tone that began to soothe her. "It's you and me. Say it."

"It's you and me," she echoed softly, returning to herself. She ran her fingers through his sweaty hair, hovering above him. "You saved me again."

"It's becoming a habit," he chuckled softly, his free hand covering his wound.

Salome scanned the bailey and was relieved to see with the Bellators' help, they were able to push the Pulauans out of the city and cut them down as they fled to their rowboats, not knowing they'd already been put to the flame. Despite the odds, they had won. They had won the Battle of Oakenshire, although she still didn't know how many lives this victory had cost them.

Jinn groaned as he pulled his breastplate off and tried to sit up, spurring Salome to slip behind him and guide his head onto her lap. "Don't move." She glanced toward the keep where all the injured were being taken but didn't see anyone from Rayma's team coming. "Where is the healer?"

When footsteps approached, she snatched one of Jinn's swords and pointed it at whoever was coming. Adonijah raised his hands, and she lowered the weapon. His gaze bounced from her to the bloody prince as he knelt beside them.

"How badly are you hurt?" Adonijah asked.

Jinn gritted his teeth as he pulled his blood-soaked shirt up revealing a slash across his lower abdomen. There was a lot of blood and Salome was finding it difficult to mask her panic. Adonijah took his canteen and poured a little bit of water over the wound to get a better look. The prince hissed, but Adonijah nodded and the tension in his shoulders vanished.

"It looks worse than it is." Adonijah started ripping pieces of fabric from a dead Pulauan's cloak to wrap around Jinn's torso. "It will need to be cleaned, stitched, and bandaged, but you'll live."

Once Adonijah and Salome wrapped Jinn's gash to stop the bleeding, the sell-sword helped the prince to his feet. With Jinn's arm over Adonijah's shoulders, they walked to the keep where Rayma and her team were tending to the wounded. The great hall where they'd celebrated Hanzo and Oifa's wedding a week ago, was now riddled with bodies, dead and alive, friend and foe. It reeked of blood, sweat, and death. Adonijah set Jinn down when he found an open spot on the floor and marched over to where Rayma was, got some supplies, and returned. Salome watched Adonijah silently take a needle and thread and look up at the prince.

"If you would prefer someone else do this -"

Jinn shook his head and motioned for Adonijah to do what needed to be done. "Try not to enjoy this too much," the prince smirked.

"I'll do my best." Adonijah grinned, then focused on the gash. After cleaning it, he carefully stitched up the wound. Salome held onto Jinn's hand tightly, grateful Adonijah was there to help him.

"That should do it." Adonijah cut the string and tied it. "I can help you to your room. You'll need to rest."

The trek to Jinn's chambers was long and somber. Salome was so relieved Jinn was safe, but her heart was heavy, knowing so many of their comrades didn't make it through the battle. She would need to give Rosalina a proper Myridian burial out at sea. She feared seeing who else might not have made it through the day.

"You should get checked out yourself," Adonijah's voice sliced through her thoughts.

Consumed with worry for Jinn, she had forgotten she, too, suffered injuries, but it wasn't anything she couldn't handle herself, knowing Rayma and her staff were busy tending to more serious wounds.

She shook her head, "I look worse than I feel." A lie, and by the look on Adonijah's face, he knew it, but he nodded and let the issue go.

Once they made it to the prince's chambers, Adonijah helped him into his bed and quickly headed for the door. Salome clasped Adonijah's forearm before he left and said, "Thank you."

Adonijah kissed her forehead. "You're welcome." And then he turned on his heel and disappeared down the hall.

Salome stood in the threshold of Jinn's chamber door, conflicted. Should she leave him to rest, so she could find the other leaders to get updates? Or should she watch over him for a little while, until someone else could take her place?

"Salome?" She closed the bedroom door slowly, before turning to face him. "Are you alright?"

"I should let you rest," she averted her gaze from his bandaged abdomen, guilt weighing heavily on her shoulders that he had been injured protecting her.

"Stay with me?" His voice was soft, his eyes expectant.

She knew she needed to meet with her brother the moment he and the pirates returned, but she couldn't bring herself to deny his humble request. Perching herself on the edge of his mattress, she gently caressed his bruised knuckles.

"What am I going to with you?" Salome's questioned seemed to catch him off guard.

"What do you mean?"

Her eyes latched onto his and there was no hiding her fear. "Jinn, promise me you won't risk your life for me again."

"You should already know I won't agree to that."

"I would never be able to forgive myself if you died protecting me," she interrupted him. "Promise me, please, promise me, you won't jeopardize your life for me again. Do not value my life above your own."

Jinn winced as he sat up, ignoring Salome's protests for him to remain in a comfortable position, and cupped her face in his hands. When she met his gaze, tears she'd been holding back slipped down her smudged cheeks. He swiped his thumb over her lips and offered a weak smile.

"I told you before, darling, if it is within my power to give, I will give you whatever you want or need," he tilted her chin up, forcing her to look at him, "but you already know I will not promise to abandon you when you need me most." She opened her mouth to argue, but he pressed his lips to hers, silencing her. When he pulled back, he whispered, "Whether in life or death, we go together. That is my promise."

Salome bobbed her head, "In life or death, we go together." Resting her forehead against his, rubbing her forearm where the freshly tattooed band in Zophar's honor sat, she knew she'd be adding more bands before the end of the war, and the thought shattered her heart.

Chapter Forty-Five

Crispin

The second the rowboat hit the sandy shore, Crispin and the pirates hopped out and stormed the beach, slicing and stabbing all enemy soldiers in their path. The Bellators were making quick work of the stragglers around the keep and when Uri's pirates saw they were surrounded, they attempted to flee to their boats, but Ondrej and Rafi had already torched them. Even if they had been able to reach their boats, Nezreen and Uri retreated, leaving them to die or face execution.

Crispin had one goal in mind, get inside Oakenshire and make sure his sister had survived. He cut off arms and legs of enemy Pulauans, leaving them bleeding in his wake, knowing one of his companions would finish them off. It took so much longer than he'd hoped to reach the bailey, but once he was there, he was struck by the smell. Covering his nose with his sleeve, he glanced around at the dead bodies lying in puddles of blood. Some eyes of the fallen were still open, forever staring upwards in terror or pain. He scanned the bodies, sifting through some of them to see if his sister's body was among them, to see if he saw any of his friends blankly staring back at him. To his relief, he didn't see Salome or any of his close companions. What he did see were faces that had been smiling around the bailey during training, and citizens from each corner of Adalore that had celebrated Hanzo and Oifa's wedding a week ago.

Dragging a hand down his face, he turned toward the keep and made his way to the grand hall where he knew the wounded were being taken care of, and exhaled a sigh of relief when he still didn't see his sister. The longer it took to find her, the more hope he had that she'd survived and was helping others.

As soon as he stepped over the threshold into the make-shift infirmary, all eyes darted to stare at him. Men were groaning and screaming as Rayma's team helped stitch them up, or in some cases, amputate limbs that could not be saved. Blood was everywhere. Tears flowed and he could sense the shattered hearts of those grieving friends and loved ones.

"She's not here," a familiar voice stated, spurring him to turn around.

Rayma wiped her bloody hands on what used to be a white apron tied around her waist.

"What?"

"Your sister," she clarified. "She's not here. She and Adonijah helped an injured Prince Jinn to his room to rest."

"Prince Jinn was injured?" Crispin had been with him less than an hour ago and it was unsettling that in that short amount of time, the prince, who was tasked with ensuring Salome's safety, found himself in need of help.

"The prince will live. Adonijah stitched and bandaged him," Rayma tilted her head to the side, pressing her hands to her hips. She looked him up and down, examining him as if to see if the blood staining his armor and face belonged to him or not.

"I'm uninjured." Crispin wiped the splattered blood she was staring at off his cheek.

"I'm glad to hear it."

He never thought he'd hear concern or genuine joy for his well-being come from the Healer from Numbio. When they had first met all those months ago in the Southern Lands, she hated him and didn't attempt to hide it. But now, something was different. Something had changed between them.

"Don't look so surprised," she huffed, as if she could read his mind. "I might not be your best friend but I'm hardly a monster."

"I didn't think you were," he offered. "Do you need help?" He looked around the room, knowing he didn't possess skills Rayma could use, but he'd do whatever he needed to do to aid her and her team.

She slipped her hand around his bicep, dragging his gaze to meet her exhausted eyes. "You should rest, Prince Crispin. You will be needed tonight."

"Tonight?"

She nodded her head sadly. "For the funerals."

Crispin could have sworn someone had taken a knife and sliced his chest wide open. "How many?"

"So far, by my count, we lost around eighty men and women today."

His head was spinning, so he sat down on the nearest bench and scraped his fingers through his sweaty, tousled hair. His bottom lip quivered, but he looked up when Rayma knelt in front of him, her normally stone-cold eyes were filled with sorrow.

"We lost good men and women today, my lord." Tentatively, she reached for his hand and squeezed gently. "We won this battle, but we will need you to be strong, if we are to win this war."

"You sound awfully close to being kind to me," he offered her a tight-lipped smile, as a tear slipped down his cheek.

Rayma flicked the lone tear from his face and smiled in return. "You freed my brother from the dungeons in Northwind. You were willing to help Heru find a way to outwit the Grim. You killed Memucan, setting me free from my prison." She held his stare and her eyes softened. "You are a good man, Crispin of Northwind. I am sorry I did not see it before."

"I don't feel like a good man right now," he whispered.

"You hurt because you care." She stood from her crouched position when someone called her name. "There are many leaders who look at their soldiers as expendable, but not you. You grieve our losses and that is what sets you apart from the rulers that came before you."

"Rayma," he hopped to his feet when she turned to leave. "I know you only came on this journey because of Heru, but I want you to know, I'm grateful you're here."

"If I didn't know any better," she smirked, "I would think we're becoming friends."

With a nod of his head, Rayma walked off to help more wounded men and women and he set off to find a quiet place where he could be alone.

Crispin's first stop was the kitchens, not for food, but for a bottle of rum. Snatching one, he stomped out and made his way to the library where he knew he'd find some peace and quiet. He didn't want to be near anyone, fearing he would look weak and vulnerable. Plopping into a wooden chair, he uncorked the liquor bottle and took a shot, welcoming the burn.

The sun was beginning to set and gave the records room a heavenly glow. This is where he found peace amidst the chaos, surrounded by ancient tomes and scattered candles. It brought back memories of his mother and how he loved helping her in the library in Northwind. *Knowledge is power.* That had been branded into his brain since he was three. Now, as the future king, he was determined to surround himself with books and wise counselors, but no text or person could have prepared him for the heaviness war brings. The death, the destruction, the loss; he wasn't sure he could manage it.

"Oden's death isn't your fault, Crispin."

He should have known Rahab would find him sooner or later. Not bothering to look up, he took another sip of rum and offered it to her, but she didn't take it.

"If it isn't my fault, then whose fault is it?" he asked, his voice hoarse.

Rahab leaned her hip against the table, crossing her arms over her chest. "He used his magic and Nezreen's shadows tracked him -"

"He used his magic to save us when I shoved us out of a window," he hissed, raking a hand through his sweaty hair.

"He could have let us die. He didn't -"

"It wouldn't be in his nature to shield himself and watch us die." Crispin reluctantly met her gaze knowing at some point he was going to have to face her. "I know you're trying to help, but his blood is on my hands. I failed to save him in the end."

She frowned and shook her head. "You dishonor his sacrifice by claiming responsibility for Oden's decisions. He knew the risks – he risked it anyway. He knew what his magic was capable of – he used it anyway."

Crispin didn't want to be on the receiving end of yet another lecture and hopped up from his seat and started to stomp away, but Rahab wouldn't be dismissed so easily. She followed him and grabbed his forearm, whipping him to face her. His nostrils flared, but she didn't relent.

"Rahab, don't -"

"He gave his life to save hundreds of lives today," her voice had a bite to it, which didn't surprise him. "He died a hero, not a victim. Do not disrespect him by feeling sorry for yourself. Mourn the dead. Thank them for their sacrifice. Live to fight another day."

A tear slipped down his cheek and he rubbed the heels of his palms against his eyes. Groaning, he pressed his back against one of the wooden bookcases and gently banged the back of his head a couple times.

"These people, men and women alike, are here to follow your lead." Rahab slipped her hand against his cheek and forced him to meet her gaze. "They will look to you for strength. Be their fortress, Crispin."

"Has anyone ever told you that your bluntness is irritating?"

"All the time," she smiled. Reaching for the bottle of rum on the table behind her, she took a swig and offered it to him. "Hail to the dead."

Crispin gulped another shot and nodded his head in agreement. "Hail to the dead."

Hours later, when the sun had set, and the wounded had been tended to, Crispin joined the others as they sifted through the bodies strewn from the beach to the bailey of the keep, searching and sorting through the bodies of the fallen, friend and foe. The enemy soldiers were piled and set to the flame, but when it came to their fallen companions, each leader oversaw their traditional burial rituals.

King Kenji murmured the ancient prayers of the Easterners as the bodies of his fallen warriors were burned on separate pyres. In accordance with their people, the ashes of the lost would be placed in decorative urns and sent back to their families to be placed in the crypts of their ancestors.

Hanzo and Oifa sent their dead wrapped in linens in a cart back to the Bone Mountains where their bodies would be buried in caves. They believed for a tribesman to go to the After, they would need to be close to the heavens, and there was no higher burial ground than the mountains.

Heru joined the surviving Numbio to bury their dead in the ground. They were formed from the earth and to the earth they would return.

The Bellators did not have traditions to follow since they were not accustomed to death in Caelestis. An Immortal, Ethereal and Bellator alike, would choose when they were ready to cross into the After and pass on to the next life. So, when Kayven and Abba had to make a decision on how to deal with the three men they lost, they opted to adopt the water burial the Myridians and Westerners cherished.

The Myridians lost two warriors, including Seraphina's twin sister, Rosalina. Salome helped wrap her friend's body and set her in a rowboat dressed in her armor, helmet, and armed with her Qata Vishna blades laid across her chest. Seraphina placed two gold coins on top of her sister's eyes before she and Salome set the boats carrying the Myridian warriors adrift.

In Northwind, the departed were buried in the mountain crypts with their ancestors. But they weren't in Northwind, nor did Crispin have Oden's body to wrap and bury, so he whispered prayers his mother had taught him, helping to usher his soul from his watery grave to the After.

Master Penn and her Keepers managed not to lose one of their own during the battle, but that didn't stop the blind warriors from offering their hands to help prepare the dead.

Once each leader had assisted their departed to the After, Crispin stood before those who remained and lifted his glass of wine. "We thank the dead for their sacrifice."

Everyone in the bailey lifted their drinks, then drank in memory of the victorious dead. Crispin knew some of the men and women gathered together wouldn't survive the war, and that thought weighed heavily on him.

Chapter Forty-Six

Salome

Several days had passed since the Battle of Oakenshire, but Seraphina still wasn't interested in leaving her chambers for training. Losing her twin was more than she could handle and even though she lashed out and pushed Salome and Kai away, they made sure she received food three times a day and forced her to bathe, even going so far as trying to braid the Qata Vishna's hair, but it just made them think of Rosalina and her impressive skills with hair and make-up.

The Qata Vishna allowed Cato to stay every night with her since the battle, so Salome's mind was put to rest knowing Seraphina was in good, caring hands with the Stormcrag. But that didn't relieve Salome of the grief and angst pent up inside her, so she dragged Kai down to the bailey to spar.

This time, Kai didn't go easy on her and gave her quite the challenge. Spinning, flipping, kicking, they began to gather a crowd who watched them spar to perfection. They'd fought one another countless times over the last several weeks and had learned one another's moves, so their sparring sessions lasted much longer than the ordinary pairing. But after going back and forth, sweat glistening across their foreheads despite the low temperatures, Salome faked Kai out and took the opportunity to land a blow to the Ryoko Naga's chest.

Salome walked over to the fallen Kai and extended her hand to pull her up. Kai flashed a rare smile and accepted the help.

"Not bad, my lady," Kai bowed her head.

"I dare say, you're a tougher opponent than Kayven," Salome chuckled.

As if mentioning the Bellator's name conjured him, the brothers sifted through the dispersing crowd and Kayven tsked.

"I dare say, I have been too easy on you, Princess," the Bellator's grin was unsettling. "What do you think, Abba? Should I show my true strength?"

Abba shrugged, "If the Princess is looking for a more challenging sparring partner, I volunteer."

Salome rolled her eyes. "Leave it to you two to get your feathers all ruffled."

"We are not birds," Kayven scoffed. "Our wings do not ruffle."

A soft voice cleared behind them and everyone turned to see Leoti standing in the bailey, her hand crossed over her chest gripping her other arm. "I was wondering... I was wondering, if I could join you?"

Salome's face softened at the sight of the Andrago who had captured Adonijah's heart and motioned her forward. "You're Leoti, right? The warg?"

Her eyes brightened and she nodded. "Yes, Your Highness."

"Call me Salome."

Leoti's doe-eyes scanned all the weapons the four of them had strapped to them and said, "I'm afraid I do not know much about weaponry and feel ill-prepared for the battle that lies ahead."

"From what I've heard about you, you are quite powerful without swords and daggers." Salome sheathed her Qata Vishna blades in the holsters on her back. "I heard you killed Prince Thanos of Gomorrah, along with his guards." The Andrago's gaze fell to the stone pavers and Salome feared she'd said something wrong. "I didn't mean to offend you, Leoti."

"Oh, no," Leoti flicked her eyes up from the ground and shook her head. "You didn't. It's just..."

Salome stepped toward her and smiled, "You may speak freely."

"I want to learn how to fight," she confessed. "I want to learn how to fight with weapons like the rest of you."

"I'm sure Kai or the Bellator commanders would -"

"I would prefer if you taught me," Leoti interrupted her which surprised Salome.

"Why me?"

"You've heard tales about me," the Andrago fiddled with the braid that hung over her shoulder and down her chest, "but I have also heard tales about you. Adonijah told me all about your time together."

In an instant, Salome stiffened as her mind flashed back to battling the Thrak on multiple occasions with Adonijah, defeating the Cornigera, and Adonijah volunteering as her champion to fight Gerd in the City of Bones. She couldn't help remembering their intimate moments as well, how his lips felt pressed against hers and how he used to look at her.

Leoti smiled, "I know he loved you."

Salome could sense Kai and the Bellator brothers backing up to give them space, but she wished they would interrupt this ambush, and sweep her away from the awkward conversation she knew she was about to have.

"I was married before I met Adonijah, but he... died." Leoti pressed on, unfazed by Salome's discomfort.

"I'm sorry for your loss," she offered.

"I've mourned Rollo and I know a piece of my heart will always love him, but that doesn't mean I cannot find love again."

"What are you trying to say?" Salome rubbed her hand along the back of her neck, shifting her weight.

"You and Adonijah cared for one another, there's history between you two, but I want you to know that I am not intimidated by that." Leoti smiled and reached for Salome's hand. "I know a part of him will always care for you, but if you would be open to it, I think we could be good friends."

The Andrago maiden surprised Salome yet again. She'd assumed she was going to stake her claim on the sell-sword or tell Salome to keep her distance from Adonijah, but instead she acknowledged their past and didn't allow it to hinder building a friendship with her. Salome immediately felt shame creep into her cheeks as she had jumped conclusions.

"I'd like that," Salome bobbed her head and smiled. "Adonijah is happy with you. It is obvious his heart is yours."

"And my heart belongs to him." Leoti pointed at the wolf dagger strapped to Salome's thigh. "So, will you teach me how to fight?"

Salome unsheathed it and handed it to her. "It would be an honor."

After spending a couple of hours teaching Leoti basic self-defense moves and how to protect herself should she be attacked, Salome made her way to her room so she could soak in a warm bath, but when she turned the corner of the hall leading to her chambers, she saw Adonijah leaning against the wall waiting for her.

"Looking for someone?" Her question spurred him to straighten from his reclined position.

"I saw you and Leoti sparring in the bailey."

She couldn't tell if he was pleased or irritated, so she marched up to him and squared her shoulders to his. "And?"

"Thank you."

"For what?" She cocked her head to the side.

"Being kind to her." His eyes met hers. "I didn't know how you would react to me and her..."

Salome slipped her hand over his forearm and squeezed. "Adonijah, I'm happy for you. She is wonderful and she suits you."

He exhaled, and the tension in his shoulders vanished. "Well, I'll take my leave then."

She nodded as he started walking down the corridor she'd just come from. "Adonijah." He turned to face her. "I'm glad you've found happiness. You deserve it."

With a smile, he bowed his head, and turned the corner, disappearing from view. And she found she meant it. She wanted him to be just as happy with Leoti, as she was with Jinn.

Slipping into her chambers, she stripped her sweaty clothes and fighting leathers off and walked into her bathroom where a hot bath was already awaiting her. She dipped her fingers in the water and sighed at the warmth. She took a breath before plunging her body into the steaming water. After the initial sting of the heat kissing her flesh, she adjusted to the temperature and leaned her head against the porcelain lip.

Her mind was restless, and even though she knew she shouldn't reach out to Niabi, especially after she'd sent the Puluans to attack them, she couldn't resist the temptation. She closed her eyes and mentally ventured to the door that belonged to her sister and instead of gently pushing the connection open, she kicked it in, like she was stampeding through a door.

"For someone who desires peace as much as you do," Salome barged into her sister's mind, vengeance and wrath fueling her, *"you certainly don't know how to pursue it."*

"What are you talking about?" Niabi's voice swam in her head, grating her already frayed nerves.

"The fleet of Pulaun ships you sent to attack us in Oakenshire," Salome gritted out. *"You speak of wanting peace for you and your unborn child, yet you send the Pirate King and his Shadow Witch after us, instead of coming yourself. You're not only a monster, but a coward as well."*

"Salome -"

"I lost someone very dear to me," Salome interrupted her sister. *"You say your quarrel was never with me or our brother, but this seems awfully personal and yellow-bellied, even for you. I thought you were a warrior queen, but I suppose those are exaggerated stories since you prefer hiring pirates to do your dirty work."*

"I have no idea what you're talking about!" Niabi's voice rumbled in her head. She could sense her sister's anger and confusion and it made her stop to think. How could she be so surprised by the attack she sanctioned? *"I never sent a fleet of Pulaun ships to Oakenshire. Up until this moment, I had no idea where you were hiding."*

Salome was now the one left confused. *"You didn't send them?"*

"No, I didn't send them." Niabi didn't hesitate and by her tone, Salome believed her. And then realized she'd just given away their position.

"If you didn't," Salome asked, *"then who did?"*

"That is a very good question," Niabi's words were laced with worry.

"What will you do?" Salome didn't want to have to admit her blunder to Crispin, but if Niabi now knew where they were, they'd have to either move quickly to prepare for war with the North or be prepared for another strike.

"If you are concerned I am going to send my soldiers to attack you in Oakenshire, you can put that thought to rest," Niabi said with a calculating tone. *"If someone ordered the Pulauans to Oakenshire, then they are within my court and will be dealt with swiftly."*

"You expect me to believe you won't attack us, now that you know where we are?"

"Only a fool would move troops in the winter months," Niabi scoffed, as if Salome was an idiot for suggesting such a thing. *"By the time they made their way to you, they'd be frost-bitten and fatigued. You might not believe me, sister, but I truly do not wish for a war. I've had enough bloodshed to last me a thousand lifetimes and I am weary."*

"Why are you telling me this?"

"Because, I meant what I told you before. All I want is to raise my child in peace."

"You will never have peace if you remain on the White Throne," Salome countered. *"Crispin will have it, whether he has to kill you to get it or not."*

Niabi chuckled sadly and it tugged at Salome's heart. *"It would seem war is in our blood. None of us ever stood a chance."*

Salome wanted to ask her more, but she felt Niabi tearing away from the connection. She'd not had anyone do that to her before. She'd always been the one to end the connection, but Niabi was putting up a tremendous fight to escape.

"As fun as this chat has been," Niabi purred, *"there are matters that require my attention. Goodbye, Salome."*

Before Salome could protest, she felt as if two hands shoved her out of Niabi's mind and when she opened her eyes, she found she wasn't alone in her bathroom.

"What are you doing in here?" Salome slipped lower beneath the water, attempting to hide her naked form, and scowled at Kai standing in the doorway.

"I knocked several times, and you didn't answer," Kai stated, as if she didn't notice Salome sitting in the bath.

"As you can see," Salome made a sweeping motion around the room, "I am occupied. What couldn't wait?"

"Harbona has requested you and Prince Crispin meet with him." Kai offered her a towel and Salome reluctantly grabbed it, motioning for the Easterner to leave.

"I know Jinn wants you to watch me, but you can at least let me get dressed in private."

Kai smirked. "Nothing I haven't seen before, my lady."

"Kai," Salome warned and the Ryoko Naga put her hands up in surrender.

"I will be in the hall to escort you when you are ready."

"Kai," Salome called out, halting her from leaving. "When Jinn and I are married, who will you be sworn to obey?"

The Ryoko Naga shrugged a shoulder. "I will serve you both. But if you wish to be technical, I am sworn to protect Prince Jinn. When you become his wife, you will be assigned a protector of your own."

Salome smiled. "Thank you for protecting him, Kai."

"It is my honor to protect and serve you both," Kai bowed her head slightly before walking out of the room.

Once Salome heard the door click, she hopped out of the tub, dried herself, and dressed quickly. The last thing she wanted was to keep Harbona waiting longer than he deemed necessary. A grumpy Harbona was not her favorite person to deal with. But once she readied herself and joined Crispin in Harbona's quarters, she was surprised to find the Seer sitting with a woman who looked a lot like Odelia. Her stunning grey eyes didn't go unnoticed, and Salome knew only Ethereals had such eyes.

Harbona must have sensed her question because he quickly introduced them to his daughter, Makeda, and Salome chuckled when Crispin's mouth fell open.

After arriving with the Immortals who aided them in defeating the Pulauans, Makeda was preparing to journey south to the Enchanted Swamp to look after Odelia, as she recovered from her stint away from her home. She'd overexerted herself by destroying Gomorrah with her magic.

Over dinner, Makeda explained how she was a member of Oden's team and was saddened to learn of his death. She offered her magical services during the upcoming battle with Northwind, but Harbona insisted she be with Odelia and reconnect with her. If another attempt on the Enchantress' life was made, he felt better with his water wielding daughter being by her side. Salome knew Harbona was trying to fit into his new fatherly role and keep his daughter safe. She didn't blame him. She would have done the exact same thing.

It was odd to see Harbona so at ease, when Salome knew him for being serious and overprotective. It filled her heart with joy seeing him interact with his daughter. She hoped after the war was won, that Harbona would finally take time to make himself happy, instead of putting the whims and wills of kings and queens before his own family, now that he had one.

After they'd eaten dinner with Harbona and wished Makeda a fair journey, Crispin and Salome made their way to their own rooms and settled in for the evening. Her body ached, her mind was exhausted, and her spirit was empty. As soon as her head hit her pillow, she closed her eyes, and dreamt of nothing, which suited her just fine.

Chapter Forty-Seven

Niabi

Niabi didn't care the members of her small council had turned in for the evening. She wanted to know who attacked Oakenshire, and she would get those answers one way or another. Comfortably seated around the wooden table in her study, the queen carefully eyed Tala and Vilora. Anaktu stood in front of the doors ensuring no one could come in or out.

Vilora picked food from between her snaggleteeth with her pinky fingernail, not bothered by Tala's disgusted glare "My Queen, will you tell us what this is all about or will you continue to give us the evil eye until we guess what you're thinking?"

Niabi's penetrating gaze shifted to her aunt, not sure if the witch had just rolled out of bed or if the disheveled look was a personal choice, she crinkled her nose and began the meeting. "A fleet of ships attacked my siblings in Oakenshire. I want to know who ordered the assault."

Neither Tala nor Vilora said a word. Niabi watched them intently, waiting to see who would speak first.

"How do you know Oakenshire was attacked?" The Andrago finally spoke, clearly confused.

"I have my sources." Niabi didn't want to reveal Salome's magical connection with her, especially not with Vilora in the room. She'd give her life for Tala, but the witch couldn't be trusted. "Someone has betrayed me, and I want to know who."

Vilora met Niabi's accusatory gaze and whispered, "No child of your womb will sit on the White Throne of Northwind, until all other usurpers have been vanquished. But I warn you, you will pay a heavy price for victory and an even heavier price for failure."

"What?" Niabi cocked her head to the side. That was the prophecy the old witch foretold almost twenty years ago.

The hag smirked, no longer lounging lazily in her chair. She squared her shoulders to the queen. "You think yourself so wise, Niabi, but you are a fool."

Tala hissed, "Watch your tongue, witch, before I claim it."

Vilora pointed at Niabi's swollen belly, "You think *that* child will sit on the throne -?"

"My siblings shall be dealt with- "

"Whether your siblings were killed the night you took Northwind or not, your heirs will never claim the White Throne," Vilora interrupted.

"What are you saying?" Niabi leaned forward, cradling her belly.

Vilora chuckled, batting scraggly hair from her weathered face. "I thought you would have figured it out by now. For your children to live, *you* must die."

Realization that she had usurped the throne from her father slapped her across the face. The old witch had tricked her with her riddles and craftily phrased prophecy, but the truth was, she had doomed Rollo the second she killed her father. "You deceived me!"

"I am the Old Witch of Endor," Vilora threw her hands up and cackled, thoroughly enjoying her moment. "Did you really think I cared what happened to you when we first met? You wanted so desperately to believe you could right the wrongs inflicted by your father that you condemned yourself."

"It's you," Niabi slowly stood from her seat, narrowing her eyes at her betrayer. "You're the one who sent the ships."

Tala hopped to his feet, unsheathing his sword and pointing it at the witch.

Vilora sighed, waving a lazy hand in the air. "I told you not to underestimate him, deary."

"Gershom," Niabi growled. "You are working for him."

"With," she corrected with a wicked grin. "I am working *with* the king."

"You mean the queen's prisoner," Tala scoffed, his brow furrowed.

"You've never been safe, Niabi," the witch rose to her feet, unfazed by Tala's weapon aimed at her chest. "And now, everything you have will be taken from you," she said so softly that it sent an unwelcome shiver down Niabi's spine.

"Or I can have you executed and put an end to your treasonous schemes." Niabi held her head high, but Vilora's hoarse laugh diffused her short-lived victory.

"It is already too late," the witch said. "Your Shadows have been poisoned against you and now serve Ophir. Your precious commander chose his brother over you and isn't here to help you." Vilora tilted her head to the side, giving the appearance of a feral animal. "You are alone."

Niabi snarled and was flirting with her knives sheathed in her sleeves, when Thrice burst into the room. Anaktu grabbed the unmasked Shadow by his throat and slammed him against the wall. Thrice reached out to Niabi, gurgling his words.

"Release him," Niabi commanded, and the Nephilim immediately dropped him. "What is it, Thrice?"

"The Shadows," Thrice's voice was raspy, but he pushed through with his message. "They have sworn loyalty to Ophir. They've freed Gershom from his prison and Ophir is on his way here to kill you. We need to get you out of the city."

Without hesitation, Vilora and Niabi launched fireballs at each other. Tala and Thrice were armed with their blades, but with fire being shot across the study, all they could do was to jump out of the way, before being struck. Niabi unsheathed her daggers, her left arm still ablaze, and kicked her desk at Vilora. Though she was a witch with fire magic, Vilora was old, and her reflexes slow, so she couldn’t move fast enough to avoid the blow of the heavy, wooden desk, and Niabi took advantage of the opportunity and ran out with Tala, Thrice, and Anaktu.

"We won't be able to get you out through the main gate," Thrice stalked down the corridor, keeping his eyes peeled for any Shadows headed their way.

"I know a way out." Niabi grabbed Thrice's arm and pulled him down a different hallway. "We'll have to be quick about it."

The four of them sprinted down the hall, remaining vigilant to a potential attack, but if there was a coup being staged, it was a quiet one. She didn't hear any screams coming from the castle staff, didn't detect the sounds of metal against metal indicating soldiers fighting other soldiers. It was deathly silent and that is what made her worry. How had she been so blind to Gershom's schemes? She was so focused and angry about him garnering foreign allies and support, for his quest for her throne, she was oblivious that he had used her own men against her.

She would make Gershom and Vilora pay if it was the last thing she did, but first, she needed to survive to fight another day.

Once they zig-zagged through the castle, they came upon a door that led through the staff's quarters. At the very end of the wing, there was a humble, wooden door that allowed passage into the city streets. Thrice had given her his black cloak to not only protect her from the chill of winter, but to help disguise her from citizens. They already had a Nephilim with them, the last thing they needed was for people to start bowing and drawing attention to them.

Niabi knew there were tunnels that led to the castle, but she was nervous about spending more time inside the keep with cold-hearted assassins on her tail. So she immediately thought of the safe house at the southeast end of the city wall. An entrance to the tunnels could be accessed beneath the house floorboards and it would lead them to safety. They just had to make it there before her enemies spotted them.

Thankfully, darkness shrouded them and the only people still out and about at that hour, were the revelers in the Night District. She would have preferred sneaking aboard an outbound ship and hatching her plan for revenge as they sailed away, but ships did not leave the harbor at night. The sailors were far too drunk or up to their necks in women to sail to the next kingdom. Instead, they'd have to make their way through the Black Forest, which didn't bother her, because she knew it like the back of her hand, but Gershom and Vilora also knew it well, and if they came looking for them there, they'd be sure to find them.

Niabi clutched her belly, and as they were scrambling toward the southeast side of the kingdom, a terracotta shingle fell from one of the rooftops and smashed on the stone road in front of them. Glancing up, she sensed them before she saw them. The Shadows, the mercenaries she'd founded and trained with for nearly two decades, had tracked them down. Slipping down from the roofs, the Shadows surrounded the four of them, successfully cutting them off from the house that was just down the street.

"Would you turn against your queen? You swore an oath to me. You bear my sigil on your arms." Niabi looked at each masked warrior one-by-one. "Would you truly commit treason knowing the penalty?"

She knew there was no use talking them down once they'd been given the order to assassinate her, but she turned in a circle appearing to plead her case only to get an accurate count of how many they were up against. By her quick count, there were fifteen of them. Fifteen to four. Not great odds, but she had faced worse. Slowly, she unsheathed her knives underneath the large cloak Thrice had given her, ready to strike the moment one stepped too close. She'd trained with these men, bled with them, and now, she would kill them without remorse. That was the way of the Shadows.

Niabi heard someone clapping and when she whipped around, she saw Vilora and Ophir appear from the darkened street. Vilora stopped clapping once she met Niabi's gaze and flashed a malicious grin. "Leaving so soon, Niabi?"

"Enough talk." Niabi slipped her hands through the cloak, revealing her knives and left arm ablaze. She whipped a blast of fire at the unsuspecting Vilora and it smashed into her chest, launching her into the air.

That was signal enough for Tala, Thrice, and Anaktu to wage war against the Shadows that surrounded them. Being severely pregnant didn't hinder Niabi from sparring with her friends-turned-enemies and she cut them down with righteous indignation. She managed to dodge a fireball. Vilora was back on her feet and the witch looked like a hornet that had been swatted one too many times. She was angry, and just like Niabi, she was out for blood. Back and forth the fire wielders went, landing blows and singeing hair and clothing. With sheer determination to see the witch burn to ash, Niabi fought on, knowing her three companions would have her back.

A chorus of footsteps stomped down the street and when Niabi looked beyond Vilora, she saw a group of about fifty armored soldiers marching toward them. They weren't going to make it out alive if those soldiers reached them, so she opted for a reckless option. She stopped firing at Vilora and aimed at the buildings surrounding them. The thought of burning a citizen's business or home made her sick, but if she was going to have her revenge, she was going to have to escape. Beams from the burning buildings fell between her and the army, but the Shadows were already scrabbling up to nearby roofs to cut them off from behind.

They had to run. She motioned for the others to follow her; they could make, it if they hurried. But someone grabbed her forearm, forcing her to stop. She looked up into Anaktu's masked face.

"Anaktu," she hissed.

The Nephilim raised his scarred hand to his mask and pulled it off his face. It had been nearly two decades since she had seen him without it and although he had aged, he hadn't changed.

"Anaktu," she whispered gently, tugging him forward. "We need to go."

Without his tongue, he couldn't speak, but he signed to her and her eyes widened.

"No," she choked up. "I will not allow it. I order you to -"

He signed with more fervor than she'd ever seen from him before. With a giant finger, he pointed for her to run, and she once again shook her head in protest, but she couldn't hold back her tears.

"I said, no!" She pulled him, but he didn't budge. "I will not leave you here. I will not -"

Anaktu wrapped his enormous arms around her and held her tightly. A whimper escaped her lips and when he pulled back, he offered a rare smile. Tala grabbed her arm and tugged her down the street.

"Niabi, we need to move, now! They're going to catch us."

"Anaktu!" She tried to fight Tala, but Thrice grabbed her other arm and together the men dragged her down the dimly lit street. "Anaktu!"

Anaktu had been captured by Andrago scouts and brought before Dichali and Niabi. The Nephilim, the last of his kind, was forced to his knees before the royals and his eyes shifted around the room in terror. It was obvious he had been mistreated while in Chua's care.

Anger flared in Niabi and she clutched the wooden armrests of her throne to keep from attacking Dichali's friend for his barbaric treatment of the creature.

"A gift for Your Majesty," Chua beamed, raising his arms in victory. "The Last Nephilim."

"What is your name?" Dichali's soft voice silenced everyone in the gathering tent, but when the Nephilim didn't answer, Chua chuckled and said, "It would be hard for him to answer without his tongue."

Niabi couldn't help herself; she shot up from her chair and hissed, "You cut out his tongue?"

"What if he mumbled curses against us?" the Andrago warrior narrowed his eyes at her. "We couldn't take that chance."

"And the slashes and bruises all over his body?" she pointed out, stepping down from her dais to approach them.

Chua shrugged lazily, "The monster is clumsy."

"As far as I can tell, you're the only monster that stands before me," Niabi spat. Before Chua had a chance to defend himself, she turned to face her husband and said, "My love, give this Nephilim to me. Spare his life and I promise he will be a loyal member of our court."

Chua balked, "You cannot be serious!"

Niabi whipped a dagger out from her sleeve and held it against Chua's neck when he got too close to her. "Friend of the king or not, you will remember your place, or your queen will remind you."

"Enough," Dichali waved his hand and Niabi lowered her weapon but her gaze on Chua didn't waver. "The Nephilim is yours, my love. But if he does not abide by our laws, then he will be executed." Niabi bowed her head in understanding. The king's glare was now directed at his best friend. "We do not

maim and torture prisoners, Chua. Next time, there will be swift punishment for the offense. Am I clear?"

Chua nodded, though his eyes burned. "My King."

Dichali motioned for everyone to leave and once they had, Niabi knelt before the Nephilim and slowly stretched her hand to his face. When he flinched, it broke her heart. She whispered, "You need not fear me. I will protect you."

"Niabi!" Tala's voice jostled her from her memories of Anaktu. "Tell us where to go!"

The Last Nephilim's eyes were filled with nothing but love as he slipped his mask back onto his face and drew his sword, nodding a silent goodbye. He turned to face the enemy soldiers dousing the fire she'd started and waited for them to attack.

She had sworn to protect him, to save him, but he was the one who had always protected her and now he was laying his life down to save hers. She couldn't allow him to do it. She broke free from Tala and Thrice's hold and darted toward him, but Tala wrapped his arms around her, halting her.

"Anaktu!" she cried, but the Nephilim stalked away, deeper into the flames to face the soldiers who had once called her master.

"He's gone, my Queen," Tala pressed his cheek against hers, her back flush with his chest. "Tell us where the tunnel is so we can get you out. Do not let his sacrifice be in vain."

Reluctantly, she pointed to the small house and once they opened the secret door underneath the rug, they descended into the tunnel. She swore she heard one final roar echo from Anaktu, but then it was snuffed out and she knew he was truly gone. Her friend and protector was dead. She swore on every dead soul she'd lost that she would make sure all those responsible would beg for Death before she exacted her revenge.

Niabi, Tala, and Thrice ran through the Black Forest as quickly as their tired legs could carry them. They escaped Northwind but hadn't had the time to grab supplies or horses. But with their skills as Shadows, they had the skills to survive the bitter winter.

The guilt of leaving Anaktu behind weighed heavily on Niabi. Other than Tala, he'd been her constant companion and silent comfort for two decades.

She'd sworn to protect him and she failed. She could still hear him roaring as he darted to his certain death to give her time to get away. She would never be able to say goodbye, she would never be able to thank him for his love, friendship, and ultimate sacrifice. Everyone saw him as a monster, a beast, an unfeeling creature, but Anaktu was gentle, caring, loving, and deserving of happiness.

Tears slipped down her rosy cheeks as they trudged through the snow with only the moon illuminating their path.

Suddenly a sharp pain ricocheted through her abdomen and stole her breath. She slammed her hand against the trunk of one of the many pine trees and waited for the pain to pass. She knew what was happening, she'd been having the contractions for the last couple of hours, but now, it was becoming unbearable.

As Tala brushed by her, she grabbed his arm and through gritted teeth said, "The baby is coming."

"Right now?" Thrice whipped around from leading the pack and caught Niabi's feral gaze.

"As inconvenient as it might be, Thrice, yes," she hissed, riding out another wave of labor pain.

Tala didn't question her but got straight to work. They were in the middle of the forest and not within walking distance of any house or village. Niabi knew the Black Forest well and knew her baby was going to be born outside on a bitter winter's night.

The Andrago helped her lay down in a comfortable position and draped his cloak over her. "I know you will shoot daggers at me when I say this, but you will need to bite down on my leather belt when you're in pain." Tala took off his belt and gave it to her. "If they hear you scream, they'll find us and Thrice and I won't be able to defend you."

Niabi knew he was right, but she wasn't sure she'd be able to do what he was asking. As wonderful as her pregnancy with Rollo had been, she remembered how excruciating birthing him was and a spark of fear flickered in her heart. Either way, she would have to do as Tala asked. Bobbing her head in agreement, she took the leather belt he offered and bit down on it hard.

Tala glanced at Thrice who looked as if he was going to be sick and ordered him to, "Keep watch and keep out of sight." Thrice nodded, not needing to be told twice, and disappeared into the dark, cold woods.

"I don't think I can do this, Tala," Niabi mumbled, biting the belt as another contraction hit her. Sweat beaded around her brow and she mentally willed herself to be quiet.

He clasped her hand and she squeezed tightly. Once the pain subsided, she opened her eyes and stared at him. "You can do this, Niabi," he said gently before adding, "and you will. Keep your eyes on me and I'll get you through this."

Niabi bobbed her head. Even though they escaped the city, her enemies would never stop hunting for her, especially knowing she'd give birth to an heir that would pose a threat to their reign.

She had two options once her baby was born. Disappear and let her enemies have her kingdom, but live in fear that history would repeat itself, and one day they'd find her and kill everyone she loved, or she could face them and protect not only her newborn, but the Andrago too. Whether she sought sanctuary from the Andrago or not, Gershom and Vilora would assume she'd be hiding there and would attack Elisor. They would kill every citizen and burn every house to the ground to find her. She wouldn't have innocent blood on her hands.

"Push," Tala whispered and her focus returned to him. "You're almost there, Niabi. You can do this."

Niabi took a deep breath of chilly air and pushed with all the strength she had left. Her head fell back in exhaustion and when she thought she wouldn't be able to push again, she heard a small, angry cry sound in the darkness.

Her eyes snapped toward Tala who held a tiny newborn wrapped in the cloak that had been draped over her. Tears filled her eyes knowing she did the impossible and after nine long months, she was finally able to meet her child.

Tala smiled as he handed her the bundle. "It's a boy."

Niabi stroked her son's rosy cheek and wiped her own tears away. "Hello, Ivaylo."

Footsteps approached and Tala jumped up, drawing his sword, but relaxed when he saw Thrice returning.

"Soldiers?" Tala asked.

"We're clear for now," Thrice reported. "I set some traps. That'll buy us some time just in case they catch up." The Shadow glanced at his queen. "We will need to move at first light. You just need to tell me which way to head."

Niabi glanced down at her son nuzzling against her chest and the choice was clear. She couldn't disappear. She would have to face her enemies, but she wouldn't do it alone. She would go to the only place Gershom and Vilora wouldn't think to look for her.

"Oakenshire," she said, and although Tala and Thrice exchanged a confused look, they didn't question her. "We are going to make a deal with my siblings."

Chapter Forty-Eight

Crispin

It'd been a couple of weeks since the Battle of Oakenshire and reinforcements and supplies were slowly trickling in. Crispin had managed to get some rest, although nightmares of the battle plagued him. He kept seeing Oden's drowned body. He was dealing with his trauma on his own, but when he heard the clashing of metal against metal coming from the bailey, he panicked, thinking they were under attack. He bolted to his window and looked outside not only to find they weren't under attack, but that his sister was once again up late sparring with the Bellator commanders.

Quick to put his fighting leathers and boots on, he made his way to the sparring grounds and hid in the shadows to watch up close how his sister and the Bellators fought. He only caught the last few movements between Salome and Kayven and was impressed with how Salome slid on her knees, bent backwards, to avoid Kayven's incoming blow. The Bellator seemed surprised by the extra effort to elude him and barked out a hearty laugh.

"Well done, Princess." Kayven nodded his head in approval as he sheathed his weapon. "You'd make a fine Bellator."

Salome bowed, a wide grin across her face. "If only I had wings, I might actually beat you," she teased.

Abba scoffed as he stepped out of the shadows. "You are far too generous, my lady. You do not need wings to beat him, just a mirror. Kayven cannot resist the opportunity to admire himself."

Salome's laugh filled the bailey and drew a smile from Crispin. He hadn't heard her laugh like that in weeks. He had only come to watch, but seeing how much fun they were having made him want to join, so he stepped out of his hiding spot, surprising them.

Salome looked him up and down and grinned. "How long have you been there?"

Crispin shrugged a shoulder. "Long enough to see you've picked up a few new moves."

Salome waved him forward, wiping sweat from her brow. "Care to step in the ring?"

His eyes danced. The siblings hadn't sparred with one another in months, and after seeing her new tricks, he was itching to face off with her again. He shrugged off his jacket and unsheathed his longsword. As he took his stance, he could see she held herself differently – with more confidence. From swapping tales of their journeys, he knew she'd trained with the Qata Vishna, and she'd been training with the Bellator commanders for weeks, so this wasn't going to be the same Salome he sparred with in the Tree House Forest. But he had also picked up a few moves. Granted his were more in the stealth department, learning from both the pirates and the Keepers during their travels, but he was confident he could still hold his own against his sister.

As they stood on opposite sides of the sparring ring, staring at one another, it gutted Crispin to realize that he'd been waiting for Zophar to count them down. Something flashed across Salome's face that let him know she'd been thinking the same thing. If only Zophar could have lived to see this day – they were back together with new skills under their belts. He would have been so proud and excited to see his wards face off. He'd probably still be secretly rooting for Salome, like he always did.

"I miss him too," Salome acknowledged.

Crispin offered a tight-lipped smile. "Commander Kayven," he didn't take his eyes off his sister, "would you start us off?"

Kayven counted them down before releasing them.

Salome used to be more defensive in nature, but she initiated the duel by running toward him. He used his sword to block the blow of her Qata Vishna blades and shoved her back.

"You learned to be defensive," she smirked and nodded in approval.

"And you learned to attack first," he took his stance again. "Let's see what else you've learned."

Both siblings had not only grown stronger, but they were faster as well. Faster in their movements but quick in their reaction time. Granted, Salome was far more flexible and agile than him, but he adapted to her movements and had more force behind his blows.

Sweat dripped down his forehead as they sparred: blocking, dodging, tumbling, kicking, punching... it was chaotic, and Crispin loved every bit of it. He wondered how she managed to survive the Battle of Oakenshire when they were being overrun by the Pulauans, but seeing her in action made him realize she was no longer the girl he grew up with in the Tree House Forest. She was a force to be reckoned with and could shake the very foundation of their world, if she truly wanted to.

"I grow bored with this back-and-forth nonsense," Kayven bellowed, a playful grin plastered across his bronze face. "We need a victor!"

"My money is on my lady," Abba said, garnering a scoff from Kayven.

"Well, of course she will win," Kayven pounded a fist to his chest. "I trained her."

"You're not even going to give me a chance to prove you wrong?" Crispin barked out a laugh.

The Bellator brothers exchanged a look before shrugging their shoulders.

"It is not because we do not believe you are a skilled fighter, Prince Crispin," Kayven began, but Crispin waved his hand in the air, cutting him off. Salome's laugh was so infectious that it spurred Crispin to laugh with her.

"Don't listen to them, Crispin," she said between giggles. "You're just as skilled -"

"Don't you start with me," Crispin pointed his sword at her, failing to hide his grin. "Best two out of three?" He wiggled his eyebrows, remembering their sparring sessions in the Tree House Forest, always trying to best the other in battle. They'd grown so much, he almost wished they could go back and enjoy those precious moments they spent together, without the titles and responsibility currently weighing them down.

Salome took her stance once more, eyes filled with mischief. "Best two out of three it is."

As he took his position, heavy boots marched toward them. He turned to see an Eastern warrior bow and say, "Your Highness, someone has arrived at the gate and claims to know you."

Crispin and Salome exchange a puzzled look. Everyone they knew was already in Oakenshire. "Who is it?"

"We aren't sure, Your Majesty," the soldier shrugged his shoulders. "She wouldn't give a name. Just said she would speak with you and Princess Salome tonight on an urgent matter."

"Bring this mysterious guest to the throne room," Crispin instructed, sheathing his sword. "Make sure they come in under a heavily armed escort."

The soldier bowed and turned on his heel to deliver the message to the guards at the gate.

"Do you know who it might be?" Salome stalked toward him, sheathing her Qata Vishna blades in their holsters.

"No, but we're about to find out." Crispin glanced at the Bellator brothers. "Would you have Harbona, Prince Jinn, and Rahab join us?" Seeing the curious look on Salome's face, he explained, "I would imagine our betrothed would want to be included in this secret meeting, don't you?"

She nodded with a knowing smile. "Let's go meet this mysterious woman of yours."

Crispin rolled his eyes and sighed. "Now don't go saying things like that around Rahab. She won't take too kindly to that introduction."

Salome snaked her arm around his and pulled him toward the keep. "You'll need someone to keep you in line when I'm not around."

He stopped, forcing her to face him.

"Crispin?" she cocked her head to the side. "What's -"

"What do you mean by that? When you're not around?" His heart was thundering in his chest; the image of her perishing in battle flashed before him and he felt his throat constrict.

She grabbed his hand, drawing his gaze to meet hers. "When this war is over, I will marry Jinn and one day be his queen. Surely, you didn't believe I would marry the future King of Sakurai and remain in Northwind with you?"

In truth, Crispin hadn't thought about it. He was so focused on the battles that lied ahead of them, that he hadn't considered what life after a victory would look like. He'd be king, yes, but he always imagined Salome by his side, heading up his small council. He felt like stomping his feet like a petulant child and demand she stay in Northwind forever, but when he thought about how Jinn and Salome looked at one another and the love they held for each other, he knew he could never impose his selfish will upon her.

"I'll still be around," she whispered. "Just not as much as we both would like."

He hugged her, her wild curls brushing against his face. "You think Harbona would give you a hippogriff so you can fly to Northwind whenever you want?"

She chuckled and he could hear the slight tremor in her voice signaling she was holding back tears. "He won't have a choice. I'll steal Zandaar if I need to; he likes me more anyway."

Crispin pulled back from her and flashed the best smile he could muster. "Of that I have no doubt."

Once Crispin was seated in the wooden throne with Salome and Jinn on his right and Rahab and Harbona on his left, he motioned for the Bellator brothers guarding the doors to open them. Escorted inside by a heavily armed group of Bellator Elite, the woman shrouded in a black hood and cloak strutted forward. Her gait seemed familiar but without seeing her face, Crispin couldn't be sure who was walking toward him. Two men followed closely behind her; one bore the resemblance of the Andrago, and the other Crispin couldn't place. He knew for sure he'd never seen them before.

The mysterious woman stopped several feet before the slightly elevated dais but didn't bow or kneel before him.

"Who are you and why have you come before me at this late hour?" His stern voice would have unnerved most guests, but the figure before him did not flinch.

"I have come to make a deal."

Her voice was eerily familiar and by Salome's reaction, he was positive she knew who stood cloaked before them.

"That's impossible," Salome whispered.

Crispin refocused on the stranger, and thought he saw a smirk beneath the shadowed hood. "Who are you? Show yourself."

The woman slowly reached up and pulled the hood back, revealing her jet-black hair and piercing green eyes. "Hello, little brother."

"You!?" He jumped to his feet and pointed at her. "Bellators, arrest her!"

The Immortal warriors leapt into action, surrounding the trio with pointed weapons, but Niabi was unfazed, and did not bother raising her hands in surrender. She held fast to her position and stared at Crispin with the same smirk snaked across her face.

"Is this how you treat your potential allies, Crispin?" she tsked as her gaze slid to the Seer. "I assumed Harbona had taught you better than that."

Harbona didn't respond, instead turned his attention to a nearby Bellator to whisper his orders and shooed him away to do his bidding.

Crispin's nostrils flared as he gritted out, "You have three seconds to give me a good reason why I shouldn't have you executed on the spot."

"Gershom staged a coup," Niabi's voice was steady and calm, unlike his own, "and I escaped before I was assassinated."

"So, your first thought was to come here?" He scoffed, crossing his arms over his chest.

"Why are you here, Niabi?" Salome chimed in with a tone of intimacy that surprised Crispin. As far as he knew, his sisters had never met, but the way they looked at one another debated that fact.

Niabi met Salome's gaze and the hardness in her face softened. "I believe we can help one another."

"Have you come to surrender the White Throne?" Crispin tilted his head up and looked down his nose at her.

His sister's green eyes bounced back and forth between him and Salome. It unnerved him at how much she resembled their mother. "I am no longer in possession of it, therefore, I cannot surrender it to you."

"So," Crispin cleared his throat, "you lost our ancestral home and what? You came here to ask us to fight for you? To harbor you? Are you delusional?"

"You want the White Throne, you can have it," she hissed. "I never wanted it; I never wanted any of it."

"You truly expect me to believe that?" He shook his head.

"What do you want from us?" Salome asked. Crispin recognized her attempts to diffuse the tension and was grateful she was his right hand.

"Let's join forces to reclaim Northwind," Niabi stared at Crispin.

"Why would we agree to that?" Crispin frowned. "Take it back yourself, *sister*."

"I swore a blood oath years ago that Gershom would not die by my hand." Her eyes drifted to Salome. "But that doesn't mean *you* can't kill him."

"So, we kill your enemy and -"

"*Our* enemy, dear brother," Niabi matched his belligerent tone. "Or have you forgotten, he too, played a role in the deaths of our mother and our brothers?"

"On your orders!" Crispin shouted and it stilled everyone in the room.

Salome slid her hand over his shoulder and squeezed, bringing him back to himself. He straightened and rolled his shoulders back.

"No apology I give will satisfy you," Niabi's voice was low, and he almost didn't hear her. "No reasoning I give will convince you that if I could go back and do everything over, I would." She met his fiery gaze with one of her own. "So, let's make a deal instead. The crown, the throne, the kingdom – take it. I don't want it."

"What do you want in return should we agree to unite?" Salome's question angered Crispin. Considering their sister's deal was insane.

"You should already know the answer to that, little sister," Niabi flashed a wicked smile. "I've told you several times over the last few weeks."

Crispin spun to look at Salome. "What is she talking about?"

Salome met his eyes and though she did not ask for forgiveness, the look in her eyes begged for it. "With my magic – I can communicate with other magic wielders. When you told me she had fire magic -"

"How long?" he cut her off.

She reached for him, "I should have told you sooner, Crispin, but -"

He slapped her hands away. "How long?"

"Since the night you arrived in Oakenshire."

"You lied to me," he whispered; betrayed didn't even begin to describe how he felt.

"Would you have been accepting of our conversations, if she had told you sooner?" Niabi posed, which only added fuel to an already raging fire.

He pointed his index finger at her, "Do not speak to me as if we are equals."

Niabi took a bold step forward, "The way I see it, we're both rulers of nothing at this point."

"You lost your crown," he hissed, squaring his shoulders to hers.

"And without my help, you'll never gain yours."

"Crispin, let's hear her out," Salome pleaded.

"Would you side with her?" He glared at Salome like a wounded animal. "Would you turn against me after everything we've been through?"

"I'm not turning against you," Salome reached for him but he eluded her grasp. "I've seen what kind of man our father was, what he did to her, and I cannot say I don't understand."

"You would have never done what she did -"

"But I have!" she shouted. "I *have* done what she has done." Tears welled in her eyes. "When Zophar died, I slit an innocent girl's throat to hurt her mother. I didn't shed a tear when Gomorrah was destroyed and if I had been on the opposite side of the wall leading the charge, I would have instructed they all be put to the sword for what they did to Zophar. I have done things I am not proud of in my anger and grief." Her gaze shifted from him to Niabi. "And if could change what I did, I would."

"She should be executed for what she's done. Not given a chance to join our ranks, so she can slit our throats in the middle of the night." He was baffled that Salome would stand up for Niabi.

Rushing down the dais, Salome positioned herself between him and Niabi. "If you order our sister to be executed for her sins, then you will have to hang me beside her, because I have committed the same crimes."

Crispin froze in place. Salome tentatively stepped toward him, slowly slipping her hands on either side of his face. "You are my king. I would give my life for you. But I have seen things, I have seen what our father did, and he was not a good man. She is not so different from us."

"Do not ask me to forgive her for the lives she stole from us."

"Crispin," she shook her head. "I am not asking you to forgive her, I am asking you to think of our people. Think of our allies. Think of the countless lives that could be spared with her help. We do not know the White Keep's layout. We don't know anything about the city, nor do we truly know Gershom and what we are facing. She does. She can give us all the information we need to take the city."

Crispin wanted nothing more than to watch Niabi hang for her crimes, but deep down, he knew Salome was giving him the counsel he needed to make the best choices to win the war and reclaim the White Throne. Despite the fact he hated her, Niabi was a force to be reckoned with and with her magic, skillset, and knowledge of both their enemy's tactics and Northwind itself, she could prove to be a powerful ally, if she didn't betray them first.

He glanced over Salome's shoulder and found Niabi waiting patiently for his decision. "What kind of deal are you proposing?"

"You can have the kingdom, but you will need to defeat Gershom and the two witches who fight for him," Niabi approached, now within an armslength of him. "I will join your ranks and battle those who betrayed me, but once the war is over, I want to be left alone to raise my son. You will never hear from me nor see me again after you become king. I wish to live out my days in the peace our father stole from me."

“You truly expect me to believe, you will freely give up the kingdom?” Crispin eyed her suspiciously and because of her proximity, he spotted her infant tucked inside of a cloth strapped across her chest.

"I'm here, aren't I?" Her voice drew his gaze from the baby. "I could have disappeared and skipped this little family reunion, but I'm here to help you. I'm here to make things right for all of us."

"I don't believe you."

"I do," Salome said, drawing a scoff from him. "I will go."

"Salome, you can't be serious."

"I'm the Hunter," Salome spun around to face him and Niabi's face flashed with surprise. "I am destined to kill those who have spilled innocent blood. Gershom's hands are stained with their blood." She glanced at Niabi. "I don't remember the White Keep."

Niabi nodded. "I can help with that."

"And me?" Crispin spat. "You would willingly ignore me?"

"I know you don't trust her -"

"That's an understatement, Salome. She killed our entire family!"

"And I will never forget it, but they're gone, Crispin. Nothing we say or do will change that," Salome grabbed his hand. "We have a chance to join forces and get our home back. Isn't that what we want?"

"If it quenches your thirst for punishing me," Niabi's silvery voice sliced through the tension in the air. "I have suffered greatly for my sins. I've lost almost everyone I have ever loved and know their deaths are my burden to bear, until I breathe my last."

"You have not suffered nearly enough." Crispin glared at her, unmoved by her speech.

"Hate me all you want, Crispin," she clasped her hands behind her back. "But to be king, one must put their grievances aside for the greater good."

He grinded his teeth, hating every second of being in Niabi's presence. "What are we up against?"

"Gershom has control of not only the Northern army, but the Shadows as well. Ophir saw to that," she revealed. "He also has two witches at his side, the Old Witch of Endor who has fire magic, and Nezreen who has her shadows."

Witches. He hated both of those witches with every fiber of his being.

Crispin rubbed the heels of his palms against his bloodshot eyes. If he didn't get some decent rest soon, he would collapse. "So, that's who attacked us."

"I found out about the Battle of Oakenshire after it occurred," Niabi nodded, looking at Salome. "And by then, I was running for my life."

"What of Uri the Pirate King?" Salome asked, arms crossed over her chest.

"A pawn in their game." Niabi sneered. "Pirate scum."

Rahab, who had remained quiet the entire time, cleared her throat drawing the siblings' attention. "Say that again."

Niabi's signature grin snaked across her face. "You're the girl my brother was so eager to defend in Northwind." She slowly and disdainfully examined Rahab from head to toe. "I would say it's good to see you again, but why lie?"

"I know pirates who possess more honor in their little finger, than you do in your entire body," Rahab hissed, tickling the hilt of the dagger on her hip.

"Honor gets you killed." Niabi kept her eyes glued on the pirate, but before Rahab could reply, the doors opened again allowing two new members to join the room.

"Father?"

Everyone turned to see Leoti sprinting toward the Andrago who had arrived with Niabi. He rushed to her and swept her into his arms.

"You're alive!" the man cried, touching Leoti's face. "I feared the worst when you didn't return."

"I'm so happy to see you!" She cupped his face and stared at him. She suddenly noticed Niabi standing with a baby strapped to her chest. "My queen, what are you doing here?"

"Niabi?" Pash's voice silenced everyone in the room as Niabi turned to face him.

Chapter Forty-Nine

Niabi

Pash was here. Standing less than thirty feet from her. She knew she should remain stone-faced in front of her siblings but something within her broke loose. Seeing him, not only alive, but again, spurred her to sprint to him. He, too, took off running and threw his arms around her when they met in the middle of the throne room.

Pash kissed her, then planted kisses on her forehead, cheek, and neck. "I didn't know if I was ever going to see you again," he whispered, resting his head on her shoulder.

Running her hands through his hair, a tear slipped down her cheek, and for once, she didn't care about looking weak. Ivaylo stretched in the wrap, startling Pash. He took a step back and glanced down at the bundle. He opened his mouth to speak but words failed him. Tears welled in his eyes as he met her gaze.

"This is Ivaylo, your son," she whispered, swiping her thumb against the tears that trickled down his face.

"He's perfect." Pash slipped his hand into the wrap and had to catch his breath when the babe grabbed his finger. "I'm sorry I wasn't there."

Niabi kissed him, silencing his apology. "We lost Anaktu," her voice cracked remembering the Nephilim.

"Wait," Pash glanced from Niabi to Crispin and Salome behind her. "What's going on here?" He looked at Niabi for answers. "Why are you here?"

"Gershom staged a coup," she explained, and his face dropped. "I've come here to make a deal with my brother and sister." She turned to face them, cupping her hand around the swaddled baby attached to her. "And do we have a deal? I help you take Northwind, and I can raise my son in peace."

Crispin and Salome exchanged a look. Niabi hoped that after their talks, Salome would be more open to her and her cause. She was well aware, especially after their run in at the White Keep, that Crispin would be less forgiving and opposed to merging, but as she watched and waited for one of them to speak, she prayed she hadn't made a huge mistake by asking them for help. There was still a chance Crispin would ignore Salome's advice and execute her on the spot. She wouldn't go down without a fight, her blades were safely tucked up her sleeves, since the guards at the front gate failed to check her thoroughly for weapons. Plus, she had fire magic and would easily watch the place burn to the ground.

Crispin cleared his throat. "You aid us in taking Northwind back from Gershom and the witches, and I will allow you to disappear and raise your son in peace."

Her heart leapt. Her gamble had paid off. Before she could respond, her brother narrowed his eyes and cut her off.

"If you step out of line, if I detect a hint of betrayal on your part, I'll cut you down where you stand. Are we agreed?"

Niabi felt Pash tense up beside her and he opened his mouth, most likely to defend her, but she flashed him a look, stifling whatever choice words he was about to spew. Looking back at her siblings, she smiled and bobbed her head. "We are agreed."

Salome descended from the dais and Niabi straightened her shoulders and waited for her sister to approach. Once they were face to face, Niabi looked her over. She had their father's curls, but their mother's skin tone and features. Her different color eyes were a surprise, and she couldn't stop staring at the intricate, green specks in her left eye.

"I will show you to your rooms," Salome said. "Unless you prefer to stay with the commander?"

Niabi glanced up at Pash and the pleading in his eyes was answer enough. "I'm sure the commander and I have much to discuss in private."

Salome nodded. A man walked up behind her, took her hand and placed it on his forearm.

“You make a lovely couple,” Niabi offered a rare compliment. They looked at her. “Don't look so surprised. I recognize a couple in love when I see one. I'm not blind.”

"This is Prince Jinn of Sakurai," Salome introduced them, and Jinn bowed his head, though his eyes were narrow and vigilant. As if to say, if you hurt her, you'll deal with me. And she couldn't fault him for it.

"Prince Jinn," Niabi said politely.

"Queen Niabi," he returned her tone, but she shook her head.

"Just Niabi," she corrected. "I have no throne anymore." She met Salome's softened gaze and motioned toward the door. "Shall we?"

Snapped out of her momentary stupor, Salome nodded and began the trek through the keep.

Her siblings and their allies had worked wonders in resurrecting the ancient castle. She was impressed with how well organized and heavily manned their rebellion was. She didn't think they were capable of amassing an army, but here she was, walking in the lion's den, grateful she wasn't facing them in battle.

"How did you escape?" Salome asked.

The question conjured Anaktu's face, and it rattled her, but she shook the image free. "Tala, Thrice, and I had to fight our way out. I lost a dear friend of mine during our flight."

"I'm sorry to hear that." Niabi was surprised to hear genuine sorrow in her sister's voice.

"Why do they call you Thrice?" Salome turned to look at the Shadow stalking behind them and he flashed a menacing grin.

"I once killed three men with one swing of my sword." He held up three fingers, "Hence, Thrice."

If Salome was impressed or intimidated, she didn't show it. "Well, Thrice, I assume you will want to be near my sister, so this is your room. Commander Pash's room is right next door."

Thrice looked to Niabi for permission to be dismissed and with a flicker of her eyes, he bowed and slipped into his quarters. "Leoti's room is across the hall from Commander Pash's chambers."

"I hope my presence hasn't created a wedge between you and our brother," Niabi said, halting Salome's departure.

Salome turned back around and gave an insincere smile. "If driving a wedge between us is your goal, I'd give it up. We have been through far too much to let you divide us."

"But you defended me," Niabi cocked her head to the side, rubbing small circles around Ivaylo's cradled form. "He wanted to execute me, and you stood up for me."

"Do not think for one second I won't strike you down, if I feel you are a threat to Crispin." The friendliness was gone from Salome's voice, replaced with an iciness Niabi knew all too well. "But I will help him make the right choices for the good of our people and allies, not the easy decisions based on emotion and grudges. He is my king, and I will die before anyone touches him."

"Let us hope, dear sister," Niabi cooed, "it does not come down to that."

"Rest well, Niabi." Salome stalked down the hall, Jinn beside her like a dutiful lapdog.

Once the couple turned the corner, Niabi closed the bedroom door and while Pash stared at her, she cast a quick glance around the space and took note of all the entrances, exits, and windows. The wardrobe wasn't large enough for anyone to hide in and there was no space underneath the wooden bedframe for an assassin to lie in wait. The fireplace was lit preventing anyone from slipping in that way. From her quick assessment, there was no real threat to worry about and with Pash in the room and Thrice next door, she knew she'd be able to rest. She needed a good night's sleep after the days of roughing it in the cold, dark forest.

"I don't know what you've heard about me," Pash's voice sliced through her thoughts, drawing her gaze, "but I am no traitor."

"Ophir told me of your brother," Niabi tilted her head in curiosity. "A brother I didn't know you had."

"He's my half-brother," Pash explained. "We share the same father."

"Why didn't you tell me about him?"

“I swore I'd never speak of him to anyone in order to protect him.” Pash sat on the edge of his bed, twiddling his thumbs between his thighs. “My father ordered men to burn his childhood house to the ground which killed his mother and grandfather. I didn't know if Adonijah had survived, but if by chance, he was alive, I knew, he would want to remain hidden."

Niabi approached him on soft feet, squeezing next to him on the mattress. "Why did you save him? You hardly know him."

Pash met her eyes and smiled. "He's my brother. I do not need to know him well to save him."

She scoffed, looking at the door and making a mental note to lock it before going to sleep.

"Why did you come here of all places, Niabi? You could have been executed on the spot."

"A calculated risk," she said without hesitation.

"You could have gone to Elisor to be with the Andrago -"

"Your father betrayed me," her eyes lit up with a fiery rage. "He stole my throne, my crown, my home. I underestimated him. A mistake I do not intend to make again." Her face softened when he placed his hand on her bouncing knee. "I did not go to Elisor because that is the first place Gershom would have expected me to go. I did not wish to bring further harm to the Andrago."

He lifted her hand to his lips and pressed a loving kiss to her skin. "We could leave this place tonight. I've been plotting my own escape for weeks."

"Why were you trying to escape?"

"To get back to you." He said it with such conviction it made her heart leap.

"Well, I do not intend to run like a whipped dog with my tail between my legs," she shook her head. "No, my love, I intend to bring Gershom to his knees for his treachery."

"Did you mean what you said to your siblings? They could have the kingdom and you'd disappear to raise our son?"

She brushed her hand down his cheek and nodded. "I've been given a second chance. I do not intend to squander it."

"So, after this war is over...?"

"We will go to Elisor and start over. You, me, and Ivaylo," she bobbed her head. "I've already spoken to Tala, and he's agreed to welcome you into the Andrago fold as long as you swear fealty to them."

"Where you go," he kissed her hand once more and smiled, "I go."

She smiled back and for the first time in months, she felt true joy and hope. Ivaylo wiggled in his wrap, letting loose a small cry.

"Would you like to hold him?" She unwrapped the newborn strapped to her chest and offered him to Pash who carefully accepted the tiny bundle.

The warmth on Pash's face filled the entire room with a palpable love that brought a tear to her eye. Gently, he kissed Ivaylo's head and whispered, "My son, you are so desperately loved. I can't wait to teach you everything I know."

Niabi leaned closer, resting her head on Pash's shoulder. Taking a deep breath, she closed her eyes, and drifted to sleep for some much needed rest.

Chapter Fifty

Salome

Niabi and her humble entourage had arrived in Oakenshire weeks ago and Salome was relieved her siblings hadn't attempted to kill each other. Reinforcements and supplies trickled in and as they did, the leaders met daily to exchange pertinent information about the war they were going to wage against Gershom and his allies, but every day, they left the room more frustrated than the day before. If Crispin and Niabi didn't start seeing eye to eye, and soon, she was going to lock them up until they swore on their lives that they would at least attempt to work together.

Although her daily routine had changed, Salome's nightly routine remained the same: training with the Bellators. Some nights, Leoti would join her to keep practicing the techniques she'd learned, but the Andrago asked for a reprieve so she could spend time with her father and broach the subject of marrying Adonijah after the war.

Tala was surprisingly kind and generous for someone who was Niabi's closest companion and most trusted advisor, but despite her initial judgment, Salome took quite the liking to him and even spent a few early mornings with him, devouring fresh pastries Jacobi had baked before the rest of the castle stirred. She listened to his stories of the Andrago and their way of life and she found his traditions and culture fascinating. She secretly hoped that one day she might be able to visit Elisor, and see for herself the beauty the Andrago offered. In a way, Tala reminded her of Zophar, and she knew, deep down, they would have been the best of friends had they had the chance to meet.

But once midnight struck, she made her way to the bailey where the Bellators were always waiting for her. An hour of drills and sparring flew by, and her strength, speed, and stamina had greatly improved since their first lesson. She wasn't sure battle fright was still an issue for her, but she didn't have the courage to ask Kayven if he thought she was ready to end their sessions. She didn't want him to tell her she no longer needed them, because that would be the farthest thing from the truth. Even if she didn't need to train with them anymore, she found their companionship not only soothing, but their presence brought her immeasurable joy when all she was surrounded by was talk of war, politics, and death.

Another thirty minutes passed, but instead of pushing through the pain, Salome motioned to Kayven and Abba that she needed a break.

"There will not be time for breaks in war, my lady." Kayven speared his sword between the pavers and leaned his weight upon it. "If you keep demanding we prepare you for what is to come, you must fight through your exhaustion. It could mean the difference between life or death."

"And if I don't get a drink of water this very moment, you'll have to explain to not only my brother, but to Jinn and Harbona as well, why you pushed me to the point of passing out," she teased as she sipped from her cup.

Kayven rolled his eyes as Abba puffed out a laugh.

"For being the Hunter," Kayven quipped, "you certainly need a lot of breaks."

"I might be the Hunter," Salome shot back with a smirk, "but I'm still mortal."

Once Salome had finished her drink and wiped the sweat from her brow, she motioned for the Bellators to resume their session, but their eyes weren't on her. Their gaze was fixed on someone behind her.

"Mind if I join you?"

Salome turned to look at Niabi sauntering into the bailey, flashing a pair of daggers in her palms. The night Niabi arrived, she learned that Salome was the Hunter, but the revelation didn't seem to faze her. Most of the leaders assumed Niabi would be on Salome's kill list but if Niabi was worried, she didn't show it. She kept her face neutral and carried herself like a true warrior queen when the other leaders rained their complaints and accusations against the Green-Eyed-Raven. Rightfully so, they didn't trust her, and they didn't want her amongst their ranks. Some, but mostly bloodthirsty Oifa, demanded they just execute her and be done with it.

Salome found it exhausting to defend her sister on a daily basis, but she didn't fault their allies for their concerns. Truthfully, she had her uncertainties, but above all else, she wished to end the vicious cycle her father started. Niabi sought a second chance to raise her family in peace and to be left alone. Would she have sought her siblings out before war came to her doorstep? Most likely not, but when she had a chance to escape and live the life she desperately wanted, she willingly put her life at risk by coming to Oakenshire. Niabi was as cunning as she was dangerous, but over the last few weeks, she'd come to learn that her sister was bold in the face of adversity and spoke her mind freely without fear of those who would oppose her.

But deep down in Salome's gut, she felt a tug, an undeniable urge to listen to what Lykos had told her when she'd reached out to him in the After. *Maybe she is not the one you are meant to defeat. Perhaps, she is the one you are meant to save.* She'd tried to shake his words from her mind, but it was impossible, as if Lykos was whispering it to her every morning when she woke up and every night before she closed her eyes. If nothing else, she owed it to Lykos to try to set things right, since their father unleashed his chaos.

As her sister approached, Salome couldn't keep her eyes off of her. There was something truly unsettling about Niabi that Salome couldn't quite put her finger on, but she was curious to see the queen in action. Maybe she would even learn a few moves from the lethal warrior. Crispin would be furious, and Jinn wouldn't be too excited to hear about their private sparring session either, but she wasn't concerned about the Bellators ratting them out.

"You sure you should be sparring so soon after having your son?"

Niabi smiled and it reminded Salome so much of their mother it stopped her dead in her tracks. "Thank you for your concern, but I've been cleared by your healers, and after weeks of inactivity, I could use the practice." She circled her blades around her hands, not at all looking out of practice.

Salome took her stance and nodded. "Show me what you've got."

Kayven and Abba stepped out of the designated training area, leaning against the wall to keep an eye on the two women and to be lookouts in case Harbona or any of the others came snooping.

Niabi stood several feet from her younger sister, her daggers in her grasp at her sides. The warm smile that had graced the queen's face moments earlier was wiped clean, and a hardened assassin stood in her place. The intensity in her green eyes sent an unwelcome shiver down Salome's spine but when her sister's left hand ignited in flames, she jumped back in surprise. She knew about Niabi's fire magic, but she hadn't anticipated seeing it in action at the beginning of a friendly sparring session.

They stared at one another silently, waiting, mentally willing the other to make the first move, but neither did. Instead, they soaked one another in, eyeing their stances, their choice of weaponry, even making eye contact at one point to feel the other out. Finally, Salome struck first, launching herself at her sister, using all the techniques she'd learned over the years. She implemented all the lessons Zophar had taught her, the Qata Vishna movements she learned from Mika, and even the few moves the Bellators had shown her. She wielded a weapon unlike any warrior Adalore had ever seen – taught by some of the most cunning warriors to take down her own blood.

But Niabi moved with the same lethal elegance having trained with the Qata Vishna, and being a Red Maiden in her own right. Her blades were extensions of her arms, and she sliced around the sparring grounds like the Andrago and Shadows. If Salome hadn't been impressed with her sister before, she was mesmerized by her now.

Salome wielded weapons – Niabi was a weapon. No wonder their father didn't stand a chance when she invaded.

"You're thinking too much," Niabi's voice cut into her thoughts. "If you don't harness your mind, you will lose every time." She dropped to the ground to sweep Salome's legs out from under her, but she had anticipated the move and hopped over effortlessly.

"Maybe you should focus on yourself more than me." Salome leapt in the air, attempting to land a roundhouse kick to her sister's chest, but only met the air when Niabi tumbled out the way.

They danced around one another, landing a few well-timed blows, but doing no true damage. It wasn't until Niabi flipped toward her that she was thrown off balance. When Niabi landed on her feet, she slammed her flaming hand against Salome's chest sending her flying and singeing her shirt.

Kayven flinched, ready to strike, but Salome held out a hand, halting him. Niabi walked over and hovered above her.

"You fight well, little sister." Niabi extinguished her hand and extended it to help her up. "You could be even better, if you let me teach you."

"Unless you can teach me how to wield fire like you, I don't think I could get any better." Salome accepted her help and planted her feet on the stone pavers.

"My fire magic doesn't make me a better fighter. It makes you believe that I am, because it's a distraction." Niabi cocked her head to the side, retracting her blades into her sleeves. "Win the battle of the mind, and you've already defeated your enemy."

"And how exactly am I supposed to do that when I don't even know my enemy?" Salome asked. She knew of Gershom and his crimes, but she didn't know the first thing about him or what would distract him enough to better her odds of defeating him in combat.

"Oh, but you do know your enemy, Salome," Niabi cooed, "and you already know what the perfect distraction will be. Us."

"Us?"

"Gershom knows he's wronged me and that I always have my revenge." Niabi sat on one of the wooden boxes used as stools and Salome perched on the one next to her. "He also knows that Vilora failed to eliminate me. He knows I'll be back, it's just a matter of when. What he won't anticipate is me joining forces with the very siblings I ordered him to hunt down. We have the element of surprise and that in itself will throw him off. He will be reckless in his decisions and in his desperation to keep the crown, he will make mistakes. That's when we strike. That's when you take your shot and kill that bastard. That's when you fulfill the prophecy and become the Hunter you were meant to be and avenge the blood of the innocent."

Salome scoffed. "For a while there, I thought I'd be killing you."

"You still might."

"Why do you say that?"

Niabi offered her a sad smile. "I am far from a hero, Salome. I have blood on my hands and though right now we have the same goals, there may come a time when you turn on me."

"I won't."

Niabi met Salome's confused gaze and stared deep into her eyes. "You and I are very similar."

"You say that like it's a bad thing," Salome whispered. "And what does that have to do with me turning on you?"

"Because if our roles were reversed and I was the Hunter, I would consider your past and what havoc you could possibly wreak in the future. Killing you would be at the forefront of my mind – just like it is on yours."

"That's -"

"Please don't insult me by lying about it. I can see it in your eyes."

Salome looked away from her, twiddling her fingers. "I have considered it."

"But?"

"But," Salome met her gaze, "you remind me too much of our mother."

"Looks can be deceiving."

"If you could go back and do things differently, would you?"

Niabi peered into Salome's eyes. "If you're asking, would I have spared our father if I had a chance to rethink my choices, my answer would be no." Her answer surprised Salome. "Had Issachar left me alone, let me live my life in peace with my husband and my son, I never would have come for him. But what he did, who he stole from me, that was something I could not, would not, forgive or forget." Before Salome could respond, Niabi continued. "Let me ask you something."

Salome bobbed her head and waited for the question.

"This prince of yours, Jinn."

"What of him?"

"What would you do, if someone murdered him before your eyes?"

Salome recoiled, but then her nostrils flared. "Is that a threat?"

"No," Niabi shook her head and patted her sister's hand to reassure her. "I am asking, if he was taken from you, what would you do?"

Salome knew exactly what Niabi was trying to get her to understand, what she was trying to get her to admit, and she was ashamed to say, she didn't blame her sister one bit, because that's exactly what she would have done. But she didn't need to admit it aloud for Niabi to guess what her answer would be.

"Am I really that much of a monster for avenging the man I loved?" Niabi asked, her eyes tearing up. "I turned my back on the White Throne and everything Issachar stood for long before I met Dichali, but he just couldn't let me be free, let me be happy. He never would have stopped hunting me, tormenting me, until I either lied down like a rodent and died, or fought back. He pushed me too far by taking Dichali. He underestimated my devotion to my husband and it cost him everything."

Salome stared at her sister, touched by the pain that filled her eyes, and realized behind that gaze was a hurting and broken woman. Maybe, just maybe, Salome could do as Lykos asked and save her before it was too late.

"I suppose I should be heading inside," Niabi broke the silence first and Salome nodded in agreement. "Until next time, little sister."

Kayven and Abba joined Salome once Niabi left.

"You trust her?" Abba asked once she was out of earshot and Salome bobbed her head, wrapping her arms around herself as the blistering cold wind whisked around.

"I hope she's wrong."

"Wrong about what?" Kayven's eyes darted to hers, clearly confused.

"I hope I'm not forced to turn on her."

Chapter Fifty-One

Crispin

Although the general consensus was to wait until winter had passed to move the troops towards Northwind, Niabi pleaded her case to the leaders that Gershom would only amass a greater army and strengthen his hold on the White City if they didn't move quickly. When Salome noted that during one of their private conversations, Niabi had said it would be foolish to move an army in the cold months, Niabi acknowledged her statement and said, "It's a risk I wouldn't have taken, but with Gershom trying to establish his reign, he's currently at his weakest. The time to strike is when he would least expect it, and in the middle of winter after staging a coup, would be the time to do it."

So, despite the heavy snow they would encounter the further north they'd travel, the leaders all agreed they'd strike hard and fast, hoping to have the element of surprise on their side and keep Gershom from strengthening his hold on the city.

Crispin hated to admit he agreed with Niabi's suggested strategy, but it was the best course, so he ordered their allies to be ready to travel in the morning.

After the meeting was adjourned, Crispin slipped out virtually unnoticed and went to the stables where Freya, the horse Zophar had purchased for him years ago, was housed. He hadn't spent much time with her and was honestly surprised to see her in Oakenshire when he reunited with Salome. Zophar had cared for her and Midnight even after Crispin had been swept down the River of Lost Souls and presumed dead. Now it was his turn to take care of Freya and Midnight. He brushed them, fed them, and made sure he swiped a couple apples to give them a sweet treat. Snow, Salome's horse, glanced over her pen and stared at him when she heard the crunching of apples, and he offered her one. Greedily, she accepted his offering and a few pets before she huddled back into her area, ignoring him for the remainder of his visit.

He chuckled and rolled his eyes. Snow was exactly like Salome. If she knew you had snacks, she would drop everything to get some and then she'd go back into her own little world and ignore you.

Midnight was just like Zophar. There was a quiet strength and kindness in his eyes that reminded him of his guardian.

When he kissed Freya's snout, she nuzzled into his neck, giving him the unspoken love and understanding he was longing for. Sometimes Crispin preferred the company of horses over people. They didn't confuse him, nor did they make him compromise what he knew to be right, for the betterment of other people.

Crispin pinned his back against the door to Freya's pen and slid down, stretching one leg out and pulling the other against his chest. He played with the hay poking out of Freya's stable before he rested his head against the door and closed his eyes. Winter's chill was brutal that afternoon. Whipping around the keep mercilessly. Certain parts of the castle were uninhabitable since they hadn't been able to repair all the damage in the outer walls. But at least the stable was intact and the horses were well cared for. They would need all the strength they could muster to make the trip north in the morning.

It would take them a few days to reach the designated location the leaders had agreed upon and set up their military camp before launching their attack on Northwind.

After weeks of planning, months of adventures, and a lifetime of waiting, his moment was coming. In a week, he could be king. The thought was as jarring as it was exciting. His life had changed drastically from the moment he stepped foot outside of the Tree House Forest. He just hoped he would lead his allies to victory.

"I know you do not trust me," the female voice he dreaded hearing disturbed his tranquil space and instantly grated his nerves, "but if we do not show a united front, your allies will waver."

Crispin's eyes narrowed as he met Niabi's gaze. "Surely you didn't drag yourself out to the stables to risk angering me."

She smirked; her boots clicked against the stone pavers as she made her way toward him. No, not toward him. Toward Freya. He was about to warn her that Freya was a biter, but as she stretched her hand toward the mare, Freya the Betrayer, tucked her snout underneath Niabi's palm, accepting her pat. If Crispin hadn't seen it with his own eyes, he wouldn't have believed it. Freya, to this day, would try to bite Salome if she got too close, so the fact that she allowed this stranger, this monster, to touch her, made him sick to his stomach.

"You're always angry, brother," Niabi's voice sliced through his thoughts, further irritating him.

"What's in your hand?" His question seemed to surprise her.

"What?"

"What's in your hand?" he repeated.

Slowly, she lifted her hand from Freya's nose and showed him her empty palm. "Is something wrong, brother?"

"Quit calling me that," he hissed, stalking past her toward the exit.

"I know there's nothing I can do or say that will earn your forgiveness, nor am I asking for it." That halted his retreat, but he didn't turn around to face her. "I have blood on my hands. I have loved fiercely and lost tragically. I tried to take the higher ground with our father, but he struck me so deeply in the heart that had I not acted, he never would have stopped hunting me."

He didn't hear her approach him until she was upon him. He turned around, half-expecting her to stab him in the chest since he'd been foolish enough to turn his back to her, but he found her unarmed with glossy eyes.

"I remember receiving news that you had been born. Even though you were father's fourth son, the kingdom rejoiced and celebrated for an entire week." Niabi's voice was soft and despite fighting it, her words drew him in. "My own son was born around the same time, but I did not send word to our mother or father, fearing what Issachar's reaction would be with me producing an heir for the Andrago throne. A baby's birth is a miraculous and joyous occasion, but for me, it reminded me that even though I was a queen in a different kingdom, out from under our father's thumb, I was still fearful of what he could do to me. He learned quickly that physical beatings and torment had zero effect on me. I was trained by the Qata Vishna, I was battered and bruised in training for years. But he was a cunning king and cruel man and knew the only way to truly hurt me was to harm those I loved most."

"Why are you telling me this?" Crispin looked at her and searched for a crack in her armor and found just a broken woman with scars that ran so deep it choked him.

"I realize you see me as I see him." Niabi tilted her head to the side, a playful curiosity. "You see me as the monster and not the wounded wife and mother who lost her husband and son. You see me as the villain, and I do not blame you. In my quest to avenge my dead, I didn't realize until it was far too late, that in order to defeat him, I'd become him." She took another step toward him, eating the remaining distance between them. Slowly, tentatively, she raised her hand and cupped his face and the touch felt like a punch to his gut. "I'm sorry

I became your villain, dear brother. My quarrel was never with you. See me for what I am and swear you will never be like me. It is a terribly lonely existence."

Withdrawing her hand from his cheek, she slipped by him, headed for the door, when he suddenly grabbed her arm and yanked her back against his chest.

"Your pathetic story might work on Salome," he hissed into her ear, fire raging in his soul, "but I am not so easily swayed." Her body tensed, but he did not relinquish his hold on her. "I will never forgive you. I will never forget that you are a monster of your own making. When this war is over, dare not show your face again, lest I take the revenge I've dreamt of since the day I escaped your villainous clutches twelve years ago."

Releasing her, he pushed past her, and stomped out into the bailey. Snow flurries danced around as he strode toward the keep, bypassing anyone who looked like they might want to speak with him. He needed to get to his room and have a moment to be alone, otherwise he was afraid of what might come flying out of his mouth.

How dare she try to plead her case with him? Was she looking for forgiveness? Mercy? Was this just part of her scheme to suck him into her story of victimhood, only to wait like a snake in the grass for her moment to betray him?

He raked his hand through his hair, exhaustion settling in, even though it wasn't nearly time to sleep. Tripping up the stairs as he sprinted toward his bed chambers, he waved off castle attendants who offered to help him up. *Unhinged.* That's what he saw reflected in their stares. The future king of the north was stampeding through the keep like he was afraid someone was after him.

Finally pushing his door open, he slammed it shut, rattling the sconces attached to the walls. Cupping his face in his hands, he trembled. His rage turned into tears that slipped down his rosy cheeks. Swiping them away, his frozen hand felt like he was scraping his face with a knife. A bath. That's what he needed. A hot bath.

Stripping as he made his way toward his bathroom, he blessed the castle attendants who had just filled his tub before sinking in, relishing the burn against his frozen skin. He tipped his head against the rim and closed his eyes.

If all went according to plan, in a week's time, he would be crowned King of Northwind. But first, he had to make it through the four-day journey to the next military camp without breaking Niabi's neck, which would be no easy feat.

He hated how much Niabi resembled their mother. Down to the tone of her voice, she was every part Bilhah, and it pained him to look upon his enemy's face and see his mother staring back at him. Crispin and Salome inherited their mother's skin tone and some of her personality traits, but they were born with Issachar's curly, brown hair, brown eyes, and obsessive need to crush their enemies.

Allowing himself to wallow for a brief moment, he thought about what his life would look like had his father been a good king and a kind father. Niabi never would have lashed out, taking those he loved. She would have inherited the White Throne, as was her birthright according to their laws, and the rest of his brothers would be alive.

Crispin glanced out the frosted window at the Ignacia Sea and it called out to him. Oh, how he loved being aboard the *Shadow of Death*, sailing across the seas, and living out every adventurous dream his childhood heart longed for. Had his father followed the laws of their ancestors, Niabi would have been queen, Lykos would have been her Master of War, Mosgalath would have found his place amongst the scholars in Northwind, Elias would have gladly accepted a position in the elite forces that protected the crown, and Crispin would have been given a command in the naval fleet. Salome and Jepthudar, the youngest of the seven, would have been given positions of high honor, although they all would have been expected to marry for power and not love.

A sudden knock on his bedchamber door throttled him from his daydream. "Enter," he shouted as he hopped out of the tub and wrapped a towel around his waist.

"Oh, seven hells, Crispin!" Salome slapped her hands over her eyes. "How are you going to tell someone to come in when you're in this state? Put a shirt on."

He rolled his eyes and slipped his clothes on and threw the damp towel at her. "You're a child."

"Moody today?" she teased and welcomed herself to sit cross-legged on his bed, wrinkling the sheets. "Are you disappointed it's me and not a certain lady pirate visiting you?"

Crispin opened his mouth to say something snarky, but nothing came out. His heart was hurting, and his stress was at an all-time high, but he wasn't sure how to tell his sister all of that when he knew she carried her own set of heavy burdens.

"What is it?" she asked, her tone now sharp.

"It's nothing," he lied.

"One of the maids told me you were running through the halls in a panic."

"I tripped up the stairs," he scoffed, waving a hand in the air to emphasize his point, "that hardly qualifies as me running through the castle in a panic."

Salome patted the spot next to her, beckoning him to come sit with her, which he reluctantly did. As soon as his body hit the mattress, she wrapped her arms around him, pulling him into a hug.

"Salome -"

She shushed him. "This is happening."

Crispin leaned into her and released a sigh that shook his entire body.

"Are you alright?" she asked and he shook his head.

"No, but I will be."

"You don't have to talk about it," she pulled away from him, eyeing him with concern, "but I'm right down the hall, if you need me." She planted a kiss on his forehead before hopping off the bed and slipping out the door. "Goodnight," she offered him one last smile before disappearing.

Crispin threw himself back onto the bed, covering his eyes with his forearm. Tomorrow morning, they would start their journey north, bringing him one step closer to Death or destiny. Without realizing it, he'd drifted off to sleep and didn't stir until first light.

Chapter Fifty-Two

Adonijah

Leaving Oakenshire and trekking north for four days was surprisingly uneventful.

Pash and Leoti brought Adonijah up to speed on the state of Northwind. How Gershom staged a successful coup and how Niabi found, joined, and became an ally to her siblings in their fight to reclaim the White Throne. Adonijah even met the former queen and Tala, her Andrago bodyguard and father of Leoti. He hated that he was nervous meeting the Andrago, but when asked about his intentions for the future, he happily poured his heart out about wanting to build a life with Leoti. She'd accepted Adonijah, and in doing so, Tala welcomed him into the fold. Especially when he found out Adonijah had been willing to die in Pash's camp for killing the Shadow that attempted to assault his daughter.

Even though he now found himself betrothed, Adonijah found everything else around him confusing. He wasn't certain if Niabi could be trusted, but he rejoiced with his brother that he had he been reunited with the love of his life, and he was now a proud father of a little boy that had his nose and Niabi's piercing green eyes.

What bothered him most about Niabi wasn't that her very presence was threatening, but that watching her interact with those she loved made her so human. He'd heard the stories about her; how she was lethal in battle and her weapons were extensions of her body. He remembered tales of how she slaughtered her enemies and purged the Black Forest of vagabonds that terrorized travelers passing through. But seeing her cuddle her newborn and kiss Pash with nothing but pure love in her eyes made his heart ache. He wanted happiness for them, but he knew the prophecy of the Hunter, just like everyone else in that camp. Salome was destined to avenge the blood of the innocent. Niabi might have had just cause to want her father dead, but she still had blood on her hands. There was a good chance Salome would still be expected to execute her sister, even though they'd come to an agreement in Oakenshire to fight together to defeat Gershom.

Over the course of the four-day journey, Adonijah observed Crispin glaring at Niabi countless times, and recognized the look of a man with murderous intent. Not even Salome would be able to prevent Crispin from driving his sword through Niabi's chest, if he set his mind to it. And he thought his family was complicated.

"You ready?" Salome asked, plopping down beside him by the campfire, startling him from his thoughts.

He bobbed his head but by the skeptical look on her face, he knew he couldn't hide his true feelings from her. She knew him far too well.

"What is it that troubles you, Adonijah?" She snatched a piece of venison off his plate, drawing a smile from him.

"Little thief."

Her smile faded when he evaded the question. "Are you worried we won't win tomorrow?"

Adonijah lowered his head.

They'd set up their military camp a couple miles outside of Northwind, still shielded by the trees of the Black Forest. They were a large and mighty host of some of the greatest soldiers in Adalore, and just off the coast, their ships awaited those who would fight by sea.

"I haven't seen my father since I was a boy," he admitted, "I'm afraid I might freeze once I see him again."

Salome slipped her hand onto his. "I know you fear his blood runs through your veins, but you are nothing like him."

"I should have told you months ago when we first met," he lamented. "I was afraid I'd lose you if I revealed my identity," he chuckled softly. "I guess I never really had you to lose." When she said nothing, he looked at her and asked, "Did I ever stand a chance?"

Salome smiled. "Had we met under different circumstances, I think we could have been happy together. But I'm no longer that girl from the Tree House Forest. And you're far more than just being The Wanderer."

"I meant what I said before, about protecting you." His eyes bore into hers, silently hoping to get his message across. "My sword will always be yours."

"All I want," she whispered, "is for you to survive this war. I want you to be happy with Leoti and maybe you'll find the peace you have so desperately been seeking."

"You were my light when all I expected was darkness. I will cherish you for the rest of my days for saving me."

She slipped her arms around his neck and embraced him. "You have been the best friend I could have ever hoped for, Adonijah." She pulled away from him and smiled. "Leoti is a far better match for you than I ever was. The way you look at one another is how great love stories begin."

"She admires you as well," he added. He felt like a weight had been fully lifted off his shoulders. Salome was right, Leoti was the best suited partner for him, and he was happier than he'd ever been.

"Well," she slapped his knee and stood up, "we better get going."

"Going? Where?" He quirked an eyebrow.

"I came to bring you to the war tent," she smiled down at him. "The leaders have gathered to finalize strategy, and I want you in there with me."

"Why?" he asked as he motioned around the camp. "I lead no army to give you input."

"There is no one I trust more to give sound advice in that room," she said without question or hesitation. "War will be waged in that room and I need to know that those with sound minds will prevail."

"I take it you're worried about your brother and sister." He snickered, drawing a labored chuckle from her.

"I'm afraid with their tempers, one will be tempted to stab the other."

"Seems like a family trait," he tossed one last piece of food in his mouth before standing up, towering over her. He motioned toward the large white tent in the middle of their encampment. "Lead the way, my lady."

As they made their way toward the tent, they spotted Niabi and Pash passing a bundled Ivaylo into Tala's arms.

"Take him to Elisor and keep him safe," Niabi instructed. Tala attempted to hand the baby back, but Niabi squeezed his forearm. "Please, my friend."

"I should be fighting alongside you," Tala's voice trembled, and Adonijah thought it sounded awfully close to a goodbye on Niabi's part.

"Should we fail to return -"

"Niabi -"

She cupped his face in her hands, forcing him to meet her gaze and listen. "Should we fail to return, I am trusting you to make sure he knows who he is and how much we loved him." Pash slipped his hands on Niabi's shoulders and nodded his head in agreement. "Promise me, you will keep Ivaylo safe and train him in the ways of the Andrago."

A tear slipped down Tala's cheek and his lip quivered as he bobbed his head. "I swear he will be safe in my charge."

Niabi embraced the Andrago and as she pulled away, she kissed his cheek. "Now, go. Get my son as far away from here as you can."

Tala cradled Ivaylo in his arms and reluctantly walked away.

Adonijah watched as the Andrago fought brimming tears, before returning his attention to his brother and Niabi. They were somber and didn't move a muscle until Tala hopped on his saddled horse and took off into the forest with their son and a couple guards as an escort. Pash wrapped his arms around Niabi's waist, and she rested the back of her head against his chest. Adonijah couldn't imagine how difficult it must have been for them to send their son away with the thought that they might not live to see him again. Pash met his gaze but didn't say anything as he clutched Niabi.

He'd nearly forgotten Salome was with him until she made her way toward them and reached for Niabi's hand. "You don't have to stay here, Niabi. You can go with your son."

Niabi shook her head and rubbed Salome's arm. "I gave you and Crispin my word and I intend to see this through to the end."

"But -"

"I was not raised to run away from adversity, no matter how tempting it might be," Niabi gently cut her off. "We are wolves, and we will take back our home." Without another word, she freed herself from Pash and marched toward the war tent, her head held high, ready for battle.

Pash scowled at Salome, which was so unlike him, it was unsettling.

"Pash?" Adonijah stepped closer to Salome, his eyes fixed on his brother. "Is everything alright?"

The commander didn't tear his gaze from Salome, but he didn't say anything. Something was clearly bothering Pash, but if he chose not to address it, then Adonijah wouldn't force him to. Without saying a word, or even acknowledging Adonijah's question, Pash stormed off to the war tent.

"I don't think your brother cares for me," Salome whispered.

"He's probably stressed. He is not acting like himself." Adonijah raked a hand through his hair and grimaced. "I hope you won't hold it against him."

Salome shook her head. "If I got mad everytime someone gave me a nasty look, I would be in a perpetual state of rage." She laughed, and it relaxed him. "Come on, we need to get in there."

"Right," Adonijah nodded.

"Leoti?" Salome called out to the Andrago and motioned her to come forward. "Join us."

Without hesitation, Leoti smiled and joined their ranks as they sauntered into the lion's den, hopefully coming out with a sound plan and without injuries.

Chapter Fifty-Three

Salome

They'd been at it for hours. Arguing back and forth, leaders from all over Adalore offered their best strategy for effectively bringing Gershom and his allies to their knees, all while the other leaders poked holes in their plans. Salome rubbed her temples, feeling a splitting headache coming on. She hadn't offered any ideas because quite frankly, she didn't have any. At this point, she could have sneaked into the White Keep on her own and driven her blade into Gershom's heart and returned to find them all in the same positions arguing over their next course of action.

Niabi stood up and placed her hand on the map of Northwind and the surrounding areas, frustration and exhaustion riddled in her features. Salome swore every time Niabi looked at her, she saw her mother staring back. It was as equally comforting as it was unsettling.

"I can lead a small team into the city undetected," Niabi raised her voice above the rest of the leaders, drawing their undivided attention, "but the majority of your army will have to attack by land and sea."

Crispin scoffed, removing his palms from the table and straightening to his full height. "You are truly a fool, if you think I'm going to let you out of our sight during battle."

"I won't be out of sight," Niabi flashed a coy smile at Salome. "Our sister will be going with me."

"Out of the question." Crispin shook his head, folding his arms across his chest.

"Crispin -" Salome attempted to protest but was cut off.

"I will not allow you to be alone with her."

"I'll go with them," Adonijah stepped forward and everyone stared at him. "From what we've already discussed," he motioned toward the map on the wooden table with figurines scattered around, "Prince Crispin, Prince Heru, Pash, Leoti, King Hanzo, Queen Oifa, the Numbio, and the Mountain Men will attack the main gate. Prince Jinn, Rahab, the rest of the pirates, Master Penn and her Keepers, the Qata Vishna, the Eastern forces, and the Bellators will attack Nezreen and Uri by air and sea. That leaves Salome and Niabi to infiltrate the White Keep and assassinate Gershom. Thrice and I can go with them and give them the backup they need, as well as keep them safe."

"I need you at the front lines," Crispin insisted. "I need all the best swordsmen battling at the main gate."

"Then I will go with them."

Salome turned around and saw Leoti holding her arm. She looked nervous, but she held her head high, mustering every bit of courage she could.

"What did you say?" Crispin asked.

"I said, I will go with them. I will be their fourth." Leoti's voice grew stronger the more she spoke, and Salome couldn't help but feel a sense of great pride that the woman who had never wielded a sword before, was now volunteering for a stealth assassination mission. Her knife skills had improved by leaps and bounds since their first sparring session and she would be more than happy for the Andrago to join them.

"Leoti," Adonijah took a step toward her, his face twisted with concern. "It's a dangersous mission, are you sure you want to go?"

Leoti furrowed her brow. "I've been training with Salome for weeks. My warging abilities would enable us to see what we might be up against on our way to the tunnel entrance, and I know the White Keep like the back of my hand. I would be an asset." Her eyes trailed away from her intended and met Niabi's stare. "And I have a no qualms in poking some holes in Gershom's chest."

Niabi grinned and nodded. "I say she goes."

Crispin opened his mouth, looking like he was going to argue just because Niabi liked the idea, when Salome cut him off. "I agree."

Leoti had made a compelling argument and she was right, she would be an incredible asset and it would free Adonijah to be where he needed to be, by Crispin's side. She knew no matter what, Adonijah would protect Crispin when she couldn't.

"What say you, brother?" Salome held his irritated glare until he conceded.

"It is agreed." He reluctantly declared. "Inform your warriors of the plan," Crispin ordered. "And get some rest. We're going to need it."

The contentious strategy meeting was finally over and the leaders were wearily trickling out of the war tent. Salome spotted Jinn across the room and his smile made her heart leap. She would never grow tired of how he looked at her. He made her feel like she was more stunning than all the twinkling stars in the night sky. His attention was stolen when Crispin engaged him in conversation.

She noticed Adonijah and Leoti on the other side of the table, whispering back and forth. Salome figured Adonijah's instinct to protect Leoti was in full swing and from what she knew about Leoti, he didn't stand a chance at talking her out of joining the assassination mission. They really were a great match.

As she was about to make her way to Jinn and her brother to join in on their conversation, she felt a calloused hand grab her bicep and yank her back.

"If you harm Niabi," Pash whispered gruffly against her ear, "you will answer to me."

Salome attempted to pull her arm from his iron grip but failed. She glanced around the room, but most of the leaders had already left or were on their way out, and Jinn and Crispin were lost in their exchange.

"Let go of me," she hissed.

"Niabi means everything to me," Pash's tone was wild, and she knew there would be no reasoning with him. She didn't want to harm him and risk jeopardizing her fragile alliance with her sister, so she kept calm and attempted once more to wiggle free of his grasp. "If you betray her, no man, woman, or deity will keep me from driving my knife straight through your heart."

Suddenly, Pash's hold on her was broken and he was thrown across the room. A loud clanging sounded through the tent as Pash fell to the fur-lined ground, pulling the map and all the figurines off the table. Crispin, Adonijah, and Leoti immediately turned to see what was going on, and some of the leaders that had left the tent reentered to see what was happening.

Jinn stood between Salome and the commander and glared at Pash viciously. Fire raged in Jinn's eyes as he growled, "Touch my wife again, and I'll gut you."

"Wife?" Crispin asked, surprised. His gaze bounced between her and Jinn. "Salome, is that true?"

The night before the Battle of Oakenshire, Harbona answered his bedroom door groggily to find Salome and Jinn. When they explained why they had disturbed his sleep, he happily waved them into his chambers. On his balcony, facing the Ignacia Sea, Harbona led the couple in their vows and bound their hands with the same rope Oifa and Hanzo had been married with.

Gazing into one another's eyes, Salome and Jinn promised themselves to one another. The moonlight lit the prince's face perfectly, and she knew, this would be an image she would never forget. A secret marriage – a secret they could share for the rest of their days.

When their lips met, something deep within her hummed and she realized her magical bond with Jinn had grown more powerful. Married magic wielders. Their connection would be deeper, stronger, clearer.

Jinn smiled against her lips. "My wife," he whispered, and she felt whole.

They spent the rest of the evening before battle together, cuddled in bed. Jinn laid on his side and stroked her hair as she ran her fingers up and down his tattooed arm and chest. They didn't get much sleep, but they laughed, cried, and shared their dreams and fears with each other until it was time to report for duty. Jinn kissed her one last time before he cloaked himself and slipped out of her room, no one the wiser.

"Salome?" Crispin's voice sliced through her memories, bringing her back to the tent full of prying eyes.

Looking up at Jinn, his face filled with apology for spilling their secret, she smiled, slipping her hand into his. "Yes," she nodded, "I'm his wife."

Stunned congratulations flooded in as their friends surrounded them, embracing them.

Adonijah helped Pash up off the ground and whispered something harshly in his ear. Pash stormed out of the tent, and Adonijah watched him leave before he turned his attention to Salome and Jinn. As he approached the newlyweds, eyes from around the room darted to them. It was no secret Adonijah and Salome had cared for one another, some thought they might eventually get married, but when Adonijah finally reached the couple, he smiled and issued his congratulations.

With a cheer, and Oifa calling for a celebration, wine was brought in, and a toast was given to bless the union between Jinn and Salome. Jinn assured them they would have a royal wedding in due time, and they were all invited to share in the revelry.

As Salome sipped on her glass of wine, a quiet sadness filled her heart as she looked around at the wondrous faces filling the tent. She wasn't naive enough to believe they would all be attending her wedding, not because they didn't want to, but because some of them wouldn't survive tomorrow's war. She used to imagine that Zophar would walk her down the aisle, that Rosalina would style her hair just right for the occasion, that her grandmother, Nym, would be there to share a piece of marital wisdom before being whisked away to the bridal suite, but they were all gone, and after tomorrow, they might have company in the After.

"You're thinking too much again," Jinn's teasing voice pulled her from her thoughts and brought a smile to her face. She hadn't noticed when everyone trickled out of the tent, but she was happy it was just her and her husband now, grateful for a moment of privacy with him.

"A dangerous thing, I'm told," she teased. "Thinking too much."

"Better to think too much," he leaned close and whispered against her lips, "than not to think at all."

She closed the gap between them and kissed him. She rested her forehead against his. "Stay with me tonight?"

"There's nowhere I'd rather be," he smiled, tilting her chin up so he could meet her line of sight. "I love you."

"I love you, too," she said softly, running her fingers through his hair.

She wanted to tell him to survive, but there was no use in stating the obvious. They'd be separated in their missions tomorrow, but the end goal was the same. If fate was on their side, and the Almighty with them, they would see another day together.

What would she do if Jinn didn't survive? She hated the thought, but hated even more that Niabi's words kept flooding her mind. What would she do if Jinn was taken from her? She had demonstrated how far her wrath extended with Zophar's death. She couldn't imagine the destruction she would be capable of, if Jinn didn't make it out alive.

Forcing her fearful thoughts out of her mind, she and Jinn walked to her tent, and didn't come out again until he had to join the others headed for the ships. With one final kiss, she watched her husband, her love, disappear into the chilly night.

Chapter Fifty-Four

Crispin

Crispin was up and dressed before the sun peeked the horizon. His boots crunched through the fresh snow as he made his way to the edge of camp, facing north, the direction he'd soon be leading an army to battle Gershom. The stillness of the Black Forest reminded him of the Tree House Forest, but instead of peace, he felt an emptiness that chilled him down to the bone. Or maybe, it was just the extreme drop in temperature that had him nervous and chattering his teeth. He had forgotten how cold Northwind got during the winter months and because it was the middle of the season, it was bitter and biting. He shimmied the white fur draped over his shoulders tighter around his body, attempting to, but failing, to harbor any little body heat he had.

The team launching the attack via sea and air left last night and he had to say goodbye to Rahab. He was uneasy. This was the first time they'd been apart since meeting a few months ago, and he wouldn't be there to have her back. But the truth was she probably didn't need his protection; she was a force to be reckoned with. He just wished he could be there to see Uri's face as she plunged her daggers deep into his scarred chest.

"Don't do anything stupid," Rahab had whispered against his lips a second before she kissed him. Her eyes were sharp, and her tone carried both warning and pleading and he knew exactly what she was trying to say without actually saying the words: I love you.

His nightmare had plagued him for weeks without fail. He felt Gershom's sword plunge into his chest; he saw the smug, victorious look on his face; he heard the screams of those he loved as he took his last breath. It ended the same way, every time, and he would wake up drenched in sweat.

"Nothing stupid." He smiled against her mouth. *"Just a little reckless."*

He slept with his arm stretched across her side of the bed, wishing she were next to him. It'd been twelve hours and he felt her absence terribly.

"You'll have to keep your wits about you today, Crispin."

Salome's voice spooked him. He whipped around and saw she was bundled up in her coat, her blue hood slipped over her braided curls, very much prepared for war.

"I've got my wits about me." He offered the best smile he could, and she shook her head, a teasing grin spreading across her face.

"Then how come I was able to sneak up on you so easily in a freshly laid batch of snow?"

"You were always the better hunter."

She pointed a finger at him, triumph in her voice, "Ah ha! You finally admit I'm the better hunter."

"Did you need me to admit it?" he chuckled, rolling his eyes. "You consistently brought food to the table when we lived in the Tree House Forest."

"It's nice when a man can be humble about his shortcomings," she giggled, elbowing his ribs playfully.

A comfortable silence fell between them as they stood side by side looking through the pine trees dusted with snow. On the other side of the ridge, the battlefield in front of the city of Northwind awaited them.

"Wife, huh?" He broke the silence and she side-eyed him.

"Are you terribly angry?"

"No." Crispin snaked his arm across her shoulders and pulled her close. "Just mad you thought of it first," he winked, drawing a laugh from her. Though it wasn't her infectious giggle, it was something and it counted.

"I won't be there to cover your ass, so make sure you watch your back," Salome cleared her throat, swiping a finger under her eye.

Squeezing her tight, he kissed her forehead and nodded. "Don't let your guard down around Niabi," he whispered. "She's not to be trusted."

"I'll be careful," she agreed, but something in her voice gave him trepidation.

"Your Majesties." Harbona bowed at the hip and when he straightened, there was a warm, familiar smile on his face. When his aura was restored, it rejuvenated his weathered appearance to smooth, youthful skin, and Crispin was still getting used to seeing him in his true Ethereal form. "The men and women are assembled and are ready to go when you command."

"And the ships?" Crispin asked.

"Leoti warged this morning and said they have set their course for the harbor."

"Good." He turned and gave his sister one more hug. "Be quick. Be safe. Come back to me in one piece."

Salome nodded, her smooth skin rubbing against his short beard. "Don't do anything I wouldn't do."

Reluctantly, he pulled back to get one more look at her. He prayed this wasn't the last time they would see each other, but before she could see any kind of crack in his facade, he motioned for her to join her small team back at camp. They wouldn't be traveling together to Northwind. She, Niabi, Leoti, and Thrice would cut east toward the coast to find the tunnel entrance into the keep. If they were successful in assassinating Gershom and Vilora, the battle wouldn't last long. What they needed was time, and a good distraction at the main gate. He would give them that and hopefully his tricks and strategy would pay off in the end.

Crispin, alongside Heru and the Numbio, Hanzo, Oifa, and the united Mountain Men, Rayma and her team of healers, and Harbona, made their way through the Black Forest. Once they breached the perimeter, the White City was within sight and it stole the prince's breath. The white spires of the White Keep built on a hill in the center of the city captured his gaze as they stretched toward the heavens. The tears welling up in Crispin's eyes could have been from the blistering cold wind that whipped around him the second he left the pines trees' protection, or it could have been spurred by the fact he'd finally made it home.

Twelve years. Twelve very long years. The last male heir of Issachar had finally come home.

"It is quite impressive." Heru trotted up to Crispin, enthralled by the sight.

"I dare say, Numbio is far more impressive." Crispin quickly wiped the tear from his cheek before his friend could notice.

"Maybe so," Heru grinned, "but you have snow."

"Is it your first-time experiencing snow?" he asked, grateful for the lighthearted conversation. Heru was good at lifting his spirits when he felt the looming shadow of despair creep over him.

"Yes, and I love it." The Numbio nodded, dragging a hand down his black beard. "But I do not believe Oifa likes it."

Both of them risked a quick glance behind them to catch a glimpse of Oifa, who appeared even more prickly than normal, flipping her lavender locks behind her shoulders.

"I don't know what would make that woman happy," Heru chuckled. They turned around before the Stormcrag noticed them staring.

"I imagine killing a few dozen enemy soldiers would put a smile on her face." Crispin laughed, but the joviality was short lived when alarm bells tolled alerting the citizens of Northwind of their presence.

The main gate was sealed shut as archers and soldiers scurried back and forth on top of the white stone wall. It glistened as the sun continued to rise high above them and appeared even more brilliant against the snow. But soon, that pristine white snow would be stained red with blood. Crispin wasn't naive to believe anything different. It would be a hard battle to win, especially since the Northmen knew how to defend their walls, but with Niabi and Pash's insight into the tactics of their military, he hoped it would give them the slight advantage they needed to come out victorious.

The night before, Cato and a small group of Mountain Men sneaked through the forest to head to the city wall. Their mission was dangerous but if done right, they'd force the Northmen to come out and face their army on level ground. Cato was instructed to take his team and tunnel underneath the main gate. Once they reached the entrance to the city, they were to put the explosives that Phex had engineered there, and once they were free from the mine, they were to detonate the explosives. If everything went according to plan, the explosion would splinter the gate, giving them a way inside and past the stone walls.

Niabi and Pash assured the leaders when they formulated these plans, that no citizens lived at the front end of the city and that the explosion would only tear down one of the military's garrisons.

As long as Crispin and his company kept the soldiers at the main gate distracted, they wouldn't notice what would truly bring their city to its knees.

Lined up on the battlefield, a hundred yards from the main gate, Crispin kicked at Freya's sides beckoning her forward. With the other leaders following up behind him flying their banners, Crispin rode as close as he dared before yelling up at the gatekeepers, not missing the hundreds of archers with their bows nocked and ready to strike staring down at him.

"I am Crispin, son of Issachar, and heir to the White Throne. Lay down your weapons or die by mine."

"Archers ready!" The commander atop the wall commanded and the bowman held their weapons taut. "Take aim!"

"Fall back," Crispin ordered, pulling Freya's reins and galloping back to his troops. "Prepare for battle!"

Hanzo and his archers readied their arrows in response to the hailstorm the Northmen unleashed, as Crispin retreated to a safe position. A smile snaked across Hanzo's face. "Let's give them our answer!" He sliced his hand through the air, "Fire!"

The marksmen let loose their arrows. While the Northmen's arrows had riddled the battlefield, the Stormcrag and Krazaks were known for their long-distance range, and easily found their targets along the stone walls.

Crispin bobbed his head at Heru and Oifa, signaling them to prepare for a ground assault. The Numbio lifted their enormous shields and as a unit began the steady trek forward, covering the Stormcrags and Krazak warriors pushing a battering ram. Hanzo and his archers fired away behind them. While camped in the Black Forest, they had used the resources provided by their allies to construct several siege towers, ladders, and ballistae. Although Crispin hated seeing his kingdom's walls damaged, he intended to use every piece of equipment they had to bring his enemies to their knees.

Hanzo had three ballistae at his disposal and had his most accurate marksmen launch enormous arrows afire at the men lining the city walls.

The stone walls held firm, but with the barrage of their persistent assault, cracks and small openings began to snake across the city's facade. Little by little, they laid siege to the White City and though the Northmen shot arrows at them, they pushed their way to the main gate and slammed their battering ram against the wood, rattling it. The Numbio held their shields in place, protecting the soldiers operating the ram, but the gate was solid and wasn't showing any signs of breakage.

Crispin whispered his prayers under his breath, as he hoped Cato and his crew had made their way underneath the gate and planted their explosives. Phex had been specific in his instructions on how to handle them and set them off. Cato nodded in understanding during the exchange, but Crispin had spent some time with the Stormcrag and knew he wasn't the fastest learner. Hopefully, they hadn't run into any problems, or worse, blow themselves up in the process. Seraphina would never forgive him, if Cato's blood was on his hands.

It wasn't long before the fresh batch of snow that glistened that morning was nothing more than slosh and mud. Crispin couldn't do anything but watch as the Northerners threw stones and boiling water down from their walls and murder holes at the soldiers doing their best to break down the main gate. Crispin knew if Cato and his team weren't successful, his army would have to find another way to take the city, hence the battering ram, but the bloodcurdling screams of his allies echoed across the battlefield, tearing his heart to pieces.

Crispin turned to Harbona. "Any word from Cato?"

Harbona shook his head. "We are waiting for his signal."

"Signal them to fall back," Crispin instructed the soldier standing next to him with a horn.

Without hestitation, the man blew the prince's command. Oifa whipped around, glaring at Crispin. Retreating wasn't in her nature, but if she didn't obey, she and her soldiers might not survive the assault from above. Crispin narrowed his eyes and told the soldier to repeat the signal. The soldier blew his horn and finally, albeit reluctantly, Oifa echoed Crispin's instructions and she and her warriors pulled the battering ram back, the Numbio shielding them as they retreated.

The Northmen let out a cry of victory, having fended off the battering ram. Arrows flitted through the sky in both directions, killing soldiers on the wall and field.

This was going to be a bloodbath. Gershom might not have had time to get reinforcements, but in truth, he didn't need the help. He had a large army at his disposal and the pirates of Pulau guarding his harbor. Perhaps, it was unwise to attack in the winter, but it was far too late to turn back now.

Chapter Fifty-Five

Salome

It took Salome, Niabi, Leoti, and Thrice about an hour to trek through the snow until they arrived at a large tree that looked completely ordinary. But this tree was actually the entrance to the tunnels under Northwind and led directly to the White Keep. Niabi circled the trunk until she found the spot she was looking for and pressed her hand against it. A section of the tree slid open, allowing them to descend a set of creaky wooden steps. She motioned her hand toward the tunnel.

"This is our way in," Niabi stated.

Salome flashed back to the night Zophar helped her and Crispin escape through the tunnels. They'd come out through a tree, but she hadn't thought about it in years. She ran her fingers across the bark and knew it was the same one from her childhood.

Zophar's smiling face consumed her thoughts; tears welled up in her eyes. She wished he could be here. If she hadn't put him in jeopardy – if she hadn't failed to save him –

"You alright?" Leoti's voice sliced through her masachistic thoughts, and she bobbed her head.

"You've been here before," Niabi's eyes narrowed. It was unnerving that she was so incredibly observant.

"It's how Crispin and I escaped you all those years ago," Salome confessed, seeing no harm in admitting the truth.

Niabi didn't say anything in response, her face stone-cold and neutral. She waved for them to follow her and for a split second, Salome hesitated. What if this was a trap? Salome wanted to believe her sister would hold up her end of their bargain, but there was always a chance she would betray her when, and if, the right opportunity presented itself. Maybe this was a huge mistake, and she should have listened to Crispin after all.

Leoti pressed her hand to Salome's shoulder. "If you've changed your mind, say the word and I'll get you out of here."

"What do you mean?" Salome turned to look at her and the Andrago shrugged her shoulders and flashed a sheepish smile.

"Adonijah made me promise I'd watch over you. Said he swore an oath to protect you and didn't want to fail you."

Salome let out a breath. That was typical Adonijah behavior. Always looking out for those he cared about. But she'd come too far to turn back now. Their friends, her brother, her betrothed – they were all counting on her to cut off the head of the snake and end the war before it truly had a chance to begin.

"No," she shook her head. "We have to go."

Although she looked as if she had something to say, Leoti conceded and motioned with her head toward the tunnel that Niabi and Thrice had already gone into.

Salome slipped inside the tree and followed the steps down, down, down into the darkness. It was cold and the only source of light was the torch that Thrice held. Niabi had explained beforehand that the tunnels had been dug out hundreds of years ago, but that over time, most Northerners had forgotten all about them. As children, Niabi and Lykos would go exploring and found their way through the ancient passageways. Built into the earth, their ancestors had fortified the tunnels with the same white stones they used to build the White City.

Silently, the four of them walked through the cobweb-filled hallways. They passed a rickety ladder and Niabi commented that they had reached the city wall. Immediately, Salome realized where that particular ladder led. The small house on the southeast side of the city that Zophar had taken them to, the hole in the floor – it was directly above her. Twelve years ago, that little house had been part of her salvation. It was all coming back to her, waves of emotions flooded her, but she pushed it to the back of her mind. Distraction would get her killed. It was a lesson Zophar had taught them in the Tree House Forest.

"Focus on your goal," Zophar would say, "Distractions will get you killed."

After another thirty minutes of walking in complete silence, Niabi stopped and turned to look at her.

"When we push through this wall," she threw her thumb over her shoulder at the dead end, "we will be inside the White Keep. Stay close to me and don't make a sound."

Nerves bubbled within her, but she steadied her breathing and nodded in agreement.

Thrice put out the torch and pushed the wall open. Light beamed into the slit as the fake door slid. Salome was the last one to slip inside the White Keep and when she did, she couldn't breathe. It had been twelve years since she'd wandered the white halls. Glancing down at the white marble floors, she could see her reflection and remembered the last time she'd done so, she was staring back at her five-year-old self.

She'd come home.

She'd come home as a warrior.

She'd come home as the Hunter.

Niabi made a sharp sound, drawing Salome's attention. With a quick nod, the four of them made their way down the corridor. There was a lot of commotion in the castle as well as the city around them. When they came upon the hallway that had windows flanking either side, one facing the Ignacia Sea, the other facing the Taybourne Mountains and the main gate, Salome stopped and glanced both ways. To her left, her brother's battlefield. To her right, Jinn at sea. She said a quick prayer before catching up with the others on the other side of the bridge.

As they approached one of the main courtyards that led to the throne room, Niabi stopped and looked around, a wariness in her green eyes.

"What is it?" Salome stood next to her and whispered.

"There aren't any soldiers posted here." The Green-Eyed Raven met her gaze.

Salome's stomach churned, an unease sinking deep into her bones.

"Where are they?" Leoti asked, her hand tickling the hilt of her sword.

Thrice turned in a complete circle, even leaning forward to look up at the second floor balcony but shook his head when he came up empty. "I don't like this."

Commotion coming from down the hall echoed their way and Thrice hissed for them to hide behind the columns positioned around the courtyard. As Salome pressed her back against a marble column, she sucked in a breath to keep quiet. The heavy footsteps of soldiers thundered through the space and she could hear the battle raging around them from both the main gate and the sea. They needed to find Gershom and they needed to do it fast, if they wanted to spare their friends.

A group of fifteen foot soldiers marched down the corridor, their leader waving them forward.

Niabi quietly unsheathed her daggers from her sleeves and nodded for Salome to arm herself. She pulled her Qata Vishna blades from the holsters on her back while Leoti and Thrice both readied themselves with their swords.

Once the soldiers were in the middle of the courtyard and within striking distance, the four of them jumped out of their hiding places and launched their speedy assault.

The soldiers didn't stand a chance as the lethal warriors sliced through them before they were able to react. In the midst of the chaos, Thrice refrained from killing one, forcing the soldier to his knees and poking a knife to his throat. Pulling his head back with a fist-full of the guard's hair, Niabi stood in front of the patrolman, her hands clasped behind her back.

"Where is Gershom?" Niabi asked, a hardness in her features.

The soldier's eyes shifted amongst them, trepidation in his gaze.

Niabi snapped her fingers in his face, motioning for him to focus on her. "I will only ask once more." Flames licked up her left hand, drawing his attention and several whimpers. "Where is Gershom?"

"The king led his troops to the battlefield at the main gate," he answered, sweat dripping down his brow.

Salome and Niabi exchanged a disappointed look. They sneaked into the White Keep to assassinate Gershom. What they hadn't planned for was Gershom having the balls to lead his army into battle and face Crispin head on.

"Please," the soldier begged, tears welling in his eyes. "I don't want to die. I have a family, please."

Thrice looked eager to slit the soldier's throat, but Salome was determined not to let that happen. Before she had a chance to tell the former Shadow to stand down, Niabi extinguished her hand and waved Thrice down.

Crouching down in front of the guard, Niabi tipped his chin up and glared at him. "Tell me where I can find the witch."

If he was fearful before, he was downright horrified now. He began to tremble, but Niabi stroked a hand down his face, soothing him. "What's your name?"

"T-T-Tobias, my lady," he stuttered.

"Tobias," she repeated so gently it even calmed Salome's nerves. "I need to find Vilora. Tell me where she is so I can kill her."

Hope. There was a glimmer of hope in the soldier's face. He nodded, "She is in the East Wing."

"Thank you." She patted his cheek and pointed down the hallway. "Go home to your family, Tobias. Do not speak of what you have seen." He bobbed his head as he scurried down the corridor and out of sight.

"You realize he might alert the others of our presence." Thrice crossed his arms over his chest and leaned lazily against a column.

Niabi stood up slowly. "I am not here to kill my people, Thrice." She glanced at Salome and flashed a malicious grin. "But I am here to kill a witch."

Salome returned the smile and an energy pulsated through her body at the thought of striking down one of Gershom's allies.

It didn't take them long to make their way to the East Wing of the White Keep and there weren't many soldiers patrolling the halls, most were called to fight at the main gate.

Niabi told them they were headed to a lounge area where she used to greet her guests upon their arrival. That's where Vilora would most likely be, considering the fact she thought herself to be of queen status now that Niabi had been run out of her kingdom. Once the guards standing watch outside the doors leading into the chamber were taken out, the four of them marched inside, and were met by a lounging Vilora and a host of twenty soldiers. Any surprise in her face at their sudden and unexpected arrival was short-lived.

"I see you have returned, niece."

Salome didn't mean to flinch. Seeing the Old Witch of Endor after learning of her description and past life from her sister was one thing but hearing her speak was another thing entirely. Her voice sounded eerily like her grandmother, Nym's. Had she taken better care of herself, not spent so much of her life harboring her anger and letting her need for revenge ravage her body, Vilora might have managed to look as elegant as Nym. But instead, the hag was wrinkled and fed off the misery and spite of anyone who drew near.

Niabi took a step forward, not looking intimidated in the slightest by the witch reclining in the ornate chair that once belonged to her. "Only one of us is walking out those doors, Vilora."

"You fool," she cackled. "You should have disappeared when you had the chance." She slowly rose from her seat, exposing her bare feet with long, cracked toenails. "Now, you will die."

Chapter Fifty-Six

Rahab

Saying goodbye to Crispin had been the hardest thing Rahab had ever done, but she made sure to keep a brave face, even though her heart was pounding inside her chest.

Once the group, consisting of the pirates of the *Shadow of Death*, Prince Jinn, Kai, the Eastern army, Master Penn and her Keepers, and the Bellators, reached the fleet, they began their short sail to the shores of Northwind to face the Pulauan armada.

Rahab noticed Prince Jinn standing by the railing overlooking Northwind, and though she wasn't one for chit-chat, she felt compelled to talk to him. Maybe it was nerves, maybe it was because they were in love with siblings and would one day be family, but she walked up to him and plopped her elbows down on the railing next to him.

"Are you scared, princeling?"

Jinn glanced at her and smiled. "Not for myself."

She nodded in understanding. "It's funny, isn't it?"

"What is?"

"Love," she smirked. "I used to be afraid I wouldn't live through a battle. Now, I'm afraid of what life would look like if Crispin doesn't survive."

"I won't be able to help her if she needs me," Jinn's eyes were fastened on the White Keep. "That's what scares me more than anything."

"Then let us make quick work of the witch bitch and that bastard she serves." She uncorked her flask and took a shot of rum before passing it to the prince.

Jinn smiled, the corners of his eyes crinkling, as he took a shot. "You will make a fine queen, my lady."

"Every lion needs his lioness," she slipped the flask back into her pant pocket.

"We are approaching where the fleet should be." Kai stomped toward them.

They glanced out into the mist, but the fog was so thick, they couldn't see anything in the open water. Rahab didn't like it.

"Maybe the pirates abandoned the city?" Kai presumed, but Rahab knew Uri better than that.

"No," she shook her head. "They're here. We just haven't found them yet -"

"Look out!" A soldier bellowed from the crow's nest, but it was too late to avoid the crash.

Out of the mist, the Leviathan, fashioned with a metal bowsprit, speared into the hull of the ship Rahab was on, splitting the ship in half, the splintering wood echoing throughout the harbor. Soldiers jumped out of the way and Rahab leapt out of the direct path of the ship, but ended up falling into the freezing Ignacia Sea with hundreds of soldiers. She surfaced and waded, looking all around for Jinn, but the prince was nowhere to be found.

The men and women who weren't able to avoid the blow from the Pulauan ship, floated in the blood darkened waters.

Once more, she tried to find Jinn, but when she realized there was a good chance the prince was dead, her heart sank. Not only would Salome be devastated, but Rahab had lost her Cloaker and her best chance at sneaking up on the Shadow Witch.

"Damn it!" She slapped the water.

Screams from the other ships in Rahab's fleet sounded, drawing her attention. Pulauan pirates were swinging from their ships and boarding the rebel fleet. Metal clashed against metal, bodies fell into the sea, splashing all around her and those who had survived the first ship attack.

Kayven and Abba led the Bellators into the sky and they dodged the explosives and battled the shadows Nezreen threw their way. When Rahab noticed which ship the shadows were coming from, she spotted Nezreen and knew if she could cut off the head of the snake, then they might be able to salvage this battle.

Swimming toward the Leviathan, she grabbed her knives and stabbed them into the hull of the ship, making her way up the side. It was grueling and tiring and by the time she made it to the deck, she was shivering and exhausted. Pure adrenaline was the only thing that kept her going. She kept seeing Crispin's face flash in her head, she felt his lips pressed against hers, and his hands roaming her body. She would make it back to him, if it was the last thing she did.

A loud explosion knocked her off her feet. When she pulled herself up to the railing, she was relieved to see Phex's trinkets were working and giving the rebels a fighting chance. The auburn-haired pirate had his reefer in his mouth and he was shouting commands for the Eastern soldiers to follow. As a unit, they launched wave after wave of concentrated explosives and managed to poke enough holes into one of the smaller ships that it began to sink, causing the pirates to abandon ship.

Hope. There was still hope.

She dragged herself to her feet, dripping along the deck as she sneaked behind unsuspecting pirates and slit their throats or stabbed them in the back. Slowly, and stealthily, she made her way from the quarterdeck to the staircase leading up to the sterncastle where Nezreen was launching her shadow assault against the Bellators.

Rahab couldn't do anything but watch as Nezreen speared her shadows as weapons. One sliced into a Bellator's chest and shredded his white wings. He plunged into the sea, dead before he hit the water. She slammed a hand over her mouth, stifling her horrified gasp. Though they'd lost one of their elite warriors, Kayven and Abba continued to lead their men and fight hard to defend the mortals they'd come to care for. Launching another round of attacks, Nezreen was fully engaged and distracted by them. It was now or never.

She sprinted up the steps, weapons drawn, ready to cut the witch down, mentally prepared for the possibility it might end up being a suicide mission, but before she could get within reach, a large fist collided with her cheek, knocking her off her feet. She hit the deck so hard her weapons flew out of her hands. Her vision was blurred, and her ears were ringing. Planting her palms on the floor and pushing herself up onto her knees, she blinked several times hoping her hazy vision would clear up before whoever hit her finished her off.

Heavy steps approached her as she crawled away, but her retreat was short-lived as she backed up into the wall, and two scuffed leather boots stopped in front of her. She squinted as she looked up and her heart sank.

"Well, well, well," Uri the Pirate King bared his teeth. "It looks like you've lost your weapons."

She spat at him. "Go to hell."

"I was hoping to see you again." He cocked his head to the side. "The one who escaped me."

Rahab found it hard to breathe. All this time, she thought he'd forgotten all about her, but he remembered her as the one who got away. She'd dyed her hair and changed her name. The girl she used to be was dead.

"If you know who I am," though she was terrified, she willed the fear from her face, "then why didn't you say something at The Sisters?"

"You've done a good job of disguising yourself, little one, but I never forget a face. Especially the face of the bitch that gave me this." He pointed to the scar she'd left across his face. "It took me a week to place you, but once I did, I knew I'd see you again. You wouldn't be able to stay away."

"Enough talking," she snarled, defiant until the end. "Slit my throat and be done with it."

"Oh, I will," he flashed a malicious grin. "But first, I think I'll take my time with you since I was robbed of that privilege years ago."

"Touch me and I'll -"

"You'll what?" Uri hissed, taking his blade and slicing her thigh, drawing blood and a muffled scream from her lips. "You have no weapons and no one here to save you." He knelt before her, grabbing her neck and squeezing, forcing her to meet his crazed eyes.

Rahab slid her hand into her pant pocket and slipped her brass knuckles on. Gasping for air as the pirate king strangled her, she used the little bit of strength she had left to punch him in the ribs. Uri roared, releasing her from his grasp. He backhanded her and she could taste the iron in the blood he'd summoned. His boot stomped down on her injured leg and even though she tried to fight it, when he ground his toe in her wound, she screamed.

Crispin's face flashed in her head, a cruel reminder of everything she was about to lose. Death had come for her before, and she defied her. Perhaps her stolen time had finally run its course, but if she was to die, she wouldn't go out sniveling in the corner like prey. She'd bare her claws and show her fangs; she wouldn't be the only one to take their last breath that day: Uri would be gutted right alongside her.

As he lowered his face toward her, a smug grin snaked across his face. Uri pressed his knee into her injured thigh. She bit her lip, refusing to give him the satisfaction of prying another howl from her.

"Yield," he whispered. "And I will make your death a quick one."

"I yield to no one."

Without hesitation, Uri slowly slid his blade down her arm, leaving a trail of blood from the tip of her shoulder down to her wrist.

Sweat dripped from her hairline, but she still refused to yield. She would rather die, than bend the knee to this monster.

"So brave," Uri cooed. "But even the brave die, deary." His eyes shifted from her gaze to her other arm. "Should I do the other one or do you yield?"

The thought of feeling his dagger slice through her skin again, made her heart tremble. She quickly glanced around to see if any of her friends were coming to rescue her, but she saw no one, and Uri laughed knowing all too well who she was looking for.

"You're all alone," he purred, a look of smug satisfaction graced his scarred face. "Your friends will not come for you. They will die here, just like you."

"She's not alone."

Rahab and Uri's focus darted toward the steps. Captain Haldane made his way up, blood streaked across his rugged face, cutlass drawn, and revenge rooted in his gaze.

"Ahhh," Uri stood up, relieving Rahab of his weight on her thigh. "The fortune teller's husband. "He straightened his shoulders to mirror Haldane's stance. "You know, I can still hear her screams. I remember the sweet taste of her blood as she agonized for hours."

"Haldane, go!" Rahab ordered through gritted teeth, but the captain refused to listen.

"I plan to kill you." Haldane said plainly. "And when I do, I'll cut you limb from limb and feed what's left of you to the sharks."

The pirate king tapped his cutlasses together, clanging the metal loudly, and stomped toward him. "I'd like to see you try."

As if someone had urged them to begin, the two pirates launched themselves at each other. She knew Haldane was skilled with his cutlass, but Uri was ruthless and significantly bigger than her friend. If she didn't get to her feet to help him, she was afraid Haldane wouldn't be a match for the Pirate King.

Chapter Fifty-Seven

Crispin

"Get those siege towers moving!" Crispin motioned to Oifa and Heru. "Maintain a distance from the main gate, just in case Cato pulls through."

Heru darted to the tower to the left and Oifa sprinted to the right one. Shouting their commands, the leaders had the two siege towers they'd constructed in the Black Forest, pushed toward the wall. There was a high probability that the Northmen would set the towers ablaze, but with Phex's input, they had put as much metal around the front of the tower as possible. It made the tower much heavier, but it gave them a fighting chance at getting to the wall where they could infiltrate the city wall.

Crispin was itching to jump into the fray, but he knew his orders, and his mission was to lead the ground assault, once they got the main gate open or destroyed. He was restless, he didn't like the fact men and women were dying and he wasn't there to help them.

"Patience," Harbona whispered, probably knowing what was flooding Crispin's mind.

"They're dying out there." He raked a hand through his hair, fighting to maintain composure in front of the men and women that were in his charge.

"It's war, my Prince. Lives are lost, but if you do not hold fast to the plan you agreed to, you will lead your men to slaughter."

Crispin knew Harbona was giving him sound advice, but it didn't relieve the guilt in his heart. If Cato didn't give them the signal soon, he was going to have to regroup on the fly and aid his allies one way or another. He paced up and down the line, hands clasped behind his back.

Heru's tower made it to the wall first. He dropped the top so his men could fight the Northerners on the wall. Oifa's tower was struck with several flaming arrows and caught fire. Crispin could hear Oifa shouting orders for the men to put out the fire, knowing they were so close to laying siege to the wall, but they weren't quick enough to extinguish the flames and she ordered the soldiers to retreat. Crispin knew that order must have been difficult for her, since retreating went against everything she believed in, but with so many lives in her hands, she had made the right decision. They sprinted back from the wall, some falling dead with arrows lodged in their backs. But once they were out of firing range, Oifa nabbed some water from a sheepskin Crispin handed her. She had dirt and blood smeared across her face and arms and she smelled like sulphur.

"Stay here," Crispin met her furious gaze. "I'll lead the next wave with the battering ram. With Heru on the wall -"

Oifa pointed a tattooed finger in his face, her eyes blazing. "The only way I won't be fighting is if I'm dead and gone. Is that clear?"

"You should rest -"

She pounded on her chest and grunted. "I will rest when the battle is won. Now get out of my way, I have Northerners to kill."

Crispin grabbed her wrist, "Wait!"

Oifa swung around, looking like she was going to punch him, but he held up a hand and pointed to the tree line. "It's the signal. Cato's ready."

She narrowed her eyes at him, ripping her arm from his grasp. "You're lucky. Men have lost hands for less."

"Forgive me," he lifted his hands in surrender. "Once the gate explodes, we will hit them fast and hit them hard. Are you with me?"

Nodding, Oifa smiled and tapped her axe. "Aye."

Crispin exhaled in relief. The signal had been given and now they had to wait for the explosion to take place. Heru had kept his men clear of the main gate and they fought valiantly atop the wall. They'd slaughtered the archers, giving them a fighting chance at getting close to the city once the gate was destroyed.

And then it happened. A thunderous boom rattled the ground beneath them and tore through the main gate, splintering the wooden doors, and flung sections of the stone wall, as if it weighed nothing. When the dust settled, Crispin saw a gaping hole for him and his men to run into the city.

The horn blew a different signal, spurring the foot soldiers to unsheathe their weapons, and with Crispin and Oifa leading, they stormed the city.

The Northerners didn't waste any time. Their soldiers bolted through the billowing smoke and charged at Crispin and his army. Now, he would get his wish to be in the thick of battle, winning back his homeland, and protecting his friends fighting by his side.

As they approached the stampeding soldiers, Crispin glanced up and caught sight of Heru and the Numbio holding their ground on top of the wall. Finally, the soldiers converged in a great crash of metal on metal. Blood sloshed in the muddied snow. Men lost their footing and slipped. Agonizing screams and final breaths flitted around Crispin. It was chaos. Adrenaline coursed through his body, spurring him to fight any enemy soldier that crossed his path. A part of him wished he didn't have to strike down his countrymen, didn't have to claim so many lives in order to take back his father's throne, but when it came down to it, it was him or them, and he was determined to walk away from the battlefield alive.

Crossbowmen let their arrows fly, downing men all around Crispin. He attempted to side-step one of his attackers, but in doing so, his enemy took an arrow to the back and fell on top of Crispin. The prince pushed the dead soldier off of him, but more fighters, both friend and foe, fell down dead or slipped in the slosh of snow and blood. Before he knew it, he was buried beneath a stack of bodies and had to claw his way out.

He thrashed through the piles of bodies, trying to get out from underneath those trampling him, because he couldn't catch his breath. He had no room to move. Suffocating. He was suffocating underneath dozens of fallen soldiers and the thought that this was how he was going to die, awakened his fight. He'd felt this sensation of drowning before when he shoved Rahab out of Kubantu's grasp and was dragged beneath the waves of the Obsidian Sea. She had saved him and breathed life back into him, but this time, he would have to save himself, if he wanted to see her again.

Slowly but methodically, he wiggled free from the arms and legs entangling him and broke through to the surface. His face was kissed by the sun and chilly air filled his lungs. He never felt more alive.

"Crispin!" Oifa shouted, pushing bodies to the side. She extended her hand and pulled him out. "You're alive!"

Crispin embraced her. Even though the battle was raging all around them, he couldn't help thanking the stubborn Stormcrag for rescuing him.

"Gershom has been spotted," Oifa pulled back and grabbed Crispin's shoulders. "He is here with the troops. If we can get to him, we can end this!"

Crispin glanced in the direction she pointed and just like in his nightmares, he saw The Bear swinging his sword, slicing down any and all in his path. He was tall with broad shoulders and looked every bit as menacing in reality, as he did when he visited Crispin in his sleep. But what was he doing on the battlefield? He was supposed to be in the White Keep, not leading his soldiers in battle.

Salome was the one prophesied to kill Gershom, even Harbona had said so months ago in the Tree House Forest. But if he was down here and she was in the White Keep looking for him, this battle would be far from over.

"Let's go," Oifa persisted. "What are we waiting for?"

Crispin grabbed the hilt of his sword and took a step in Gershom's direction, but the sting of The Bear's blade and the crack of Crispin's ribcage echoed in his head, thwarting his attempts to fight him.

"I can't." Crispin shook his head. "I can't fight him."

"What do you mean?" Oifa looked baffled and glared at him with disdain. "He's right there! We could end this war right now."

"Harbona told me if I fight him, I won't survive." Crispin hated to admit it aloud and hoped Oifa didn't think him to be a coward. "Salome is the only one who can kill him. It's the prophecy."

At that, Oifa's face softened, and she nodded which shocked him. "Then we will find another way."

As Oifa glanced around, Crispin caught sight of Adonijah sprinting toward Gershom, longsword clutched in one hand and a dagger in the other. He looked like a man willing to lay down his life to settle a score.

"Damn it," Crispin hissed. He couldn't fight Gershom and live, but he couldn't watch Adonijah duel him and meet the end of The Bear's blade. He was going to have to help him.

"Push our men forward," Crispin pointed at the section of wall that had exploded. "I'll meet you there." With a nod from Oifa, Crispin jogged across the battlefield, cutting enemy soldiers down, and praying he wouldn't be too late to save his friend.

Chapter Fifty-Eight

Niabi

Vilora's short stature and her non-threatening stance didn't tame the adrenaline pulsing through Niabi's veins. She knew the power her aunt harnessed, but she also knew the same power hummed through her. She would destroy that deceitful witch with the very magic she unwittingly stole from her all those years ago, in the cabin that appeared out of nowhere. She'd been a fool for listening to Vilora. The witch had played on her fears and in allowing her emotions to control her, Niabi didn't decipher the witch's double-sided prophecy and paid a hefty price. Rollo deserved better. Dichali deserved better. She deserved better. And now, after all this time, looking into the face of the woman who had set her up for defeat and deceived her into believing she had an ally who understood her pain, she was itching to strike her down and tear her limb from limb.

With a snap of her fingers, Vilora unleashed the Shadows guarding her. They pointed their spears and swords at the four invaders, who had also unsheathed their weapons. They were clearly outnumbered, and Niabi knew some of the soldiers; she's sparred with a handful of them on a daily basis for years. They were skilled warriors and could generate quite a fight, but Niabi wasn't accustomed to losing and knew her sister wasn't either.

In the blink of an eye, the assault was launched. Niabi ignited her left arm and fired, roasting two Shadows. Their screams would undoubtedly haunt her nightmares, but she didn't give them a second glance as she whipped around, flying around the room like a twister of flames, slicing and stabbing anyone who crossed her path. She knew Salome, Thrice, and Leoti would handle the Shadows. Her eyes were fixed on her own prize: Vilora.

Vilora's glared at Niabi and smirked, both her hands ablaze. "Has my student come to play?"

"No," Niabi snarled. "I've come for your head."

"Then come and take it!" Vilora blasted two enormous fireballs at Niabi, but she tumbled away, dodging the attack.

Launching her own flamed attack at the witch, Vilora was forced to hide behind her chair, taking cover as best she could. Niabi was skilled with her blades, but the witch didn't know how to wield a sword. She relied heavily upon her magic, albeit strong magic, but that wouldn't stop Niabi from chopping her to pieces for her treachery.

Niabi integrated her magic along with sword play so she was confident in her abilities. Slamming her hand down on the tile, she zipped a blast of fire toward the chair Vilora was crouched behind and lit it up. The witch screamed as she scrambled from her hiding place, which was exactly what Niabi wanted her to do. With a quickness, Niabi sprinted toward her aunt, weapons drawn, ready to strike her down, but Vilora laughed and shot a blast of fire that nailed her square in the chest.

There was blood all over the white marble floor and the room smelled like death.

"You thought you could defeat me, Niabi?" Vilora's voice drew her distracted gaze. "You really thought you were stronger than the Old Witch of Endor?"

Niabi lifted herself up onto her elbows and stared up at Vilora. Her hands were cradling balls of fire and the smirk on the witch's face meant only one thing. She was aiming for the kill.

"Any last words, niece?"

But before Niabi could respond, Thrice sprinted toward the witch, his sword in hand, but at the sound of his rushed footsteps, Vilora turned one hand toward him and blasted an orb of fire into his chest, knocking him off his feet. Thrice screamed as his leathers ignited, but Leoti ran up quickly to help him.

Enraged, Niabi took advantage of Vilora's distraction and hopped up, landing on her feet. The witch spun around and placed her hand against Niabi's chest and issued her flames to consume her. Niabi grabbed Vilora's throat with her own flaming hand. "Have you forgotten, Vilora?" she hissed, relishing the fear in her aunt's eyes. "Fire doesn't burn fire." Niabi plunged her dagger into the old woman's chest.

Vilora gasped for air as Niabi released her, letting her crumble to the floor in a pool of her own blood. "I should have known you would be my undoing," she rasped, meeting Niabi's gaze one last time. "You are cursed. Anyone close to you ends up dead."

Those words stung Niabi more than she would ever admit. She didn't offer a response. She just stood over Vilora and watched as the life drained from her face. Her eyes were glossed over, and she stared blankly at the ceiling. Grabbing Thrice's longsword, she slammed it down across Vilora's neck, claiming the witch's head.

Thrice groaned, wrenching Niabi from her aunt's lifeless body. She slid over to him and grabbed his hand. Leoti had managed to put out the fire before it consumed him, but he was badly burned, and parts of his flesh were welded to the clothing that remained around his torso.

"He needs a healer," Leoti whispered as Thrice dipped in and out of consciousness. "There is nothing more I can do for him."

Salome knelt beside them, her eyes roving across his charred chest. She stared at Niabi and she shook her head. Niabi was all too aware of what that meant. Thrice wasn't going to make it. He was in bad shape. His death would be slow and painful and the thought that her friend, one of her most loyal protectors, wasn't going to make it out of the White Keep as a victor, soured her stomach.

Leoti's eyes bounced back and forth between the sisters, silently reading into their exchanged looks. "We can't leave him here to die," her voice cracked. "He needs a healer."

"He won't make it in time." Niabi spoke the truth, but it didn't sting less.

"We have to try to save him," Leoti was indignant. "We need to get him to one of the medical bays. I can make a salve that will help him until we can get him to a healer."

Niabi wanted to put her foot down and remind her they had more important matters to tend to, especially with a war raging all around them, but when she heard Thrice hiss in pain, her heart shattered. She'd known him for years and he'd risked his life to help her escape the coup Gershom had ignited. She owed him.

Niabi glanced at them, gaging the interest in the new mission. "If we all carry him, we can get him to a medical bay."

Salome bobbed her head in agreement, sheathing her weapons, and grabbing one of his legs.

Together, the trio carried Thrice as quickly as they could down the twisting corridors. If there was a chance to save Thrice, they would do everything they could to do so.

When they finally reached the apothecary, Niabi and Salome hoisted Thrice's heavy body up onto a wooden table in the middle of the room. There were jars filled with liquids and creatures, even eyes and bones and teeth. Salome looked around the room with upmost horror, but Leoti weaved around the room as if it were a second home. She speedily examined the shelves, grabbing different glass containers to concoct the salve for Thrice's gooey chest.

"You'll have to hold him down." Leoti rolled her sleeves up and grabbed a glob of the balm, spreading it across her palms. "This will sting him at first and I don't want him to move."

Niabi pressed down on Thrice's shoulders and Salome put all her weight across his legs. With a quick nod of affirmation, Leoti started applying the salve, and just as she predicted, Thrice started jostling around. Even in his unconscious state, he fought them as if they were torturing him. He let out a scream and the three of them glanced at the entrance, hoping no one heard him.

Leoti grabbed a piece of cloth and stuffed it in his mouth. "I'm almost finished." She went back to slathering the salve across his chest and abdomen.

If he survived, he would have severe burn marks, but knowing Thrice, he'd probably give himself another nickname to gloat of his brush with Death.

Once Leoti was finished applying the balm, she wiped her hands clean before taking the cloth out of his mouth. He wasn't shaking or fighting them anymore, the worst of the sting over. Thrice laid so still Niabi feared he was dead, but the slight rise and fall of his chest gave her hope that her friend might make it.

"Now what?" Salome asked, leaning against a wall of shelving, pointing at the bag Niabi had stuffed Vilora's head in. "Gershom isn't in the White Keep. The witch is dead, but we still failed our mission."

Niabi rubbed the heels of her palms over her eyes. "Then we make our way to the battlefield."

"And what? Hope we spot him amongst thousands of soldiers?" Salome shook her head.

"We'll rest here for a little while." Niabi brushed hair out of Thrice's face. She didn't see his face often. Shadows always hid behind their masks, but once he abandoned the Shadows, he ditched the uniform. He was quite handsome with his dark locks and facial hair. She wished he would open his hazel eyes and promise he would be alright. She had lost so many friends and loved ones already. Did she really have to lose him too?

"And then?" Salome questioned, stealing her from her thoughts.

"Then we find Gershom, one way or another."

CHAPTER FIFTY-NINE

ADONIJAH

The second Adonijah caught sight of his father across the battlefield, hacking his allies to pieces, he didn't hesitate to chase after him. Gershom was bold to leave the White Keep, but he had always been a vain man. Adonijah knew the only reason the old man was fighting amongst the troops was to establish his dominance and have his men spread tales of their victorious king. But Adonijah didn't particularly care why Gershom was fighting, he was just elated to set his eyes on him, after all these years of plotting. For it would be the last time he saw his father, his mother's murderer, whether he gutted Gershom or fell prey to his sword, it would be over one way or another.

Northern soldiers and Shadows blocked his path, and he was forced to battle several soldiers before he came within striking distance of Gershom. He clanged his blades together, making a loud noise, which captured his father's attention. Slowly, The Bear turned around, blood smeared across his face. His hair was the same, shaved on the sides with a chestnut bun streaked with white hair. He was missing an ear, which was surprising, but those eyes – no matter how desperately he tried, he couldn't forget how haunted and enraged Gershom's eyes were. The Bear flashed a menacing smile as Adonijah pointed his sword at him.

"Do you remember me?" Adonijah circled, keeping pace with Gershom as he moved, maintaining a safe distance between them.

Gershom cocked his head to the side, "Should I, boy?"

"I am Adonijah, son of Satara," Gershom's eyes widened as Adonijah continued, "and I'm here to kill you."

Gershom laughed. "After all these years, you've finally come home, my son."

Adonijah spat on the ground, taking his fighting stance. "I am not your son."

"Oh, but you are, Adonijah. My blood flows through your veins and whether you like it or not, you will always be mine." Gershom circled his sword around his hand, not looking remotely interested in a fight. "Lay down your weapons, Adonijah. Join me and I will make you my heir."

"If memory serves me correctly, you already have an heir."

Gershom barked a laugh. "Pash is nothing more than a disappointment. That's why I sent for you all those years ago. I was going to make you my heir and teach you everything you needed to know to one day take my place and rule in my stead. Your brother is useless to me. Has too much of his mother's southern blood in him to make him a well-suited successor. But *you*," Gershom took a step toward him. "You were special and I knew I'd finally gotten it right." He was now within striking distance, but something about the way he spoke and moved gave Adonijah pause from striking him down. "What happened to your mother was a pity. She wasn't supposed to get hurt."

As if snapping out from some hypnotic spell, Adonijah snarled and swung his sword at his father who blocked the blow. "But she did," Adonijah stilled, meeting Gershom's gaze. "And I've waited all these years to avenge her."

Gershom sighed. "Have it your way then."

Gershom pushed Adonijah back and whipped his longsword around, forcing Adonijah to be on the defensive. He blocked blow after hammering blow, until he tripped over a fallen soldier's leg and tumbled to the ground. Still fighting his father's barrage as he tried to scramble to his feet, he found himself in an extremely vulnerable position. Gershom kicked a batch of muddy snow at Adonijah, temporarily blinding him. It gave The Bear enough time to disarm his son and point the tip of his blade to Adonijah's chest, just above his heart.

"I would tell you to yield, but we both know I won't spare you," Gershom smirked.

"Then run me through," Adonijah spat viciously. "Do it!"

A wicked gleam flashed in Gershom's eyes as he thrust his sword forward. Only the tip broke through Adonijah's flesh before Gershom was tackled to the snow, dragging his weapon along with him.

Adonijah winced in pain as he put his hand to his wound. He pulled away and his hand was coated in blood. He glanced over at Gershom, searching for whoever pushed him in time to save him. His stomach dropped when he spotted Pash hopping up next to their father.

"You!" Gershom growled, grabbing his sword and rushing toward Pash. "I should have killed you years ago!"

Adonijah got up with every intention to help his brother, but Ophir suddenly stepped between them with a vicious wrinkle creasing his bald head.

"Frowning ages you, Uncle." Adonijah couldn't help himself and relished seeing Ophir's head redden in rage.

"I'll enjoy gutting you like a pig." Ophir swung his sword, initiating their duel.

Adonijah had to hand it to his uncle. Despite his age, he was still light on his feet. Harbona had warned him at the Hidden Tavern months ago, that he'd meet the Shadow who he had brawled with again. He just didn't expect the bald man he exchanged punches with would turn out to be his blood relative. But blood or not, Adonijah wouldn't lament striking him down.

Risking a quick glance at Pash battling with their father, Adonijah knew he would have to make quick work of Ophir, if he was going to help his brother take their father down. Adonijah and his uncle's swords clashed loudly, and Ophir grimaced at the contact. Sweat beaded around his head and his arms shook. Capitalizing on Ophir's rare show of fatigue, Adonijah used his sword to parry Ophir's away and rammed his shoulder into his uncle's chest, knocking the wind out of him. Ophir threw a punch, but Adonijah dodged it as he snatched his dagger from his belt and lodged it into the Shadow's chest.

A grunt escaped his uncle's lips as he sank to his knees. Adonijah grabbed the knife and began walking past Ophir, but his uncle grappled for the small blade in his boot, spurring Adonijah to slip behind him and with a swiftness, placed his hands on the man's head and snapped his neck, letting him fall to the bloodied snow in an odd position.

One down. One to go.

Adonijah rushed toward Pash, but fighting Ophir had not only delayed him, but distanced him from the fight. Pash and Gershom fought with fervor, anger, and a deep-rooted animosity that it was difficult to tell who the better swordsman was.

Pushing people out of his way, Adonijah stormed toward them, but when Gershom landed a well-timed blow to Pash's weapon and plunged his sword into Pash's chest, Adonijah's world slowed. Gershom's mouth moved, but he didn't hear what his last words to his brother were. Gershom retrieved his sword and marched toward the main gate, signaling his personal guards to surround him.

Adonijah sprinted to his brother and cradled his head. "Pash, I'm here. I'm here." Pash's hazy eyes met his and it was at that moment, Adonijah knew he wouldn't be able to save him.

"Tell Niabi, I love her." Pash strained to get that final message out as his breathing turned ragged. Adonijah wasn't an expert, but by the way he sounded, he was positive Pash's lung had collapsed and was slowly filling with blood.

"I'm sorry, Pash," Adonijah whimpered, tucking his head against his brother's. "I'm so sorry." But Pash didn't respond and Adonijah couldn't feel him moving, couldn't hear him breathing.

Reluctantly, he pulled back and saw Pash was gone. Overwhelmed with grief, Adonijah roared up into the sky, before turning his tear-stricken face toward the fleeing Gershom. Adonijah lowered his brother down and grabbed his sword. He was going to drive his blade straight through his father's back. He would make him suffer for what he'd done to Pash. He would -

Arms grabbed him from behind and without looking to see who it was, Adonijah swung his sword, barely missing Crispin's chest.

"Let him go!" Crispin shouted before pushing Adonijah out of the way of an incoming blow from a Northern soldier. Crispin stabbed the guard before turning back to him. "I need you to fight, Adonijah. Leave Gershom to Salome. If you go after him again, I can't follow."

Adonijah wanted to disobey, wanted to rebel, wanted to knock Crispin out of his path and charge after his father, but he knew the prophecy. He knew if anyone could kill Gershom, it was Salome. He had to trust her. Had to give her a chance to set things right. Him bolting after Gershom put him and Crispin in a precarious position, and they were going to have to fight together, if they were going to make it back to their allies. So Adonijah let his father go and allowed his grief and anger to fuel him, becoming a wrecking ball on the battlefield.

Chapter Sixty

Rahab

Attempting to stand, Rahab felt the full extent of the wounds she'd sustained. Her thigh had a nasty gash across it and her pants were soaked in her blood. Her sleeve had been shredded and the long cut that ran the length of her left arm was leaving a puddle of blood next to her.

Haldane groaned when Uri sliced his inner thigh.

"Get up!" Rahab commanded herself.

Uri slashed Haldane's other leg, bringing the pirate captain to his knees.

She was about to watch her friend, her captain, be murdered. But something snapped inside of her, propelling her to pull herself to her feet, using the wooden railing as an anchor. Pure adrenaline and hatred fueled her, and like a caged animal that had been freed, Rahab ran toward Uri whose cutlass was pointed at Haldane's chest and jumped on his back. She didn't wait for the pirate king to react to her assault because if he got the drop on her, she and Haldane would both die. Wrapping her hands around Uri's head, she twisted with all her strength until she heard a loud snap. Then she and the pirate fell to the wooden floorboards.

She rolled onto her back in excruciating pain. She couldn't hold back the tears any longer as Haldane dragged himself over to her.

"He's dead." She breathed a sigh of relief when she saw the pirate king lying a foot away, eyes glossed over, neck twisted in an unnatural angle.

Haldane stroked her face, tears in his eyes. "Aye, lass. You saved my life."

"How disgustingly touching," Nezreen hissed. Her attention and shadows fully fixed on them. "You might have killed the king," the shadows twisted around their limbs, pinning them to the floor, "but you will not live to tell the tale."

Rahab fought against the shadowy bonds but to no avail. There was no breaking free from the blind witch's dark magic.

"Any last words, pet?" Nezreen waved her hand in the air, summoning one of her shadow tendrils to stroke Rahab's cheek like a passionate lover would.

Before Rahab could answer, several blades sliced through the air toward Nezreen, but her shadows alerted her to the attack, and she ducked out of the way. Blinking twice, Rahab didn't understand where the knives had come from. No one else was on this level of the Leviathan. But it was then, Master Penn and Kai stepped out of thin air, weapons drawn and ready.

"Oh, it's you," Nezreen sounded bored. "I thought you would have crawled back to The Sisters like a whipped dog by now, Penn." She cocked her head to the side, her sightless gaze fixed on Kai. "And who is your friend?"

"Fight me, you bitch," Master Penn growled, baring her teeth at Nezreen.

The witch's shadows flared around her, all pointed at the ends like spears. "Gladly." With a wave of her hand, the shadow spears sliced down toward the women, forcing them to duck and dodge as they tried to get closer to the witch.

Rahab was wholly transfixed by the duel and how incredibly graceful Master Penn moved, not being struck once by Nezreen's shadowy attack. Kai was death itself, dancing around the ship, slicing pieces of shadow like she would a sea monster's tentacles. She was so distracted she didn't realize that Jinn was kneeling before her until he grabbed her and hoisted her up into his arms.

"We need to get you out of here," he whispered and tucked his arm underneath her knees.

"It's about damn time you showed up," she hissed with his movements.

"My apologies. Battle delayed me." Jinn flashed a wicked smile before he glanced at Haldane. "Captain, can you walk?"

Haldane nodded, pain rippling through his features, though he refused to acknowledge it. "Aye, I can walk."

"Seraphina and the Qata Vishna are waiting for you below. They will get you to safety and to a healer." Jinn started walking toward the steps but stopped when Kai screamed.

Nezreen cackled as she wrapped her shadow tentacles around Kai's body. She was squeezing her, cutting off her air. Kai's face was turning blue, and her weapons were on the floor, just out of her reach. Master Penn attempted to help the Ryoko Naga but in her moment of distraction, Nezreen struck. Pinning the Master of Keepers to the floor with her shadows, Nezreen flashed a malicious smile.

"Your fear is delicious," the witch cooed, breathing in as if she could indeed taste their fear.

"Help them," Rahab ordered Jinn.

"You've already lost a lot of blood, Rahab."

"Put me down and help them!" She punched his chest. "I swear I'll gut you the second I have the chance if you let them die."

Jinn gently placed her on the floor, eyes glued to hers. "Keep out of sight."

Nezreen stalked around the two women being strangled by her shadows and crowed, "I look forward to destroying The Sisters next. Those who do not swear fealty to me, will be put to the sword, and I do enjoy it when they refuse to bend the knee. I have learned to crave the sound of pained screams and tortured souls."

"You won't -" Penn's voice was cut off when the shadow around her neck tightened.

"Goodbye, Penn," Nezreen smiled, closing her fingers together, forcing her shadows to squeeze. "Tell Neempo I said -"

But she didn't get to finish that sentence because Jinn uncloaked himself standing directly in front of her and whipped his tachi blades across his chest, beheading her. As soon as her severed head bounced on the wooden floorboards, her shadows disappeared, releasing both Kai and Master Penn.

Rahab rubbed the heels of her palms against her eyes. It was over. They'd actually defeated both the pirate king and his witch. Tears rolled down her cheeks.

Someone's hand swiped at her cheeks. Opening her eyes, she met Haldane's equally relieved gaze. Everyone they had lost, everything that had been stolen from them – they'd had their revenge. It was over. She slipped her arms around his neck and pulled him into a full-blown hug. The captain's shoulders tensed, but a split second later, he wrapped her in his arms and laughed.

"Why are you laughing?" she mumbled into his shoulder.

"I never thought I'd get a hug from the likes of you," he smiled against her cheek.

"I knew the princeling would make me soft."

Haldane barked out another hearty laugh as he pulled away from her. "Aye, but being soft doesn't make you any less fearsome. It just makes you more human."

Two thuds hit the deck, rattling the floor beneath her. Kayven and Abba, their faces and arms streaked with blood and glistening in sweat, glanced around at their injured comrades and surveyed the two dead monsters.

Abba made his way to her, dropping down to one knee. Tossing his head to the side to remove his dark hair from covering his eyes, he smiled and extended his hand. "You look like you need to see a healer, my lady."

"Captain Haldane is also injured," Rahab motioned to the blood on the pirate's pants.

Abba nodded in understanding as several more Bellators landed onto the deck. A smug smile crossed his bronze features, as if to say, I'm already a step ahead of you.

Rahab huffed and accepted his outstretched hand. "If you bolt into the sky and make me sick, I'll be forced to fight you."

A small laugh escaped the Bellator's lips as he lifted her in his arms and held her tightly against his armored chest. "Are all mortal women as feisty as you and Salome?"

She grinned, "Is that your way of saying you like us?"

"I suppose it is." Abba looked up into the sky, wings stretching for take-off. "Hold on tight, my lady."

Chapter Sixty-One

Niabi

Niabi wasn't sure how long they'd been hiding in the apothecary, but Thrice still hadn't stirred. At least he wasn't groaning or screaming in agonizing pain. His chest was angry looking, but Leoti assured her he would survive, as long as they weren't discovered. Thrice was an easy target and wouldn't be able to defend himself should soldiers burst through the doors.

Salome paced back and forth; her hands perched on her hips. Her boots crunching against the floors was an irritating sound that grated Niabi's nerves, but after a while, she tuned her out and sat in a comfortable silence, drowning in her own thoughts.

She prayed Tala and Ivaylo had crossed into Andrago territory. She hoped Pash was still holding strong on the battlefield, even though she currently felt like a complete failure in her mission. She and Salome were tasked with finding and eliminating Gershom. Though they'd killed Vilora, their expectation in ending the war quickly was dashed. Niabi racked her brain, trying to formulate the best strategy to get them to the front lines without having to battle soldiers scattered throughout the city streets. There wasn't a tunnel that would take them to the main gate, and they didn't have horses to speed their journey. And of course, there was the issue with Thrice. They couldn't leave him behind, but they also couldn't stay held up with him, hoping their allies would come for them.

"Someone is coming." Salome's voice ripped Niabi from her thoughts.

Niabi unsheathed her daggers from her sleeves, ready to kill anyone who walked through that door. But the footsteps that neared, passed by and continued down the corridor. She and her sister exchanged a look before Salome slowly opened the door an inch to peek at who was marching by. Salome's shoulders stiffened and she waved Niabi forward. When Niabi glanced out, she understood why her sister's body posture had changed so abruptly.

"Is that -?

"Gershom," Niabi hissed softly. He and his small entourage were headed in the direction of the throne room. He had blood and dirt smeared all over his armor and for a moment, Niabi believed maybe luck was finally on their side. She whipped around to meet Leoti's gaze. "You stay here and watch over Thrice. We will deal with Gershom and come back for you."

Leoti's brow furrowed and Niabi could sense the Andrago was itching to disagree and argue her case, but for whatever reason Niabi didn't quite understand, the warg nodded her head in agreement. "Be quick about it," Leoti said and clutched the hilt of her longsword tightly.

Niabi's eyes collided with Salome's. "Are you ready?"

Salome grabbed her Qata Vishna blades off her back and smiled. A wolf, if Niabi ever saw one. "Let's finish this."

When the coast was clear, Niabi and Salome slipped out of the room and waited until they heard the click of the latch behind them before slipping down the hallway. Stealthily, the sisters made their way toward the throne room. The irony hadn't escaped Niabi that the very same place she had been given to Dichali in marriage as a death sentence, the same place she'd killed her own father, was the same place she'd face off with The Bear and claw his eyes out for his treachery.

Niabi and Salome crept behind statues and columns until they came upon the double doors that led into the throne room. Four soldiers stood guard outside the room. Easy pickings for her and Salome. With a quick nod, she and Salome threw daggers across the hall and downed the four men, ensuring they were all dead by slitting their throats.

As Salome bent down to grab her daggers lodged in the chests of two soldiers, Niabi kicked the doors open like a battering ram against the main gate. Sauntering inside what used to be her throne room, she caught Gershom's stunned look as he reclined in her throne.

"You!" he seethed.

Niabi smirked. "Afraid you're down a witch." She tossed Vilora's head on the floor before flexing her left hand, igniting it. "Nothing to say? How unlike you, Gershom." She cooed and cocked her head to the side.

Seeming to regain himself, he snarled, "We both know you can't kill me without forfeiting your own life, Niabi. Perhaps, we should quit with the theatrics."

She flashed a wicked smile. "It's not me you should fear."

Salome walked in as if on cue, Qata Vishna blades drawn, blood splattered across her face, arms, and fighting leathers.

Gershom had the audacity to laugh, swatting his hand around like he was shooing a pesky fly. "You think this *girl* can defeat me, Niabi? I killed my own son for power – this girl won't stand a chance."

Niabi couldn't help the gasp that escaped her lips causing Gershom to grin in great satisfaction.

"Oh yes," he crowed. "Pash is dead."

Flames licked up Niabi's arm with every intention to burn him to ash, but Salome stepped between her and Gershom, blocking her from attacking him. Niabi knew Salome was trying to prevent her from breaking her blood oath, but it did nothing to quench her rage.

"I am Salome." She narrowed her eyes, making sure he noticed her blades held out to her sides. "I've been looking for you for quite some time."

Gershom turned to look at her and his face paled when he noticed her two different color eyes, one containing the mark he'd spent the majority of his life afraid of. Salome smirked. "And I hear you've been dreading to meet me."

"You're the Hunter?"

Salome nodded. "Unfortunately for you, you won't be leaving this room alive."

"Just like your sister, you've underestimated me." He whistled, and Shadows stationed in an adjoining room filed in, surrounding the sisters, weapons drawn.

Niabi and Salome wielded their weapons, back-to-back, and when the Shadows launched their assault, they fought together. They flipped, spun, dove, kicked, sliced, and struck the shadows, battling them down dead. Oddly, it felt right fighting side by side with Salome. They fought as a unit, using their combined skills to take down a host of highly skilled Shadows.

Bodies were scattered around the throne room, staining the white marble floors red. Salome and Niabi were the only two that remained unscathed. Standing face to face, Niabi smiled, proud of how effortlessly she and her sister fought together. She knew in accordance with their agreement, once Gershom was defeated, Niabi would disappear and never show her face again, but getting to know Salome had her rethinking living a life of obscurity. She found herself wanting a friendship with Salome and maybe, just maybe, once the dust settled, they could have that. She wouldn't be so lonely thinking she was the last of the White Wolves of Northwind. Perhaps, in time, Crispin too would come around and they could wash the slate clean.

Movement from over Salome's shoulder caught Niabi's attention, ripping her from her brief moment of hope. Gershom stood on the dais, a bow drawn taut, with an arrow nocked and aimed directly at Salome. With a wicked and triumphant grin, The Bear released the arrow. Niabi grabbed Salome by her shoulders and spun them, so they switched positions. The arrow pierced Niabi's back, lurching her forward into her sister's arms. The horror written across Salome's face echoed the pain that ricocheted through Niabi's entire body. She'd been shot before and stabbed countless times, but this was by far the worst pain she'd ever experienced.

Gershom hissed and Niabi could hear him nocking another arrow, either to finish her off or strike his true intended target. Salome lowered Niabi to the ground quickly and carefully before launching an attack on Gershom before he had a chance to take another shot.

Crawling to one of the columns to lean against, Niabi couldn't do anything but watch as her sister battled Gershom. Despite his age, he still moved like a warrior in his prime and landed several punches to Salome's gut and chest, knocking her weapons out of her hands and bringing her to her knees.

"Get up," Niabi commanded, though she was positive Salome was too far away to hear her strained voice.

Gershom hovered over Salome, grabbing her hair and tugging her to meet his gaze. With her neck exposed, Gershom took the sword clutched in his right hand and swung with all his might, but Salome punched him in the groin and wiggled free from his grasp, escaping the blow. Tumbling away, she hopped to her feet, grabbed Gershom's head and slammed it down on her rising knee. With a howl, Gershom fell to the floor, his nose broken and bloody.

"You bitch!" he screamed, snatching his sword and stalking toward Salome.

She was light on her feet, dodging his reckless blows, allowing the old man to tire himself. Niabi knew Gershom trained for hours almost daily so his stamina was excellent, but Salome too had been endlessly training for this very moment, and if Niabi was a betting woman, her money would be on her sister to come out victorious.

Salome unsheathed the white wolf dagger attached to her hip and blocked what would have been a lethal blow. Using his momentum against him, Salome danced out of his way, spinning to his back and slicing his side as she passed. He hissed, fire raging in his eyes. Niabi knew that look: desperation. He was tiring and instead of adapting to his enemy, he fell prey to her.

"I shall never yield to you!" Gershom stood to his full height, towering over Salome by several inches.

"I never asked you to yield." Salome snatched her Qata Vishna blades up from the floor where she'd dropped them and spun them around her hands, beckoning him forward. "I will take no prisoners and leave none alive."

Niabi coughed, drawing Salome's attention. Her eyes were hazy and blood trickled down her back and pooled underneath her.

Taking advantage of the distraction, Gershom charged at Salome, his sword swinging down at her. Shoving her blades up just in time to block his attack, she kicked him square in his chest, and knocked his sword from his hand, making sure it wasn't within reach. He crawled away from Salome, but Niabi noticed he'd pulled a small knife out of his belt, but before she had a chance to warn her sister, he whipped around and stabbed Salome in the side, drawing an ear-piercing scream from her.

"No," Niabi teared up at the grimace crossing Salome's face.

Gershom once again towered over Salome. He retrieved his knife from her body and pointed it against her throat. "I will finally put an end to Issachar's line after all these years."

"Crispin -"

"Can't kill me, foolish girl," he interrupted, flashing a wicked grin. "Only the Hunter can kill me, and it doesn't look like you'll be doing that. You failed." Poking the dagger into her neck, drawing a bit of blood, he whispered, "Do tell your father who sent you."

With surprising quickness, Salome smashed her arm against his, pushing the knife away, leaving a small slice against her throat. She jumped up and took the small dagger she kept hidden in her boot and stabbed it into the side of his neck. "Tell him yourself," she growled in his ear before letting him fall to the floor, clutching at the hole in his neck.

As he gurgled on the floor, writhing in pain, the life slowly draining from him, Salome picked up Gershom's longsword and with a mighty swing, she claimed his head from his shoulders.

Niabi sighed in relief, but when a wheezed cough escaped her, it drew Salome to her. Salome clutched her side, blood staining her clothes.

"You need to get out of here," Niabi motioned toward the doors leading out of the throne room. "You need to get Leoti and Thrice."

Salome knelt next to Niabi and gently pulled her from the column to look at the injury she'd sustained. The arrow was still stuck in her back and when Salome reached up to touch it, Niabi winced and shook her head. The way Salome looked at her, Niabi knew she looked just as bad as she felt.

"Tell me what you see," Niabi instructed.

"There's purple splotches veining from the wound."

Nightshade. The tip of Gershom's arrow was poisoned. That's why she felt as if life was slipping away from her. Niabi rested against the column and glanced around at the sea of dead bodies. This throne room had seen more death than any other room in the White Keep. Niabi was starting to believe the room was cursed.

Salome grabbed her arm and with an exhausted groan, she attempted to help Niabi to her feet. "We need to get you out of here. Rayma will -"

"It's too late for me, Salome."

"We can -"

"Salome," Niabi's voice was calm but firm. "The arrow was poisoned. There's no saving me." Niabi saw the desperation to save her deep in Salome's eyes, but Niabi offered her a loving smile. "It's ok, Little Wolf."

The tears Salome was holding hostage finally escaped at the use of the nickname Lykos coined for her. "You took the arrow meant for me."

Niabi coughed, resituating herself even though it didn't ease her pain. "Surprising, I know. The villain has a heart after all."

"You aren't my villain." Salome grabbed her hand and squeezed. "Not anymore."

A tear slipped down Niabi's face. "Tell my son, I love him."

"I swear he will be cared for, Niabi." Salome sliced her hand and let her blood drip onto the marble floors. "I swear to you, Ivaylo will know of you and Pash. He will know you loved him and that you both fought courageously."

"And died with honor?" she whispered, and Salome nodded. Niabi's bottom lip quivered, the burning pain consuming her, drawing a small groan from her. She grabbed her sister's hand, not caring of the blood that now seeped onto her. "Stay with me?"

Salome bobbed her head. "Until the end."

"I need you to do something for me."

"Name it."

"Bury me in Elisor with Dichali and Rollo." Her eyes welled up. "And tell Crispin that I'm sorry. For everything. He will make a fine king."

Salome swiped a tear that slipped down her dirt-stained cheek. "Consider it done," she whispered.

Niabi painfully reached over and embraced Salome. "I wish we could have had more time, sister."

She closed her eyes, taking a deep breath as her body numbed to all the pain she'd been battling a moment before. When she opened her eyes, she found herself lying in a field of wheat. A light breeze whisked through, guiding her to stand up and walk through the farmlands. The sun was beginning to set and hues of purple, pink, and orange streaked across the sparsely clouded sky. For miles, all she could see was row after row of honey-golden barley dancing side to side as the wind led her forward. After what seemed like a small eternity, Niabi finally reached the edge of the field and came upon a grand white tent. She'd never seen this place before, but she instinctually knew where she was: The Great Beyond. And this tent flooded her with a familiarity that spurred her heart to leap within her chest.

Could it be?

She forced her feet to move closer, to see if the hope ricocheting through her was well warranted. The nearer she drew to the humble abode, the more at peace she felt. Before she reached the flapped entrance, a man stepped outside and the sight of him made her fall to her knees as tears streamed down her cheeks.

"My heart and my soul." The gentle voice washed over her like waves across the sand.

Slowly, she looked into Rollo's green eyes. Her son stroked his hand down her cheek and flicked her tears away. "I've missed your face," he smiled.

"Rollo," she threw her arms around his neck and squeezed. Wildly, she raked her hands through his hair, over his face, and kissed both of his cheeks. "My moon and my stars."

Rollo rested his forehead against hers and he whispered, "We've been waiting for you."

"We?" Her eyes met his and he nodded. His smile was punctuated by his dimples and gave him that boyish look she'd longed to see one more time.

"We."

Niabi glanced over Rollo's shoulder and saw Dichali standing at the entrance of the tent. Her breath was stolen at the sight of her late husband and with Rollo's help, she scrambled to her feet and ran toward the former Andrago king. Wrenching his arms open, she leapt into his awaiting grasp, and laughed. She kissed his lips, his cheeks, his forehead; she laughed, she cried, she nearly screamed.

"It's you," she whispered against his lips. "Oh, how I've missed you, my love."

"We will never be parted again," Dichali smiled, and it filled her heart with a happiness that she had yearned for years to feel again. "We can be a family again."

She bobbed her head. "We can finally be at peace." Wrapping her arms around Dichali again, she closed her eyes and inhaled his pine and tobacco scent. She had made it back to them. She'd finally made it home.

Chapter Sixty-Two

Salome

Salome held onto Niabi and didn't release her until she couldn't feel her sister moving anymore. After a minute of cradling her, she reluctantly leaned Niabi back against the column, resting her forehead against hers.

"May Death guide you to those you loved and lost. Until we meet again, sister." She dragged her middle finger from her forehead down to her chest.

It was then her own breathing became labored. Remembering she too had been injured, she placed her hand against the stab wound in her side, drenching her fingers in blood. If she didn't get it taken care of soon, she might be seeing her sister sooner than she expected. Her heart ached as she looked at Niabi's lifeless face once more before she struggled to her feet. Grabbing Gershom and Vilora's severed heads, she stuffed them in the same bag, and dragged it with her as she made her way down the hallway.

Though she'd killed Gershom, and Niabi had put an end to the Old Witch of Endor, no one else knew, so the battle raged on at the main gate as well as at sea. As she trapsed through the corridor that had windows on either side giving her views of both the mountains and the sea, she was relieved to see the Bellators still flying around, giving her the hope that their forces were holding their own against the ruthless Pirate King and his Shadow Witch. But as she took a closer look at the winged warriors, she noticed they weren't fighting, but patrolling. Had they defeated the pirates?

She whipped her head in the other direction where her brother led the foot soldiers and saw that the battle continued to rage, and flames licked up the white stone walls. She needed to get to Crispin, she needed to show everyone that the city was now under a new rule, with the death of their masters. Feeling lightheaded, she sat down on the floor before she fell and hurt herself. Steadily taking slow, deep breaths, she calmed her nerves and purged her fear of dying, to think through her options. She would never make it through the city to the battlefront on foot and she didn't have Snow to get her there either.

"Jinn?" She extended the bridge between them, hoping he answered. If he was silent, if he didn't respond, she wasn't sure if she could handle losing him after watching her sister die in her arms. *"Jinn, my love?"*

He wasn't answering; he was always quick to respond. The deafening silence made her head spin. He couldn't be dead. Her husband couldn't be dead. Dragging herself up to peer out the windows overlooking the sea, she stared at the ships. There were some on fire, there was one that was sinking, and if her eyes weren't deceiving her, there was one ship that was completely split in half and inoperable. How could that be.

She couldn't give up. She had to get to Crispin somehow to deliver Gershom's head, even if she got there pale, frail, and on Death's doorstep, she would come through for her brother.

As she shakily stood to her feet, she felt a warmth flood her head.

"Salome?"

"Jinn?" Her bottom lip quivered at the sound of his voice. *"You're alive. I thought when you didn't respond that you..."*

"I'm here, darling." He picked up when she trailed off, and her heart was filled with relief. *"Where are you?"*

"I'm still in the White Keep." She couldn't help the pained groan that escaped her lips.

"You're hurt."

"Where is Kayven? Or Abba?" She didn't confirm or deny her injury to him, he couldn't get to her fast enough to help, so there was no need to worry him. *"I need them to get me. I'm sitting in a long corridor of windows."*

There was a brief pause before Jinn answered. *"Abba is taking Rahab to see the healers."*

"Is she alright?" Her heart dropped. If the pirate didn't make it, her brother would be devastated.

"She'll be fine." Jinn's voice soothed her. *"Kayven is making his way to you now."*

"Thank you." She clutched her side.

"How bad is it?" he asked. *"And before you tell me you're fine, I can sense your pain through our bond."*

She leaned her head back against the wall. *"Gershom stabbed me, but I'll be ok."* Why did that sound like a lie?

"Is he dead?"

"Yes." Her lip quivered, Niabi's dead body flashed in her mind. *"Niabi is dead. She took an arrow meant for me and I couldn't..."* She sucked in a breath before explaining, *"It was poisoned, and she was gone before I could save her."*

"I'm sorry," his voice soothed her, wrapping around her as if he were sitting next to her.

"Are you safe?" she asked.

"The Pulauans have been defeated and though we suffered casualties, both the Pirate King and Shadow Witch are dead." She sensed a bubbling pride stirring within him and couldn't help but smile.

Another groan escaped her lips as the burning in her side started to throb. She felt cold. Perhaps the hallway filled with windows was lettingthe chill in, or perhaps she'd lost too much blood and was dying. She looked up and down the hallway, feeling someone's presence. When she didn't see anyone, she realized Death was with her, standing in wait to claim her soul and usher her away.

"Salome?" Jinn attempted to mask the panic in his voice but failed. *"Don't. Don't give up."*

"When we first met," Salome shifted into a more comfortable position, stretching her legs out in front of her, *"I thought you were the most handsome man I'd ever laid my eyes on. There was something about you, how you looked at me, how you spoke, how you moved that hypnotized me and drew me to you. I tried to fight it, tried to fight falling for you, but it was like fighting to breathe or refusing to eat. It was impossible for me not to love you, Jinn."*

"Why does it sound like you're saying goodbye?"

"I have loved you in this life, and I will love you in the next." A tear slid down her cheek. She shivered, feeling like her fingers and toes were submerged in ice, and noticed her hands were turning blue.

"Stay with me," Jinn's voice rang out. *"Salome, stay with me! Please!"*

Death was near. She had bided her time, she'd been patient in claiming Salome's soul by shepherding other souls to the After, leaving Salome for last, and now, she could sense Death closing the gap between them. She closed her eyes, taking in a deep breath to steady herself, knowing this was the end for her. Quietly, she slipped into darkness and Jinn's voice was snuffed out.

CHAPTER SIXTY-THREE

RAHAB

"Ouch!" Rahab winced, fighting the urge to slap the needle out of Rayma's steadily working hand. "I'd prefer if you didn't enjoy inflicting so much pain on me, Healer."

"For being a fearsome pirate," Rayma shot back, flicking her eyes up for a fraction of a second, before returning to her work stitching up Rahab's thigh, "you complain an awful lot."

Abba cleared his throat and took a step forward. Since he'd flown her to the medical tents, he had refused to leave her side, which both touched and irritated her. "Would holding my hand help?"

Rahab glared at the Bellator's extended hand and shook her head. "Not necessary. I've been through worse."

"By all that grumbling, you wouldn't know it." Rayma rolled her eyes as she finished the last stitch. "You'll be back on your feet in no time, but you'll have to use a cane for a few days to let your leg heal properly."

Rahab scoffed and crossed her arms over her chest. "I won't be using a cane."

Rayma cleaned her hands before packing up her medical kit. "Then I suppose you'll really resemble a pirate when you start limping around like one."

"That's a vicious stereotype," the pirate narrowed her eyes, but Rayma didn't back down.

"Then prove me wrong. Use the cane."

The tent flap opened and when Rahab looked up, relief flooded her seeing Crispin standing there.

"Hello, princeling," she smiled, a tease embedded in her tone, "or should I call you king now?"

He huffed a chuckle, her comment seemed to rattle him from his stunned silence. It was then she noticed he was carrying a head by the hair, it hung by his side and its face was frozen in horror for the rest of eternity. She jutted her chin toward the severed head and said, "Most men bring flowers or sweet treats for the woman they love, but I suppose this head will do."

Crispin's eyes flared, mischief and warning dancing in his expression. "That mouth of yours."

"Tempting, I'm sure," Rahab smirked.

"Is she alright?" Crispin ignored her comment and addressed Rayma. Once the Healer nodded, his body seemed to relax.

"She'll have to use a cane to help her walk until she's fully healed," Rayma narrowed her eyes at the pirate, making sure she understood these were non-negotiable instructions. "But she'll be back to seafaring and plundering before you know it."

"You don't have to talk about me, as if I'm not in the room, Rayma," Rahab straightened, cracking her back, as the Healer gathered her medical supplies.

"Ah, so you do listen?" Rayma griped and Crispin laughed.

"And what's so funny?" Rahab glared at Crispin, fire flaring inside her chest.

Crispin dropped the head, his eyes glued to the pirate. "Leave us, please."

Rayma and Abba left without pause or argument. Once the flap of the tent swooshed back into place, Rahab opened her mouth to say something snarky, but Crispin's lips crashed against hers, and whatever insult she was about to spew was forgotten. They'd had their fair share of passionate encounters, but the way he kissed her this time was raw, wild, and filled with relief. She cupped his face, dragging him closer to her, but when she winced from her freshly mended injuries, he jumped back, raking a hand through his disheveled hair. His lips were swollen, his eyes hungry, but there was a tentativeness in his posture that made her heart ache.

"I'm fine, Crispin," she said softly.

Gently, he caressed her thigh, seeing the stitches holding the red, angry flesh together. "Who did this to you?" His fiery gaze met hers. If there had been an army between them and the person who had maimed her, she had no doubt Crispin would have torn them all to pieces to avenge her.

Pressing her hands to his face, dragging the tips of her fingers down to his chest, she said, "There is no one for you to harm. I took care of it myself."

The storminess in his expression seemed to subside, but only by a fraction. "Who did it?"

"Uri." She smiled, the realization that the pirate king was dead suddenly impacted her. "He won't ever hurt anyone again."

Crispin nodded, beaming with pride. "When they told me you'd been injured..." he sucked in a breath, steadying himself, "...I thought the worst."

"You think you'd get rid of me that easily?" She tsked, drawing a much-needed laugh from him. "You'd be bored without me."

He swiped pieces of her sweaty blue hair away from her face. "Of that I have no doubt." With an impish grin, he slipped one arm carefully underneath her knees and cradled her back with the other. Lifting her up into his arms, he kissed her forehead and said, "I think you'd be far more comfortable in my tent."

"Is that so?" she snickered, slithering her arm around his neck.

"I'll make sure you get all the rest you need," he winked.

"Prince Crispin." Kayven's voice sliced through the room and drew their attention. The warrior's face was forlorn, and Crispin's breathing quickened. She could feel his heart thrashing against her waist.

"What is it, Commander?" Crispin asked, though his voice seemed shaky.

"It's your sister," Kayven whispered, a scratchiness in his throat.

"What about my sister?"

"The Healers are working on her, but they can't seem to wake her." Kayven straightened his shoulders back, but it didn't mask his fear or his watery eyes.

"Go to her," Rahab patted Crispin's chest. When their eyes met, her heart nearly ripped out of her chest. If she could relieve him of his pain, she would have jumped at the chance. "Go," she nudged him gently, spurring him to action.

Crispin set her back down on the table and kissed her forehead before he motioned for the Bellator to show him where his sister was. Rahab wasn't the praying sort, but she whispered to the Almighty, hoping He was listening, hoping that He would spare Salome and let her live.

Chapter Sixty-Four

Crispin

Crispin followed the Bellator commander to a tent very similar to the one he'd been visiting Rahab in. Neither man spoke a word as they walked a few tents down but as soon as Kayven stopped and pointed to the flap, Crispin couldn't seem to make himself walk inside. He just watched the flap waft in the light breeze, catching glimpses of Rayma's feet scurrying around the table where he knew his unresponsive sister was lying.

"Prince Crispin?" Kayven's voice brought him back from the depths of his mind.

"What happened?" It was all the prince could think of asking, buying himself some time to avoid looking upon his sister.

"She reached out to Prince Jinn through their bond, said she needed someone to come get her." Kayven rubbed a hand against the back of his neck. "She needed a way to get to the front lines, to bring you Gershom's head and to end the bloodshed. But when I got to her..."

"What?" Crispin pressed, his chest constricting his air flow.

"I expected her to be waiting for me with a triumphant smile, but she was lying on the floor, clutching her side. She had been stabbed and by the looks of it, lost a lot of blood." Kayven swiped a single tear that slipped down his bronze cheek and cleared his voice. "I tried to wake her, but she did not stir. I had Durmas fly Gershom's head to you, and I brought her here, hoping Rayma could help her before it was too late."

Crispin patted Kayven's shoulder, not knowing how to respond. He knew Kayven and Abba had grown quite fond of Salome, seeing as they spent a lot of time together in Oakenshire, but he never thought he'd see a mighty Bellator shed a tear for a mortal. Either Kayven was terrified and was trying to mask it, or he knew there truly was no hope of Salome living and Crispin was here to say goodbye.

"And Niabi?" Crispin found himself asking. The thought she was the one to stab Salome crossed his mind.

"Dead." Kayven met his gaze. "We found her body in the throne room, a poisoned arrow in her back."

Hearing Niabi was dead didn't flood him with relief or joy like he expected it to. Instead, he felt a deep sorrow squeeze his heart. For a moment, he thought Niabi was invincible, that no one could kill her. But knowing she fought for him to be king, knowing she gave up the throne for a life of obscurity, humbled him for some reason. He might not have cared for her, and he certainly hadn't forgiven her, but in the end, she'd earned his gratitude.

Rayma whipped the tent flap behind her as she stomped outside. Her sudden presence startled Crispin.

"How is she?" He dared to ask, but she shook her head slowly.

"I've done everything I can for her," Rayma wiped her bloody hands on her apron. "I'm sorry."

Crispin's bottom lip quivered as he rubbed the heels of his palms against his eyes. Rayma slipped her hands around his wrists, bringing them down from his face, forcing him to meet her compassionate gaze.

"Go to her."

"I failed her."

Rayma shook her head. "Your sister did what she promised to do. She saved hundreds, if not thousands of lives today." The Healer motioned for him to go inside the tent. "I cannot promise she will make it through the night, but I will do everything in my power to help her. I suggest you say your goodbyes, just in case."

How could he say goodbye to his best friend? How could he say goodbye when they still had so much left to accomplish together?

Crispin dug deep within his soul to force his feet to move. He moved the flap and took a deep breath before plunging into the tent and resting his eyes on his sister's still form. Her breathing was light, the only sign she still had a fighting chance to wake up. She'd been stripped of her armor and fighting leathers and had a piece of cloth covering her chest and another one concealing her lower extremities. She looked so much like a corpse being prepped for burial than a warrior fighting for her life. Her body was bloody, and dirt stained her paling face. He noticed multiple bruises beginning to form on her face, hands, and torso and a deep-rooted rage stirred within him. He approached her body and gripped the edge of the table, hovering above her.

"Wake up," he whispered, his voice breaking. "Please, Salome, wake up."

Nothing happened. She didn't move, her breathing didn't change, her eyes didn't flutter. Oh, what he would give to see her look up at him and smile, say something snarky, and wrap her arms around him. But she didn't. She didn't respond at all.

I suggest you say your goodbyes, just in case.

Crispin batted Rayma's words from his mind as grief and hopelessness settled within him. He shook his head and slammed his hand on the table, rattling Salome's body. "Wake up!" he shouted. He grabbed her by her shoulders and shook her a little bit, his tears raining down on her. "Salome! Salome! Wake up, Salome! You can't leave me! I can't lose you," he sobbed.

His knees gave way and the soft ground broke his fall. He didn't care that everyone outside could hear his cries. He didn't care that they would think he'd come undone, because the truth was, he had.

Flashing back months ago when he and Salome were first approached by Harbona, she didn't want to go to war. She was content with the Tree House Forest, but he forced the issue. He wanted them to battle their enemies and come out with the kingdom, crown, and throne. It had been his obsession for twelve years and now that they'd won the war, now that he would bear the crown, sit on the White Throne, and rule over the Kingdom of Northwind, he realized he hadn't considered what it would cost him. They'd already lost Zophar but losing his sister too – his heart just couldn't bear it. She didn't deserve an end like that.

If he could go back, he would have left her in the Tree House Forest. He would have made sure he kept both Zophar and Salome safe and more importantly, alive. But he couldn't go back. He couldn't change their fates. He didn't protect them, and in the end, couldn't save them.

"Please," Crispin grabbed Salome's cold hand and kissed it. "Please, wake up. Come back to me."

Rushed footsteps entered the tent and stopped as the flap whipped opened and closed. Crispin turned to see who had interrupted his private moment with his sister and saw both Adonijah and Jinn gawking at her body.

Jinn stepped forward; his eyes fixed on his wife. If he noticed Crispin crouched on the ground, he didn't acknowledge him. The prince cupped Salome's face and rested his forehead against hers, tears unapologetically streamed down his face. He whispered something to her that Crispin couldn't hear but knew just like he had his moment with his sister, Jinn would need his time as well.

Crispin pulled himself to his feet and proceeded to leave the tent but stopped next to Adonijah. He put his hand on his shoulder. "Rayma said we should say our goodbyes," Crispin whispered. "She might not last the night."

Adonijah's teary gaze met Crispin's and he shook his head. "Your sister is far too stubborn to leave us behind."

"I'm having her taken to the White Keep," Crispin explained, glancing over his shoulder as Jinn cradled Salome's body. "If nothing else, she will be in the home of our ancestors one last time."

Without waiting for Adonijah to respond, Crispin stomped out, and unless it was important, everyone left him alone.

It was going to be a long, sleepless night.

Chapter Sixty-Five

Salome

When Salome opened her eyes, she was no longer in the white stone corridor. She was sitting at a long white table and across from her was the most beautiful woman she'd ever seen. Her white, long braid draped over her pale shoulder. Her purple eyes were zoned in on Salome, and even though she looked young, there was no mistaking who she was and that she had roamed Adalore for an eternity.

"You've been following me for quite some time," Salome initiated the conversation. "It looks like your patience finally paid off, Lady Death."

Death smiled and it was laced with a friendly familiarity that surprised Salome. Every time she thought about Death, she fought it, but sitting before her now, she was flooded with peace.

"I've been watching you, Hunter," Death spoke and her voice was melodious. "I wanted to see for myself, if you were worthy."

"Worthy of what?"

"Living."

"What does that mean?" Salome tilted her head to the side before scanning the stark room she was in. She visited her brother, Lykos, in the After before, and this didn't look remotely like the same place. "Where am I?"

Death motioned her hand around the space that had no windows or doors or furniture other than the table and two chairs. "This is the Void. This is my home."

"Why am I here?" She refocused on Lady Death. "Am I not dead?"

It was Death's turn to look confused. "Your soul has not decided whether to release you or not."

"You mean, I could go back?" Salome didn't want to get her hopes up, but she couldn't help it. If there was a chance she could see Jinn again, see her brother again, she would do whatever she could to find her way back to them.

"Those who come to the Void are between life and death," the goddess explained like a mother would speak to her child. "Your body is in need of healing. If your friends are able to find you in time, this door will open, and you will be free to return to the mortal world." She motioned toward a door on her left that hadn't been there before.

"And if my friends don't find me in time?"

"Then the other door will open, and you will be welcomed to the After to see those who came before you." A second door, this one to Death's right, appeared.

Salome dragged her gaze from the door and stared into Death's violet eyes. "Why not just claim me? I've felt your presence for months. What is it you want from me?"

"I do not want anything from you. I have been your constant companion since the day you were born." Death pushed her seat back and slid to her feet. She floated toward Salome and only stopped once she was before her. "I have followed each Hunter since Malachi and have ushered them all to the After when their mortal lives came to an end. But you," she smiled, "you were the first Hunter who fought me; the first Hunter who defied my presence. You did not welcome me, nor did you let your fear of me deter you from risking your life to save others. You surprised me, mortal."

A rattling sound from one of the doors drew Salome's attention. She could hear her name being called. Walking toward the doors, she found the one leading back to the land of the living shook. Light flickered behind it.

"Salome!" the voice cried out again. "Salome!"

She recognized the voice, and she slammed her hand on the door and cried out, "Crispin! I'm here! I'm here!"

"He can't hear you." Death was now standing beside her, arms clasped behind her.

"But I can hear him."

"He's trying to wake you from your slumber." Death turned to face Salome and she mirrored her stance. "Should you sense my presence again, Salome the Strong, know that I've come as your friend and protector. Not your enemy."

"What did you call me?" Salome cocked her head in confusion.

"When the mortals sing their ballads and tell their tales of your great victories, they will refer to you as Salome the Strong, the first female Hunter, and in time, when another Hunter is needed," Death met her gaze with a bright smile, "hopefully they are just as worthy as you are to bear the title."

Salome shot back to when she was in the Isles of Myr and had become the newest Red Maiden. She was instructed to pick one of the Five Virtues and though all of their voices were pleading their case, it was Strength that she chose.

May Strength be your protector and may her eagle guide you on your path.

"Salome, come back to me, darling." A gentle whisper wisped through the room, drawing Salome's attention. "Come back to me."

"Jinn?" She touched the door and felt a growing warmth beneath her palm.

"They're waiting for you," Death said.

The door leading to the mortal world grew brighter, so bright, Salome was forced to squint, and Death began to fade from view.

"We will meet again, Salome the Strong," Death's voice rang out around her. Though the words seemed ominous, Salome felt a wave of peace wash over her and she knew the next time she met Death, she would greet her like an old friend.

Salome's eyes shot open, and she found she was lying in a bed that felt like she had been resting on a cloud. Scanning the room, she recognized the white stone walls and the window that looked out over the White City. She didn't hear the sounds of battle raging around Northwind, nor did she smell the burning wood from the ships in the harbor. Scooting up so she was leaning against the white oak headboard, she finally noticed Jinn and Crispin on the other side of the room, slumped on the couch against the wall, sleeping. They didn't look like they'd even taken a moment to bathe or scrub the evidence of battle from their armor.

She pulled the blankets off her and noticed she was in a plain white smock. Her body was clean and when she lifted the smock to examine her stab wound, she found an angry, swollen wound that had been stitched to perfection. Another scar to add to her ever-growing list, but she was alive, and that's all that mattered.

She wasn't sure how long she'd been unconcious, but her back ached, and all she wanted to do was stretch her legs. Draping her legs over the side of her bed, she slowly put her feet on the cold tile floor and applied her weight, making sure she didn't fall flat on her face. With some difficulty, she made her way toward her balcony, grabbing a fur tossed over a chair, and wrapped it around herself before slipping out the door. The cold burned her lungs as she breathed in the salty sea air whipping through the city. Snow was peppered across rooftops in the city below her and memories of her growing up in the White Keep flooded her. As she scanned the surrounding areas, she caught sight of the gardens she loved running through as a child and made note to visit as soon as she could.

"Thinking of escaping, Princess?"

Salome turned to see Kayven perched on the railing of her balcony. She hadn't noticed him at the far end of the patio and smiled. He tucked his wings behind him and returned her smile with a bright one of his own. His hair was pulled back in his typical half-up, half-down style and he had fresh cuts and bruises on his face and arms, but other than that, he was in prime shape.

"It is good to see you on your feet." He hopped up and walked toward her.

As soon as he was within reach, she wrapped her arms around him and to her delight and surprise, he gently squeezed her back.

"You mortals with your physical displays of affection," he teased, though he didn't release her until she pulled away.

"Admit it. You've grown fond of our ways," she grinned, attempting to hide the wince she whimpered from straining her injured side.

"You should not be out of bed when you clearly need rest," he chided, but she waved him off.

"I needed some fresh air." She brushed wild strands of her hair from her face. "How long have I been out?"

"Two days." He rested his elbows on the railing and she did the same. "Those two in your room refused to leave your side even though we begged them to. Thank the Almighty you woke when you did. Everyone in the keep was beginning to smell them."

Salome barked out a laugh. "It's nice to know they care." She bumped him with her shoulder, drawing his golden gaze. "What happened after I passed out?"

"Once I found you, I flew you to Rayma. I knew by your coloring that I might be too late, but I had to try." Kayven's face darkened. She rested her hand on his forearm, bringing him back from whatever memory haunted him. "I made sure one of my men delivered Gershom's head to your brother at the front lines and the fighting ended. The city surrendered seeing Gershom was dead and the people welcomed Crispin as their true king. Apparently, rumors had spread through Northwind over the last few months that Issachar's son lived, and they were relieved he'd come to defeat Gershom, who had always been seen as an enemy of the people."

Resting her head against his shoulder, she said, "Thank you for saving me."

In a rare display of affection, the Bellator pecked her head before snaking his arm across her shoulders and tugging her close. "Out of all the mortals I have met, you are by far my favorite."

"And out of all the Immortals I've met, Abba is by far my favorite." She tried and failed to hide her smirk and before long they were both laughing.

"Salome!?"

Footsteps thundered inside her chambers as Crispin and Jinn had woken up and noticed her empty bed. Kayven opened the door, and she stood in the threshold as her husband and brother rushed around the room frantically, until they noticed her. Their faces were filled with relief and Jinn rushed to her, slipping his arms around her and gently picking her up, kissing her. She raked her fingers through his hair, pulling back from his kiss, swiping the tear slipping down his cheek.

"I thought I had lost you," he whispered.

She shook her head. "I heard you calling for me."

There would be a time when she explained the Void, and everything she talked to Death about, but all she wanted to do now was kiss him, and by the look in his eyes, she knew he felt the same way.

Jinn's lips met hers and she could feel his longing for her, she could sense his stress melting from him, and she deepened their kiss until Crispin cleared his throat, reminding them they weren't alone. With care, Jinn set Salome back on her feet and she walked toward her brother who still had dirt smeared across his face.

She sniffed the air around him and crinkled her nose. "You could have at least bathed in the two days I was asleep," she teased and the tension he was holding in his shoulders loosened.

"Brat," he chuckled and wrapped his arms around her, kissing her forehead.

"We did it," she whispered, and he nodded.

"We did it."

Remembering Rahab had been injured and Abba had flown her to Rayma, she asked, "How's Rahab?"

"Bandaged and having to use a cane until she heals, which she gripes about, but she's recovering." Crispin pulled back from her and slipped his hands around her face. "You scared me. What happened to you?"

Salome, Crispin, Jinn, and Kayven spent the next couple of hours catching up on their versions of the battle. They reflected on those they'd lost and that's when Salome informed Crispin of how Niabi died. How she sacrificed herself to save her and that her last request was to be buried with her kin in Elisor. Crispin agreed without question and even teared up a little bit when she delivered Niabi's last words to him. Salome planned to fulfill her promises to her sister as she took her last breaths; she would make sure Ivaylo was cared for and that he grew up knowing who his parents were.

Once she was dressed and able to walk more than a few feet without needing to catch her breath, Salome reunited with her friends. She swapped stories with Adonijah, Seraphina, and Cato. She hugged Kai and kissed Abba on the cheek. She danced with Harbona, laughed with Oifa and Hanzo, and drank her fill with her future sister-in-law, Rahab. As a group, they toasted their dead and buried them in the mountain crypts, honoring their sacrifice.

Crispin's coronation and wedding to Rahab was celebrated across Adalore and the people of Northwind feasted for a week in their honor. Although Rahab wasn't a huge fan of the title of queen, she was extremely excited when Crispin made her the Commander of Northwind's armada and ensured the crew of the *Shadow of Death* had high ranking positions in the fleet and enticing pay to keep them in the White City. All of them readily accepted, except Captain Haldane, who returned to Pulau and became the new Pirate King, swearing he'd right Uri's wrongs in honor of his late-wife, Palma.

Adonijah and Leoti journeyed to Elisor, where they were determined to help Tala raise Ivaylo. Salome promised to visit as soon as she could and if Ivaylo needed anything, he would have it. She knew her nephew would be in good hands with the Andrago, and Crispin offered Tala an ambassadorship to Northwind, should he ever wish to return.

Oifa and Hanzo took the united Mountain Men tribe back to the Bone Mountains where they established a peaceful world for their people. Within a few weeks of being in Fennor, Oifa and Hanzo discovered they were expecting a child and the couple that used to loathe one another, rejoiced, knowing with their child, a new age had truly dawned. Equally Stormcrag and Krazak, their heir would continue the work of unity between the ancient peoples.

Heru and Rayma tearfully said goodbye to one another before the prince returned south with the Numbio. With Harbona and Lavena pulling some strings, they ensured Heru could visit Rayma and Inaros in Caelestis whenever he wanted, and that the Immortals would keep Rayma protected from the Grim, breaking the curse.

Though the Qata Vishna bid their Red Maiden farewell and sailed back to the Isles of Myr, Seraphina remained with Salome, fulfilling her oath to Nym to protect her granddaughter. And wherever Seraphina went, Cato went as well.

Harbona remained with Crispin and Rahab as their advisor. Once Odelia was well, she and Makeda joined him in the White Keep, finally mending their familial bond.

The Bellator commanders returned with Lavena to Caelestis, but as a parting gift and with Harbona's blessing, Salome got to keep Zandaar, the hippogriff. Kayven and Abba made her promise that she wouldn't fly alone at night. She only conceded to those terms once they agreed to visit her in Sakurai, whenever they had the chance. She owed the Bellator brothers everything; they saved her when no one else realized she was drowning. They would always hold a special place in her heart.

Master Penn and her Keepers hitched a ride with Captain Haldane and returned to The Sisters where they christened a new Sovereign. Penn and Haldane had grown quite fond of one another during the course of their journey and as the pirate established his new reign in Pulau, the Master of Keepers did everything in her power to aid him and improve relations between their kingdoms.

Though it was difficult saying goodbye to the friends who had become her family, Salome knew they'd all join her and Jinn in Sakurai for their royal wedding the following year. But what she'd been dreading for weeks, what she had refused to think about until that moment, was having to say goodbye to her brother before she boarded Jinn's ship to Sakurai.

Standing face to face on the docks, the winter chill gone and the crisp, floral air replacing it, the siblings stared at one another in complete silence. She wasn't exactly sure how to say goodbye to her best friend.

"Make sure you don't let that crown go to your head," she teased, pointing at the silver crown resting upon his curls.

He rolled his eyes and clicked his tongue. "You're worried about *my* head getting inflated? What about you, Salome the Strong? I've already heard two different ballads about your victory in the North."

She shrugged a lazy shoulder, feigning indifference. "Three, but who is counting?"

"Brat," he laughed and pulled her to his chest, squeezing her tightly. "How am I supposed to say goodbye?" he asked softly, tears filling his eyes. "How am I supposed to be happy for you, when my heart is breaking?"

"Out of everyone I have known and loved, you will always be my favorite." She hugged him, not wanting to let him go. "Take care of him, Rahab." The pirate queen nodded, stretching her hand across Crispin's chest once Salome released him.

"I will," Rahab promised and Salome knew she would keep her word.

"I will see you both soon."

With a final kiss and hug, Salome walked up the gangplank with Jinn and boarded the *Jade Warrior*. Sailing out of the harbor, taking one last, long look at Northwind, she let loose the breath she'd been holding onto, and waved at Crispin and Rahab until she couldn't see them anymore. Jinn slipped up next to her and rested his elbows on the railing.

"We will visit them often," he smiled. "You might be the future queen of Sakurai, but I know where your heart lies."

Salome tunneled her hand into his and squeezed. "My heart is with you, my lord."

"You flatter me," he raised her hand to his mouth and kissed it. "I swear to you, we will come back. This is your home, and I wouldn't dare take that from you."

Salome pushed up on her toes until her lips met his. "A secret for a secret?" she said softly against his mouth.

He flashed a crooked smile and nodded, wrapping his arms around her waist and pulling her to his chest. "You first."

Mark of the Hunter Trilogy

Acknowledgments

Holy Guacamole, the trilogy is complete!!! I started writing this story when I was fourteen and honestly, gave up on my dream of being a published author. Thank God, my husband, Brad, convinced me to give it another go. My fourteen-year-old self would be in awe of us at thirty-two.

If you have a dream, pursue it! If you gave up, it's not too late to try again. If I can do it, you can do it.

Thank you, the reader, for giving my work a chance. I appreciate YOU! Thank you for your support and for reading (and hopefully loving) my work. It has been such a dream come true to put all the stories running wild in my head down on paper. I am so excited for you to follow my career and fall in love with the characters who take up all my free time.

Be on the lookout for my new books! And don't worry, one day soon, we will return to the Ten Kingdoms of Adalore on a new adventure!

And as always, I want to thank God. Without Him, I would be lost and on a different path.

To my husband and best friend, Brad. Thank you for every bit of encouragement, support, and love you send my way. Without you, I would have given up on my dream years ago.

To my daughter, Remi, thank you for telling me how much you love me. You will never know how much that means to me.

To my son, Archer, thank you for your hugs throughout the day. They are my favorite interruptions.

To my daughter, Roux, thank you for bringing all the sass and smiles. It fueled me.

To my Mom and Dad, thank you for all your love and support. Mom, thank you for encouraging me to read and write from such an early age and for helping me edit my work! Dad, thank you for seeing my talent before I saw it myself.

To my sister, Logan, thank you for playing video games with me whenever I needed a break from work!

To my brother-in-law, Matt, thank you for your friendship, and for believing in my success before I published a single word.

To my friend, Mercedes. Thank you for your past ten years of friendship and for being the godmother to my three children. I love you, girl, and I'm so grateful for our talks.

To my book loving, writing sound board of a friend, Pier! You are an amazing friend, and I appreciate all your encouragement, support, and for being the best hype woman around!

To my Midnight Tide Publishing family, THANK YOU for welcoming me into the fold! Elle, thank you for your help and answering all my random questions like the true Mama Bear that you are! Brindi, thank you for our light-hearted chats when I'm feeling down! Jenny, thank you for brightening my day and hyping me up! Lou, Hannah, Whitney, Nicole, Stephanie, and everyone else at MTP, you rock!

And to my incredible street team! Thank you for encouraging me, supporting me, and loving my characters and books! It's a dream come true!

Also By Morgan Gauthier

Fantasy:
Wolves of Adalore (2021)
The Red Maiden (2022)
The Raven and the Wolf (2023)

Contemporary Romance:
Aloha, Seattle (2021)
The Maine Attraction (2022)

About Author

Morgan Gauthier lives in East Tennessee with her husband and best friend, Brad, and with their three children, Remi, Archer, and Roux (who are 5 years old and younger!). If five people wreaking havoc in the same house wasn't enough, Morgan also has three dogs, Potter, Skye, and Bubba.

Her first book, *Wolves of Adalore*, was published in 2021 and is the first book in a YA Epic Fantasy Trilogy. The *Mark of the Hunter Trilogy* is official complete and totally binge-worthy!

Morgan also writes Contemporary Romantic Comedies. *Aloha, Seattle* and *The Maine Attraction* are now available, and she is definitely planning on writing more in the genre.

If Morgan isn't writing or reading, she can be found binge watching Netflix shows, playing video games, attempting to cook like Gordon Ramsay (not even close to his level), and practicing archery.

You can follow her on:

Instagram: @authormorgangauthier

Facebook: @authormorgangauthier

Goodreads/Amazon: Morgan Gauthier

Pinterest: @authormorgangauthier

TikTok: @authormorgangauthier

Website: https://morgangauthier2.wixsite.com/morgangauthier

More MTP Books

A jaded girl. A persistent genie. A contest of souls.

Recent college graduate Dolly Jones has spent the last year stubbornly trying to atone for a mistake that cost her everything. She doesn't go out, she doesn't make new friends and she sure as hell doesn't treat herself to things she hasn't earned, but when her most recent thrift store purchase proves home to a hot, magical genie determined to draw out her darkest desires in exchange for a taste of her soul, Dolly's restraint, and patience, will be put to the test.

Newbie genie Velis Reilhander will do anything to beat his older half-brothers in a soul-collecting contest that will determine the next heir to their family estate, even if it means coaxing desire out of the least palatable human he's ever contracted. As a djinn from a 'polluted' bloodline, Velis knows what it's like to work twice as hard as everyone else, and he won't let anyone—not even

Dolly f*cking Jones—stand in the way of his birthright. He just needs to figure out her heart's greatest desire before his asshole brothers can get to her first.
COME TRUE: A BOMB-ASS GENIE ROMANCE is the romantic, fantastic second-coming-of-age story of two flawed twenty-somethings from different realms battling their inner demons, and each other, one wish at a time.

Do fairies exist?
This is the question Lainey asks herself after her sister's brutal murder in Central Park. Armed with her sister's diary and the mysterious entries within, Lainey's quest for answers leads her to Phoenix, a surly but handsome fae. The answer to Lainey's question reveals a truth that will change everything she thought she knew about herself and the world she lives in. A sacrifice must be made to break a curse that locked the gate between the human and faerie realms.
Leaving the only world she has known, Lainey finds herself surrounded by evil queens, curses, and magical creatures. Together, Lainey and Phoenix must find a way to break the curse that doesn't result in Lainey's death—like her sister's. Do fairies exist? The answer will change Lainey's life in ways she never imagined.

Ingram Content Group UK Ltd.
Milton Keynes UK
UKHW042113280423
420980UK00019B/242/J